"Who'd you say this was?"

"Damn it, Rocco, cut it out. This is Chapin, Chapin Hope."

"Okay, Hope, now you listen if I've got to spell it out for you. What you're involved with is no ordinary problem. A goddamn murder charge *and* a newspaper series on a whole network of conflict-of-interest accusations. You've been around long enough to know you can't expect anyone to advertise their association with you after the kind of mess you've let go public. Make it all go away, Senator. Make it never have happened. Then give us a call. Until then, Senator, you're the goddamn invisible man."

ESTABLISHMENT OF INNOCENCE

"IT'S ALL THERE—PACING, DRAMA, CHARACTERS . . . SEX . . . FULL OF POLITICAL SHENANIGANS AS CURRENT AS TODAY'S HEADLINES."

—The Washington Star

"BIZARRE . . . ENTERTAINING . . . THE AUTHORS DO NOT DISAPPOINT."

—Minneapolis Tribune

Establishment of Innocence

Harvey Aronson and Mike McGrady

A BERKLEY MEDALLION BOOK
published by
BERKLEY PUBLISHING CORPORATION

G.P. Putnam's Sons
200 Madison Avenue
New York, N.Y. 10016

Library of Congress Catalog Card Number: 75-21938

SBN 425-03288-4

BERKLEY MEDALLION BOOKS are published by
Berkley Publishing Corporation
200 Madison Avenue
New York, N.Y. 10016

BERKLEY MEDALLION BOOK ® TM 757,375

Printed in the United States of America

Berkley Medallion Edition, JANUARY, 1977

This is for Izzy and Pat

1

A small red light winking in the corner of the rearview mirror. Chapin Hope's eyes lowering to the speedometer. Then the siren, frail in the distance. Seventy-five—damn it, that was pushing it. Still, he kept his foot off the brake pedal, letting the Mercedes slow of its own accord as the mirrored pinpoint became a beacon and finally a black-and-white patrol car.

The siren did not let up and Chapin wondered whether he should pull over to the shoulder of the road. He never had before. Why start now? The senator from Stony Harbor votes "No"—the "Noes" have it. Vindication was prompt as the police car went mute, struck dumb by the small brass emblem attached to the rear bumper of State Senator Chapin Kirk Hope's car. As he pulled by, the trooper waved. It was a friendly wave, almost sheepish, but Chapin didn't return it. The son of a bitch should never have bothered him in the first place. Not on Long Island. His country.

Geographically, Brooklyn and Queens were part of Long Island, but that was geography, not reality. Chapin Hope's Long Island, the real Long Island, began where New York City ended. The real Long Island was a glacial slope that ran 110 miles east from Queens County. Bordered on the north by Long Island Sound and on the south by the Atlantic Ocean, Long Island extended into the sea like the twin-forked tail of a great whale, Orient Point on the north tip and Montauk Point on the south.

The senator was traveling from east to west, coming from a conservation-committee meeting on the North Fork and heading for a bar near the New York City line. It was half past four on the afternoon of the third Friday in November, one of those dismal, dank days that cast a gray mist over the small-town landscape of eastern Long Island. The South Fork was more celebrated, was famous for its rockbound wave-etched bluffs and for the summer glitter of the Hamptons, but Chapin Hope preferred the North Fork. It was gentler, the last stronghold of Long Island potatoes, of cauliflower auctions, of green fields that scented the spring with strawberries.

1

The road ran from farmlands to housing developments, from yesterday to today. Through the windshield, overlapping grays shadowed the fields and the houses. Too early for snow, but there was snow in the air. Chapin reached down to the climate-control knob and his eyes took in the speedometer again. It was moving back toward seventy. Actually, there was no reason to hurry. Plenty of time.

He stopped at a diner outside Riverhead. In the parking area a long-haired young woman wearing a black sweat shirt and men's dungarees was stepping down from a Volkswagen microbus. Chapin studied her, then looked quickly away—she had caught his stare and returned it with an added ingredient, mockery.

Once inside the diner, he ordered a black coffee to go and then carried it into a phone booth, where he dialed the first of three calls.

The machine in his Albany office informed him that State Senator Chapin Kirk Hope was away on official business and would be back on Monday morning and would the caller be kind enough to leave a message at the sound of the tone? He waited for the tone, then hung up. The machine was working.

The second call was to his wife, Thalia.

"I'm sorry, Thal," he said. "I'm stuck here in Albany."

"I thought you had a meeting in Greenport—"

"I couldn't get to it," he lied. "Something came up."

"Oh, Chape, we were counting on you—"

"I really couldn't help it," he said. "I won't be able to get out of here until late tonight. Some committee nonsense has come up and there's no way to say no. If I don't get it done now, I won't have any time with the boys over the weekend. I don't want to have to come back here on Sunday."

"You work too hard." He could imagine Thalia pursing her lips. "But you know what you have to do. The boys are going to be let down. We planned quite a dinner for you. Baked clams."

"Look, I'll wrap this up as quickly as I can," he said. "The minute I hang up, I'll put this machine on. I won't even stop for telephone calls."

"Try not to be too late," she said. "And drive carefully. They're talking about snow."

The third call went to a cocktail lounge. The Pumpkin was one of dozens of night spots decorating Jericho Turnpike in Nassau County near the Queens border.

"Hello," he said. "Is Ginny there?"

"Who's this? Harry?"

Chapin recognized the voice of the Pumpkin's manager.

"Yeah," he said. "Come on, Baldy, I want to sell her some insurance."

"Just a second," Baldy said, laughing.

It took almost five minutes to get Ginny to the phone.

"I don't need insurance," she said, "but there is one little thing you may be able to do for me."

"That's why I'm calling," he said. "I'm going to be able to make it after all. When's the best time?"

"Whenever you get here is the best time."

"You don't have to tell me."

"But around eight is when I'm getting off."

"I'll be there."

"Oh," she said. "I finally got the stuff—"

"Not over the phone," he said. "Tell me about it later."

"Okay, I'll see you at eight . . . Harry."

"Right . . . Gertrude."

He knew she would be grinning as she left the phone. That grin. From the very beginning Ginny had understood that she could never call him by his correct name in public. He had picked the name Harry because it seemed the exact opposite of Chapin. (Harry Hope—wasn't he a character in a play he once saw? A degenerate or maybe a drunk?) The last name was no problem; last names were seldom used at the Pumpkin.

Ginny not only understood the necessity of the disguise, she even seemed to enjoy the deception. Late at night, however, in her apartment, she always made it plain that she was hoarding his real name for her private pleasure. When they were making love, she would say it over and over again—ChapinChapinChapinChapin-ChapinChapin—almost as though since its use was rationed, it had become more valuable to her. To him as well; never before had the name gotten such splendid use.

The coffee was still hot as he carried it outside. He poured a third of it onto the blacktop and took the rest into the car. Thalia had been right about the weather; a talcum of snow dusted the road.

Once again the car seemed to take control of the driver. From time to time Chapin glanced down at the speedometer and forced himself to slow down. He was too eager, eager as a kid taking a cheerleader to the prom. The image raised the kinds of questions that had been plaguing him more and more in recent months. Do kids still date? Then: Are there still proms? And later: Are there still cheerleaders? Probably. Ginny had been one. And that was not so long ago.

Instead of picking up the expressway at Riverhead, Chapin

stayed with Route 25. There was time to kill and he enjoyed the changing vistas. Just beyond Riverhead there were crusted winter fields north of the road and the fenced-off pastures of the Grumman Aerospace Corporation on the south; signs on the fences prohibited the taking of photographs. He had mixed feelings about the Island's ties to the defense industry; it had sent men to the moon and it had provided thousands of jobs—however, in more recent years it had also provided thousands of layoffs.

It took less than a minute to drive past the community of Ridge. Chapin had once attended a meeting there; the farmers and nursery owners had been upset by herds of stunted deer feeding off their property. Then he came to the Smithaven Mall, an enclosed and climatized mecca that cost $20,000,000 to build and now contained more than a hundred stores, a Calder mobile nobody understood, and a waterfall of glycerine droplets flowing down nylon strands. All that and Macy's, too.

Then the sprawl of high ranches and split levels and colonials, a world of quarter-acre plots and fenced-in dreams. The land—that was the key to everything. The land still represented the American dream to people who rejected the cities they came from, who formed civic associations and bought play gyms and fertilizer, who screamed about school taxes and downzoning, who voted for the Chapin Hopes because the Chapin Hopes would protect them from the invaders—the blacks, the radicals, the bomb throwers, the fetus killers, and everyone else who threatened the established values and, therefore, the land.

Traffic accumulated as he drove through the townships of Smithtown and Fishington and Huntington. Route 25 was called Jericho Turnpike now, and it became a tangle of shopping centers and gas stations and pizza parlors and bargain marts and motels and bars.

Chapin Hope stopped for gas just across the Nassau County border. He drove slowly through Syosset and Hicksville and Jericho and Westbury. And, finally, he was driving up to the Pumpkin. Despite his attempts to slow himself down, he was early. Ignoring the empty parking spaces near the Pumpkin's entrance, Chapin parked the Mercedes against shrubs on the far side of the field.

It was time for the disguise. Sitting in the car, he unknotted his somber maroon necktie and replaced it with the wider and more vivid tie he carried in his attaché case. Next he reached into the glove compartment for a black velvet bag and, once outside, he slipped the bag over the Senate shield and tied the drawstring. He felt as guilty as if he had put on a mask.

Three-quarters of an hour early. He didn't want to seem anxious, didn't want Ginny to realize just how anxious he in fact was. The

4

situation bordered on the humorous. Here he was, forty years old, hair graying over the ears, small hard gut starting to press against his belt, two sons in junior high school, and he was afraid to walk into this dive and let a cocktail waitress know how much he liked her.

Game playing, sure, but he couldn't stop it. He walked across the turnpike to the Express Diner. The only person there, the counterman, was sitting on a stool at the far end of the counter, not bothering to look up from a fresh copy of Saturday morning's *Daily News*.

Although Chapin's name had often appeared in the paper, his picture was rarely used. State senators were simply not that important. Actually, power was in no way equated with a picture in the paper. At least, not power as Chapin knew it. And there were times—now was one such time—when anonymity was an advantage.

"How about a cheeseburger?" he said.

"Give me a minute, will ya?"

Chapin was tempted to give the son of a bitch forever, but he kept his silence as the counterman finished the paper. A moment later, as he asked for French fries and a small Coke with his cheeseburger, it struck Chapin that this was the exact order he might have placed two decades earlier when this whole business—Ginny, game playing, the rest—would have seemed more comprehensible. The cheeseburger was cardboard, the Coke was too sweet, and when he looked at the French fries, all he could see were cholesterol and calories.

Still he lingered. Every cell in his body was urging him to get up and rush to Ginny but he sat there pushing the food from one side of the plate to the other. Ginny, Ginny, Ginny. Despite himself, Chapin sighed audibly. He had never been able to come to grips with this side of himself, the Harry side. It was the Harry side that kept an Off-Track Betting phone account. The Harry side that had spent four years carrying on an affair with a thirty-five-year-old divorcée who served as administrative assistant to an upstate senator. The Harry side that once spent a ludicrous half hour in the company of an eighteen-year-old black girl in a Manhattan massage parlor.

Ginny was not the first extramarital liaison. Nor, in all probability, would she be the last. But there was a difference. The others had been diversions. They had been the fodder of the entertainments he later presented to his closest friends, his only two close friends, in the locker room of the club after a long day of golf.

The three of them had been friends since childhood. Chapin and Greg and Norris. Greg—L. Gregory Hammer—was Chapin's law

5

partner, the firm's specialist in criminal defense and general flamboyance. Norris Whitlaw was a construction company president whose county and town accounts were the envy of the building trade.

The three of them had become friends on high school playing fields and they still met for games. They all played golf at Fox Hollow and late in the day, muscles aching pleasantly, martinis starting to take hold, they would sit in the locker room and begin the show. "I once knew a girl who . . ." anyone could begin. Needless to say, the stories never went beyond the locker room. Each man understood the importance of discretion and each also understood the importance of the outlet, of being able to tell someone else. The act of telling served as antidote to the experience. It also helped establish one's credentials as a regular guy who, despite success and reputation, understood the vagaries of the modern world.

"Something wrong with the food?" the counterman said.

"Just one small thing," Chapin said. "It tastes like shit."

"Well, you don't eat it, you don't have to pay for it."

The counterman seemed genuinely apologetic and Chapin was immediately sorry about his reaction—that was more like his Harry side than his Chapin side.

There was no way he could tell Greg and Norris about Ginny. No way. He imagined them in the locker room, Leroy bringing in the second tray of iced Beefeaters, and him starting in. Telling them about a red-haired cocktail waitress who had been married at sixteen, divorced at eighteen, and who knew everything there was to know about sex at age twenty-five. For instance . . . no, no way. The one thing he was not going to do to Ginny was turn her into a locker-room story. Not the way she made him feel. Not now, at any rate. Oh, perhaps someday—he didn't kid himself about that; the end of passion was inevitable, only the duration was a matter of conjecture—maybe then he would find a way to refer to it without cheapening it. Hell, it wasn't as though Greg and Norris were insensitive men.

By seven forty-five Chapin had run out of thoughts. He left two dollar bills next to the barely touched dinner and walked back across the turnpike to a spherical building painted a grotesquely luminescent orange and topped by a winking neon sign, THE PUMPKIN.

As he walked into the bar, Chapin felt a familiar uneasiness. He knew that at this time, the hour separating the last of the office workers and the first of the night people, the Pumpkin would be at its emptiest. Still, he felt uneasy. His sole protection was the fact that anyone recognizing him here would probably share in the embarrassment.

6

It was always midnight inside the Pumpkin and it took his eyes a long moment to adjust to the dimness. The decor, pure cocktail-bar modern. Chairs in tan plastic, square tables set too close together, a chrome railing stretching the length of the bar, a squat piano, red brocaded walls, Ginny.

Her back was toward the door but the hair was unmistakable. That hair. Red hair falling over the brief black-and-white costume. Ginny was seated at the elbow of the bar talking to a tall brunette. As he approached, the taller woman whispered to Ginny and Ginny spun around to greet him. There was something about that movement, the quickness of it, that seemed almost guilty.

"You're early," Ginny said, squeezing his hand.

"Is that a crime?"

"No, but I've got some bad news. Baldy's short-handed and he asked me if I could stay a little extra. Just for the rush, just to handle coats. He knew you were coming but he was practically begging."

"Maybe we should make this another night."

"Go ahead," she said, "and I'll tell everyone who you are."

"Blackmailer."

It was a shared joke but Chapin could pick up the urgency in her voice. It was that above all else, that thing in her voice, that he would never be able to tell anyone else about. It was a source of genuine wonderment, the fact that a woman could take such pleasure in him, that a woman could want him as much as he wanted her.

"The usual, Harry?" Baldy called out from behind the bar.

"The usual," he said.

"It's on us tonight," Baldy said. "I'm really sorry about Ginny. The other girl, the new one, called in sick and I'm really short-handed."

"As long as you're not short-armed," Chapin said, letting the Harry side have its way.

The usual was a Seven and Seven, a drink that Chapin found barely swallowable. But it was another part of the Harry disguise. Harry was an insurance salesman who hit Long Island every couple of weeks and spent his nights dallying in bars; the Seven and Seven suited Harry as did the *double entendres* and the bad jokes and the backslapping manner.

"Oh, Harry, say hello to an old friend." Ginny was introducing him to the tall brunette. "I don't think you've met Charlotte."

"I don't think I'd have forgotten it."

That was Harry talking. But Charlotte, now that Chapin had a chance to study her, did seem vaguely familiar. Charlotte had a full figure and the kind of leggy good looks that he associated with chorus girls. The only flaw was the makeup—there was too much of

7

it. Too much aquamarine shadow around the eyes, too much redness on the cheeks. Even as he came to this conclusion, however, Chapin realized that it was right, right for a place like the Pumpkin —but dead wrong for a face that naturally striking.

"Now I am sorry that I've got to run," Charlotte said. "I've heard so much about you. That's all Ginny talks about these days. I'd love to stay and see if you live up to your notices."

"Then it's just as well you're running along," Ginny said. "Competition I don't need."

"I don't think you have to worry," Charlotte said, and she blew them both a kiss as she left. The two men who were the only other customers at the bar turned to watch her—she was the kind of woman who would have drawn the same sort of attention if the place were crowded.

"Hey, watch it," Ginny said, turning his face back in her direction with the tips of her fingers.

"You heard your friend," he said. "You don't have to worry."

Ginny laughed and led him to a small table across the room from the piano. She sat with him then, her left thigh pressed against him, and he wondered whether the warmth affected her the way it did him.

Chapin looked around the room. A writer for the *Daily Islander* —Long Island's leading newspaper—had done a funny column recently on the Island's leading "cheaters' bars" and had rated the Pumpkin sixth. Three years earlier the same writer—who obviously didn't mind repeating himself—had done a rating of "lonely bars" and in that one the Pumpkin had finished third. Chapin had now been there often enough so that he would have thought up a different label. To him the Pumpkin regulars were neither lonely nor cheating; to him they were, simply, Instant People.

The routine never varied. Tonight at eight fifty-five he would be there, sitting with Ginny, toying with his Seven and Seven, and the place would be quiet. At nine P.M. it would be filled with people. One moment the Pumpkin would be an empty shell. The next moment it would be buzzing with the small talk of realtors and funeral directors and salesmen and defense executives and off-duty cops and countergirls and department-store buyers and secretaries and beauticians. The men would be married and the women would be either widowed or divorced; all, however, would be Instant People.

Even as he imagined the Pumpkin's nightly performance, the prelude began. Bobby Kelly materialized at the piano carrying a bourbon on the rocks with his left hand and a melody with his right hand. Bobby was in his fifties, aging badly; a small taut-skinned

8

man, pale-eyed and balding, possessed of a plaster smile and a voice that reminded Chapin of stag parties.

Bobby placed his drink on top of the piano and, using both hands now, tried a few ripples and chords. Then he swung into "Hail, Hail, the Gang's All Here" and it was almost as though the song made it happen. Instant People. "Is everybody happy?" Bobby asked. There was the usual scattering of affirmatives and negatives as he moved into the basic repertoire of piano bars everywhere: "More" and "Strangers in the Night" and "The Shadow of Your Smile" and "These Foolish Things" and "Yesterday."

Ginny was in the cloakroom as some of the Instant People began singing along and others moved out onto the tiny dance floor. By this time Bobby Kelly had acquired his usual retinue of sidemen. The empty-eyed blonde sitting to his immediate right was using drum brushes against an upturned beer tray. The red-faced man to Bobby's left was slapping his palm against the piano top. Other patrons were rapping fingers against the bar, spoons against glasses. Ridiculous. Chapin had always despised group dynamics, had once walked out of an off-Broadway play when a cast member had tried to draw him onto the stage. But this was the Pumpkin and Chapin tried to do what Harry would have done; he kept time to the music by tapping his fingertips against the table.

And now, with everyone behind him, Bobby sailed into his specialty numbers—putting risqué lines into popular standards. Chapin felt like a visitor from outer space. Still, he continued to keep time.

Ginny wove her way through dancing couples, sat down beside him, pressed into him again.

"Did I tell you I got the stuff?"

"I'm not sure about that," he said, taking a swallow from the Seven and Seven. "I'm not sure I can go ahead with that."

"It's the very best kind."

"It's not that," he whispered. "It's the whole idea."

"It wasn't easy, getting this stuff," Ginny said. "That new law you were so hot for. . . ."

"Don't. Don't even tell me how you got it. The less I know, the better. I'm not even sure—"

"Oh, honey, stop being nervous," she said. "There's not going to be anyone else there. There's nothing like it to . . . relax you. Everyone uses it these days. I went to a party the other night, a straight party, and they put hash in the brownies."

"Wonderful," Chapin said.

Hash in the brownies. New York had the toughest drug law in the nation, a law strongly supported in the Senate by the Hon. Chapin

Kirk Hope—and now they were putting the stuff into brownies. What next, Girl Scout cookies? The idea of a grown man being afraid to try pot would seem absurd to many people. But the conflict was not easily resolved. After lecturing at schools, churches, and civic halls throughout the state on the evils of drugs, on the need for more stringent legislation, he was now preparing to get stoned.

It was even worse than that. It was not just a matter of agreeing to try marijuana. He had initiated it, had actually asked Ginny if she knew how to get some. She did. And she had. And now they were going to get stoned and they were going to make love and what bothered him most was that he could hardly wait.

At ten o'clock Ginny came to the table with her coat over her arm.

"Baldy says now's all right."

"You're making me feel guilty," Chapin said. "You're going to lose all those tips. You've done all the work and now someone else is going to get the payoff."

"And I'll have you."

"Ginny, that's such a nice thing—"

"And besides," she cut him short, "Betty said she'd divvy up with me."

That was her sense of humor and no matter how many times she did it—undercutting a seemingly sentimental remark with a sharp-edged punch line—Chapin was caught off-balance. He had no right to look for sentiment. And actually one of the qualities he prized most in Ginny was a certain toughness of mind; forget that it was an indication she had been around the block a few times. It also happened to reflect an independence notably absent from the women who inhabited his ordinary world.

By now they had worked out the procedure. Ginny drove Chapin in her car the three blocks to the Nassau Overlook apartment complex (IF YOU LIVED HERE, YOU'D BE HOME NOW, said the sign). Chapin found an excuse—or, rather, Ginny allowed him an excuse—to remain in the car while she went in and paid the baby-sitter. He sat in the dark, finishing his cigarette, as the sitter came out, a young girl slowly walking across the open quadrangle to the identical apartment building on the other side.

Only when she was out of sight did Chapin leave the car. He flipped the cigarette ahead of him, stepped on it, walked briskly toward the nearest building. He pressed a button opposite Ginny's name, looked away from the bright lobby lights, and as the buzzer sounded, he pushed open the plate-glass door and turned right toward the apartment. He thanked God it was on the ground floor; he felt at his most naked now, during this walk from parked car to apartment, and an elevator ride would have been intolerable.

10

Sensing this, Ginny always left the door ajar. But this time it did not matter. As he was reaching out to the door, another door, this one on the opposite side of the hallway, opened and a soft, oversized young man appeared. He was bundled up against the cold and he was carrying a tiny white poodle in his arms. The two of them wore matching scarves.

"Good evening," Chapin said, but the young man failed to respond. Without so much as a grunt of greeting, he moved on toward the entrance. Inside her apartment Ginny was waiting.

"Laura's sound asleep," she began.

"Damn it!" he said. "Your friend across the way—the poet?—he saw me coming in here. I knew this was a mistake. I shouldn't be coming here. We should be going to motels."

"Oh, Chapin, you have such trouble coming here—how would you feel checking into a motel?"

"I guess I'll have that drink now."

He followed her the half-dozen steps to the kitchenette. He was pleased to see that the bottle of Chivas Regal he had brought the last time was still almost full. But he was not pleased to notice the frozen-dinner tray that had been left on top of the kitchen counter; how did a kid manage to survive on stuff like that?

In the living room Chapin relaxed with the scotch as he and Ginny followed their usual ritual. Ginny rarely drank alcohol, at least when she was with Chapin, and tonight she had opened a can of Fresca for herself. As always, Ginny chose the easy chair. The first time he had come to the apartment, Chapin had asked her to sit beside him on the couch and she had said no—no, she would much rather be looking at him. He now understood this to be a necessary part of her lovemaking ritual.

It was an interesting phenomenon. Ginny constantly turned away from the appearance of sensuality. Her off-duty wardrobe featured high-throated blouses and dresses slightly longer than the mode. Her appearance was always ladylike, and Chapin had learned early that an off-color story or a four-letter word other than "damn" was more apt to stir a blush than a laugh. It was as though he had to deal with two distinct people—a lady in the living room and a whore in the bedroom. It was a combination he found very much to his liking.

"How are things in Albany?" she asked.

He smiled at the question; that, too, was standard. There was an insistence on observing all the niceties, on manufacturing a certain quota of small talk. And, as always, he went along with it and talked about everything except the desire that dominated his thoughts.

"Oh, you know," he said. "Gray. Cold. Dull. Nothing. Snow today."

11

"Does anyone know yet what the governor's going to do?"

"He hasn't said yet," Chapin answered, "but I wish to hell he'd make up what he calls his mind. The speaker's climbing walls. If he'd just say something, anything, maybe we could get some work done for a change."

"I'm not sure that's such a good idea," she said. "I've seen some of the work you people do; most often I'd just as soon you all stayed home."

"How about the abortion law? The most liberal abortion law in the country."

"Yes, and you voted against it."

"Only after I knew it would pass."

It was impossible to explain the process to someone looking at it from the outside and Chapin seldom made the effort. Well, with his sons he would sometimes try. But people who never had to go out and win votes tended to look on elective office the way they looked on other jobs; you did well and you wouldn't get fired. Nothing was further from the truth.

What was important was not the way Chapin Hope voted but what ultimately happened to the bill. Thus it was of absolutely no significance that he voted against a liberal abortion bill, which he personally favored. What was important was that the abortion bill did, in fact, finally pass.

He knew that there were times when some people—Ginny, his own children—considered him a representative not of some geographical area so much as a representative of the Dark Ages. What they never realized was that he was a mirror, a reflector of his constituents' wishes.

And this was a constituency that could tolerate a war in Asia more easily than the thought of a poor person accepting welfare; this was a constituency that strongly supported the restoration of capital punishment but was against stores opening on the Sabbath. It also happened to be a constituency that had elected Chapin Hope a half-dozen times by increasing margins.

"Are you ready to try the pot?" Ginny asked.

"I'm crazy to do this."

"You don't have to."

"You want me to."

"Consider it part of your education," she said. "You should know what you've been voting against."

"Well, then," he said, "I'm glad I didn't vote against child molestation. . . ."

"Not funny."

12

"Okay," he said. "But first let me pay you for it—I know this stuff doesn't come cheap."

Whenever he did that, whenever he reached for his wallet in either a literal or a figurative sense, Ginny froze. She had explained to him that first time together that he must never put a price tag on her or her affection. That was why he never let her know about his part in arranging the loan she had been able to obtain from Federated Security, the $4,000 loan she had needed to pay for a new car.

"I told you not to worry about that," she said. "Besides, the pusher always gives out the first sample free. How else am I going to get you hooked? Hey, how do I even know you're not a narc? I mean, if you were a narc, Chapin, and if I took money from you, if I sold you some of this stuff, it's my understanding that I could, under your beautiful new law, get one to five, with time off for good behavior. But if I give you some, the only thing I'm going to get is high."

She went to her bedroom then, and Chapin went back to the Chivas for a refill. He was well into it when Ginny returned. She was wearing the blue satin dressing gown with the slits up the sides. He noted the change of costume with pleasure because the blue dressing gown was, he had learned, a reliable signal that lovemaking would follow shortly.

Ginny opened a Marlboro cigarette box and shook the contents out onto the coffee table. Scattered among the machine-made cigarettes were a few of less symmetrical design. Ginny picked up one of the handmade sticks, lit it, inhaled deeply, and handed it to Chapin.

He looked at it for a long moment, long enough for the overly sweet smell to reach his nostrils. What the hell? He took it and in imitation of Ginny and a thousand bad movies, he drew deeply, bringing the smoke down into lungs that had been battered by cigarettes for the past twenty years. Nothing.

"My turn," Ginny said.

He would have to learn the etiquette; he passed the joint back to Ginny, watched her take another deep breath, and then it was his turn again. Oh, if he could be seen now—by his sons, by his fellow legislators, by the backslappers at Rotary, by anyone at all in his other world. The thought struck him as amusing and he laughed.

"Are you starting to feel it?" Ginny said.

"I'll tell you the truth," he said. "The only thing I'm feeling is slightly absurd. But don't worry; it's not the first time. Do you mind if I have another drink?"

13

"Let me get you one," she said. "You just keep working on the grass."

He started another joint but he was happy when the fresh drink arrived. He still felt nothing from the marijuana. If there was any effect at all, it was simply to make him more thirsty. He thought back to their great debates over marijuana in Albany, and the recollection of grown men spending weeks debating the weed struck him as the height of absurdity. He smoked two—no, three—of the things now without a single pleasant sensation. Thank God for the Chivas.

Ginny, meanwhile, had gotten herself a second—could it be a third?—Fresca, and was lighting up still another stick, which she seemed to be keeping to herself this time. That was all right, perfectly all right. Maybe he was old-fashioned, but Chapin knew that no one ever drank a bottle of booze and then had to sit around for hours wondering whether he was going to feel anything.

While the marijuana seemed to do nothing, the Chivas had thoroughly relaxed him. Never had he felt so ready for a woman, even for Ginny. As if on cue, Ginny began to send out signals that she was ready for him.

The process was so basic, even crude, that Chapin still had difficulty believing it was intentional. What was happening now, what happened each time they made love, seldom varied. Ginny was settling back deeper into the easy chair, stretching her legs out in front of her, and somehow, as always, the blue dressing gown had become hiked up over her knees. There was no nice way of describing it—she was sitting across the room from Chapin and she was exposing herself and immediately he felt his own response.

"Not yet," she said to him, and there was a sudden sharpness in her voice. "Chapin, I want you to try another one first. For me. It will make everything so much better for me."

"But it doesn't work. It doesn't do anything for me."

"That's what everyone says the first time," she said. "You'd be surprised what it's doing for you, what it's going to mean in a few minutes."

"I can't wait much longer," he said.

"I know, darling, soon, soon."

The stick was lit and handed to him. The room filled with the smell now, a musky smell very much like incense, and Chapin decided to smoke this last one as rapidly as possible. He knew that the delay would only add to their pleasure. But, God, their time together was so limited that he hated to waste it on anything except the act of love itself.

14

He inhaled the smoke deeply, held it, hoped that it would do something, anything, so that Ginny would not be disappointed in him. Nothing. Across the room Ginny was lying back sleepily, staring at him through the haze, waiting, and now the entire lower half of her body was naked. He could not take his eyes off that patch of silken auburn hair, the sight of her legs opening and closing in a hypnotic rhythm. The lamp beside her chair seemed to be wavering, seeming at first to be far away and then to be coming closer, and maybe that was it; maybe that was what the kids meant when they claimed to be high. But what made him feel truly high, higher than any mere visual distortion, was the sight of Ginny, the sure knowledge that she was finally ready for him.

"Not yet." Her voice was ghostly, distant. "Make it last, Chapin."

Make it last? He wanted nothing more than to stub out this butt and move over to her. He had never felt so good in his life, so relaxed, so ready. Somehow, magically, Ginny had taken the blue robe off and now it was draped across her body like a towel. Looking at her, Chapin could almost feel that marvelous slipperiness, the welcome awaiting him, the way he would become lost in her. Surely she, too, could wait no longer. Across the room her mouth seemed slack, the lips slightly parted, and the brightness of her eyes was seen in the wavering lamplight.

He knew what was to come. The way her lips would become soft with kissing, the way her skin would be oiled to his touch, the way her eyes would become unfocused as she allowed the waves of pleasure to wash over her. And the ChapinChapinChapinChapin-Chapin as she came onetwothreefourfive times, a string of fire-crackers going off, each accompanied by throaty screams and only later would he realize that he had been responsible for creating all that pleasure.

Now was the time. He need only touch her wrist and it would start and he would carry her into her bedroom and mount her and plunge into her and thank sweet Jesus for finally showing him something about loving a woman.

Chapin crushed out the final smoke and got up. He took the first step toward her and his legs turned to rubber and the last thing he remembered was the feeling of falling.

Three hours later Chapin was able to drag himself back to consciousness, but only with the most painful effort. At first he was aware only of the ache; it seemed to be a hangover of championship quality. Then he opened his eyes. He was stretched out on the couch of Ginny's living room; Ginny was in the chair across the room, coiled into a small ball, snoring gently. She was wearing slacks and a sweat shirt.

"What time is it?"

"Oh, thank God," she said, coming out of her sleep with startling swiftness. "Chapin, I was so worried. A dozen times I almost called an ambulance."

"That would have been fun," he said. "But what time is it?"

"Over there." She nodded. "Just past two."

"Oh, no," he said. "My head is coming apart. Was it the pot or the booze?"

"Well, it was probably wrong to mix the two," she said. "But I tend to think it may have been the cocktail table. At least that's what your head hit when you fell."

Getting to his feet was pure pain. Almost equally painful was the realization of what had happened or, more precisely, what had not happened. He had spent four hours in this apartment and he had not once touched Ginny; he had spent the evening with the woman he loved and he had not once made love to her.

"I was right all along," he said.

"Chapin, we've got to get you back to your car," Ginny said. "You were right about what all along?"

"About pot," he said. "It should be illegal."

2

Leaving the apartment, leaning against Ginny, staggering, bumping into an elderly man walking a dog, trying to apologize, mumbling. The man looked at Chapin with fright, and Chapin fought an urge to run to the car.

"Easy, easy does it," Ginny said. "That doesn't matter; he's not even from my building."

Chapin tried to lighten it.

"Yeah," he said finally, "but I think that damn dog recognized me."

"That's better." Ginny leaned over and kissed his ear. "Much better."

"Damn it," he said.

"Ummm?"

"What a waste."

"I know." There was that note in her voice. "I wanted you, too."

She reached out with her right hand then and trailed a finger across his lap. It was right, just right, precisely the kind of gesture Thalia could never have made. With Ginny it was spontaneous, natural, part of the way she was. In his mind he could still see her facing him in the apartment, her eyes covering him, her legs coming out of the blue robe.

"Pot!" he said.

A few minutes later, as they parked beside a chocolate Mercedes in the Pumpkin lot, they were both laughing. It was nearly three A.M. and there were only a few cars waiting for their owners. The kiss was long and hard and finally tender.

"Don't worry," Ginny said. "Next time we'll make up for everything."

"Next week?" He was annoyed by his inability to keep the eagerness out of his voice.

"Whenever you're able to," she said.

They stood between the two cars talking for a few more moments and then they said good-bye, calling each other Harry and Gertrude.

Ginny turned toward the Pumpkin entrance; she would make her good nights while he left the parking lot. Chapin waited for her to leave before walking around to the back of his car and lifting the black bag from the State Senate shield. It was such an effort to bend over that he wondered whether he would be able to drive home. Still, he took the time to unlock the attaché case and switch ties. Ludicrous, perhaps, but it could not be helped. What the hell, Superman needed a whole phone booth.

Chapin leaned back against the cushions, waited for his head to clear. Nothing was what it seemed to be in life. Except Ginny. She was herself. But Chapin could think of no one else on earth who was entirely what he seemed to be. According to Ginny, one of the Pumpkin regulars, a short-bearded man who passed himself off as an engineering executive, was actually a rabbi with a well-to-do Westchester congregation. Chapin's high school baseball coach had been a not-entirely-secret homosexual. Just the other day, during a legislative investigation of loansharking, Chapin had been impressed by more than one of the hoodlums who stood up to plead the Fifth Amendment. They had looked and acted very much like successful businessmen and the fact was that any one of them could have belonged to Chapin's country club with no difficulty.

Driving was going to be difficult, but not driving was impossible. Chapin kept the lights off as he drove slowly through the lot and before leaving, he paused to take one last look through the half-curtained front window of the Pumpkin. He was rewarded by a snapshot glimpse of Ginny sitting at the bar talking to a brunette. It was an effort to focus in on the two of them but he recognized the other woman as the friend Ginny had spoken to earlier in the evening. Charlotte, yes—where had he seen her before? A civic meeting, a political rally?

A good memory is standard equipment for a politician, or should be, at any rate. Well, that would give Chapin something to think about on the drive home. Maybe his memory was going. He had read somewhere about men having trouble with their memory after the age of forty. Now where had he read that? Damn it. Forty. Wasn't sexual potency supposed to start going then, too? Well, he hadn't felt any symptoms in *that* area. For all the good it had done him that evening.

It was snowing, large flakes that dissolved as they hit the pavement. Jericho Turnpike seemed deserted and he made good time as he sped east toward the expressway. Jericho Turnpike was getting to be an old derelict of a road, beaded and bangled with bars and gas stations. Good real estate, though—he wished he had been in politics back when it was being developed. Or, rather, shortly before it was developed. That's when a man could make a fortune.

The terrain improved the closer Chapin came to his home. The expressway flowed through flat high-ranch and split-level developments, but the road north toward Stony Harbor wound uphill past larger homes shrouded in thick woods. A sign: INCORPORATED VILLAGE OF STONY HARBOR. NO STOPPING, NO PARKING, NO PEDDLERS. A turn to the right, another, and he passed the mailbox that marked the beginning of a long winding driveway. In the moonlight, snow jeweled the trees bordering the driveway and glistened against the white façade of the colonial home. When Chapin had purchased the home new a dozen years earlier, it had been worth $80,000—but he had been helpful to the builder on a zoning matter and had gotten the house for $50,000. On the current market it was worth at least three times that figure.

Chapin enjoyed his home. No, he felt comfortable with it, at ease with the large beam-ceilinged rooms, the solid furniture. Before going upstairs, he sat at the counter in the spotless kitchen and drank a Tab. Then to bed.

"Chapin?" It was a sleepy murmur.

"Yes, dear, go back to sleep."

"What time is it?"

"One thirty," he lied. "Go to sleep."

Thalia mumbled something about the boys, then nestled back into her blanket. She must have gone to sleep without a pill or she wouldn't have stirred at all. She usually went to bed immediately after the eleven o'clock news, frequently accompanied by sleeping pills.

Chapin stood at the window for a moment, staring at the silent snow and the glistening trees. Then he turned back to the bed and reached under his pillow for the flannel pajamas. What would Ginny think of the pajamas? She probably would have laughed; she would have found so much of his life here humorous.

The luminous face of the digital AM-FM clock-radio on his night table read 4:03 as he hunched between the covers. Was Ginny asleep? They had never spent an entire night together and he had been thinking about that. Damn it, that was something they should be able to work out. There was no reason she couldn't get time off and come up to Albany. He imagined it. Dinner at L'Epicure and then a nice drive over to Saratoga, over to that new Holiday Inn in Saratoga. Why had he waited this long?

He closed his eyes and Ginny came back to fill his mind. She was with him then, repeating his name over and over. He could feel her presence in the room, the way she would touch him here and there. For a moment State Senator Chapin Kirk Hope, Republican-Stony

19

Harbor, tensed in his bed. Then he reached down and put his hands in his pajamas.

Winter sunlight washed the room and splashed against his face. He looked at the clock and came fully awake as he was able to make out the numbers: 11:30. Oh, God, his head. A hangover. No, it was worse than that. Thalia's bed was made and a note had been propped against the lamp on the night table: "Beauty Parlor. Home at 1 P.M." The note had been written neatly in green ink on her personal stationery.

Christ, but they were a matched pair. Mr. and Mrs. Proper. The only thing saving Chapin was his Harry side; Thalia would never understand that. But if she could, or if she had her own Harry side, they might both be a lot better off. Patterns, it was all patterns. Shop at Saks and Bonwit's; golf in the low nineties; subscribe to *Time* and *Town & Country*; join the Book-of-the-Month Club; serve as chairman of the Stony Harbor Garden Club and director of the Voters' Registration Committee of the League of Women Voters; find time to teach Sunday School at St. Stephen's Episcopal Church; give to the Friends of the Stony Harbor Library; support the town drug council. It was the same basic mold that had attracted Chapin when they met at Penn except then there had been something else, a hint of untapped passion. A false hint. The first time they made love Thalia had been a virgin; at the time he considered this an example of her admirable self-restraint but now he had come to believe she was only following her natural instincts.

Thalia no longer gave off hints of passion. Her slimness had become angularity and the flavor was antiseptic. She reminded Chapin of those alarmingly bright-eyed, all-American suburban types who spoke up on behalf of dishwashing liquids and discount houses for the benefit of television audiences.

Thalia would have been a natural for commercials. Her teeth gleamed and so did her stemware. The house was always in perfect order. But to give credit where credit was due, Lupe, the latest in a series of sleep-ins, was proving a gem. As Chapin came down the stairs, Lupe had just finished doing the living room and was dragging the vacuum cleaner into the dining room. She said that Mrs. Hope had told her to make fresh coffee for him and that the pot was on in the kitchen. If he wanted anything else, she'd be happy to prepare it for him. "*Café bueno*," Chapin said in an accent that drew a broken-toothed smile from Lupe.

The boys heard him and came running from the den, where they'd been shooting pool. Chapin Jr. was fifteen; Tommy was thirteen. Chapin took pleasure in simply looking at them—each had his father's brown hair and his mother's gray-green eyes and the even features that could have come from either parent. They had no exceptional talents and no exceptional problems and that suited their father fine.

"Hey, Dad," Tommy was saying, "c'mon, we're playing eight ball, you can take the winner."

"Okay," Chapin said, "but give me a couple of minutes to get some coffee down. Listen, guys, I'm sorry I didn't get home in time for dinner last night."

"No sweat, Dad," young Chape said. "Like my social studies teacher says, government should be a full-time job."

"You know, he's right."

"I don't know if I told you about him," the boy went on. "His name is Mr. Steiner and he's pretty good. Uh, he wants to know if you'd come in and speak to the class."

"Sure, if it's okay with you," Chapin said. "I mean, are you sure it wouldn't embarrass you?"

"Are you putting me on?" the boy said.

Chapin couldn't stop himself from reaching over and squeezing the boy's shoulder—at the same instant he realized that it was a gesture that he had picked up from the governor. The teacher's name was new to him. Steiner. Probably Jewish. Most likely another one of those liberal Democrats who seemed to infest teaching staffs. Oh, so what? If they lived in the district, they usually wound up voting for him. All it took was a man-to-man handshake and the basic we-all-believe-in-the-same-thing routine. And a speech to the class about ethics in government and the need for a responsible citizenry. And what the hell, Chapin really did believe in these things.

"Hurry up, Dad," Tommy was calling.

It was another world. This was Senator Hope at home. Saturday in the suburbs. This was sneakers and white athletic socks and light tan chino pants and a cocoa-colored crew-neck sweater. This was a day for shooting pool and watching a football game. Was there anything that would intrude? No, about the only thing he should do was check with Greg on what was new at the office. Hope, Hammer & Battalini. Jack Battalini was a junior partner, added to the firm less than a year ago. The name Battalini was of vital importance in an area where Catholics represented the most populous religious grouping. Jack handled most of the divorce cases; Chapin specialized in zoning and land law; Greg took charge of the criminal cases.

Chapin stood at the refrigerator long enough to taste at a glass of orange juice. No he was not ready for that. He poured coffee from

21

the electric ceramic pot into the oversized mug that the boys had gotten for one Father's Day or another. The mug was carried to the counter, where Thalia had left a plate of chocolate-covered doughnuts and a copy of the *Daily Islander*. Two things happened simultaneously. He reached for a doughnut and saw the front-page headline.

COCKTAIL WAITRESS
MURDERED ON LI

Shock was immediate. As he drew his hand back, the doughnut fell straight down and splashed into the coffee. COCKTAIL WAITRESS. . . . What would seem oddest in retrospect was that the headline had been sufficient; he did not have to see her name to know that it was Ginny. He did not have to read that awful first line: "The mutilated body of red-haired cocktail waitress Virginia Hanson was. . . ." The story started on the front page and was continued on page three. It was relatively short and had probably been rushed into print just before the paper's deadline. Chapin read the story not word by word, but syllable by syllable.

COCKTAIL WAITRESS
MURDERED ON LI

by Robert J. O'Malley

The mutilated body of red-haired cocktail waitress Virginia Hanson was discovered at 5:30 A.M. today in the bedroom of her blood-strewn Mineola apartment. Police said Mrs. Hanson, a twenty-five-year-old divorcée who lived alone with her eight-year-old daughter but was known to have several men friends, had been badly beaten and then "butchered" by an ax-wielding assailant. Her daughter, Laura, was unharmed.

Police discovered the body after being called by Roland Feebe, a writer, who lives across the hall from Mrs. Hanson. According to police, Feebe phoned after being awakened by the sounds of a violent struggle in the waitress' apartment. He said the struggle lasted for about fifteen minutes. Just after he called, Feebe told police, he heard the apartment door slam and someone run into the hall. He said he was afraid to open his own door. Police later found Laura Hanson crying in the bedroom closet in her apartment. She said she had run into the closet when she heard the fighting. Signs of struggle were evident throughout the kitchenette, living room, and Mrs.

Hanson's bedroom in the four-room, ground-level apartment, part of the Nassau Overlook apartment complex.

"I never saw anything like it," said Ptl. Frank Cappobianco, one of the officers first to arrive on the scene. "The place was drenched with blood." Det. Lt. Charles Brownstein, chief of the Nassau Homicide Division, described the killing as "one of the most brutal murders I've ever seen. The victim was literally butchered."

Mrs. Hanson was employed as a cocktail waitress at the Pumpkin, a bar-restaurant on Jericho Turnpike less than a mile from her home. It was listed in a *Daily Islander* article recently as one of Long Island's leading "cheaters' bars." Early today police were tracing Mrs. Hanson's movements prior to the murder and checking into her personal life.

Lt. Brownstein said the police were hoping for a quick break in the case. "We already have some leads," he said. Brownstein said there were no signs of forced entry and that the murder victim probably knew the killer.

As police began sifting evidence, Roland Feebe sobbed in his apartment across the hall from the murder scene.

"It's just terrible," said the thirty-one-year-old writer who has authored several children's books and is currently working on a book of poetry. "I don't know why anyone would want to hurt Virginia. She had no enemies and she minded her own business. She was a wonderful person."

The coffee and the doughnuts remained untouched as Chapin read through the story two more times. Virginia Hanson. He had never thought of her as Virginia; just Ginny. Virginia Hanson was a woman he didn't know; Ginny was someone who had given him pleasure—pleasure and love.

The words were all wrong. COCKTAIL WAITRESS. There was a hardness to that, a cheapness. It was why he had never thought of her in those terms. Cocktail waitress. No. And then the other word, the impossible word. MURDERED. Ginny murdered. And the rest. "Blood-strewn . . . butchered." Someone had beaten Ginny and cut her up with an ax. Some dirty, stinking lunatic had butchered Ginny, his Ginny. It was so unthinkable. Someone had actually cut into that soft, fragile, loving body with an ax. Someone who was still alive, still running around loose. And he, Chapin, had been with her just a few hours before it happened. Maybe even less than that.

The paper began to shake in his hand and he smoothed it out against the counter. The sense of loss, even the sense of horror, were being replaced by a sense of fear. A shiver of pure fright sliced through his stomach. He traced his finger across the news story. There it was: ". . . police were tracking Mrs. Hanson's movements prior to the murder and checking into her personal life."

He was involved in both categories. Or was he? Well, someone named Harry was. Detectives were probably talking to people from the Pumpkin now and someone was bound to tell them about Harry. Surely someone already had. Bobby Kelly knew Harry and so did Baldy, the manager. Even that Charlotte could identify Harry. And that fag writer across the hall—what was his name? Feebe—the queer son of a bitch had stared right into him. He probably had already given the police a description.

Still, would they be able to trace him? They'd be looking for Harry the salesman, not for State Senator Chapin Hope. But you could never tell. And what did that detective mean about a quick break? Maybe Ginny had met someone else when she went back to the Pumpkin. No, he couldn't believe that.

Suddenly Chapin was aware of a tug at his sleeve.

"C'mon, Dad, you said you were gonna play."

"Not now," he said, pulling away. "I have to do something."

Ignoring the hurt on the boy's face, Chapin rushed out of the kitchen and ran back up the stairs to the privacy of his bedroom. He picked up the phone on Thalia's night table and dialed Greg Hammer's number.

3

Forty miles west of Stony Harbor, on the second floor of an old apartment building overlooking a municipal parking lot in Hempstead, Robert O'Malley did not have to be told what had happened to him. Nor did he have to be told what to do. Nothing. Absolutely nothing. The important thing was to lie there with your eyes shut and not move a muscle. That way nothing would break.

O'Malley tried to gauge the extent of the damage. There are some who say it feels as though your tongue has grown a coat of fur. O'Malley felt that to be a serious misstatement of fact. His tongue had grown three sizes larger than his mouth but it was completely numb. Actually, the fur seemed to be growing between his teeth.

Nor was there any truth in the contention that a hangover dulls the senses. O'Malley's senses had never been more keen. The wintry, midmorning sun, finding a tiny gap in the double curtains, seemed explosive. And O'Malley found himself praying that the phone would not ring; he feared the sound might be fatal.

But, then, a hangover was as much a part of O'Malley's morning as a shower. During the past eleven years there had been only one period when he had awakened without pain. That had been at the marina at Varadero Beach, where he had been covering the exodus of Cuban refugees, and the Miami skipper whose boat he was on discovered that he had neglected to lay in hard liquor. For six unforgettable mornings O'Malley had awakened with an uncoated tongue and unblurred vision; it had been the worst week of his life. Finally, deliverance had come in the form of a bottle of rum he had obtained in a trade with one of the young, pistol-packing Castro soldiers who made sure no one left the dock area. The bottle had cost him a Kodak Instamatic, but was well worth it. As O'Malley later explained to an editor, he took lousy pictures.

This particular morning, however, seemed especially disastrous. Last night had been the dead woman. How many drinks had it taken to get beyond that one? He remembered cutting the seal on a new quart bottle of Jack Daniel's and he did not remember throwing the empty bottle into the sack on the kitchen floor. In all probability, then, he had taken less than a quart. Good. That was something in his favor.

He was trying not to think about the killing but there was no way to keep the details from returning. Well, there was *one* way. If he could only manage to get up and get the first drink down.

First one eye was opened and then the other. Except for the single spot of sunlight, the room was dark, dark by design. There was nothing in the room that O'Malley cared to see. An undistinguished bureau, its top drawer forever stuck shut; an out-of-date calendar, turned to December of the previous year; an oversized bed that sagged like a hammock beneath the 320 pounds of the man once considered the best investigative reporter north of Drew Pearson.

O'Malley was an unregenerate Old Journalist. He was incapable of using the word "I" in a news story and he would not have known how to insert an adamantly personal opinion. He had no concern at all with inner motivations, stream of consciousness, literary style, or pop psychology. Nor did he ever find it necessary to "pipe"—to varnish the truth. He would go to a great many lengths to get a story, but he would not make one up. He felt the reporter's job was to get as much relevant information as possible and then to present it in an orderly and understandable fashion. Anything less than that—or more than that—did not interest him.

Bias was the reporter's enemy and O'Malley did not, under most circumstances, even go to the trouble of forming an opinion. Except during national campaigns, politics was a bore. One year he exposed a State Liquor Authority scandal, and the next year he pried into the efforts of politicians to get kickbacks from Long Island defense contractors. And for that one, just eleven years earlier, O'Malley had been given the Pulitzer.

That same year his marriage had ended. Not coincidentally, that same year he had taken up steady company with a bottle. The photograph of him accepting the Pulitzer showed a lean, boyish man with the dark curly hair and bright blue eyes of an Irish tenor. Now, if O'Malley were to describe himself in a news story, it would be as "a large shambling man" or perhaps as a "bearlike figure." A reporter less sensitive to physical appearance might settle for a simple adjective: "fat."

As he lay in bed, staring through darkness at the ceiling, wondering whether he dare reach under the pillow for a pack of cigarettes, O'Malley found that he could not stop the night before from intruding itself on the morning after.

The memories had long ago become superabundant. The images that survived now were the kind you would prefer to bury. The roughest ones—Newark going up in flames, a civil rights worker shot through the head in a car outside Selma, a village napalmed in Vietnam, cops clubbing down a cripple in Chicago—stayed with him the longest; and he knew the memory of the night before would never be erased.

O'Malley had gotten a ride from headquarters with the chief of Homicide, Detective Lieutenant Charles Brownstein. He had noticed that the young patrolman standing outside the apartment door seemed unusually pale. There was a second man there, a neighbor, who turned out to be a poet, and he had been holding a blanket up to his face like a small child and he had been crying.

The reporter had followed the detective into the apartment and both men had had to step over a human arm that lay beside the welcome mat in the foyer. The amount of blood staining the living-room rug and splattered over two of the walls made O'Malley doubt that it could have all come from one victim. It was then he tasted his dinner a second time and knew he was going to vomit.

"Hey, buddy, don't go in there," a young patrolman had said but O'Malley made it to the bathroom and bent over the toilet. When he straightened up he saw that a severed head had been left in the sink, an eyeless head with startlingly red-orange hair, and he was sick a second time.

"I tried to stop him from going in there," Cappobianco, the patrolman, was explaining to Brownstein. "The head's in there in the sink."

"You'll have to be more careful, Bob," Brownstein said. "The boys haven't had time to go through the place yet. This has to be the worst one I've ever seen. The very worst."

O'Malley had spotted the bottle of Chivas Regal on the counter separating the kitchenette and the living room. If ever he needed a drink, it was then. Even as the thought crossed his mind, a detective called out from the kitchen area: "Oh, Jesus, you're not going to believe what's in here."

O'Malley had seen more than enough. He had also seen a half-dozen roaches in the ashtray. He went to the poet, who was still weeping into the blanket, and asked for the nearest phone. The man introduced himself as Roland Feebe and led O'Malley to his apartment across the hall. It was white from floor to ceiling—white carpeting, white furniture, white phone. A small dog—even he was white—yipped nervously as O'Malley picked up the phone.

"You can forget about your front page," he said to the night news editor. "You can stick it in the garbage can."

"What've you got, Bob?"

"An ax murder," he said. "The goriest goddamn killing I've ever seen. Some lunatic hacked a cocktail waitress to pieces."

27

"We've only got fifteen minutes. Twenty at most."

"Okay, I'll get what I can."

He reached into his jacket for the folded sheets of copy paper he used instead of a notebook, groped further for a pencil stub that quickly became an extension of his right arm. He asked Feebe questions as they walked back to the victim's apartment. Feebe was shaken but, like most people, he didn't mind having his name in the paper. He gave O'Malley the victim's name, age, occupation, and a little of her background.

"Did she live alone?" O'Malley asked.

"No, oh, God!" Feebe said. "Where's Laura? Laura's her little girl."

"Did you check the bedroom?" Brownstein asked Cappobianco.

"Just a quick check," the patrolman said. "I'll take another look."

As Cappobianco went toward the bedroom, O'Malley's eyes moved from one object to another in the living room. The pencil never stopped moving: "Grn walls. . . . 20 x 14 . . . inexp . . . $190? . . . no books . . . Wyeth print waterfall . . . blood on 2 walls. . . ."

"The kid's okay," Cappobianco called from the bedroom. "Just shaken up. She's been hiding here in the closet. She didn't see anything, just heard her mother screaming."

"Keep her there!" Brownstein said. "Keep her there till we're through out here." He turned toward the medical examiner. "Doc, you got anything in that bag that would knock the kid out, I mean *out*?"

"I think so," the examiner said. "How old is she?"

"Seven. No, eight," Feebe said. "Just turned eight."

O'Malley added that to the loose string of notations and headed back toward Feebe's apartment and the phone.

"This is O'Malley again," he said. "Smitty on rewrite tonight?"

"No time for rewrite," he was told. "I'm going to put you right into the machine and we'll move it out back in takes. It'll have to go out the way you dictate. Okay?"

"Fine."

"Okay, I'll hook you into the machine. Wait for the buzz."

That damn buzz. It was all too mechanical for O'Malley. He didn't like the idea of talking nonstop but the machine came with a voice-activated device that automatically shut down the recorder after seven seconds of silence. What bothered O'Malley most was the absence of any human reaction. It was like shouting into a storm. With Smitty you'd get a "nice work" or a "you're up" but with the machine all you ever got was a click and a long empty silence.

Buzz.

"The mutilated body of red-haired cocktail waitress Virginia Hanson—H-A-N-S-O-N—was discovered at five thirty—five three oh—A.M. today in the bedroom of her blood-strewn Mineola apartment, period. Police said. . . ."

Flipping rapidly from one scrawl to the next, resorting to the journalistic shorthand familiar to any reporter racing a deadline, O'Malley dictated the story almost precisely as it was to appear in the paper two hours later. A deskman would be able to edit the story in seconds—the only marks he would make were to indicate paragraphs and capitalization. Though unapplauded, O'Malley's effort was something of a bravura performance—there would be no wrong names, no incorrect ages, no inaccurate quotes, no overly gruesome descriptions. But all of the available facts would be there, presented in an orderly fashion, and anyone reading the story would understand the horror of what had happened.

As he came to the end of his story, the reporter heard Feebe talking to himself in a singsong voice.

"I don't know why anyone would want to hurt Virginia," Feebe was saying. "She had no enemies and she minded her own business. She was a wonderful person."

O'Malley tacked it onto the end of the story. It was the kind of sentiment someone always expressed in the wake of violence, but it made an adequate kicker. Then he said "Thirty" into the phone, a hangover from a time when men sat down at typewriters to do news stories, and he walked back one last time to the murdered woman's apartment.

"Brownie, I'll see you tomorrow," he said.

"Not until noon," Brownstein said. "Seriously."

"I don't expect to be conscious until noon."

The homicide chief allowed himself a half smile. When they first met, O'Malley had just graduated to the *Daily Islander* from an upstate daily and Brownstein had just been promoted to detective. Although Brownstein worked at giving an equal break to all the reporters, those early ties could sometimes be a help. O'Malley had been the only reporter still at headquarters when the murder victim was discovered and Brownstein had offered the lift to the scene. Now Brownstein arranged for the reporter to be driven back to headquarters in a patrol car.

O'Malley would not push the chief and Brownstein knew that. It would have been wasted effort. No one pushed Brownstein. He had worked his way from patrolman to detective in thoroughly unmeteoric fashion, one small step and then another. Brownstein's real talent was for hard work, for intelligence and reliability instead of genius. He had gotten ahead, not by being dazzlingly right, but by never being glaringly wrong.

Brownstein's name had been mentioned in hundreds of news stories, which—along with the fact that he had a night-school law degree—made many consider him the logical replacement for the incumbent Nassau district attorney, Norman Galton, if and when Galton decided to leave the office. O'Malley was not one who felt that, however. He knew that Brownstein never promised more than he could deliver, knew that he would never announce the verdict before the evidence was collected. How could he be a DA?

There were other reasons why O'Malley knew Brownstein would never sit in the big office. The Homicide chief had no use for politicians. He didn't seek the publicity that came his way. While some cops would turn in their mothers if it meant a name in the headline or a picture in the paper, Brownstein never even gestured. If O'Malley was a reporter, Brownstein was a cop.

Brownstein did nothing impetuously or emotionally. Even late that night in the murdered woman's apartment he showed little reaction. He had never stopped directing the police photographer and the medical examiner and the fingerprint men and the blood technicians—he had orchestrated the symphony, but had not reacted in any purely human way to the tragedy at his feet. No, not true—there was that moment when he had suddenly shouted to Cappobianco to keep the kid away.

As O'Malley was leaving the apartment, he stopped to talk briefly with Leonard McCoy, the county medical examiner.

"Tell me one thing, Doc," he said. "How're you going to figure the cause of death on something like that?"

"It's a beauty," the examiner conceded. "We won't say anything until we get all the pieces back and start looking them over. But I'll tell you this much—you can say that it's definitely a homicide."

"Can I quote you on that?"

"Well, it's either a homicide or the most thorough suicide on record."

The medical examiner's humor was not surprising; McCoy was a man who took great delight in showing newsmen through the county morgue. O'Malley was sure that the doctor was delighted to be involved in a crime this macabre.

The reporter shook his head and left. Unlike some fat men, O'Malley moved with utter gracelessness. One might conclude, rightly, that the weight was an acquisition of recent years and he had not yet gotten used to the burden. O'Malley seemed unaware of his appearance. His suits could have been cut from circus tents—the narrowness of the lapels and ties reflected not only an earlier era but also the fact that he had long ago given up any notion of concealing his bulk.

The weight was one reason why people, even people on the paper, tended to speak of O'Malley in the past tense. The drinking was another reason. He had won the Pulitzer and so there would always be a measure of respect, but the kind of respect one might accord a former all-American or a once-popular crooner or a dinosaur. O'Malley's editors considered him something of a calculated risk; and so he had been taken off the riots and wars and national stories and major investigations and placed back where he started, on a police beat. More often than not, the risk paid off and the job on the ax murder was just one of many examples.

Still, the younger reporters on the paper were not that impressed. Alcohol is the cement that holds together most newspaper myths, but these are myths from another time. Most of the young reporters, look-alike journalism-school graduates, seemed interested in raising families and financing mortgages and becoming part of the community. In their eyes O'Malley was as obsolete as an antimacassar.

Some stood grudgingly in awe of his capacity for liquor. But what they didn't see, what only one person in the world ever saw, was the effect of the drinking. And this particular morning after, O'Malley was having a difficult time making it as far as that first cigarette.

"Are you okay in there?"

"Don't ask."

The first words are the hardest. It was a croak. Teddi Bennett stepped in to survey the damage. Teddi lived on the fifth floor, and three mornings a week, sometimes four, she got off the elevator at the second floor. It was a body check, a way of making sure that O'Malley had not come down with some exotic fever or, more likely, was not lying dead of a richly deserved coronary.

If Teddi missed the rendezvous more than two consecutive mornings, O'Malley would ride the elevator up to the fifth floor and knock on her door and ask to borrow a cup of whatever came to mind. They had never formalized the arrangement, had never even thought it through, but the morning visits were a ritual and rituals hold together the days for people who live alone. Even the hangover was a ritual and without it, O'Malley would feel incomplete, as though an old friend had stepped out of his life.

She was not O'Malley's friend because of any mutuality of interests, or because of any notable intelligence, or because of any enduring beauty. She, too, was a past-tense figure. She had danced

31

at the Latin Quarter when that was what tall blond girls aspired to; she had worked as a high-priced call girl in Manhattan until age caught up with her.

Now forty-one, Teddi tended bar at the Blue Barn in Syosset, where an endless stream of potentially wayward husbands could admire her slimness, could ignore the wrinkle lines appearing around the eyes, could forget that the platinum was bottled. Teddi lived on the fifth floor and she was Robert O'Malley's friend, his only friend, and she was there if he needed her.

"What hit you?" she said. "You look even more awful than usual."

"You're not going to believe this," he croaked.

"Try me."

"Well, eleven men came in here last night and tied me up," he said, not bothering to turn his head toward her. "They forced me to drink an entire bottle of booze. It was a horrible experience."

"Well, it looks like you put up a struggle," she said.

O'Malley's clothes, resembling nothing so much as huge deflated balloons, had been left wherever they had been removed. Teddi picked them up, emptied the pockets out onto the bureau, wadded the clothes together, and deposited them on the floor of a closet already piled high. She put fresh water in the kettle and turned on the gas burner; O'Malley detested instant coffee but anything else was unthinkably complicated.

"Bob, I knew that girl in your story today."

"That Virginia . . . ?"

"Ginny Hanson," she said. "We worked the Intimate Room together two, three years ago. She was a good kid, Bob. What really happened to her?"

"Imagine the worst. That's what happened."

"It was really an ax?"

"Believe it," he said. "Chopped up like firewood. They don't have the weapon but the doc says it has to be an ax or something like it. A cleaver, maybe. He says no knife would have done it."

"She was such a nice kid, really," Teddi said, "although she never did have any taste in men."

"Yeah, I'll take that as gospel."

"She lived for her kid," Teddi said. "Her Laura. I'll tell you, nothing else counted. She liked sex but even that didn't count when it came to Laura. Just getting enough to feed the kid and pay for the sitter—the rest was nothing. I don't think she ever had a piece of real jewelry in her life. She was very bad with men. I never saw anyone have such lousy luck. Remember that Jericho Turnpike deal, the housewife hookers? Ginny was picked up there."

"Tell me again what a nice kid she was."

"Don't be mean, Bob. Taking tricks has got nothing to do with good or bad. If some guy started waving an ace in front of her, all she saw was a new dress for the kid. I don't think she ever even looked at half the guys who were paying her for it. And when she got caught, she stopped on the spot. She never went into court—but she had to do some favors for someone in the cops, you know what I mean, and he kept the record clean. I know that Ginny got her kicks, okay, but not from the kind of things that guy wanted."

"Now it's getting interesting."

"I wish I could tell you more," Teddi said. "But Ginny never spelled it out for me."

It was time to try the coffee and O'Malley sat up slowly. His naked feet found their way into the slippers and he started to lumber across the room toward the bathroom. He was wearing a red nightshirt and when he came back five minutes later, he was in a terry-cloth robe and his hair was wet over his forehead. The coffee.

"Did this Ginny ever get serious with a guy?"

"Constantly," Teddi said. "But only with the worst types, the worst types for her. I mean we could be working a bar filled with bachelors and she'd locate the one married man there and not only that but he'd turn out to be in the Mafia. I never saw anything like it. She had a *knack*."

"Well, it finally paid off."

The coffee was staying down. Good. O'Malley added a jolt of whiskey to the unrinsed cup, swallowed it, found some copy paper and a pencil, started taking notes.

"It didn't make sense to me," Teddi was saying. "She'd work overtime to get some change for the kid. Then she'd be going with some guy who is married for twenty years, a walletful of pictures of his kids, a potential gold mine, if you know what I mean, and she'd never hit him up for a penny. Of course, I haven't seen her in over a year—hey, Bob, you're not using my name, are you?"

"You know better than that," he said. "Let me ask you this— what was her drink?"

"Rum and Coke sometimes," she said, "but more often it was just plain Coke."

"Would she ever drink Chivas Regal?"

"No way. Not then anyway. She said that scotch tasted like cough medicine."

"Well, whoever sliced her up last night was drinking Chivas."

"He has expensive taste."

"Well, if I were tending bar these days," O'Malley said, trying to keep it light, but failing, "I wouldn't be going home with anyone

33

who was ordering Chivas. Not for a while, anyway.''

"Thanks, Bob," she said. "Seriously, thanks. But don't worry. I'm not going home with anyone these days.'' She stood and gestured that it was time for her to leave.

"Thanks for stopping in, Teddi.''

O'Malley watched her as she left. She still had the good wheels—he made the observation academically; he was appreciative but uninvolved. One night almost ten years earlier they had spent a night together, and they had never done it since. It was not that it had been unpleasant or unsuccessful or undramatic or unanything. Maybe it was just that a mutual curiosity had been satisfied and there was no need ever to mention the incident again. And later Teddi had become much more than lover, she had become a friend. When O'Malley felt the need for sex—which was not as often as it had once been—he arranged for a hooker.

As the door closed behind Teddi, O'Malley added a fresh splash of bourbon to the coffee cup. He then sorted out the pills. A nineteen-gram lecithin, a 1,000-mg vitamin A, three vitamin E's, one vitamin B-12, three multipurpose vitamins, all washed down in a single swallow of booze. Silly really. But O'Malley had read of too many alcoholics hit by malnutrition and he often thought how embarrassing that would be, a 320-pound man starving to death.

4

By noon, when O'Malley drove up, there were three orange-and-blue Nassau County patrol cars parked outside the Pumpkin. Inside, Lennie Davito—Leonardo, to both police and reporters—was creating a composite picture of the suspect. Using a metallic clipboard and magnetized facial characteristics—sets of eyebrows, lips, noses, and so forth—he was slowly putting together the thoroughly ordinary face of Virginia Hanson's last known escort.

Brownstein was watching quietly as three middle-aged men, apparently regular customers, assisted Leonardo in his efforts.

O'Malley recognized the man using the bar phone as Baldy Davits, a man who had specialized in managing bars like the Pumpkin all over Long Island. The reporter heard a few sentences, realized that Baldy was wheeling and dealing for a replacement for the late Virginia Hanson.

"Anything yet, Brownie?"

"A man was here with her last night," Brownstein said. "We're getting his description now. So far we've got two dozen people who saw him or think they know something about him."

"Like what?"

"Well, he seems to be a quiet type—but maybe that just means quiet for this place," Brownstein said. "Good-looking . . . refined—but again, that may just mean refined for here, and that might also apply to Jack the Ripper. Leonardo's working on the sketch now and you'll get a copy as soon as it's ready."

"Yeah, that'll get a good play," O'Malley said. "By the way, who are my colleagues?"

"So far, believe it or not, you're almost alone," Brownstein said. "I hear the *Newsday* man is on his way and the *Press* has decided to do it by phone—they say they're short on Saturday. Some TV people are coming out."

"Yeah," said O'Malley. "Some kid who gets his hair done in a beauty parlor will stand in front of the joint and make a speech about crime in the suburbs. Beautiful."

Brownstein grinned in response.

"Another thing, Bob," he said. "We'll be setting up a special police number for anyone with a lead. I'll get that to you as soon as I know what it is."

"Have you got the description now?"

"Approximately six feet tall, one hundred and eighty pounds, approximately forty years old." Brownstein was reading from a small loose-leaf notebook. "No identifying scars or characteristics. Claims to be an insurance salesman. Claims to be from New Jersey. Uses first name of Harry but no one recalls last name. Last seen wearing a gray suit, a white shirt, and an orange print tie."

"Could be anybody."

"I know," said the chief. "Another thing, though; we did find out there was sex involved. The ME said there was semen in the vagina."

"Well," O'Malley said, "at least you know a man did it."

"What we know," Brownstein said, "is that a man had intercourse with her last night. Which reminds me, Bob, I know that you and I can work together and I'm willing to give you what we get as we get it. The exception, the only exception, is anything that might hurt us, hurt the case, if it is given out. If you should come up with anything, I'll expect the same break."

"No problem," O'Malley said. "I think I can even give you a little something now."

"Yes?"

"Well, I can tell you that she was one of the Jericho Turnpike originals. . . ."

"A hooker?"

"That's my information."

"Frankly, Bob, I think we would have had that. We ran a check on her and she comes out clean."

"She had a helpful friend."

"Who?"

"I don't know," O'Malley said, "and I'm not going with it unless I do know. But I've been told that one of the investigators made a trade with her, a favor for a favor."

"Who gave you that?"

"I can't say, Brownie, but it's reliable. My feeling about Virginia Hanson is this—she may have been a little off, may have even been a little nympho, but that's mostly guessing. What I do know is that she had a genius for picking wrongos."

"And how much of that is speculation, Bob?"

"I didn't bring an affidavit with me, Brownie, but I think that'll hold up."

36

Baldy had put the receiver back in the cradle. Judging by the expression on his face, he had failed to locate a replacement. O'Malley walked over and showed him his police press pass.

"Yeah, I read your story," Baldy said. "What's the matter with you guys? I've seen you before, either here or somewhere, and you can't mention the Pumpkin without putting us down. You had to dig up that cheaters'-bar shit again. It's not as if we don't buy ads in your goddamn paper—"

"I don't give a rat's ass about what you buy," O'Malley cut it off there. "And I'd just as soon you didn't waste my time trying to bullshit me. Every time that cheaters'-bar stuff gets into the paper, you've got to take on another bartender. When you see what I'm going to put into tomorrow's story, you're going to have to send out for ropes to hold back the crowd. Now, if you'll just pour me a bourbon—Jack Daniel's is fine—we can get on with this. Who knows? You may even get your name in the paper."

"Look, O'Malley"—pure weasel—"all I'm asking is that you say something nice about the place. Would it kill you to just once write something nice?"

"Why don't you start by telling me what kind of woman this Virginia Hanson was?"

"She was a lady," Baldy said. "I mean that and you can put that right there in your paper; she was a genuine lady."

"That's not what I hear."

"Well, you hear wrong, friend. She worked here a year, and the only guy I ever saw her leave with was this guy Harry. She never did nothing out of line. She came in here, she did her job, and that was that."

"How about Harry?"

"Harry's not a regular," Baldy said. "The regulars come here all the time, hate to miss a night. It's like what you might call a social club. You know, like everyone belonging to the same family."

"Let's not get carried away," O'Malley said.

"Well, Harry wasn't no regular. He stopped in about eight months ago for the first time. Ginny took one look at him and that was it."

"So Harry did take her home?"

"Ginny had a thing for him," Baldy said. "He was the only one. When she told me he was married, a family man and all, I told her to be careful, to go easy, but she said it didn't matter. There's nothing dumber than some nice girl flipping over a guy with a wife and kids, but this Harry comes back every week or so, and if the situation don't bother them, why should it bother me?"

"Did this Harry seem to have any peculiar traits?"

37

"I'll tell you something, O'Malley, you want my honest opinion, Harry didn't do this thing. He always behaved himself. He had a good word for everyone and always stayed more or less to himself. Except for Ginny, of course. And he never had more than two drinks. . . ."

"Chivas—am I right?"

"Never," Baldy said. "Harry's drink is Seven and Seven, never nothing else, and not much of that, never more than two and generally he didn't finish the second."

"Who could?" O'Malley said. "That's a kid's drink."

"Then there's a lot of kids coming in here."

"I understand Harry sold insurance?"

"What can I tell you, pal? If a customer tells me he sells insurance, then he sells insurance. And that don't sound to me like a story someone's gonna make up. We get plenty of those, you know—it's a line with some guys, they enjoy telling broads they're from the FBI or the CIA and that's the reason they can never be reached at home, if you follow me, but I never heard of anyone trying to impress a broad by saying he sold insurance."

"Tell me about the way he looked."

"I already went through that with that Leonardo guy," Baldy said. "Isn't that amazing, the way he works? You know who Harry reminds me of? He reminds me of Jack Lemmon, the movie star, only maybe not that good-looking, you know, more gray in the hair, but still and all very nice-looking."

"How about his car?"

"I never noticed it."

"But you say he left with Virginia Hanson last night?"

"Yeah, but they went in Ginny's car, and then Ginny brought him back about closing time. She said that when she came in—"

"Wait a minute—Ginny came back here *alone?*"

"Yeah, but she was just here for a couple of minutes. That wasn't unusual. She'd bring him back to get his car and then she'd come in to say good night."

"Last night did she leave with anyone else?"

"Oh, no, she left alone," Baldy said. "She just stopped in for a few minutes."

"Did she speak to any other men?"

"Nope. The place was all but cleared out then."

"Did she seem frightened of anything? You know, worried about anything?"

"Not in the least," Baldy said. "In fact, she was in a very good mood, kept laughing and saying that something funny had happened. She was talking with me and Charlotte and—"

"Does Charlotte work here?"

"Nope, she's what you could call a semiregular," Baldy said. "She comes in now and then, you know what I mean. She's kind of a friend of Ginny's, which says something about Ginny because Charlotte's a good-looking head. Lots of times good-looking broads bug each other. Anyway, Ginny said she had just been through the funniest night in her life; at least it would seem funny when she could sit down and tell us all about it. And then she just went off by herself."

O'Malley finished his drink. It didn't look as though there would be a second one. He rolled the copy paper up and jammed it into his pocket. He had a lot and he had nothing; he had enough to fill the space in the next day's paper, but he didn't have an inkling of what had actually gone on. The police still didn't have the weapon; Brownstein said they were searching the entire apartment complex in case the murderer had dumped it somewhere on the grounds. What haunted O'Malley was the Chivas in the Hanson woman's apartment. Who was drinking it? Was it possible that there was more than one person involved? No. O'Malley was sure the crime had to be the work of one man. There couldn't be two people on the face of the earth capable of doing what he had seen.

5

Whenever he was faced with a confusing situation, Chapin Hope's first instinct was to take the matter to committee. He realized nothing was ever resolved in committee—who was it that said a helicopter looked as though it had been designed by a committee—but he also knew that a committee could produce options. And, at this moment, options seemed in desperately short supply.

The committee would have to be a three-man body. Himself, Norris Whitlaw, and Greg Hammer. All had been friends since boyhood; all were Stony Harbor residents; all were tied together by dozens of business interests. And yet, anyone looking at the three of them would be more impressed by the differences than by the similarities.

Although Norris Whitlaw headed the sizable Long Island construction firm bearing his name, it was somehow difficult to connect him to the heavy machinery he owned and the massive buildings he put up. Norris Whitlaw favored Italian suits with pinched waists and flared lapels. His hair was tinted a perpetual auburn and worn fashionably long. Wherever he went, Norris exuded a soft intermingling of harmonious scents, Aramis and success.

Greg Hammer—one-third of the law firm of Hope, Hammer & Battalini—was the Island's leading defense attorney. Flamboyant in personality, he was a brisk killer in court. He was as tough-minded as Norris was soft, a realist instead of a dreamer, and the only reason the two of them could get together on any level was Chapin Hope. Chapin was the intermediary, the translator, the bridge. That was Chapin Hope's talent—it explained much of his success as a politician—he had always been a cement that held together dissimilar materials.

On this particular Saturday morning it required three telephone calls for Chapin to reach Norris Whitlaw. One to Norris' home, a second to his office, a third to the Cadillac rolling south on the Sagtikos Parkway, a fourteen-mile belt running north to south on the Island.

"What're you up to, Norris?"

"Eighteen years old. Legs you wouldn't believe. Untouched by human hands. . . ."

"This time of day?"

"This whole weekend," Norris said. "Rhoda thinks I'm off on an overnight to Downingtown, a last weekend of golf with the boys. What it's going to be is a weekend with Donna, my new receptionist."

"Very impressive," Chapin said, "and I hate to interrupt anything like that but I've got to see you."

"Sure, Chape, something to do with the apartment project?"

"I can't say anything over the phone, Norris. This is something I've got to see you about."

"That sounds serious."

"Could be," Chapin Hope said. "Could be. The truth is, I don't know how serious. But I want to sit down and talk it over with you and Greg."

"Fine, how about tomorrow night? We're all getting together at your place for dinner, right?"

"It's more urgent than that," Chapin said. "To tell you the truth, Norris, I was thinking about right this minute."

"Well, old buddy, how about thinking in terms of tomorrow night? Right this minute happens to be taken. You wouldn't want to interfere with the happiness of a beautiful eighteen-year-old girl?"

"Norris, this is important."

"You think this isn't, Chape? Look, give me some idea of what it's all about. . . ."

"Norris. . . ."

"Whatever you're talking about, I'm sure it'll keep. . . ."

"Norris, do me one favor."

"Sure, Chape."

"Just forget it."

Chapin Hope put the phone back in the receiver and stared at it for a long minute. One down, one to go. Chapin didn't think that the phone was tapped but one never knew. No one in politics made such assumptions anymore. Not since Watergate. For all he knew, his phone carried more bugs than a derelict. He kept his call to Greg Hammer brief.

"I might need some legal advice," he said.

"Well, you've come to the best."

"Listen, hotshot, this time I'm serious."

"And you think I'm not?"

"Greg, will you stop and listen for a minute—"

"Hey, something really *is* bothering you."

"Affirmative."

41

"Well, listen, I'm gonna watch Notre Dame today. Why don't you come over and we can have a talk?"

"Greg, can we find another spot? You know Priss—she'd want to know what it's all about."

"It's *that* important?"

"It could be," Chapin said. "You can tell me."

"Right, okay," his law partner said. "Look, it's off-season—why don't we meet at the club? We should have the place to ourselves."

"Fine," Chapin said. "And Greg. . . ."

"Yeah?"

"The sooner, the better."

"I'm on my way."

Chapin left a note for Thalia and yelled a brief apology to the boys: "I've got to run—save me a game." Thalia had taken the Mercedes for her beauty-parlor appointment—she laid claim to it whenever he was home, leaving him with the wagon. Except for the fragmentary exchange late the night before, he and Thalia still had not spoken to or seen each other. It was just as well; Chapin had the feeling that she would be able to look right into him and discover the truth. The note would annoy her—not that she would miss him, simply that he had done something unexpected.

Chapin spurred the station wagon along the road lining a bluff that jutted above Long Island Sound. The day was bright and the unseasonably warm sun was burning off the morning fog. Through the bare branches he could see Connecticut, a distant blur beyond the whitecaps that flecked the water.

Never before had he appreciated his partnership with Greg Hammer as he did at that moment. He was inwardly disturbed that Norris could not tear himself away but Greg was the one who was needed. During the last three or four years Greg Hammer had established his credentials as Long Island's foremost criminal lawyer. "Suburbia's answer to F. Lee Bailey," a Long Island *Press* columnist had called him. And why not? Greg had all the requisites —native intelligence, a strong ego, a flair for cross-examination, a firm belief in pretrial investigation.

Like other superlawyers, Greg also had an uncanny instinct for realizing which cases were *worth* taking. It was an instinct that paid dividends for the firm. During the summer Greg had attracted statewide attention by winning acquittal for a priest accused of killing a Rosary Society president with whom the good father had clearly been having an affair. The priest could barely pay expenses but Greg had figured—correctly—that the case would be worth a fortune in new business.

Greg's Buick was in the parking field when Chapin arrived. He must have raced there—either Greg had detected his desperation or, more likely, he had turned the drive to the club into a small contest. Chapin found himself hurrying through the building. In the lounge two men were sitting in easy chairs watching the big television game. Chapin's steps echoed on the stairs leading down to the locker room. He had never been there when it was quiet and empty, and the silence seemed to accentuate the dankness of the room. He missed the trays of drinks, the smell of liniment, the sound of showers, the bustle of white-jacketed waiters. He walked down the empty locker-sided corridors and in one of them L. Gregory Hammer was sitting on a bench, pouring whiskey out of a leather-covered flask into a small silver cup.

"Up yours," Greg said, offering him the cup and taking a tug from the flask.

"Thanks for coming, old buddy," Chapin said.

"So maybe now you'll tell me what's up."

"It's so goddamn silly. . . ."

"Now I know it's serious," Greg said. "Whenever a client tells me something is silly, I know it's anything but."

"I don't even know how to begin. . . ."

"Oh-oh, they tell me that, too. But—and this may interest you—they always find a way."

"Well, did you see the *Islander* today?"

"As much as I could stand. I glanced through it—that's about all it's ever worth."

"The murder story, the one on the front page?"

"Yeah."

"You read it?"

"Who wouldn't read it? Somebody chops up a cocktail waitress, everybody's going to read it. I don't know anyone who skips by the cunt stories. . . . Hey, what's the matter with you?"

"The woman in the story wasn't like that, Greg. She happened to be a decent human being."

"And you know this for a fact?" Greg was staring at him.

"I knew . . . I . . . uh. . . ." What the hell was the matter with him? "I knew her."

"You what?"

"I knew her."

"You knew her."

"Yes."

Greg wiped the top of the flask with a sleeve of red Banlon and took another swallow.

"And did you also happen to kill her?"

43

It was as if a gun had gone off at close range.

"What?"

"Very simple, buddy. Did you kill her?"

"What the hell's the matter with you, Greg? What kind of question is that?"

"Look, Chape, you're smarter than that. You call me up all hot and bothered. You have a problem. Such a big problem you can't tell me about it on the phone. You don't even want to tell me about it at my house. Now you ask me if I read about a murder, and you tell me you know the victim. I mean, cut the shit, Chape. We're not talking about Elizabeth Barrett Browning, we're talking about a cocktail waitress. So you knew her. Well, old buddy, did you happen to know her in the biblical sense?"

Chapin was not ready to answer that one, not that quickly. If it was that clear to Greg, then it would be that clear to everyone. He found himself staring at a man he had known from childhood and suddenly coming to the realization that somewhere along the way Greg had changed. Even the rugged good looks were fading; the jawline was beginning to lose definition and the once-thick, curly blond hair was disappearing into graying sideburns. He recalled the line that had appeared next to Greg's photo in the high school yearbook ("a halfback with humor so wry, our Greg's a regular guy"). Well, along with the hair, Greg's charm and sense of humor also seemed to be wearing thin. Chapin could feel the nerve tic in his cheek and he turned quickly to keep it from Greg.

"Enough, Chape, you were banging her—why don't we just move on from there?"

"Yes, damn it, I was having an affair with her."

"So I'll ask you again; did you kill her?"

"No, my God, no."

"You probably had plenty of reason to," Greg went on. "If I know the type, and I'm happy to say I do, she was probably hitting you up for a few bucks. Correct me if I'm wrong. Maybe she was threatening to put in a little person-to-person call to Thalia. . . ."

"You didn't know Ginny," Chapin said. "She . . . Ginny . . . was a . . . a . . . well, she was a hell of a fine person."

"And I'll bet she wasn't bad in the sack."

"You may not believe this"—even as he said the words, Chapin knew they were sounding pompous—"it just wasn't like that. I really respected her."

"Beautiful," Greg said. "She was Joan of Arc and you did it to *Clair de Lune*. So why do you need me?"

"Because I was with her last night." The bastard. "That's why I need you."

Greg's sigh started with an upward rolling of eyes and ended in a lip-blown sputter. It was the sort of sigh a parent makes when a guilty child finally admits to an act of wrong-doing. It was also a sound that more than a few of L. Gregory Hammer's clients heard during their first audience with him. It established, usually indelibly, who had the upper hand.

"Okay," Greg said, "now let's go the rest of the way. I don't want to play Perry Mason with my own law partner, but if I'm going to represent you, you might as well tell me everything. Let's start from the beginning."

Chapin told him. Dispassionately, chronologically. He started with that first night he stopped in the Pumpkin. He recalled the first moment he saw her, the hair, the smile. He recalled the times they had met after that. The phone calls. He was aware that Greg was listening at times without comprehension and he wanted desperately to explain his feelings. The best he could manage was, "Nobody ever made me feel like that."

He described his disguise, his Harry disguise. The loud tie, the drinks, the off-color jokes, even the velvet bag for the Senate seal. And with Greg doing nothing more than asking an occasional prompting question, he went through an account of the night before—from the time he first drove into the Pumpkin parking lot to the time he drove out of that same lot a half-dozen hours later.

Only two things seemed to surprise Greg. The first was that he had never discovered the Pumpkin himself. The other was that Chapin had wanted to try marijuana.

"Pot? Jesus H. Christ, Chapin, I don't believe it. That's for kids and weirdos. The next thing you're going to tell me is that you painted a fucking flower on your car."

"It was just one time. . . ."

"But, hell, Chapin, you may not know it, but you're the original Mr. Clean. You were one of the major supporters of that damn law."

"That's one reason I decided to try the stuff," he said. "You mean you've never tried it?"

"As a matter of fact, I never did. I'm a true-blue American. I drink," he said. "Did anything come up in her apartment? Are you sure you didn't push her around? You didn't even have an argument?"

"Nothing like that," Chapin said. "I don't think we were ever happier together."

"She wasn't cockteasing? She wasn't giving you a hard time?"

"I'm telling you, Greg, she was never like that. Besides, nothing even happened. I passed out before anything happened."

"For how long?"

"I don't know. An hour, maybe two."

"And no one else was there? No one came in while you were passed out?"

"She would have told me."

"What about her daughter?"

"She was asleep."

"Does she know you, who you are?"

"No."

"Think now. Did she ever meet her Uncle Harry?"

"No, she was never awake. Ginny was careful about that."

"Well, if you can't be good, at least be careful. . . ."

"I need advice, Greg. I don't need cheap shots."

"Just a minute, Senator, I'm not through yet," Greg said. "All right. You're absolutely sure the last time you saw her was through the window of the bar as you drove away?"

"Of course I'm sure."

"You didn't go back to her place?"

"No."

"Didn't park outside her apartment and watch her come back with some other guy?"

"No."

"Didn't see her come back with somebody else and wait there until he left and then go in to give her hell?"

"God damn it, Greg. . . ."

"Take it easy, Chape."

"Take it easy!"

"Chape, if you think this is rough, you've got no idea what may be waiting for you in a courtroom someday. Relax—I said *may*-be."

"My God, are you really asking me these questions? You really are playing Perry Mason. Greg, this is me, Chapin. Chapin Hope. You've known me all my life, Greg. You know what I've accomplished; you know what I stand for. Or at least you should by now. If you don't, no one does. Christ, Greg, you're supposed to be my best friend."

"That's the reason I'm putting you through this." Greg took a long pull from the flask, without taking his eyes off Chapin's face. "I am your friend but you called me as a lawyer. I'm going to be both."

"Well, then, lawyer, you should still know me well enough to know I had nothing to do with what happened to her, to Ginny. My God, that was terrible, horrible. Whoever did that had to be insane.

46

I'm in no way connected with it. I'm innocent. That's the whole point—I am innocent."

"Bullshit! That's precisely *not* the point!" Greg slammed a hand down on the bench in front of him. "Maybe you should pay more attention to this side of the business, Chapin, because you don't know the first thing about criminal law. That's right—not a goddamned thing. I'm not talking about what they teach in the briefcase factories, but the way it is. This isn't some goddamned zoning change, this isn't the good old boys from Rotary getting together to make a tax deal on golf-course property. This is a capital crime. Murder. M-U-R-D-E-R. A very sordid, sloppy, bloody murder. Somebody chopped up a cocktail waitress and a lot of people want to know who did it. And if anyone gets around to you, finally, and formally accuses you of doing it, your innocence is going to be about as important to you as the fact that you have blue eyes. Get that through your head. Innocence doesn't matter. It's never whether a defendant is innocent that counts, it's whether he can demonstrate that he's not guilty—or at least convince the jury that there's a reasonable doubt."

"I'm getting the message. . . ."

"Hell, Chapin a defendant may never be able to establish his innocence. No one ever finds him innocent. They just find him not guilty. Once you get into a courtroom, it's a game. It's all a fucking game."

"That's enough."

"Okay, so just don't give me any more of the . . . senatorial bullshit."

"It's just that I wanted you to know I didn't have a thing to do with what happened."

"Okay. Now can you prove it?"

"If it ever came to it, I think so. Yes, I think I can."

"How?"

"The people who saw me in the Pumpkin and were there when I left her off—they know I didn't go back with her."

"It may help, but it doesn't mean you weren't in her apartment later on."

"Thalia could help," Chapin said. "Thalia woke up for a minute when I came home. She asked me what time it was—it was close to four but I told her one thirty."

"Well, that will help you more with Thalia than it would with a jury," Greg said. "Juries hardly ever listen to a defendant's wife. The presumption is that she'd lie for him no matter what."

"Come on, Greg, do you think someone could accuse me of this?"

"No? Then why are we sitting here talking about it when we could be watching a football game?"

"Well, it would be bad enough—God, it would be the end—if my name is even brought into this thing. You know, that's all the newspapers would need. They'd love it."

"Yeah. 'Senator Dated Murder Victim.' Terrific. Great for circulation."

"It wouldn't do a hell of a lot for my family life either. What worries me is that people are going to give the police my description. Or at least the description of a man named Harry who is going to look an awful lot like me."

"Which people?"

"More than I care to think about. The clowns over at the Pumpkin. Baldy, the manager, for one."

"What's his last name?"

"I have no idea. Then there's Bobby Kelly, the piano player. Anyone else who hangs out there and who ever bothered to look at me when I was with Ginny. I don't know. Certainly the fag poet who lives across the hall from her place. Feebe."

"Yeah, he could be trouble," Greg said. "Are you sure he's queer?"

"According to Ginny. Why?"

"That kind of information can always come in handy. Okay, anyone else? How about the other broad, the one your friend introduced you to?"

"Charlotte? Definitely."

"That's all?"

"All I can think of."

"And there's nothing else that places you at the scene, nothing the cops could call evidence?"

"Nothing I can think of."

"You're sure? Think hard, Chape."

Chapin was still shaken by Greg's hard grilling. Greg's tone was so lacking in sympathy, so arrogantly superior, that it made him feel stupid, even guilty. Chapin was rattled. He started to repeat again that he could remember nothing more, then froze as a picture flashed into his mind.

He saw himself sitting in the living room with his second or third scotch, and Ginny across from him, looking at him and fingering the opening in her can of Fresca. Ginny playing with the can and then, a second later, a small cry as she looked at the drop of blood welling from a tiny cut on her finger. Blood. Ginny's blood. He had made a

48

brief show of tending the wound, had pressed it for a moment as though to stop the bleeding, then had wiped her smear of blood from his fingers onto his trousers. The gesture was so unlike him that Ginny had made some kidding remark about his spotting his immaculate image. The trousers were still hanging in his closet.

Greg was watching him. "Remember something?"

Chapin flushed. Stupid, stupid. There probably had not been enough blood to leave a stain, surely not enough to be noticeable. Greg was still making him feel guilty as well as foolish. He would check the trousers before saying anything.

"No, Greg. The whole experience is just too painful to think about."

"There is no other person, no other detail of the evening that's just too painful to tell me about, is there?"

"Nothing. No one."

Greg looked steadily at him for a moment in silence, as though giving Chapin a chance to reconsider his answer. Finally he spoke.

"Okay. Well, if you are brought into this, you're going to have a lot more to worry about than some bad publicity and the way your wife and kids take it. That's for sure, and it's something you better start facing."

"Just how bad do you think it could get, Greg?"

"I can total it up for you, Chape. Item one: You were screwing her. Two: You were seen in her company just prior to the murder. Three: Any jury in the country will look at the situation and figure out its own motive. Furthermore, there's no way you can prove you weren't with her when she was killed. Most important of all, you're a state senator and there's something about your position and your life that brings out the vigilante instincts in any DA or newspaper or jury. Face facts, you'd be one hell of a suspect."

Chapin let the fear come out then and it tasted sour. His face felt hot and his hands were wet.

"I know," he said slowly. "I guess I knew that all along."

"Okay," Greg nodded. "We understand each other. Now you have two choices. You can either go to the cops before they come to you, or you can play it tight, say nothing to nobody, and hope they never get that close to you."

"Do you think they will?"

"My feeling is it's going to depend on the cops handling the case. If it was here in Suffolk County, I'd say they'd never find you. But this guy in Nassau, Brownstein, is tough. Still, I think you've got a chance. They'll probably figure out that Harry is just an alias but they can't have any idea yet they're looking for a state senator named Chapin Hope."

49

"So what do we do?"

"Well, even if you go to them, your name gets into the papers. No one could keep that secret. So we'll take a calculated risk and play it cool. Maybe you'll get lucky. And in case you don't, we'll have a little time to figure out some angles."

"I could use a breathing space," Chapin said. "Maybe in the meantime they'll get the real killer. Christ, I wish I knew who he was. I'd—"

"Maybe he knows who you are," Greg said.

"What do you mean?"

"Maybe she told him about you. Maybe he's somebody with a grudge against you."

Chapin felt himself wrestling with a new fear. "Jesus."

"Yeah," Greg said. "But as far as anybody blaming you is concerned, there's one solid plus we haven't even mentioned yet."

"A plus?" It had seemed to Chapin to be a day constructed entirely of minuses. Greg's wink did not dispel his doubts.

"If they do find you, buddy, you'll have one of the country's very best defense lawyers representing you."

Chapin tried to break his own tension, tried to reclaim his equality with Greg for the first time in this ordeal of a conversation.

"What're you going to do? Call in F. Lee Bailey?"

"Don't joke, partner. Like I told you on the phone, I'm the best."

He really wasn't kidding. He was serious. The press clippings had finally gotten to him. Of course, there was always the possibility that it was not ego, that Greg had become one of the best defense attorneys in the country. We really don't know much about each other, Chapin thought.

Greg was laughing. Apparently his thoughts about Chapin had been following a similar line.

"Marijuana?" He shook his head. "I still can't believe it."

"Neither can I," said Chapin.

"Here," Greg said. "Have another drink."

6

Saturday night. Chapin Hope lying on his side, eyes staring at the luminous numerals on the digital clock-radio less than two feet away.

12:06.

Thalia's steady, rhythmic breathing in the adjacent bed provided a counterpoint to the merry-go-round of his own heartbeat. How to go to sleep? Chapin remembered a recent article in the *Reader's Digest*—"Think Yourself to Dreamland." The author, a psychologist, had recommended his own surefire technique: Go to sleep a little bit at a time. Begin by concentrating on a fingertip or maybe just a single toenail. The fingertip or toenail was told to relax, to go to sleep, and then a larger area—perhaps an entire hand or foot—was coaxed into limpness. Chapin gave it a try, whispered, "Go to sleep, thumb," felt preposterous, abandoned the plan.

12:27.

Sleeplessness was a new phenomenon to him. He had always been one of those fortunate people able to pull his car over to the side of the road and fall into a deep but brief sleep in a matter of seconds. But tonight, nothing. It was everything that had happened—especially the conversation with Greg. That had been like a mugging.

12:43.

Chapin noticed that Thalia's breathing pattern changed as her sleep deepened. It seemed to go through a spontaneous degenerative process, breaking first into a series of soft nasal explosions and then into long snoring whistles before steadying itself again. There had been another article on sleep, this one in the Sunday *Times Magazine*. The author questioned the reality of insomnia, maintained that even though a person felt wide awake through the night, the probability was that he was constantly dozing off, catnapping, accumulating enough sleep to see him through another day.

1:07.

Chapin tried desperately to slow down his thinking. But it would have been as easy to slow down a roller coaster. No, *two* roller coasters. One ran into the past—a cocktail waitress with red hair and soft lips. The other hurtled forward—a politician involved in a crime he didn't commit. A crime committed by someone who, for all Chapin knew, might be a danger to Chapin himself or to his family. It was too bad lie-detector evidence wasn't admissible in court. Sill, police sometimes used lie-detector tests to guide them in investigations. But what difference would that make? Just being involved in the case would be enough to ruin him. All the public had to know was that he had been having an affair with Ginny.

1:23.

People were like that, even people who fancied themselves as broad-minded and cosmopolitan.. There was no room in their philosophies for Ginny, for the truth about their relationship. One night Ginny had spelled that out for him, had said it all: "Did it ever occur to you that there's no one on earth we can tell about this? Not even our closest friends. Don't kid yourself. Your pals wouldn't understand it, not for a minute. Not unless you made it dirty. And you know what everyone would tell me? 'But he's married.' As if I didn't know that. Everyone would say the same thing, that it's pointless, that there's no future. Okay, then let's just settle for that. Let's not need a future."

1:35.

He had agreed, but there had still been bad moments. He was too used to plans, to schedules, to goals, and had found it difficult to abandon suddenly all notions of a future. And such notions split his head in half. His pleasure in Ginny, hell, admit it, his happiness with her, was a threat to his marriage, his family, his career. Oh, sure, there had been moments when he was tempted to give all that up for Ginny. But what would he have done? Gone out West somewhere to become the world's oldest apprentice lumberjack? Or run away to the Florida Keys, where he could get a job as a charter-boat deckhand and she could work as a barmaid?

At those moments when he grasped Ginny's potential for erasing his everyday world, Chapin had felt panic. After all, he was no Nelson Rockefeller with his billions to fall back on. He was no Teddy Kennedy, who could walk away from personal disaster and pick up his political career. One night when he was with Ginny, the impossibility of their relationship had surfaced in his mind and driven him to commit small acts of cruelty. Ginny had put a halt to it.

"Oh, Chape," she had cried, "stop it! Please, stop it! If you feel that way, all you have to say is one word. 'Good-bye.' Say that, and you'll never hear from me again. I promise. That's all it would take. But don't do *this*, Chape, please. What we have together is so

52

fragile, so very fragile. Don't stomp on it."

2:00.

She had never used the word "love," but that was because of him. Chapin knew she wanted to—damn it, so had he. As it was, the truth of what she was saying had shocked his emotions; he didn't quite realize what was happening to him until the tears leaked down over his cheeks. In all of the years of their marriage Thalia had never seen him cry. Nothing between them had ever seemed that important.

6:15.

He must have slept. Either that or he had stopped looking at the clock every few minutes. No matter. At dawn the difference between a memory and a dream is minute. It had been a long night crowded with memories and dreams, and the sheets beneath him were soaked with his perspiration.

Chapin eased his feet into the slippers beside his bed and turned to look at Thalia. Fast asleep; she'd be that way for another two or three hours. Excellent. He was thinking about the Sunday papers; especially the *Islander*.

The sun had not yet risen above the tree level as Chapin Hope padded down his long blacktopped driveway to the mailbox. The grass had turned to a frosty stubble and the November trees had given up most of their leaves; Chapin made a mental note to tell the boys to tear up the tomato vines and cornstalks in the back so the ground would be ready to turn over next year. Next year? God. He reached into the mailbox for the *Islander*, and his hands started to shake. The entire front page was filled with a drawing of the suspect, a "computer-assisted composite police sketch"—*of himself*. The headline: SOUGHT IN MURDER.

In the kitchen Chapin put the paper on the counter and stared at the front page over his instant coffee. Would anyone else make the connection? The hair was wrong, too full and too curly. He hadn't had hair that thick since high school. Either the police artist or the assisting computer had also given him a slight whisker growth, had made him swarthy. Maybe that was because it had been the end of day when the eyewitnesses saw him and there had been no chance for a second shave.

There was no way to throw out the front page of the paper—but perhaps he could alter the drawing. He removed the front and last pages from the paper, kept them folded, and bent a single sharp crease across the center of the drawing. Next he rubbed the front page between his hands, adding a network of small wrinkles to the nose and eyes. He left the too-bushy hair and whiskery chin untouched and returned the pages to the paper.

Then he shaved.

Several hours later Robert O'Malley was studying the same drawing on the front page of his newspaper. What drew his attention was a small technical observation. The drawing lacked harmony. In real faces there was a balance that inevitably escaped the computer.

"Doesn't look like an ax murderer to me," he said, handing the page to Teddi Bennett.

"Jesus, I dunno," Teddi said. "That's Ginny's type all right. Those clean-cut bastards always got to her."

The same edition was delivered to Detective Lieutenant Charles Brownstein. He had spent considerable time the previous day studying the drawing, and now he repeated the process.

"I've seen this man," he said to his wife. "I can't help but think I've seen him somewhere."

The drawing was seen by Roland Feebe. He felt the lips were all wrong.

It was seen by Norris Whitlaw and it never occurred to him that it was a sketch of his best friend. He thumbed past it quickly. On page three, however, there was a photograph that captured his full attention. It was an old picture taken from a high school yearbook, and it showed a slim young cheerleader, ponytail whipping to the side, mouth open in mid-yell, legs tucked up beneath her. Norris studied the picture and spoke to his eighteen-year-old companion. "I can't understand why anyone would kill a girl this young—he must be some kind of a degenerate."

Thalia Hope skipped past the drawing without a second glance. She did not like to read about violence. In the world she had fashioned for herself, things like ax murders never happened.

And the sketch was seen by Greg Hammer, who immediately went to his phone in the study.

"I don't want to scare you, Chape," he said, "but the picture worries me. It's too close. I won't be surprised if someone makes the connection. Yeah, we've got to be ready in case that happens."

7

"*Norris*, please pass the salt."

Rhoda was asking him for the second time. The first time she asked, her husband's face had been locked in a smile prompted by a recent memory. Very recent. Earlier that same afternoon, as a matter of fact. This time he passed the shaker.

"You must have had *some* time in Downingtown," Rhoda went on. "You haven't heard a thing I've said ever since you got home this evening. I'll bet you guys never left the bar. . . ."

"What did you shoot?" Greg asked.

"I'll tell you about it later," Norris said. Dinner at the Hopes'. Thalia had selected one of her specialties—sole Albert—and Lupe had taken care of all the trimmings. The men knew that the serious conversation would come later, when they were alone, and now they sat back, contenting themselves with small mutterings of agreement and disagreement as the women carried the conversation at the dinner table. Not surprisingly, the talk soon found its way to the story of the hour, the cocktail-waitress ax murder.

"It hardly seems possible that something like that could happen," Thalia said.

"It's awful," Priscilla Hammer said.

"It's like some horror movie," said Rhoda Whitlaw. "Thank God it happened in Mineola, not here, or I'd be frightened to death. Thank God those things always happen somewhere else. I don't really think it would happen to someone like us."

"I'm not sure I follow that," Priscilla said.

"Well, a woman like that," said Rhoda, "the kind of life she was leading—that undoubtedly had a lot to do with it."

"What kind of life was she leading?" Norris said.

"Come off it, Norris," Rhoda said. "She was a cocktail waitress. Divorced. Working in bars. God knows what was going on in her private life."

Rhoda sailed on, oblivious to the way that Chapin and Greg were staring down at their plates. Norris took up the slack.

"Good old Rhoda," he said. "Always jumping to conclusions. I saw a picture of her in the paper tonight and she didn't look so terrible to me. To tell the truth, she looked like a nice kid.''

"She looked so . . . common," Rhoda said.

"Listen to the paragon." Norris was addressing the table. "Whenever Rhoda says someone's common, then I know she's worth a second look."

"Oh, come on now," Priscilla broke in. "What did she do that made any of what happened her fault? What could she possibly do to bring something that terrible onto her?"

Usually Priscilla Hammer remained silent. It was generally felt that Greg talked enough for the two of them. It was also the consensus that when Priscilla bothered to say something, she made sense.

"Exactly," said Norris. "Leave it to Priss."

"Of course we don't have any idea what really happened," Priscilla said. "My guess is that she was one of those super-feminine women, you know, too feminine for her own good. Someone like that can get trapped in life—there's always some man around trying to do them in. And in this case the man was an insane killer. Imagine, dying like that. . . ."

"Well, as you say"—Greg was disturbed by the expression on Chapin's face—"we don't really know anything except what we read in the papers."

"You men—all three of you—you'd like to know someone like that." The predinner cocktails had taken hold of Rhoda. "I don't know any man sitting in this room who's so much of a saint that he wouldn't—"

"That's enough, Rhoda," Norris warned.

"Oh, listen to him, will you? As if he's. . . ."

Rhoda stopped short, seeing the anger on her husband's face. There was a silence then, six adults listening intently to the scrape of silver on porcelain. Slowly, carefully, the conversation was restarted and guided into safe areas—the onset of winter, the possibility of another fuel shortage, the children, the new indoor tennis court in Fishington, movies, potential winter vacations, and, of course, politics.

"Chape, when are you going to make up your mind to run for Congress?" Norris asked. "You've been stuck up there in Albany long enough—and once you get the nomination, there's no way you could lose."

"Believe me, Norris," said Chapin, "there are ways I could lose."

"I don't mind telling you," Norris went on, "business has been great and we don't have to kid ourselves, not here, not with friends.

The reason business has been great is the work the county's been throwing my way. And we all know who's responsible for that.''

Chapin held up his hand.

"You do your job well,'' he said, "and I do mine. There's nothing wrong with that. Not one thing. That's the system.''

"Well, the system is working pretty damn well then,'' Norris said. "If I get the bids on the police academy, hell, I'll have to put a couple dozen more men on the payroll. Without you, Chape, I'd still be putting in patios with my dad. So anytime you want to run for higher office—Congress could just be another stop—you know I'll be there when it counts.''

"He couldn't afford to,'' Greg said.

"What's that supposed to mean?'' Norris asked.

"What Greg means is that I couldn't afford to,'' Chapin explained. "Actually, Norris, it'd be an enormous step backward for me. And for you, too. There's an old joke where the husband says, 'I wear the pants in my family—I make all the important decisions. My wife decides where we're going to live, where the kids go to college, how we spend our money, what we're having for dinner. Me, I'm in charge of world peace and disarmament.' Well, let's just let the boys in Washington decide what to do about world peace. I'll just sit here and worry about the unimportant things— like where we're going to put a new highway or build a jetport.''

"But that must eat at your ego. . . .''

"Norris, you don't know anything about my ego,'' Chapin said. "Jesus, I've got my own little committee in Albany that has more to do with what happens to your dollar than the President of the United States will ever have. Why should I leave that and become a freshman Congressman, one of five hundred faceless idiots who—''

"Why don't we take a little break?'' Thalia broke in. "Lupe has already set out the brandy in the library—I'm sure you gentlemen have some business to discuss while we ladies go and powder our noses.''

The patterns seldom varied. Even though the six of them were close friends, even though it was a casual Sunday supper, the men wore ties and the women were in long dresses. Sometime in the distant past it had been decided that the proper way to end dinner was with the sexes dividing and retreating to separate alcoves. It was expected that the women would discuss child rearing, room decorating, and other matters of no immediate interest to the men. The men would get business matters out of the way. And then, in an hour or slightly less, the two groups would rejoin over coffee and the conversation would center on matters of mutual interest, what

57

Chapin thought of as the three G's—golf, gardening, and gossip.

The brandy snifters were waiting beside the fireplace and Chapin bent over to touch a match to the newspapers beneath the birch logs. The host then turned to close the twin doors to the library and Norris started in.

"Three guesses where I spent the weekend?"

"My only guess is that it wasn't Downingtown," Greg said.

"Right on the first guess," Norris said. "I spent the entire weekend in Patchogue."

"That sounds very exciting," Greg said. "What was the matter? You couldn't find accommodations in Speonk?"

Chapin carried his brandy to the fire and he stared down at the flames. He tried not to hear the conversation that he had heard a thousand times before.

"The accommodations were just fine," Norris said. "Remember when I told you about hiring the new receptionist?"

"Yeah," Greg said, "the jailbait."

"So you shacked up with a teenager?" Greg pushed on.

"I won't lie to you," Norris said. "We spent the night together but nothing happened. Not yet. She's still a virgin."

"I hate to interrupt this," Chapin broke in, "but there *is* something I've got to talk to you about."

"It sounds serious," Norris said.

"Wait'll you hear," Greg said.

"I'm afraid I've bought myself a pack of trouble," Chapin went on. "And I've got a feeling that I'm going to need all the friends I've got."

"You can count on me, old buddy," Norris said, "and I mean for anything. What's the matter? That Babylon crowd giving you trouble again?"

"Nothing as simple as politics," Chapin said. "God, if only it were politics, I'd know what to do. I told Greg about it yesterday, Norris, and I wanted to tell you, but you were otherwise occupied."

"Chape—"

"It doesn't matter now, Norris. I just want to make sure you understand this isn't to go any further than the three of us. I mean that. Not even Rhoda."

"Don't worry about me," Norris said.

Chapin pressed his lips together and then plunged.

"The girl who was murdered?" he said. "Ginny Hanson. The waitress? Well, I'm the one they're looking for. The one in the picture."

"What!"

"I didn't do anything," Chapin said. "I'll answer the big question at the top—I didn't kill her. I didn't hurt her in any way. But I was the one who was with her Friday night, the night she was killed, and I'd been seeing her for a few months. We were having an affair.''

''You've got to be kidding,'' Norris said. ''That's . . . that's crazy.''

''It's no joke,'' Chapin said.

''My God!'' Norris gulped his brandy and shook his head. ''Okay,'' he said finally, ''whatever I can do, just name it. Hey, wait a minute, wait just one minute. An alibi—I could give you an alibi. You can say we were together this weekend.''

''Don't be silly,'' Chapin said.

''Not too fast there,'' Greg said. ''Let's not say no to anything, not until we know where we're at. That's a generous offer, Norris, and we'll just hold it in abeyance for the moment.''

''I knew I could count on you,'' Chapin said. ''Both of you.''

''One other thing, Norris,'' Greg said, ''if anyone starts asking about Chape, don't say a word. Nothing.''

''What're friends for?'' Norris said. ''Hell. Chape, I know you couldn't hurt anybody.''

''Not Chape,'' Greg said. ''Chape's a lover.''

''You better believe it,'' Norris chimed in. ''Jesus! A cocktail waitress! That must have been something else.''

''Easy, Norris,'' Greg said.

''It's okay,'' Chapin said. ''Ginny was great, Norris. Let's just leave it at that—at least for now. What bugs me is that there's a madman out there—someone would have to be a madman to do something like that. I couldn't read the story without feeling sick.''

There was a moment of silence, a moment of contemplating horror, and then Norris picked up the conversation.

''Hey, it'll probably all blow over. If it's any consolation to you, I never even thought of you when I saw that picture.''

''Good.''

''Besides, there are a couple of other things we should discuss before the ladies get back.''

''Like what?'' Greg asked.

''Well, one thing I wanted to ask Chape about,'' said Norris, ''is that we got the invitations to that one-hundred-and-twenty-five-dollars-a-plate dinner for the esteemed leader of our neighboring county, Rocco Porcina. I mean, is that one absolutely necessary? It's not even Suffolk County. And paying one hundred and twenty-five dollars to hear Rocco talk—hell, that's like buying a color television set and watching Lawrence Welk reruns.''

''You can think whatever you want about Rocco,'' Chapin said, "but at least he gets the job done. I only wish Suffolk had someone who knew how to get it all together."

"Personally, he's impossible."

"Personally doesn't matter," Chapin said. "Rocco knows more about politics, about the way things get done, than the whole Kennedy family in their best year. You've been picking up a lot of work, as you said, and some of it is from Nassau County. There's no sense in annoying people. In fact, if I were you, I'd take a full table and buy a page in the program."

"C'mon, Chape, you're talking about three thousand dollars."

"No, I'm not. I'm talking about getting things done. I'm talking about politics."

"Norris," Greg interrupted, "Chape's telling you stuff I thought you knew."

"Figure out how much new business fell your way from Nassau County last year," Chapin said. "Figure it out carefully because *they* are adding it up—believe me, they are. And when you have it all figured out, figure on getting ten percent of it back to them. Somehow. But get it back."

"Okay," Norris said. "I was just asking."

"And I was just telling," Chapin said. "Now, is there anything else we have to worry about before the ladies come back?"

"Just one other thing," Norris said. "The high rise? How long is it going to be before we can start thinking about putting up the building?"

"Too early," Greg said. "Norris, it's too early to even talk about that. We got the zoning changes only a couple of weeks ago."

"By the way," Chapin said, "forget that I even asked, but what'd that cost?"

"Peanuts," Greg said. "Under five thousand."

"Well, how long before we can put up the building?" Norris persisted.

"Easy does it," Chapin said. "My feeling is that we should be prepared to wait at least four years. By then no one's going to remember that it was ever zoned any other way. Patience. We wait this one out and we're sure to get back ten for one, minimum."

"There's something else we should think about," Greg said. "We don't have to decide anything now, but we should ask ourselves whether we'll want to sell our homes before the high rise goes up."

"What do you mean, sell our homes?"

"Norris, this may come as a small surprise to you, but some people aren't going to be too happy when they learn that someone is going to build a ten-story building on seven acres of land just off

60

Stony Harbor's quaint and historic Main Street. There's going to be a stink and residential property values may just decide to depreciate.''

"I never thought about that," said Norris. "In a way, it's like we're fouling our own nest, isn't it?"

"You might say that," answered Greg. "And the question is, should we unload the nests while they're still unfouled?"

"We have plenty of time to figure that one out," Chapin said. "I can't get concerned with it now; that damned murder keeps coming up in my mind."

"Wow!" Norris said. "I just thought of something. Suppose somebody does connect you. It could affect our whole setup, it could. . . ."

There was a noise at the library doors and Greg was the first to get to his feet.

"We can carry on that discussion at a later date," he said loudly. "Here come the ladies—ah, radiant as always."

8

The composite portrait drew them out of the woodwork. On the Monday following the killing, Detective Lieutenant Charles Brownstein heard from an evangelist's daughter who reported seeing the devil kill Virginia Hanson in a peculiarly vivid dream. The following day Robert J. O'Malley was contacted by a former American Legion post commander who informed him that the murder was the work of black terrorists. And in the weeks that followed there were other calls, understandably anonymous, from psychics, visionaries, and giggling teenagers.

The two men came at the crime from different directions. It was the Homicide chief's feeling that sooner or later there would be a break. Until then he would keep pushing—chipping and chipping at the plaster until the wall crumbled. O'Malley's calm, on the other hand, was of a more superficial nature. Inside he was burning. The reporter craved a lead the way he would want a shot if he were suddenly cut off from booze. It had been that way ever since the moment he glanced at the sink in the murdered woman's bathroom.

For O'Malley there was also a more immediate goal—his editors had released him from the regular police beat to concentrate on the cocktail-waitress killing. There was the feeling of freedom coupled with the pure satisfaction of knowing that the bastards needed him. In general, O'Malley despised his bosses. They were the new breed in American journalism—executives rather than editors. They ate in the company's new executive dining room, battled for the numbered parking spaces, thrived on conferences, labored for masthead mentions, received profit shares, and talked endlessly of team efforts. When O'Malley first came to the paper, he kept a half-filled paper cup beside his typewriter and no one ever said a word. Maybe that was because the managing editor, Gunner Harris, had kept a bottle beside his typewriter.

The good old days. O'Malley's fondest remembrance of Gunner was of a trip they had taken to Atlantic City to accept some award for the paper. Gunner had drunk himself to sleep soon after their arrival and when O'Malley woke him at seven that evening to go to dinner, the managing editor had picked up the phone, dialed room service, and ordered bacon and eggs and a Bloody Mary.

"What the hell are you doing?" O'Malley had asked.

"Ordering breakfast," Gunner had answered.

"What do you mean, breakfast? We're going to dinner."

"Dinner, shit," Gunner had said. "At seven in the morning?"

"It's seven o'clock at night," O'Malley had said, going to the hotel window and opening the shade. "Look, it's seven o'clock at night and the goddamn sun is setting."

O'Malley would never forget Gunner's answer. The managing editor had looked out the window and cleared his throat.

"Bullshit," he had said. "The sun's rising."

O'Malley had just been slightly surprised that Gunner wasn't able to stop the sun's downward path and make it back up his words. The men who ran the paper now would never have understood Gunner Harris. Nor did they fully understand Robert J. O'Malley. But they knew what he could do. They knew that he made them all look good on the Hanson story, that, in fact, he had done a job none of them would have been able to do. So, after one of their twice-daily editorial conferences, they decided to take a calculated risk.

"We've decided to turn you loose on the ax murder, Bob," Custer Yale, the new managing editor, told him. "Don't disappoint us."

"Gee, Mr. Yale," he had said, "I'll sure do my best."

"Someday you're going to go too far with that stuff," Yale said.

And now the bastards were on his back because he hadn't come up with a handle. Those first two weeks O'Malley's stories were mostly variations on a familiar theme: "Police today were looking for new leads in the ax murder of cocktail waitress Virginia Hanson." Stories that did little more than keep the big story alive. The exceptions included a story on the fear and intensified security at Nassau Overlook, the apartment complex where the murder occurred. There also was a profile on Leonardo, the police artist, and a good feature on the murder victim fashioned from bits and pieces gotten from Teddi and from others—most of them persons who had been interviewed on both sides of Long Island's cocktail bars. Many of the bar people knew Ginny at least casually but none had ever seen her outside the clubs. The consensus seemed to be that Ginny Hanson had been a "nice person" and you can go only so far with that kind of information.

What O'Malley had learned was that Ginny had been an intensely private person. He had been unable to turn up any close friends—he was especially frustrated in his efforts to locate Charlotte, the brunette Baldy Davits had mentioned. The only nonrelative he talked to who seemed to know Ginny personally was Feebe. The murder victim's baby-sitter, a high school senior, had never exchanged more than a sentence or two, had never even seen any of Mrs. Hanson's men friends. Feebe was less than useless: "She was interested in literature," he told O'Malley, "and she adored Fitzgerald, especially *Gatsby*."

Only two relatives could be located. O'Malley managed to speak to both the dead woman's ex-husband and the maternal aunt who claimed Laura Hanson after her mother's slaying.

Don Hanson, the ex-husband, had settled in San Diego, where he was working as the greens keeper for a municipal golf course. A friend had sent him stories about the murder and he had not been particularly surprised. "She was always a nut," he said. O'Malley asked him if he had any interest in seeing Laura. "I was never even sure she was mine," he said.

The reporter had better luck with the aunt, Brigid Grady, a handsome woman in her late fifties who broke open a six-pack and sat with him in the kitchen of her brick home in Floral Park, just over the county line in Queens. "You couldn't blame Ginny for being a little wild," she said. "Her parents both died by the time she was thirteen. Her mother, God rest her soul, was my sister and it was only right I take her in. She was a little wild but a good girl. She helped around the house and I'll tell you something, she got good marks in school. My husband and me—he's with the Transit Authority—we both loved Ginny and we both love Laura. Laura's in school now, which reminds me, if she comes home while you're here, don't say anything, okay?"

O'Malley had nodded and accepted the second can of beer.

"I know Ginny had men," the woman went on, "but she was no tramp. Listen, it's different than when I was young. Nowadays you see all this stuff in the movies, even on the TV, all these young people living together without getting married. Who knows? Sometimes I wonder if maybe they've got something—don't put that in the paper, though, huh? But Ginny was always a free whatayacallit, free spirit. Her real parents, rest them, never had much time for her and when she came to us, my husband and I were both working. Hanson? That was some mistake; he was a sailor and she was sixteen and she met him at the penny arcade in New York. What'd she know?"

"Did she ever talk about the men she was seeing over the last couple of years?"

"No, I knew she had them, but we never said anything. I figured they were probably married but listen, that was her business. Take this Harry, the one whose picture we saw in the paper, she never even mentioned his name. I asked Laura and she says she never saw anyone looked like that. Well, Ginny would have made sure of that. Look, your name is O'Malley, you're Irish, you should understand. Ginny had a soul. If you ever saw her with Laura, you'd understand what I mean. She spent a lot of time with Laura, doing things together. Laura knew she had a mother who loved her.''

O'Malley's reaction would have startled the reporters who sat near him in the city room. He reached across the table and squeezed Mrs. Grady's hand.

The profile of Ginny Hanson was a solid piece of work; all that was noticeably missing was any clue to the identity of the killer. The composite sketch continued to produce reactions but no solid leads. O'Malley listened patiently to a Westbury divorcée who claimed that the sketch was a picture of her ex-husband, who, it subsequently turned out, was three months behind on his alimony payments. Not only was the resemblance minimal, but the ex-husband lived in Florida and had not been north of Orlando in six months. In another case a homeowner in a split-level development in Syosset called to report that the sketch looked just like his next-door neighbor. The neighbor turned out to be fat, bald, mustachioed, and the proud owner of a German shepherd that had a talent for tearing up recently planted lawns.

Nothing. All roads came to dead ends. Including searches made by both O'Malley and the police for the brunette who had been at the Pumpkin with Baldy Davits when Virginia Hanson stopped in on the last morning of her life. "As far as we know," Brownstein said, "she and Davits were the last people to see the victim alive prior to the murder. And Davits isn't much help. Also, if this Charlotte was a friend of Miss Hanson's, as Davits claims, she might know something about 'Harry,' whoever he is."

"Maybe they both belong to the same disappearing club," O'Malley said.

"It's a possibility," Brownstein said. "I've had a couple of men scouring the bars, but they haven't gotten a thing. Even Davits doesn't know Charlotte's last name."

"Yeah," O'Malley said, "last names are one of the things you don't ask about in those places. You can't even be sure the first names are the right ones."

O'Malley had been making his own checks at cheaters' bars and had gotten nowhere. Charlotte was known to the regulars at several of the bars, but only in a limited sense. That is, no one could provide a last name or a home address.

Teddi had seen Charlotte at the Blue Barn a few times but they had never exchanged more than a few words.

"She hasn't come in lately," Teddi told O'Malley, "but a couple of times when I saw her, she came in with Ginny. I could ask around."

"I already have," O'Malley said, "but go ahead. If she does know anything, I'd like to get to her before the cops do."

O'Malley spent several consecutive evenings at the Blue Barn on the chance that someone might have a lead for him. More than that, however, it was to try to get a feel for a world that was somewhat foreign to him, to try to understand something more about the world that was once Ginny Hanson's.

The Blue Barn was divided into two large rooms. One area contained the bar, several booths, a few small tables, and a cleared area for dancing to the music of a four-piece band. At the end of the bar area three steps led down to the large dining room. The bar belonged to the roamers and the cheaters and the aging singles, the sexual drifters, and the dining room was given over to couples, some of them married, the customers Teddi called "the straights." Those from the dining room would occasionally move out onto the dance floor, clutch at each other for a few moments, then walk primly back down the steps to their surf-and-turf dinners.

O'Malley had yet to make it from the bar to the dining room. Teddi kept the glass fresh and guided him toward all possible sources. Some nights the pickings were notably slim. His second night in the bar the only other customer was a middle-aged woman with bleached hair who was making a scotch sour last. No, she had never met Ginny Hanson, but she wanted to show O'Malley something that would interest him. She opened a large handbag and inside was Pepe, a Chihuahua who accompanied the woman everywhere.

"This woman I met has a bitch," she informed O'Malley, "and she was gonna pay me for Pepe's services."

O'Malley studied the dog gravely.

"Well, I don't suppose," he said, "she'd have to pay too much."

"Listen, it's not the size that counts," the woman said. "Anyway, we turn Pepe and her dog loose together in the living room, and nothing, I mean nothing."

"It wasn't what you'd call love at first sight?"

"The son of a bitch couldn't get it up," she said.

"You ought to get that dog checked out." O'Malley stood up to leave. "Maybe he's queer."

As he stood up to leave, O'Malley could see that the woman was mulling over the possibility. What do you do for a homosexual

Chihuahua? O'Malley grinned at his own response to that one. Introduce him to Roland Feebe's toy poodle or maybe just to Roland Feebe. O'Malley hated homosexuals.

The next morning, too early, O'Malley was summoned to Custer Yale's office. It had to be trouble. Yale talked to him only when it was absolutely necessary. Their relations had been strained ever since Yale, at the age of thirty-four, had been elevated to the managing editor's job. One of his first moves had been to call in the old hands for a friendly pep talk.

"Just what is it you want out of the *Islander*, Bob?" he had begun.

"Huh?"

"I'd like to know what your long-range goals are," Yale had gone on. "What you'd like to have someday at the paper."

"Well, someday," O'Malley had said, "I'd like to work for adults."

That first conversation had done away with the amenities. Custer Yale no longer tried to soften the reporter with flattery and that is the way O'Malley wanted it.

"I want you to start working on a hard-assed piece on the Homicide Division," he said.

"What are you talking about?"

"Look, Bob," Yale said, softening, "this one isn't my idea. It comes all the way from the main office. They think it could be a hell of a story. After all, there's an ax murderer at large and nothing's happening. It's about time someone started getting some results on this one—it wouldn't hurt us to tighten the screws on Brownstein."

"On Brownstein? Someone's been seeing too many reporter movies."

"Well, Bob, if you won't do it, it's just possible we could find someone who will."

For a few seconds O'Malley felt one of his periodic urges to step around Custer Yale's desk and break his nose. But, as always happened on such occasions, he thought about his alimony obligations and the price of Jack Daniel's. What he did not have to think about, simply because it was much too visceral a matter to require thought, was his commitment to what he did for a living.

"Look," he said. "Brownstein's a good cop. He's the best there is."

"That may be," Yale said, "but he's not getting anywhere. Hell, he hasn't even found the weapon."

"He may have to find the murderer first," O'Malley said. "Let's give it another week. Brownstein deserves at least that."

"Another week, sure." Custer Yale didn't bother keeping the

triumph out of his eyes. "We'll give him another week but there better be a break by then."

O'Malley never mentioned the encounter to Brownstein, but word got back to the Homicide chief. And that same afternoon he called O'Malley.

"It was nothing," the reporter said.

"It's television," Brownstein said. "All those police shows."

"Yeah," O'Malley said. "Maybe what you need is a wheelchair."

9

The secretary who sorted the city-room mail had to bend the envelope to fit it into O'Malley's box. It was a tan ten-by-thirteen-inch envelope of the sort used for mailing manuscripts and photographs. The mailing address had been scrawled in red crayon and there was no return address. The last name was misspelled: O'Mally. Instinctively the reporter looked for the postmark and found one of those U.S. Postal Zone imprints. Progress, it was always getting in O'Malley's way. The date at least was clear: December 16.

The reporter took the envelope to his desk with the rest of the mail. Press releases from the Police Benevolent Association, the Long Island Environmental Council, the Long Island State Park Commission, the North Shore Performing Arts Foundation, the National Safety Council, and a Manhattan publicity man who handled second-rate entertainers. O'Malley tossed the releases unopened into a wastebasket and studied the manuscript envelope. Like most people accustomed to receiving mail from the public, O'Malley picked up vibrations from envelopes. And from the minute he looked at this one, it disturbed him.

He ripped it open. Two items were clipped together. One a newspaper clipping, was Leonardo's sketch of Harry, the suspect. The other was a nine-by-twelve glossy photograph of a distinguished-looking man with even features and brown hair graying at the temple—O'Malley picked up a slight resemblance to the actor Jack Lemmon, a more notable resemblance than to the police sketch. Written across the face of the photograph in black ink were the words "Yours Ever, Chape."

O'Malley placed the two pictures beside each other. Close enough. And then—like a kid taking the toasted marshmallow from the fire at the last possible moment—he turned over the glossy. And there, printed in the now familiar red crayon, were these words: "Chapin Kirk Hope, State Senator, Suffolk County."

The breath came out of O'Malley in a whistle. The glossy was Hope, all right. No wonder that sketch had bothered him. He had encountered Hope only twice, both times on stories in Albany, but like most of the old hands at the *Islander*, he was aware of the man and his reputation. Chapin Hope was a quiet power in the Suffolk Republican organization. He had established a political protectorate in his district; he was becoming something of a force in the state legislature. Basically conservative, he was nevertheless attractive to moderates. Probably because of the clean-cut image, the straight-arrow reputation. A second whistle. Chapin Kirk Hope. A state senator, a goddamn state senator. Once again O'Malley remembered the horror in Virginia Hanson's sink and he stared at the face in the photograph and tried to make a connection.

"Son of a bitch!"

He said that out loud and his left fist came down onto the desk, cartwheeling papers to the floor. The noise drew the attention of nearby reporters and one of them, Debbie Jahnsen, a recent graduate of the Columbia University School of Journalism, snickered to the young man on the other side of her, "O'Malley's on the sauce again." Debbie was known to be having an affair with Custer Yale, a circumstance that had in no way slowed her advancement on the paper. As he lumbered from his desk, O'Malley stopped briefly in front of the young woman's desk and looked down at her.

"Custer said to tell you he can't make it tonight," he said.

His destination was the *Islander* morgue. "Morgue" was the old name, the one that O'Malley would use until the day he died. It was the appropriate name; the morgue was a repository for trivia past. At the *Islander*, however, they had started calling the morgue "library" and there was a movement afoot at the highest echelons to refer to it as "research center." Instead of the crammed file cabinets of days gone by, there was a long counter manned by a corps of young men and women who had little more to do than push buttons that activated mechanical information retrievers and other buttons that illuminated microfilm screens and copying machines. Dutifully O'Malley asked one of the clerks for the clips on Chapin Kirk Hope. "He's a state senator," O'Malley added. Sometimes that was necessary. The new "library" used distinguishing descriptions to avoid confusion in cases of similar names. When the new system had been initiated a few years before, one file envelope had been labeled: "Christ, Jesus, Religious Leader, Deceased."

At the clerk's touch the machine disgorged a drawer containing two narrow envelopes filled with the bric-a-brac of Chapin Hope's public life. O'Malley carried them back to his desk, where he spent the next hour drinking coffee out of a plastic mug crusted with dregs of bygone days.

The earliest clip reported the marriage of Lieutenant Chapin K.

Hope to the former Thalia Louise LeMay of East Aurora, New York. Both bride and groom, according to the story, were graduates of the University of Pennsylvania, where Lieutenant Hope was a member of the ROTC. The story added that Lieutenant Hope, a prelaw student at Penn, was serving with the judge advocate's office at Fort Bragg, North Carolina. The bride's father was a druggist in East Aurora. The groom's father, Bertram W. Hope, was a prominent Long Island realtor and a former treasurer of the Suffolk County Republican Committee. The best man was L. Gregory Hammer, a boyhood friend of the groom. O'Malley halted on reading that name—yes, Hammer and Hope were still law partners. O'Malley had never met Hammer but he was aware of his growing reputation and several months earlier he had filled in for a colleague covering the trial of a philandering priest whom Hammer had saved from a murder rap. He had watched the lawyer dismantle the key prosecution witness and he had been impressed.

The clips indicated that Hope attended law school following his discharge and that he had opened the office with Hammer soon after being admitted to the bar. Probably bank-rolled by his old man, O'Malley speculated. O'Malley considered law and politics the most corrosive combination in American government. If Hope had been a carpenter, he wouldn't have had a chance. As it was, his political career was well under way within two years of his going into practice.

First the Fishington Town Board, then the legislature. It was all in the clips—the campaign close-ups, the elections, the public posturing in between.

Fishington—State Sen. Chapin Kirk Hope (R-Stony Harbor) highlighted Fishington Town's Memorial Day observances yesterday with a speech calling for a "new belief in old principles—a reaffirmation of faith in the ideals on which America was founded."

The ceremonies at the war memorial in front of the Town Hall culminated an hour-long parade by Boy and Girl Scouts, veterans' posts and their auxiliaries, and fraternal and civic groups. Hope, a native of the town, which comprises the major portion of his constituency, said he had gone to high school with men who died in Korea and whose names were inscribed on the memorial.

Pointing to the memorial, Hope declared that "excesses such as flag burning and street violence can no longer be tolerated under the guise of freedom. Such acts have nothing to do with freedom. Such acts desecrate the very principle of

71

freedom for which these brave men—men with whom I shared my boyhood—died. For their sakes we have to come back to America—to this nation under God.''

Stony Harbor—The Stony Harbor Lions Club announced today that State Sen. Chapin Kirk Hope has been chosen as the organization's ''Man of the Year.'' . . .

Albany—A bill calling for the return of prayer to New York public schools was introduced in the legislature today by Sen. Chapin K. Hope (R-Stony Harbor). In proposing the measure, which political observers give little chance of passage, Hope said he was responding to appeals from ''the overwhelming majority of my constituents.'' . . .

Bridgeport, Conn.—A bistate effort to halt the pollution in Long Island Sound was launched yesterday by New York and Connecticut legislators. Named as chairman of the group was Long Island State Sen. Chapin Kirk Hope (R-Stony Harbor). . . .

Albany—A bill heralded as the toughest antidrug legislation in the nation was signed into law today by Gov. Rockefeller. The bill was strongly supported in the Senate by Suffolk Republican Chapin K. Hope. . . .

Washington, D.C.—A delegation of high-ranking Republicans came away beaming yesterday after an hour-long meeting with Vice President Agnew. ''The Vice President understands the needs of suburbia as well as the needs of the nation,'' said the group's spokesman, State Sen. Chapin K. Hope (R-Stony Harbor). Hope said Agnew had agreed to speak at a $100-a-plate county GOP dinner next month.

Most of the clips went on in that vein, except for a few indicating Hope's interest in zoning matters and his continuing involvement in local politics. Another one of those pious bastards, thought O'Malley, another fraud. The reporter had learned long ago that there were no Mr. Cleans in politics; the system simply didn't permit it.

O'Malley took another look at the glossy. He wished to hell there was some clue as to its origin. The sender could have been someone with a grudge against Hope or even a Democrat with a warped sense of humor; the other possibility: It could have been someone with inside information on the murder. That signature—''Yours Ever,

Chape''—maybe the sender was someone who knew Hope intimately, some woman scorned.

Chapin Kirk Hope. O'Malley stared at the photograph, looking for some sign of depravity, even a hint of viciousness. But all he saw was blandness. He was looking for Jack the Ripper and finding Jack Armstrong.

10

As much as possible, Detective Lieutenant Charles Brownstein did his own legwork or personally checked that done by his assistants. He saw cops who became administrators as vaguely tragic figures. It had to do with an ethic his mother, Sarah, instilled in him as a child: "Do your own dirty work; nobody else is gonna do it for you." His parents had operated a liquor store in the Jackson Heights section of Queens and when Brownstein was eleven, his father was shot by a holdup man who took $176.28 from the cash register and a bottle of Gallo from a shelf near the door. His father lingered for a year, a near vegetable, and his death came as a relief. The gunman was never caught.

Sarah Brownstein moved out of the neighborhood but kept up the store. Charley helped out Saturdays and summer vacations and he was there, holding a broom, the day his mother reached under the counter, drew a revolver, and wounded another holdup man, this one a knife wielder. When Brownstein came out of the Army with three stripes and a European Theater patch, he told his mother he was going into the Nassau County Police Academy.

"Good," she had said, "now you push them around."

On a Thursday night four weeks after the Hanson murder Brownstein made a stop that had been made once before by a subordinate officer. Initial reports showed that a man answering the description of the suspect had been in the Empress Diner, just across Jericho Turnpike from the Pumpkin, on the evening of the murder.

Yes, the counterman was saying, he was the one who had been working that night; he was the regular on the four-to-midnight shift. And it was that Harry character all right; he looked just like the picture.

"I remember him because there was nobody else at the counter," the diner man said. "Like I told the other detective, he ordered a cheeseburger, fries, and a Coke, and he didn't touch them."

"How come?"

"That's what I asked him and I'll tell you what he said, he said the food was shit, so I told him to save his money, he didn't have to

74

pay. Listen, it ain't my fault the stuff they put in hamburger these days, that's the way they come. Anyway, when I told him that, he seems sorry he said anything. He takes a coupla bites, you know—like when your wife burns something and you don't wanna hurt her feelings? Okay, he takes a coupla bites, and then he leaves a fifty-cent tip.''

"You ever see him before?"

"No, I told the detective that, not before or after either. But that ain't surprising, even if he hung out across the street. But he's not the type guy who eats in diners."

"Oh?"

"He was a restaurant type. Good places. Like no offense, but you don't eat in diners much either."

The counterman knew something. Brownstein's hobby was good food and he thought briefly about the meal that was waiting for him at home. His wife, Violet, had promised *coq au vin* and he was going to break open the Chablis that was on ice. There would be just the two of them; their daughter, Jackie, was away, studying law at Boston University.

"You're right," he told the counterman. "That's good, very good. What else did you notice about him?"

The counterman was flattered.

"I don't know. Like I said, he seemed, uh, preoccupied. And, oh, yeah, he kept fiddling with his tie. I remember that because the tie didn't fit the shirt."

"I'm not sure I follow that."

"Well—I know this because I wear those wide ties myself—you can't really wear them with those button-down shirts. The other kind of collar, the slot collar, you've got room for the knot. But this Harry had it all wrong—he was wearing a button-down shirt and you could tell the collar wasn't wide enough for the tie."

"You should have been a detective," Brownstein said. "I've got men on the force who—"

"It's the job," the counterman said. "Most nights it's like this, maybe two or three customers. I've got nothing but time on my hands. One thing I try to do, I try to figure out what customers do for a living. And sometimes I ask them and you'd be surprised how often I'm right. I'd have been wrong about you, though—I'd have figured you for maybe an accountant. Now take this Harry; I didn't ask him but I remember trying to peg him."

Brownstein leaned forward. Like most detectives, he shared the counterman's hobby. The police phrase for it was "making somebody."

"What did you guess about Harry?"

75

"Well, that's another reason I remember the tie," he said. "The tie threw me off. It didn't go with the rest of him. The tie was what you might get with a salesman or a real estate guy."

"Or an insurance man?"

"Sometimes, but this guy was more conservative. You should have seen his threads. Now you're talking about one of those two-hundred-dollar suits, you know. And it wasn't just the suit, it was the way he carried himself. You know what I mean, his style. Almost snotty. To tell the truth, I was surprised when I read in the papers that he's an insurance man."

"That's just what he said," Brownstein interrupted. "We have no idea what he really is."

"I can't see him selling anyone a policy. I pegged him for a high-class lawyer, maybe somebody with the county. Not one of those loudmouths you see in the clubs but a high-class type. Like you remember Eugene Nickerson, he used to be county executive. Well, he came in here once and this Harry reminded me of him only not *that* classy."

"Fine." Brownstein shook the man's hand. "And thanks. You've been very helpful."

"Anytime," the counterman said. "You need anything else, gimme a call, just ask for Hy."

Brownstein had meant what he said about the man being helpful. Driving away from the diner, the detective chief allowed himself what he considered a luxury; he gave in to a flash of intuition and allowed it to lead him along a particular line of thought. A politician. Why not? A new avenue to explore. Brownstein had little use for politicians and he wondered whether his feeling about them was detouring him from more logical routes. A politician. Wouldn't that be something? If it had not been for the *coq au vin* and his profound distaste for acting on impulse, Brownstein would have turned around and gone back to the office. Instead he continued home to the chicken, followed by a well-ripened Brie, followed by an hour with the chess game he was playing by mail with the Los Angeles Homicide captain he met at a police convention in Denver. Still later he joined Violet in watching a James Bond movie on television. He laughed several times during the movie, invariably at spots not designed to provoke intentional laughter.

And at nine the next morning he was in his office—alone with a hunch and the contents of an inlaid wooden box that his men had found at the bottom of a drawer filled with expensive lingerie in Virginia Hanson's apartment.

The box contained eleven newspaper clippings. Three, yellow and ragged now, concerned the Jericho Turnpike prostitution scandal. As he fingered the old clippings, Brownstein recalled some of the details. Most of the hookers had been suburban housewives supplementing their pin money without their husbands' knowledge. Although the identities of the Johns had been kept from the press, they had included more than a few prominent Long Islanders. When O'Malley first linked the late Virginia Hanson to the scandal, Brownstein had made inquiries among acquaintances in the district attorney's office. No one recalled the name Virginia Hanson. If someone had covered up for her—and the three clippings in the wooden box lent credence to O'Malley's information—they had done a thorough job.

Brownstein doubted that the clippings had any connection with the killing. They went back too far. And the more recent clippings followed no distinct pattern. One centered on a campaign to halt pollution in Long Island Sound. Another reported how six Long Island legislators had voted on the state's abortion law. Six of the clippings dealt with New York's stringent narcotics law—the legislative debate and the bill's passage. These six clippings occupied Brownstein's attention; his original thought was that there might be a narcotics tie-in in the case. Dope was always a possibility in cases involving bar people and the search of the slain woman's apartment had turned up some possible related leads—an unprescribed bottle of tranquilizers in the bathroom cabinet and a small plastic bag of marijuana in a Tampax box. The department's Vice Squad, however, assured him that the Pumpkin was not a dope joint.

"It's a pickup place but it's clean," the squad's commander told him. "Once in a while we might find a few free-lance hookers moving in there, but that's it."

Virginia Hanson had no police record and she was unknown to all but one of the contacts used by the Vice Squad narcs. The exception was a bead-wearing bartender who had once worked with her and who described the murder victim as a "straight snatch." He added that drugs were not her "karma." And that it was his opinion that she was "into balling."

Brownstein managed to translate this with some assistance from one of the younger men in Homicide. The bartender was not the only one who saw fit to mention Virginia Hanson's interest in sex. One witness showed up at Brownstein's desk three weeks after the slaying and identified himself as Crazy Oscar, a Massapequa used-car dealer.

"Ginny was wild in bed," he said.

The dealer had been certain that his name would come up in the investigation sooner or later; he wanted to make sure that his name didn't also come up in the newspapers. There was a small matter of a wife and five children. Brownstein agreed to keep his name out of the papers if he checked out clean, which he did. Crazy Oscar had known Ginny for six months and he said he was the one who ended the relationship.

"I was getting too involved," he said. "That's my one rule—don't get involved. You do that, you start getting emotionally committed, and things get out of hand. That's the way you get all fucked up. I'll tell you, Chief, it wasn't just the family; I was beginning to screw up the agency."

"Maybe you can tell me," Brownstein had said, "what was so special about Virginia Hanson?"

"Well, first off, the sex was fantastic." He stopped there, uncertain whether to elaborate on this point or not. Brownstein watched the light catching in Crazy Oscar's pinky ring and said nothing. "Like once my family was away and I brought her home and we had a session in the pool, you'd think I was making it up. I tell you, Chief, I almost drowned and it would have been worth it. But it wasn't just that. It's the way she had with a man, the way she made you feel. No woman ever made me feel like that before."

"How did she take it when you broke up?"

"Okay." Brownstein looked at the heavyset, balding man in front of him and wondered why Virginia Hanson would *not* take it okay. "She said she understood perfectly. In fact, she said that was part of what she liked about me, the fact that I could do things like that without a second thought. Once she told me that it was my ruthlessness that attracted her. Ruthlessness, that's the word she used, but I thought that was bullshit. I used to try and give her things. One time a car right off the lot, a genuine cream puff, but she wouldn't take the time of day from me. She was a crazy broad, a crazy fucking broad. I mean, you'd never marry someone like Ginny but I'll tell you something else, Chief, when I read about the murder . . . oh, forget it."

"Go on."

"Well, I cried like a baby."

In the days that followed, Brownstein began to write off drugs. He knew that tranquilizers and other pills had become as common as Band-aids in most medicine cabinets; he also knew that marijuana rivaled liquor as a social adjunct in some suburban circles. And there was nothing else to link Virginia Hanson with drugs.

It was hard to believe that the clue had been provided by a short-order cook in a second-rate diner—but there it was. The clippings were spread out in front of Brownstein now and he could see that they weren't about narcotics and abortion and pollution. What they were about—and now it seemed so obvious as to be almost vocal—was politicians, most likely a single politician, one particular politician.

Brownstein did not rush from one clipping to another. He began with the antipollution story and listed the names of every political figure in the story from the governor down to local assemblymen. He picked up a second clipping and checked the names there against the names on his list. Two names matched up; one was the governor and the second was a state senator from Suffolk County. The governor's name failed to appear on the third story but the state senator was there again.

Why had he not thought of this before? Was he getting old? Would he have to stop strangers on the street and ask for their help? The name now leaped out of the stories at him. The same man who had been appointed chairman of a bistate committee to protect Long Island Sound had also voted against New York's liberalized abortion law and supported the state's narcotics legislation.

Brownstein did not know Chapin Kirk Hope but he had heard of him. His memory was of a clean-cut type, one of those law-and-order politicians. The clips filled in some of the gaps—a Republican from Stony Harbor, an easy winner in a conservative district.

Well, he had his man. Now what to do with him? Detective Lieutenant Charles Brownstein stacked the newspaper clippings together and returned them to the large envelope in which they were being kept. He drew a cup of plain hot water from an electric coffeepot atop a small file cabinet and—using a teaspoonlike caddy he had found in Bloomingdale's housewares department—he brewed tea from a canister kept beside the pot. The blend was his favorite, Earl Grey, discovered six years earlier during a vacation in London.

At his desk he inhaled the aroma and then he sipped the tea. He finished the cup before he picked up the phone.

"Vito," he said, "don't make any noise about it but see what you can get me on a state senator from Suffolk named Chapin Kirk Hope. Right, Hope."

11

Main Street sliced through the southern tier of Stony Harbor, a flow of commerce running a half mile east from the bay to St. Stephen's Episcopal Church, where it ended in a crossroad. That first afternoon in town O'Malley parked at the village dock and fortified himself against the cold with a belt from the flask of Jack Daniel's he kept in his glove compartment beside the first-aid kit.

An elderly man sat on the bench in front of him and beyond the man the water was steel blue in the sharp December afternoon. On a slight bluff at the water's edge there was a patch of green and it stirred memories of O'Malley's last visit to Stony Harbor. On a clear spring day some years earlier he had watched a long line of teenagers complete a five-mile hike from Pershing Senior High School to protest the war in Vietnam. Sailboat masts had dotted the harbor like toothpicks then and the breeze from the bay had scented the morning with salt cologne. The kids had come marching out of that clean day into the green park with their youth and pride on display and O'Malley had tried to swallow his cynicism but it was no use. He looked the other way and his eyes rested on a gaggle of middle-aged shrews wearing military caps, with flags sewn across their breasts, protesting the protesters with catcalls, and he knew they would have it their way. The speakers had included a student, a rabbi, and a peace-group representative. O'Malley had interviewed the protesters, the counterprotesters, the uninvolved shopkeepers, and he had written a story that gave everyone equal space and then he had gotten drunk and put the entire scene out of his mind.

Chapin Hope had not been present and that fact had been no surprise. The clips made it plain that Hope understood his constituents and when the issue was Vietnam, he had always retreated to the old bulwarks. He supported "the values that made this country great" or "the ideals on which America was founded."

O'Malley stood there now, staring at the empty bandstand and remembering that morning in the park and the kids' faces. In those faces he had seen something of his own youth, a youth that was as irretrievable as one of those small waves disappearing in the harbor.

Then he stuck his ungloved hands in the pockets of his coat and began walking the length of Main Street. Christmas decorations were looped from lamppost to lamppost and they enhanced the small-town feeling. It was a feeling fast disappearing from Long Island communities as the main streets fell beneath the advance of climatized shopping malls. Stony Harbor's main drag was an anachronism that survived for one reason.

Money, O'Malley thought. There were enough people with enough money, people who valued the character of the village over the convenience of a shopping center, people who wanted to preserve the past as a badge that set them apart from the others on the commuter trains and the crowded parkways.

During his walk O'Malley passed three antique stores, two real estate offices, a five-and-ten, a liquor store, a hardware store, a marine-supplies store, a sizable clothing store, a boutique, a soda parlor, a German delicatessen advertising "Homemade Clam Chowder," a quick-order pizza place, a French cleaner's, two banks, a coin-operated laundry, a movie theater, and a weekly newspaper office that sidelined in "Job Printing."

Nothing seemed out of place. The health-food store, the La Vie Art Gallery, the stationery store, the craft-and-hobby shop, a food market sufficiently behind the times so that one clerk was always available to carry a customer's groceries to the car.

There were also two bars on Main Street. One, the Rap, was all too obviously a kids' hangout. The other, Bobo's, was just as obviously a bucket-of-blood joint. Government was represented on the street by the post office building and the ivy-decorated village hall. A small, modern professional building stood out beside the village hall and the sign listed a dentist, a pair of doctors, an accountant, and the law offices of Hope, Hammer & Battalini.

After walking the length of Main Street and back again, O'Malley drove through the village, up and down side streets, then detoured to Pinnacle Lane, to Chapin Hope's house in the northernmost section of Stony Harbor, a five-minute walk from the sound. O'Malley drove down to the beach, to a padlocked gate and a sign: PRIVATE BEACH—RESIDENTS ONLY.

He parked there, beside the gate, and drained the remaining bourbon from the flask. He had a sudden impulse to toss the empty container against the sign but resisted it. Stony Harbor was an incorporated village of 6,000 residents with its own twenty-man police force, its own sewage plant, an annual budget of about $1,200,000. From the clips O'Malley knew the village was a microcosm of white-upper-middle-and-would-be-upper-class America, the sort of place where all zoning is predicated on "pre-

81

serve the residential nature of the community.''

O'Malley wondered how a man accommodated himself to this world. But, then, O'Malley had grown up in a Brooklyn neighborhood forever teetering on the edge of slumdom. His old man had been a longshoreman who was struck by spinal problems in his late thirties and hit by the booze in his early forties. O'Malley had grown up hating the kind of people who could afford to travel on the ocean liners his father unloaded. He had always, in his bones, despised the Chapin Hopes—but he had always sensed there was no way to bring them down.

Well, if the son of a bitch was guilty of murder, O'Malley would find his vulnerable spot. In fact, for the first time in years, O'Malley was actually looking forward to a story. The day he received the photograph he took it to Roland Feebe, Ginny Hanson's pudgy neighbor. Feebe, who had seen Harry only for a moment in the corridor, felt that the picture was the right one.

"He has a certain quality, don't you think?" the poet had said. "Almost spiritual. I mean, it's difficult to believe that this man could be responsible for . . . the incident. Of course, passion makes some people do the strangest things, doesn't it?"

"I suppose so."

O'Malley resembled a man who had just seen a fly die in his soup and excused himself an instant later, refusing Feebe's offer of a glass of sherry. His next stop had been the Pumpkin.

"I ain't a hundred percent positive," Baldy Davits started off. "You know, I wouldn't swear to it in court."

"No one's saying anything about court," O'Malley had said. "All I want to know is, does it look like him?"

"Like I say, I wouldn't want to swear to nothing, but yeah, that's Harry all right. A little younger, maybe, but that's him."

O'Malley had returned to the office, had taken the picture and the file in to Custer Yale.

"I wish we knew who sent the damn thing," O'Malley had said.

"Don't worry about that now." Yale was ecstatic. "Just get on this thing. A state senator. Too much. *Too* much."

"We've got to get more than this," O'Malley said.

"Sure." Yale seemed preoccupied. "Sure. Listen, I'll be right back. I want to show this to Cliff."

Cliff was H. Clifford Kline, the onetime *Life* magazine hotshot who had edited the *Islander* during the past year. He, in turn, called the publisher, Leland Birch, and he called the main office in Chicago. It was difficult to imagine who would be called after that. At any rate, Yale came back smiling. O'Malley could have whatever it took. This was his baby. Let's get this guy, this Chapin Hope.

Only one thing bothered O'Malley. That was the fact that he and Custer Yale seemed to be in a state of agreement. When they agreed a second time—both felt it was not the right time to tell Brownstein about the photo—O'Malley felt sharp misgivings.

It was Yale's fear that Brownstein might release the information to competing newspapers. O'Malley had additional motivation. He preferred working alone. He abhorred pool reporting and he resented the team concept that was becoming prevalent at most large dailies. He had never in his life used the word "scoop" but that was his goal. He did not want to be part of an *Islander* team; he wanted to be out on his own doing the one thing in the world he did better than other people.

O'Malley knew he could be more flexible on his own. Although he never "piped," he had few scruples when it came to obtaining the information. Like most good investigative reporters, he tried to stop short of criminal action in his search for the facts. Most times he was successful.

This time he had asked for $3,000 up-front money and the check had come through within an hour. As O'Malley came back for the expense money, he couldn't keep the satisfaction from flickering across his face. That was a mistake.

"Remember, Bob," Yale had said, "watch the booze."

"Sure, Custer." O'Malley had known it was too good to last. "And you watch your ass."

"What's that supposed to mean?"

"Oh, something I heard," O'Malley said. "I heard that your pal Cliff doesn't like his executives dipping their pens into the company inkwells."

"I'm supposed to know what you're talking about?"

"Everyone else does," O'Malley said. "That J-school broad you've been banging has been talking about it."

"That's enough, O'Malley." Yale had turned crimson but hung on for the last word. "Remember to call in."

Call in—the editor's litany. The theory was that reporters were children who would be lost without the benefit of constant direction. "All you've got to do is go out and buy fruit," an editor had once told O'Malley, "but I've got to decide whether you should buy apples or pears or oranges." O'Malley felt that there was also a fear, the fear that the world would end and no one would bother to tell the news desk.

The reporter converted the check into traveler's checks and a walletful of ten- and twenty-dollar bills, then took a room at the King's Court Motor Home six miles south of Stony Harbor. Twenty-six dollars a night. For blond furniture and Magic Fingers beds and color TV and room service. And, most important for O'Malley, the security of impersonal surroundings. There was a reliable supply of liquor and, when necessary, food, and, always necessary, anonymity.

After checking in at the motel and setting up his Olivetti on the bureau, O'Malley sized up the terrain. Main Street by foot and then the drive through the village and Chapin Hope's neighborhood. He saved Bobo's bar for the second day. It was O'Malley's experience that where there was booze, there was talk. And where there was talk, there was sometimes information.

Of O'Malley it might truly be said that he never met a bar he couldn't like. But nothing in his checkered past had prepared him for Bobo's. It was not so much the ambience—the semilight, the stale-beer smell, the clicking of the balls on the coin-operated pool table—because all of that was familiar enough. Even more familiar was the barmaid, an untidy young woman who seemed to be supporting catawba melons in her bra. What was remarkable, even for a neighborhood saloon, was the quality of the conversation.

In three hours the closest O'Malley came to a coherent discussion was a brief exchange with an outpatient from the nearby veterans' hospital, a grizzled and bleary-eyed old man who confided to O'Malley that he was being constantly pursued by teenage girls.

"You wouldn't think it to look at me, right?" the old man said.

"Well . . . no," O'Malley admitted.

"All they want is my body," he said.

The conversation did not notably pick up with the arrival of the other regulars, silent, badly shaven men who drew circles with their fingers in the puddles left by the beer glasses. In a single afternoon O'Malley had never heard so many failures rationalized, never heard so many jokes first told in grade-school urinals.

O'Malley did his best. He monopolized the pool table, winning it from a lean white-haired man in a torn windbreaker, a regular who seemed to suffer no undue embarrassment when a pint bottle of red wine fell from his coat and broke on the floor. He lost finally to a huge woman wearing a mackinaw and he retreated gratefully to the bar, where he bought a round for the house.

The drinkers were a close family unit, close enough so that they seemed able to communicate fully with one another through a series of grunts. O'Malley knew it would be impossible to break into the family in a single afternoon but he didn't relish the thought of a second day in Bobo's. To see if the process could somehow be accelerated, he bought a second and a third round for the house, a house that, at its peak, consisted of Windbreaker, Mackinaw, the outpatient, a dozer, and an off-duty village cop with a .38 dangling from his belt and a rolled-up copy of *Penthouse* magazine protruding from his hip pocket.

There did not seem to be a source in the place. At six O'Malley switched over to doubles and he could feel them working. When they had done enough work, he asked whether anyone knew Senator Hope. The only response came from the outpatient.

"All them politicians are fulla shit," he said.

For that invaluable bit of information O'Malley bought his last round and shrugged his shoulders. To hell with it.

"Whataya wanta know about Hope for?" the cop asked.

O'Malley decided it was time to take a chance. He reached into his wallet and handed the cop his *Islander* press pass. He told him he was doing a feature story on the village and he understood Hope lived there.

"Don't mess with Hope," the cop said. "I crossed him once and I'm not about to do it again."

"Well, I'm more interested in life in a small town, that kind of thing."

"This place is like Peyton Place," the cop said. "You gonna put that in the paper there?"

"I heard that," O'Malley said. "Being on the force, you must really know what's going on."

"I'm telling you."

"We've got to get together then," O'Malley said. "I'll have to have some pictures of the local police and you'd do as well as the next one."

The patrolman's name was Jerry Walsh; he had been a bouncer-bartender at a topless bar on Jericho Turnpike when he heard about the opening on the Stony Harbor police force. He still worked nights at the bar.

"You say I shouldn't mess with Hope?"

"I wouldn't," Walsh said. "Not again. I stopped him once late at night for speeding, fifty-five in a thirty-mile zone, so I chewed his ass. The next day the chief calls me in and chews my ass. He tells me if I ever bother Senator Hope again I can count on being a bouncer full time. So now I make believe that Mercedes is invisible. I'll tell you, I don't think he ever goes below fifty."

"And he's part of this Peyton Place scene?"

"Senator Hope? You gotta be kidding. Hope's as square as they come—I mean, God only knows what those guys do up in Albany but you never hear a whisper about him down here. He's a big man over at the church."

O'Malley signaled the barmaid—one for himself, one for his new friend. The cop seemed to be having some trouble formulating his next thought but it finally came out.

"Uh, do you pay for this kind of stuff, this information?"

"Sure do." O'Malley found a twenty in his wallet and slid it down the bar. "This is just a down payment."

"Well, let me tell you, then," Walsh said, "if you're into that Peyton Place-type stuff, you might as well forget about Hope. He is not your man. But I can tell you who is—his partner, the lawyer, he's gotta be the biggest swordsman this town ever saw."

"Battalini?"

"Hammer," he said. "I told you I work at this topless place—El Dorado—I see Hammer coming in there twice, three times a week. You don't mind my saying, he drinks about the way you do, nonstop, and also throws around more money than God. But he is some swinger."

"Gregory Hammer?" O'Malley said. "Gregory Hammer, the big-shot lawyer?"

"Big-shot swinger is more like it," the cop said. "You see a lotta guys coming on with the topless dancers but you never see one of 'em making out. Except this Hammer. I don't know his secret but more than once he walks out with the dancer. Also his car gets around the neighborhood, if you know what I mean."

"His *car*?"

"Say a guy's out of town on business; don't be surprised to see Hammer's Buick parked in that driveway the same night. That big Buick gets around this town. It's what you call common knowledge. Hey, you're not gonna say that I was the one who told you that?"

"Hey, Jerry, you think I don't protect my sources? Your name doesn't come into this without your specific okay. His wife must know that, about . . . ?"

"Who can tell? Some broads are smart enough to look the other way. And these guys are making a big buck. You ever see Hope's house?"

"I may have driven by it."

"Well, that's one house you're not gonna see from the road," the cop said. "He's got a driveway longer'n some county roads. And there's the Mercedes *plus* a new station wagon. I'm telling you, you drive by that place and you can practically smell the money."

Money. That was the key to Chapin Hope. Everything about the man came down finally to money. The house, the car, the wife, the whole goddamned village—everything surrounding Chapin Hope floated on a reservoir of money. O'Malley did not consider this precisely a revelation: The politician of any substantial rank who hadn't made his fortune in this day and age wasn't really trying. But at least it was a starting point.

"There's three of them hang out together actually," Walsh was saying. "The other one is this guy Norris Whitlaw, the building contractor."

"Is he an ass man, too?"

"I think so," the cop said. "I don't know for sure, but he's a real dude, and I've heard some talk."

Driving back to the King's Court Motor Home, O'Malley wondered what the secret of Hope's financial success would be. Probably not the defense-industry payroll—that was for politicians with federal muscle. Kickbacks from local contractors were possible, although Hope seemed slicker than that. Most likely the answer would have something to do with real estate. That's where the gold was in the nation's most populous demographic division, the suburbs. Most of the suburban bonanzas of the past two decades had been made by men who understood what could happen to land values when an area filled up rapidly with people.

In the motel O'Malley sat on the edge of the bed, debating the wisdom of a nightcap and studying the Magic Fingers coin box with skepticism. He started jotting down notes—reminders, actually—on the back of the postcards bearing photographs of the swimming pool in front of the King's Court Motor Home. He reminded himself to run a check on Hammer. He wrote down the name Norris Whitlaw. Then he scrawled two words in capital letters—"SEX" and "MONEY"—and connected them with a single line. After another moment's reflection he bisected the line with a large question mark.

The reason for the question mark was looming large in O'Malley's mind. His experience was that most men were barely able to handle one character failing at a time, that the man who divided his attention between two major corruptions was a *rara avis*. O'Malley had observed the phenomenon in Las Vegas—the gamblers bent feverishly over the crap tables, barely noticing the net-stockinged young women bringing them booze. Later, when they had been sufficiently burned, then there would be time for women, but it was rare that a man's passions were strong enough to be divided. It was the same over the long haul; he had read, for instance, that compulsive gamblers, perpetual plungers, were likely to have low sex drives.

In his own experience, and with the sort of contacts he had

developed over the years, O'Malley had always found it chancier to get authentic information on a man's extramarital affairs than on his financial affairs. So he would begin by concentrating on the latter—in the morning he would begin looking into an area he was expert at exploring. And if his theories were right, a thorough knowledge of Chapin Hope's daytime financial entanglements could lead to a revelation of his capability for ruthlessness in controlling those entanglements when they became a threat. And that knowledge could present a corollary to Hope's nighttime sexual entanglements and the lengths to which he might go to protect himself in *that* arena.

But an ax murder, for Chrissakes? O'Malley had long ago ceased being surprised by what people could do to each other, especially when they felt cornered. And for the moment, Hope's financial dealings represented the only reasonable avenue of investigation available and one in which O'Malley thoroughly knew the terrain.

Before turning out the light, O'Malley finally surrendered to curiosity and dropped a quarter into the coin box at the head of the bed. He followed the printed directions carefully and in a few seconds the entire bed began to tremble, shudder, and heave beneath the 320 pounds of Robert J. O'Malley. In less than a minute he was seasick and only with some small difficulty did he manage to escape the vibrating bed. As he stood there, a huge figure in outsized boxer shorts, waiting for a mechanical bed to come to its senses, O'Malley once again reflected on the fact that he had been born in the wrong century.

12

"Good morning." The voice on the telephone was cheerless. "It's eight o'clock."

O'Malley put the motel phone back in its receiver and picked up his watch from the bureau. It was seven minutes past the hour and he understood why the telephone voice had that weary, mechanical quality. Majority America wakes up by eight o'clock; the voice must have delivered dozens of wake-up calls by the time it reached through O'Malley's sleep.

The reporter picked up the phone a second time, dialed room service, asked for a pot of coffee, two orders of scrambled eggs, two large orange juices, a rasher of bacon, and a side order of sausage.

As he showered, O'Malley considered the day ahead. He doubted that there would be any quick breaks. He had started too many investigations and he knew that the first few days were a matter of setting up the apparatus, of lining up the sources.

O'Malley had never met an investigative reporter who was better than his sources. It had been a source—an overworked, underpaid secretary in a defense-plant office—who had called O'Malley one night ten years earlier and handed him his Pulitzer on a platter. Or who at least handed him the exposé that won journalism's big apple. (The award also stemmed from the amount of money the *Islander* spent on the story and the fact that the paper was overdue for a Pulitzer.) All the big exposés of the past decade—from Watergate and My Lai on down—were not the results of hard work and digging; primarily they came about because someone somewhere decided to spill the beans. The probing and checking came afterward, but the key reporting was done by the source.

O'Malley had seen it happen to others as well as himself. The reporter would be sitting at a desk in the clutter of a city room, suffering through routine assignments—a Public Service Commission release concerning a hearing on a proposed hike in electricity rates or a roundup story on upcoming school-budget votes. And then the phone would ring and the caller would be an ambitious young staff assistant who felt he wasn't moving up the ladder rapidly enough; or it would be a girlfriend who had just been jilted; or it would be a politician just passed over by the party hierarchy.

Hell, the fact that O'Malley was in Stony Harbor at all was due to a source. An as yet anonymous source who had contacted him by mail. A source who could be male or female, powerful or humble. But a source who was no friend to Chapin Hope. And a source who had done more with a manila envelope than O'Malley had done in weeks of probing.

Now it was time to line up other sources. In the next few days O'Malley would call up a half-dozen men who either barely knew each other or had never met. They would be joined only in the mind of a reporter trying to penetrate the defenses that surrounded Chapin Hope.

There was a knock on the door and O'Malley searched for a towel large enough to maintain minimal decency. He settled for the blanket and opened the door for a young man carrying a breakfast tray. As he put the tray on the table, the young man glanced around, seeming confused.

"I think the kitchen made a mistake," he said. "I've got two breakfasts here."

"I'll let you know when you make a mistake," O'Malley said, signing the tab.

Before beginning breakfast, the reporter took the telephone directory to the table with him. This was no simple task. The directory was in a leather binder that had been chained to the bed stand. Were there actually people who stole telephone directories? At any rate, O'Malley had no intention of looking up a series of telephone numbers while hunched over the bed stand. He solved the dilemma by tearing the book into two sections and taking the sections to the table with him.

At home O'Malley would have done with his instant coffee and vitamin pills. But he had learned that nothing improved his dietary practices quite so much as an expense account. Nor did the high calorie count set before him stir any guilt pangs; O'Malley had never yet heard of a diet that didn't advise the dieter to begin the day with a good solid breakfast.

Later, carrying his last cup of coffee to the phone, O'Malley started his calls. Not until then did he fully appreciate what he was up against.

The first call went to Buzz O'Neill, director of the Fishington Town Recreation Department. An ex-cop and a former president of the Police Benevolent Association, Buzz had come to O'Malley for favors more than once in the past. O'Malley was certain that Buzz, a lifelong Republican in the area, would be acquainted with Chapin

Hope. What he didn't know was how closely.

"Count me out," he told O'Malley. "I don't know what you think you've got on the senator and I don't want to know. It just so happens that the senator got me this job—my kids get fed every night because of him. Even if I knew anything, and I'm not saying I do, I wouldn't tell you about it."

The next call went to Kenneth Powledge, director of security for the twenty-three Long Island branches of Madison National Bank. Powledge, a former agent for the Federal Bureau of Investigation, had been friendly with O'Malley for more than fifteen years, first at the bureau and then at the bank.

"Chapin Hope?" Powledge said. "Are you serious?"

"It's serious, all right."

"Christ, Bob, Hope is chairman of the Appropriations Committee. You know what he could do to us if he wanted to? I'm not even talking about what he could do to me personally, although if it came down to that and Hope wanted me fired, I could start clearing out my desk this minute."

"Yeah, well. . . ."

"I'd like to help, Bob. I've never turned you down before."

"Suit yourself." Then O'Malley did something he hadn't wanted to do. "I sure am sorry it's Chapin Hope," he said. "But they can't all be Lee Harvey Oswald."

There was a silence for several seconds while Powledge considered. Finally he spoke: "I guess I'd forgotten that. Okay, we'll have lunch, but no promises."

"The John Peel Room?"

"No," Powledge said. "My bosses go there."

"How about the Westbury Chef instead?"

"Okay," Powledge said. "Tomorrow at one o'clock."

O'Malley could have reminded Powledge of more than one favor but the one had been sufficient. The relationship between a reporter and his source was a two-way street. When the story appeared, both usually profited. In one case Powledge had given O'Malley a story he felt was being neglected in the bureau. He had given him a second because he felt he was being pulled off a case for political reasons. He had fed O'Malley information on a third occasion because he knew the reporter would shake the tree hard enough to bring down a few more apples. And there was something O'Malley had left out of a story. One day in Dallas in 1963, when Kenneth Powledge had been among the FBI agents who failed to prevent a nightclub owner named Jack Ruby from getting too close to an accused assassin in a police basement, O'Malley had not mentioned his name.

The reporter's third call went to Wolf Barrios, the county Democratic leader. This call was routine and unpromising; O'Malley was constantly surprised to discover how little politicians ever knew about the opposition.

"Sure," Barrios said. "Why don't you come over and we'll talk. But I can tell you right now what we've got on Hope and it's zilch. I don't trust the bastard, but he *is* Mr. Clean. He's been beating our brains out over there for—what, ten, twelve years?—and it's getting so bad we can't even find young lawyers to run against him anymore. Listen, we'd love to have something on him."

"Well, if you hear anything, let me know."

"Sure, Bob."

O'Malley's next call went to Jerome Miller, a salesman for Manhattan Life Insurance and a former district director for the Internal Revenue Service. Jerome Miller was the most reliable kind of source, a mercenary. O'Malley reached him at his office.

"Hello, Miller, this is Fox."

"Yes, Fox," Miller said. "Give me a number where I can call you."

"I'm in a motel," O'Malley said. "Call me at 555-8888. Room forty-two."

"I'll be back with you, Fox."

It took more than ten minutes and when the phone finally rang, O'Malley was staring into an empty coffee cup.

"Okay, Fox," Miller said. "I'm in the coffee shop across from my building. If they've got this phone tapped, they've got them all tapped. What's up?"

"The usual," O'Malley said. "I'm going to need some help."

"How much help?"

"The whole *schmear*."

"It's getting harder."

"I take it you mean it's getting more expensive."

"That's exactly what I mean," Miller said. "It's not me, it's my man."

"How much does he want?"

"Five."

"The last time he was happy with three and a half."

"And sirloin was seventy-nine cents a pound," Miller said. "Times change. And he has problems; he says it's getting very tight."

"All right," O'Malley said. "Five. But I want everything he can get his hands on."

"Right," said Miller. "Who's the prizewinner?"

"Chapin Hope," O'Malley said. "State Senator Chapin Hope, Republican, Stony Harbor."

"Consider it done," Miller said.

"Let's make a date now," O'Malley told him. "A week from tonight in Stony Harbor. Eight o'clock. I'll be at a bar called Bobo's. It's right on Main Street; you can's miss it."

"No one will recognize us there?"

"Jerome," O'Malley said, "if anyone recognizes you there, you've been hanging around with the wrong crowd. And I mean the wrong crowd."

The first steps were always the most difficult, O'Malley thought as he put down the phone. Merely setting up contacts could be a job; sometimes it took days just to hit the right source or set up an appointment. Most reporters looked on this phase of a story as drudgery. But to O'Malley it was not without its satisfactions.

And so it was with a sense of comfort born of routine that O'Malley got dressed and drove into Stony Harbor to begin his own legwork at the Village Hall. In the clerk's office a frail gray-haired woman brought out property maps at O'Malley's request, some of them dating back to 1641, the year of Stony Harbor's incorporation. O'Malley pinpointed the senator's property—lots 45, 46, and 47 in School District Six.

"Could you tell me who owns lots forty-eight, forty-nine, and fifty?" he asked the clerk.

"There is no lot forty-eight," she said. "But forty-nine and fifty belong to the Morgenthaus."

"That must be the Clancy Morgenthaus. . . ."

"Oh, no," she said, "that's the Norman Morgenthaus."

"Of course," he said. "The Norman Morgenthaus."

This parcel of information was jotted down for use at O'Malley's next stop, the county offices in Riverhead. As he left Stony Harbor and started his drive south toward the expressway, O'Malley heard the voice on the car radio making endless comments about the day's unseasonable warmth. Fifty-six degrees and rising. The warmth, on the heels of the previous day's snow, probably accounted for the heaviness of the fog. O'Malley had the feeling that the world was ending precisely one hundred yards in front of his slowly moving vehicle; the road was being unrolled in front of him like a carpet.

The fog added an element of uncertainty to a road the reporter had often traveled. He tested himself against the fog—guessing which road signs would suddenly appear, calculating the arrival of overpasses and crossroads—but he did too well at the game, so well that he stopped playing it.

Driving from north to south on Long Island is not unlike sliding down a large economic graph. In Hope's North Shore neighborhood the homes began at $80,000 and a man couldn't hope to survive on less than $40,000 a year. And now, as he approached the center of the Island, O'Malley could no more ignore the evidence of economic decline than could he ignore the gradual flattening of the hills.

The fog was welcome here; it blotted out the dreariest of suburban landscapes. Unfortunately the vistas were etched permanently on the reporter's mind. Without being able to see the details, he remembered them. He knew he was driving through the bare developments planted on the potato fields of yesteryear. He knew the too-large homes with the too-small windows; the false pillars supporting nothing that required support; the cedar shingles that faded to asphalt on the sides. It would be another decade, maybe two, before the new shrubs and young trees provided any softening effect. Until then, fog didn't hurt.

The voice on the radio was saying sixty-one degrees, still rising. The fog had come in from the north, had rolled in off Long Island Sound in huge unswirling chunks of gray, and at times the chunks were so thick that O'Malley drove on instruments, guiding himself by the arc lamps flanking the road and by the twin row of slowly moving taillights stretched out before him.

In the fog O'Malley missed his turnoff. No matter. It gave him time to think. Immediately ahead the stark outlines of Pilgrim State Hospital loomed darkly out of the thinning fog. Pilgrim State was a Dickensian relic, a mental institution built in a more morbid era. The reporter saw only the silhouette, the gloomy outlines, the slight tint of color where he knew the red tile roof to be.

As the fog thinned, he noticed that the parkway borders were deeply rutted, scarred by the wheels of thousands of cars gone lame since the fall reseeding. With each passing mile the trees became slighter and now, in the southern sector of the Island, they were all dwarfed, stunted by the sandiness of the soil. The homes, too, seemed stunted, as though the soil had been too depleted to support second floors or modern concepts. This was not Chapin Hope's district; O'Malley wondered whether the senator knew anything of these people and their lives. Clothesline supporters and patchy lawns and tricycles left in driveways. This was a world inhabited by the intermittently out-of-work, the assemblyline laborers who did well only in times of war, and those who went north every day to repair the oil burners and the dishwashers and the home-alarm systems and the swimming-pool lighting setups.

O'Malley emerged from the last tatters of fog to a sun that was curiously bright. The houses here were painted flat colors, oranges and greens, too bright to qualify as pastels, too garish to qualify as taste. Although the South Shore villages had been built beside an ocean of some size, they gave no evidence of past spendor. Danny's Used Auto Parts. The Knights of Columbus Hall—Bingo Every Tuesday Night—$1,000! Franklin H. Harris Cesspools Cleaned and Built.

The trees were small, the homes were small, and even the people seemed small—maybe because of the way they walked, heads bowed, as if searching the sidewalks ahead for some carelessly discarded treasure. O'Malley knew this world all too well. It reminded him of the Brooklyn streets he knew as a boy; it was a world that Ginny Hanson would have known, too; but Chapin Hope would think he was on another planet. Postage-stamp lawns, stucco bungalows, numbered streets, chain-link fences, garbage cans in full view, polyethylene sheets tacked over the lawn furniture and the bedroom windows.

O'Malley took the next road north and headed directly for the county center, a modern complex centered on a great glassed-in lobby. His immediate target was the county clerk's office, where he was a sufficiently familiar figure to draw a small buzz of recognition. Putting on his most phlegmatic expression, O'Malley walked down a long line of desks, each carrying the name of a different locale—past Smithtown and Port Jefferson and Setauket and he stopped at Stony Harbor.

"I'd like to see the property records for District Six."

"Certainly."

The woman returned almost immediately with three huge ledgers, the individual listings of every parcel of property in the entire school district.

"If you tell me whom you're interested in, perhaps I can help."

"Oh, I'd rather not," O'Malley said. "It's lots forty-nine and fifty."

"Certainly, that's right here."

Opening one of the volumes, she pointed out the lots in question. They were owned by a Norman Morgenthau and taxed at the rate of $3,700 annually. O'Malley reached for a pencil and allowed his eyes to wander to the notation directly above Morgenthau's. Lots 45, 46, and 47, three adjoining lots owned by one Thalia Hope. The previous year Thalia Hope had paid $3,000 in taxes on property with an assessed valuation of $30,000. O'Malley multiplied that figure by four to come up with the approximate value of the Hope home.

"If you don't mind," O'Malley said to the clerk, "I'd like to thumb through these ledgers."

"That's your privilege," she said.

For more than an hour O'Malley thumbed through the ledgers and allowed his eyes to wander over the names of the senator's neighbors. He picked out a television playwright, a political cartoonist, and several names that rang distant bells. The names were, for the most part, pure WASP: as far as O'Malley had been able to determine, there were no blacks in Stony Harbor and any Jews or Catholics were recent arrivals. The original developer of the village had excluded not only blacks and Jews and Irish; he had, in an act of breathtaking bigotry, barred all "Mediterranean types" as well.

One item in the ledger was of more than passing interest to O'Malley—the recent downzoning of a seven-acre parcel of land just south of Main Street. The land was owned by the Thalia Corporation.

That did it for the first visit. On his way out O'Malley stopped in the lobby just long enough to call the *Islander*'s Albany Bureau on the pay phone. There were some corporation links he wanted the bureau—which had been told to work with him—to check out. Specifically he wanted to know what corporations listed as directors either Chapin Hope, Gregory Hammer, Norris Whitlaw, or their wives. He gave the Thalia Corporation as a starting point.

Driving back to Stony Harbor, O'Malley felt the pleasant glow he associated with facts beginning to fall into place. He had decided to have a late lunch at the soda parlor-luncheonette in Stony Harbor. Bobo's had been a bust as far as gossip was concerned; maybe he was using the wrong kind of hangout. When he entered the soda parlor, O'Malley's glow increased—one of the men sitting at the counter was Buzz O'Neill, the town recreation director he had phoned that morning. They spotted each other simultaneously, and O'Neill immediately jumped up and hustled O'Malley to a booth at the back of the shop.

"What's the matter, Buzz," O'Malley said, "you don't want your friends to see me?"

"They can't miss you," O'Neill said, "but they don't have to know what we're talking about."

O'Malley was about to answer when a waitress approached the booth. "What's good here?" he asked instead.

"They make terrific westerns, don't they, Lila?" O'Neill said, winking and smiling at the waitress. O'Malley ordered coffee and a western on white toast.

As the young woman left with the order, so did O'Neill's grin. "I won't help you, O'Malley," he said. "I mean that. Neither will a lot of other people in this town who owe the senator. I'll tell you something else, if you were gonna do a story about the good things he's done, you wouldn't have room in that scandal sheet of yours to put it all down."

"I didn't say what kind of a story I was doing."

"Don't snow me, O'Malley, the *Islander* only does one kind of story on Republicans. I don't know what you think you've got on the senator, but people around here are gonna know it's typical pinko-*Islander* bullshit."

"So set me straight," O'Malley said. "Tell me about his good deeds."

"I'll tell you someone you should get hold of," O'Neill said. "Talk to Sonny Castor—he'll tell you all you need to know about the senator."

"Sonny Castor?"

"Sonny's got a dredging and bulkheading outfit that works outa the harbor. As a matter of fact, he bulkheaded the village park. Well, last year Sonny had some problems and he got into trouble with the shylocks. Big trouble. The way I heard it they called Sonny up one night and told him they were gonna cut off his wife's hands."

"So what's that got to do with Hope?"

"It probably helps that Sonny's a town committeeman, but he went to the senator, he told him about it. Now I ain't saying the senator knows any shylocks, but you meet a lot of people in politics, you make a lot of contacts. What I'm saying is that the next thing you know, the shylocks give Sonny an extension. Not only that, but the senator arranges a loan for him with a regular bank. And we're not talking pennies, we're talking twenty-five big ones."

"I see what you mean," O'Malley said, deciding to play along. Either O'Neill was an idiot or thought O'Malley was one. Committeeman or not, James (Sonny Castor) Castorina was periodically assessed by the Suffolk rackets bureau as well as by the U.S. Justice Department's eastern district strike force. He had what law-enforcement officers call a "low profile." No police record, nothing to prove that he was directly involved in the rackets. But some of his associates were known hoods, and there was no question that he had mob ties. Senator Hope's intervention meant only one thing to O'Malley; Mr. Clean had his own line into the organization. And he also had Sonny Castor in his pocket.

"And that's just one example," O'Neill said. "The senator has helped a lot of other people. Working people. Business people."

"Give me an example."

"Okay. You know the House of Lords?"

"The big restaurant on the hill?"

"Right. I know a maître d' there; he told me how they were having a lot of trouble when they got started. Money problems, and there was some mix-up with the liquor license. Well, the senator helped them both ways."

"You mean he's got a piece of the place?"

"No, no, he helped them get a mortgage. And we're talking six figures."

O'Malley nodded. The House of Lords was one of a half-dozen oversized restaurants constructed the year the state legislature started considering legalized gambling. O'Malley knew that the basements of these restaurants were loaded with gaming tables—roulette, baccarat, craps, the works. All they needed was legislative approval, and they'd be ready to go. The senator didn't miss a trick.

"Believe me," O'Neill said as he left, "the senator's a good man. Ask anyone."

"I will," O'Malley said before biting into his sandwich. The next minute he was thinking that O'Neill was right about one thing. The soda parlor made a hell of a western.

The maître d' at the Westbury Chef rushed forward and greeted Robert J. O'Malley as if the fat man were a long-lost son. In a way, O'Malley was. Over the past year his luncheon appearances at the Chef had been infrequent. But during his tenure as one of the *Islander*'s stars he had been a leading expense-account customer at the restaurant. In addition, he had on several occasions persuaded an *Islander* columnist to plug the place and use the maître d's name in passing.

"Some libation, Mr. O'Malley?"

"A special."

"Like old times, Mr. O'Malley," the maître d' said. The special was a double martini served over ice in a glass slightly larger than a water tumbler. It was the first of two such drinks O'Malley would order with lunch. As it arrived at the table, so did Kenneth Powledge.

It was like old times, all right, O'Malley thought. At the age of fifty-three Powledge still resembled the special agent he had been for most of his adult life. He was proof that while you can take the man out of the FBI, you can never quite take the FBI out of the man.

Hell, Powledge still wore the bureau uniform—dark gray suit, conservative narrow tie, and—something of an oddity in the flamboyant world of men's fashions—a white shirt with a starched collar.

"Chapin Hope," Powledge said, shaking his head after they greeted each other. "I'd like to know what you're drinking these days."

"The same," O'Malley said, pointing to the special. He raised the glass. "Chapin Hope," he said.

"You never change," Powledge said, sipping the tomato juice he had ordered. "What are you looking for, Bob?"

"Anything you want to tell me."

"That's not good enough," Powledge said. "If you're just on a hunting expedition, count me out."

"We're not hunting. We've got him cold—I'm just looking for some extras."

"How cold is cold?"

"Freezing, but you don't want to know. I'll just tell you that it's very big and very dirty."

The barest flicker of a smile touched Powledge's face. "That's all I need to know," he said. "I'll tell you the truth, you've just made my day. I never did like that sanctimonious prick. What did you want to know?"

"Everything."

Powledge reached into his jacket pocket for a large flat wallet. Inside was a notebook with a built-in pencil. Before starting to read from the notebook, Powledge glanced at the diners sitting at nearby tables. Although he apparently saw nothing to upset him, the security chief kept his voice low—low enough so that O'Malley had to ask him to repeat several points.

"His deposits at Madison come to one hundred and fourteen thousand dollars plus," said Powledge. "That's one hundred and nine thousand in a joint savings account with his wife, Thalia, and, ah, approximately five thousand in their joint checking account. But that's not the sum total."

"How's that?"

"We're not his only bank," Powledge said. "In fact, we once ran a security check on the senator and—"

"Something wrong?"

"Wrong? No," Powledge said. "Let me tell you about Hope's credit. He's one of the two or three men who can get unsecured loans from the bank. He's walked out with anything from one hundred thousand to one hundred fifty thousand, and I'm not sure whether anyone even asked him to sign an IOU. He wouldn't have a better credit rating if his name was David Rockefeller."

"Well, he makes a good buck."

"So do I. But if I want to borrow money, the bank wants me to put up my house and my car for collateral. But then there's a big difference between Chapin Hope and Ken Powledge. The big difference is that one of us is chairman of the Appropriations Committee."

"I can see where that would help a credit rating. . . ."

"Yeah," Powledge said, "and it didn't hurt that he almost single-handedly kept city banks out of the suburbs until we had a chance to build up our branches. The only reason I ever ran a credit rating on the senator, I was curious why he wanted a loan at all. Anyway, I found out he's worth another hundred above that."

"Hundred?"

"Hundred *thousand*," Powledge said. "He keeps accounts in a few banks. Let me put it this way. If the senator wanted to, he could put his hands on a quarter of a million by tomorrow noon."

"How's he making it?"

"I hate to tell you."

"What?"

"I hate to tell you, but I assume you'd find out anyway."

"Probably."

"He makes most of it through his law firm," Powledge said. "His clients are all people who do business with the state but a big source of income is banks."

"How's that work?"

"Nothing under the counter," he said. "It's all a matter of record. The fact is he's getting legal fees from half the banks in New York State. Whenever there's a zoning change, whenever a bank needs a law firm, they put in a call to Hope's office."

"Wait a minute, you mean Hope represents banks himself?"

"No, not in a million years," Powledge said. "The bank people rarely see the senator, except up in Albany when they're pushing one bill or another. No, the law firm sends this fellow Battalini to do the financial work. A financial wizard he's not—in fact, his real specialty is divorce cases—but that doesn't affect the law firm's bills. The bills to the banks are steep—not illegal, you understand, but steep—and no one ever complains."

"It's funny," O'Malley said, "but I haven't come across this wrinkle before."

"It's not all that new. Banks have never been reluctant to do business with state senators."

"Live and learn," O'Malley said. "What other sources of income?"

100

"It's hard to say. Almost everything goes through the law firm. I've gone over the checks for the last six months but they don't mean much to me. My guess is that Hope's on the boards of some of the corporations doing business with his firm—but that's hardly illegal."

"Still, it would be interesting. Listen, Ken, I'd like to see the checks."

"I'll get you copies," Powledge said. "But, Bob, this isn't an easy one. Not for me. If Hope hears anything, I can start looking for work."

"I'll give you a hell of a reference."

"Very funny."

"Let's order," O'Malley said.

"I hear the shrimps stuffed with crabmeat are very good," Powledge said.

"All I can tell you is they go great with the martinis."

The evening before meeting with Jerome Miller, O'Malley placed a call from his motel room and drew Custer Yale from the nightly editorial conference at the *Islander*.

"How's it going, Bob?"

"Not bad," O'Malley said. "The senator's got his fingers into the cookie jar up to the shoulder. The only thing is I'm going to need another five thousand dollars."

"*Five* thousand?"

"For information," O'Malley said. "It's a straight buy from an old source."

"What kind of information?"

"If all goes well, my bedtime reading tomorrow night will consist of State Senator Chapin K. Hope's income-tax returns for the last five years."

"Income-tax returns?"

"We've used them before," O'Malley said. "It's called investigative reporting. They're the one place most of these people don't tell lies—everyone's afraid of Internal Revenue."

"What in the hell do we want income-tax returns for?" Yale was saying. "What're income-tax returns going to tell us about whether Hope killed Virginia Hanson or not?"

"For Chrissake, Custer, don't make me give you a journalism lesson. When we're through, we're going to have everything there is to have on Chapin Hope. When we lay out the full story, the last thought he's going to have is suing us for libel."

"Well, I can't authorize five thousand dollars," Yale said. "It's just not that easy."

"Why don't you speak to the boss?" O'Malley said. "And when you're talking to him, be sure to tell him I've already told my source that he's going to get the money."

The $5,000 was authorized before O'Malley put down the telephone. At eight o'clock the following night, he was at Bobo's, leaning against the bar, watching a pool game between a heating contractor and an outpatient. Jerome Miller, sullen and apprehensive, came in shortly after the hour, took the stool beside O'Malley, and ordered a draft beer that he never touched.

"You'll get the money by the weekend," O'Malley said.

"No rush," Miller said. "But I've got to warn you, this may be the last time. Things are getting tight over at the service and my man is talking about leaving."

"Well, it was nice while it lasted."

"Nice, but slightly illegal."

"Is that so?" O'Malley said. "Well, now, let's see what goodies you brought this time."

"Not now," Miller said. "Not with all these people. . . ."

"We couldn't be safer," O'Malley said, tearing open the envelope. O'Malley, starting to leaf through the income-tax returns, ignored Miller as he left the bar and walked out the front door.

It was all there, all outlined in an accountant's code. A gross income, the previous year, of $111,000. And the sources. Income from the law firm and a list of corporations paying money to Chapin and Thalia Hope. Corporations involved in land transactions around the new jetport site. Corporations involved in a golf course in Greenlawn, a racetrack site in the Hamptons, shopping centers in a couple of other places.

Lead piled on top of lead—enough to keep a reporter busy for months. As he put the tax forms back in the envelope, O'Malley decided to do without a refill. He left a dollar bill on the bar and started back for the motel, back to the best bedtime reading he knew. Oh, there would be nothing in the tax returns to hint at violence, nothing to indicate a morbid interest in sex, just evidence of a man intent on making a buck.

It was enough. It was a start.

13

The two New York State legislative bodies, the Senate and the Assembly, convene every year on the first Wednesday after the first Monday in January. On that day legislators, aides, reporters, lobbyists, clerks, stenographers, pages, messengers, and assorted camp followers come to Albany and fill it up. The legislative session lasts until March or April and is frequently reconvened later at gubernatorial whim. It results every year in the consideration of some 15,000 bills, 1,400 of which find their way to the governor's desk and 1,100 of which become the law of the state.

This is a not-inconsiderable accomplishment considering the amount of time most legislators spend in Albany. A normal work week begins when they arrive late in the day on Monday and comes to a rather abrupt end, as a rule, on Wednesday, when most lawmakers return to their wives, families, jobs, and constituents.

On the second Wednesday of the brand-new year, as the planes, trains, and highways filled with departing people, Chapin Hope stayed in Albany.

He felt as lonely as an undergraduate who remains on campus over the holidays, but he needed the time. Time to think, to get away from *Islander* stories about the crime, to remove himself from all reminders of Ginny, and, for some uncertain reason, to get away from Thalia.

A week earlier he and Thalia had experienced their first genuine argument in five years. Thalia had clipped a news story chronicling the rising cost of living and had given it to Chapin along with a request for a twenty-five dollar weekly raise in her household allowance. Chapin had responded with a rare show of temper, quickly comparing his wife—by no means favorably—to such notorious financial villains as Franklin D. Roosevelt and George Meany. Thalia had briefly yelled back and left the house. Afterward Chapin wondered why he had gotten angry; he knew her request was reasonable and presented no financial strain.

Although Albany was a temporary ghost town, Chapin would not be entirely alone. In a few hours there would be dinner with Judson

Larned. Judson had been inviting Chapin to dinner for years and was only too happy to delay his own departure from the state capital to accommodate the senator. Larned, a former Assembly speaker and the best-paid lobbyist in Albany, had made reservations at L'Epicure, a meeting place for jockeys and tanned blondes in the summer, for power brokers in the winter.

Chapin did not bother returning to his hotel room after work. It was a short walk from the Capitol to the Clinton but the voice on the radio was talking about a windchill factor of thirty-five degrees below zero and no walk was short enough in that kind of weather. Instead he strolled through the emptying Capitol and listened to the sound of his footsteps echoing back from granite heights. The building had been designed to resemble a French town hall but was actually a hopeless hodgepodge of styles, an unharmonious mix of building materials. There was onyx from Mexico, Siena marble from Italy, red granite from Scotland—the people in New York State couldn't even get together on the kind of rock they wanted to use; small wonder they had trouble with abortion reform.

Chapin's favorite walk was up the Western Staircase, past all the carved heads known as the Gallery of Greatness. There was something comforting about finding yourself in the company of Washington and Jefferson and Hamilton and Franklin and Lincoln. Nor was he intimidated by the Poets' Corner—the sandstone reproductions of Bryant and Longfellow, Whittier and Walt Whitman. Whitman had been another Long Islander, like Chapin Hope.

Still not thinking about a destination, Chapin found himself in the third-floor press room, an ancient chamber usually jammed with reporters straining to find excitement in the normally juiceless process of lawmaking. Now the room was quiet. With no one to watch him, he went over to the *Islander* desk, where he spotted a rolled-up copy of the day's paper. Hope picked up the tabloid and searched out the only story that mattered to him. With every page he turned there was a small feeling of relief. Each day the story seemed to slip farther back into the paper and become smaller in size; it was no longer large enough to support a by-line. Today's story reported the absence of new clues and repeated the special police telephone number.

Chapin picked up the headset at the *Islander* desk and dialed Judson Larned's hotel suite.

"Judson, it's too cold to go all the way to L'Epicure," he said. "Why don't we just go across the street to the Ambassador?"

"It's your stomach," Judson said, punctuating the sentence with the booming laugh that was his trademark.

"But it's your expense account," Chapin said, "and think of all

104

the money I'll be saving you."

"I'll make the reservations," Judson said. "See you at seven."

Reservations, as it turned out, were something of a redundancy on a night this cold. The restaurant was all but deserted. Larned was waiting with his hand out and at the table beside him there were two iced drinks.

"I ordered us a brace of Beefeaters."

"Amazing," Chapin said. "You even got the brand right. Tell me now, how'd you know about that?"

"Who knew?" Larned said. "In the event that you wanted something else, I was fully prepared to make the ultimate sacrifice and drink it myself."

Again that booming laugh. One of the things that made Larned Albany's top lobbyist was his genuine love of the process, the fact that he never had to fake the laugh.

"Do you want to tell me who's paying for dinner tonight?" Chapin said. "Then we can get the business out of—"

"Hey," Larned said, "maybe this is purely social. Maybe this is just for the pleasure of your company."

"I hope not," Chapin said. "I've been down lately, Jud—something I don't even want to talk about—and I don't think anyone should be paying for the pleasure of my company."

"Well, maybe I can think of a way to cheer you up. But first, some sustenance. You picked the Ambassador—what do you suggest?"

"Well, having eaten here before, I'd suggest that we send out for a pizza."

The stab at humor was rewarded by another volley of laughter. Chapin felt his spirits brightening.

"Chape, I'm having a little party later on, if you're interested."

"A party?" Chapin said. "On Wednesday night in Albany?"

"It's what you might call a private party," Larned said. "Two friends of mine are stopping by here and joining us for coffee—both of them lovely young women who—"

"You know I can't do something like that," Chapin said. "You know I can't be seen with anyone. . . ."

"You're not going to be seen with anyone," Larned said. "Relax. This isn't what you think it is. One of the girls is my secretary. You've met Peggy? The other one is a friend of hers, Laura; she's a bright kid just home from Vassar. Believe me, everything's on the up-and-up. If you like Laura, we'll stop by Peggy's apartment later and have a few drinks, that's all."

"You had me worried for a minute."

"Let me do the worrying," Larned said. "You forget, I was up here for ten years myself. I know the ropes. But I'll tell you something, Chape—in the old days the guys didn't take themselves that seriously. I'll tell you, they knew how to have fun in those days. And I hear that was nothing compared to Al Smith's time."

There was a second martini, then a third one with dinner. Chapin ordered a ham steak, a cut of meat that the Ambassador staff had not yet figured out how to ruin. Larned ordered what he always ordered —filet mignon, well done, with sliced tomatoes. He sent the filet back twice for "more fire" and then there were brandies.

"I guess it would be wrong if I didn't at least tell you who was paying for the feed," Larned said.

"I was curious."

"It's the dairymen."

"Ah, the dairymen, a spendid group," Chapin said. "By that, of course, I refer to the fact that they contributed a few thousand dollars to my last campaign."

"*Five* thousand dollars," Larned said.

"As I say, a splendid group."

"Chape, I don't have to bullshit you," Larned said. "These guys have appreciated your support up here in the past and they're looking forward to it in the future. You happen to be a very big man in their book and they know that in life you have to pay for anything of quality."

"They've been very generous."

"Chape, it's a pleasure to do business with you," Larned said. "Some of these guys up here, you'd be surprised. I have to make a small spiel about the nutritious value of milk and, as you may have guessed, I haven't touched a drop of the stuff in thirty years."

"I'm not exactly known as a milk fancier myself," Chapin said.

"Well, as you know, the dairymen are, by and large, little people, your basic small businessmen, and it doesn't hurt anyone politically to support them."

"I've always—"

"We know that," Larned said. "And, Chape, you're gonna find these guys more than appreciative in the only way that counts. What they need now are some quality sponsors on the new price package. I'm going to send a kit over to your office tomorrow, you know, the usual stuff, the arguments. . . ."

"Jud, I'm having some trouble following this."

"It's not too complicated," he said. "In a couple of weeks the Senate is going to vote on whether to okay a price increase beyond the current ceiling. I mean, they're sure to okay something but the dairymen tell me they need another three point four cents a quart. . . ."

106

"Jesus, Jud, that's going to sound inflationary as hell to a lot of people."

"What doesn't sound inflationary?" Larned said. "I mean, think what we're spending for dinner tonight. We'll go forty dollars easy and this is a greasy spoon. The dairymen think they're being very reasonable. Let me let you in on a secret, Chape—they've got charts that show that within five years the price of milk is gonna be a dollar a quart. Within five years!"

"A dollar for a quart of milk?"

"That's what they say."

"Jud, this time I don't know," Chapin said. "I know I've gone along on the price increases before, but every time we okay one of those things you know who gets nailed on it; it's always some guy who can't afford it. Look, it's one thing to vote for price increases; it's another thing to take milk out of a baby's mouth."

"Chapin, one of the first things I ever learned up here is that babies can't vote."

"But mothers can." Chapin was tired of his condescending tone, and he was thinking of his argument with Thalia. "I'll tell you, Jud, this time I think you'd better count me out. I can't go along with another price increase this session. You'll have to tell those guys they're getting greedy."

"Wait a minute, Chape. We both know how generous they can be."

"Fine. This time let them be generous with the customer. They've been watching the oil boys."

"Everyone's been watching the oil boys," Larned said. "This country never had a peacetime shortage of anything until the oil boys showed us that shortages are big business. It only works with a necessity, of course—but milk happens to be a necessity."

"Oh, Christ," Chapin said, "don't you people ever learn anything?"

"Don't give me that 'you people' bullshit." Larned was angry. "Look, before you knew how to fix a traffic ticket, I was running this place. I mean, *running* it."

"Bug off, Judson. I'm tired."

Chapin had no idea how things managed to get out of hand so quickly. As he watched Larned get to his feet in a fury and leave the table, Chapin saw the possible disappearance of at least $5,000 in nontaxable income, $5,000 in an unmarked envelope. As Larned hurried across the dining room of the Ambassador, he was joined by two women. Chapin remembered one of them, the brunette, the secretary, but the other was a blonde in a turquoise knit dress—she was a Vassar coed about the same way Zsa Zsa Gabor was. Well, he was losing that, too. Chapin felt an instant of regret. That blonde—was she the kind of woman who would leave a hole in a man's life or would he have trouble remembering her name the next morning? Where were his friends? It had taken just a single gin-laced phrase to send Judson Larned scurrying off into the night.

Who else was there in the whole damn town of Albany? Just politicians. Chapin knew dozens of men who radiated an easy warmth, not one who seemed capable of friendship. Politicians, they never offered to scratch your back until their own back had developed a rash.

Ginny—maybe she had been the only friend, the only person who had not profited through knowing Chapin. How long would Greg and Norris hang around without the business ties? Ginny, she was the only one, and what a hole she had left in his life.

Every time he thought of Ginny, Chapin felt a fresh flood of anguish. Somewhere there was still a butcher loose, a madman who enjoyed rending human flesh with a hatchet. Chapin's thoughts flew from one fragment to another—from the certainty of the madman to the possibility that the madman had seen Chapin, from the danger to everyone to the specific danger to Thalia and the kids. God, what was he doing up in Albany?

No night was longer or lonelier than a midwinter night in Albany. It was incredible that a city of this size could not support a live theater, a sports arena, or even a movie theater near the Capitol. Chapin took a cab to Central Avenue, to the only cluster of neon around, and stopped outside a bar, the Body Shop. The only person in sight was the barmaid, a stocky young woman with a limp.

"Is there a dancer?" Chapin asked.

"That depends," the barmaid said. "Is there a customer?"

"I'll have a Chivas."

"You get three guesses," she said, "and you've already used up one of them."

"Scotch?"

"Very good," she said. "Some people don't get it in three tries."

"Is there a dancer?"

"I guess that depends on your definition of dancer," she said, and then turned to a curtained alcove at the rear of the room. "Hey, Penny, you're on."

Chapin carried his drink to the bare wooden platform in the center of the room. He sat on one of the wooden auditorium chairs and rested his drink on the stage. As the jukebox selections changed, the dancer arrived.

She was a short woman with heavily muscled legs and breasts

that reminded Chapin of bananas. She was balanced on the highest pair of platform shoes Chapin had ever seen, the kind of shoes a girl could fall off. As she arrived, she treated her only customer to a smile broad enough to reveal a mouthful of bad teeth, and then she started running her tongue from one side of the mouth to the other.

Penny didn't even make a gesture toward Terpsichore. The music was loud with a beat too heavy to ignore, but ignore it she did, strutting to the sound of some private drummer, never taking her eyes off Chapin, never giving her tongue a moment of rest.

"Still cold out there, honey?"

"You better believe it," Chapin said.

"Well, it's gonna get plenty hot in here." As she said that, Penny looped her thumbs into the sides of her G-string and lifted it away from her body. "Would you like it to get hot in here?"

The dancer stooped in front of Chapin. She reached for his drink and drained the glass. When she stood up, her G-string was on the stage at her feet. Confronting Chapin now was the densest, blackest bush of pubic hair he could recall ever having seen; he wondered how she had managed to conceal it behind the G-string.

"Now, honey," she said, "isn't there something you'd like to put in there?"

"What?"

"I said isn't there some little thing you'd like to put in there?" she said. "Most of the boys take a dollar bill and roll it up and put it in."

"I don't entirely follow you."

"One of those dollars," she said. "Just roll it up and put it in. You know how to put it in, don't you honey?"

Now she was sitting on the stage in front of him. Slowly, in a manner she undoubtedly considered tantalizing, she opened her legs wide. Chapin Hope, desperately wishing he were somewhere else, rolled up a dollar bill and inserted it into the woman.

"Oh, that's right, darling," she said. "Put it all the way in. Oooh, that feels so good."

Chapin could taste the ham steak he'd had for dinner, and he got to his feet. He hurried to the door, and the telephone beside it caught his eye. Without seeming to think, he picked up the phone and dialed a number. Beside him, back at the stage, he could hear the dancer laughing.

"Yes?" The voice on the other end of the line was heavy with sleep.

"Margaret, this is Chape. I've got to see you."

"Just a minute," the voice said. "Chape? Just a minute. Let me wake up. . . . Chapin, is that really you?"

"Margaret, I've got to see you."

"Chapin, you called me at this time to tell me that?"

"I've never needed to see anyone so badly in my life."

"Chape, maybe we can get together for lunch next week."

"I need to see you now," he said.

"Are you all right?"

"I know what you're thinking," he said. "The way I just cut things off—I've been so ashamed of that."

"Chape, for Christ's sake, that was *four* years ago."

"Was it? It seems—"

"Chape, I can't talk," she said. "There's someone here now."

He put the receiver back in the cradle and left the bar. Outside, most of the neon signs had been turned off and the snow was swirling on Albany's main drag like prairie dust in a windstorm. There was not a cab to be found. Chapin could see a pair of headlights coming his way, the only sign of life in the night, and he stepped out into the snow to flag down a stranger.

14

O'Malley, now an unfamiliar figure at the *Islander* offices, showed up on the Thursday separating Christmas and New Year's and thumbed through the accumulation of press releases until he came to the envelope holding his holiday bonus and then he turned to the telephone. The switchboard operator got him the Albany trunk line and he dialed the number he had gotten from the bureau chief there—Chapin Hope's private line.

In O'Malley's judgment the call was melodramatic but necessary. He felt that he had enough material for a dozen conflict-of-interest stories, enough material at least to damage Hope politically and perhaps even to wreck him. There was still nothing to link Mr. Clean to the ax murder or even to suggest he was the sort of man who could have gone crazy enough to commit such an act. But there were still the photograph and the reporter's instincts, and now that O'Malley had the muscle to back up a confrontation, it was time to do some of the things they don't teach at journalism school. The first thing he was going to do was stick a tack in the senator and see what happened.

The reporter called at a propitious moment. Hope's secretary was out to lunch and it was the senator who picked up the red desk phone.

"Chapin Hope here," he said.

"Hiya, Harry," O'Malley said.

"I beg your pardon."

"Come on, Harry, cut the shit," O'Malley said, deepening his voice.

"I'm afraid you have a wrong number. This is Chapin Hope."

"Look, Harry, I've got no time to play games. Let's just say that I know something that might prove embarrassing . . ."

"Stop right there," Hope said. "I really think you've got the wrong party."

"I got the right party, Harry. We both know that. Now, this information I'm talking about, it's worth plenty to you."

"I have no idea who you are." Hope was trying for a hard, crisp

111

tone of voice but he could not conceal the quaver. "I don't know any Harry, and I can't imagine what you're talking about."

"Well, gee, Harry, all the fellows at the Pumpkin told me to say hello."

For the first time there was a pause at the Albany end of the conversation.

"What?" Hope said finally.

"You heard me right, Harry," O'Malley said. "Now if you want to hear more, I'll tell you what you do. You get your ass back to Long Island. Tonight at ten o'clock you find yourself a spot at the bar of a place called the Blue Barn. Got that? The Blue Barn. You won't have any trouble finding it, Harry. It's right there on Jericho, just a couple of miles past the Pumpkin."

"You're making a big mistake."

"You're the one who made the mistake, Harry. Don't make a second one. Ten o'clock. The Blue Barn. At the bar. Just be there. I'll do the rest."

O'Malley hung up. Hope was cool, all right, but he'd be at the Blue Barn at ten o'clock. He had said nothing on the phone really—nothing, but everything. If he had not been Harry, he would have hung up before O'Malley made it to the second sentence. The reporter then readjusted his headset and dialed nine to get the outside line. When he heard the tone, he put in the call to Teddi Bennett.

At a quarter to ten Chapin Hope slowly pulled the Mercedes into the parking lot behind the Blue Barn. He hadn't told anyone he was coming down to the Island. Maybe he should have called Greg—but Greg would have sent over his investigator and Hope did not feel up to a crowd scene, not yet.

When he had received the phone call from O'Malley, Hope had stared at walls for four hours and then simply walked out to his car, gotten behind the wheel, and, not stopping for supper, he had headed for Long Island. He drove as if he were programmed—no stops, no awareness of scenery. Moments after leaving the Tappan Zee Bridge, he could not remember having driven over it. When he left the Long Island Expressway and turned onto Jericho Turnpike, the ride became dreamlike. Not exactly a dream, more a vision remembered, a kind of *déjà vu* feeling that only heightened as he drove into the parking lot. The signs were different—BLUE BARN instead of PUMPKIN—but the buildings were as interchangeable as he knew the people would be. Instant People.

The lot was crowded and the Mercedes came to a stop at the far end of it. Not thinking then, not having to think, Hope reached into the glove compartment for the velvet cover and put it over the license-plate emblem. As he walked through the side entrance, Hope was again overcome by a feeling that all this had happened to him in some earlier incarnation. He stood at the edge of the corridor staring out toward the bar, the picture of a man looking for his date, but the smile on Hope's face vanished as he considered the reason he was there.

He saw a woman with red hair on the dance floor, a slim woman in a black dress with her hair piled high, and it was not a vision that Hope could handle easily. But then her partner spun her around and she was in her late fifties, a hard-faced woman wearing too much lipstick, and her blue-bordered eyes studied Chapin Hope from north to south in cold appraisal.

The Blue Barn was jammed. Surprisingly so, Hope thought, unless Thursday was its night. Each of the lonely bars had one special night; the Pumpkin's had been Monday. There was never a logical reason for the choice of night but people looking only for the warmth of other people seemed to know instinctively where to go on any given evening. Fridays were for everyone; Saturdays were for married couples; Sundays were dead; but weeknights were turned over to the Instant People—the divorced and widowed, the single and the errant. The searchers.

On this Thursday night the jollity was just slightly deafening. The tinkling of glasses, the steady buzz of talk, and music, music, music. The combo played from the head of the small dance floor, just inside the steps leading up to the dining room. Piano, drums, bass, guitar, and trumpet. The guitar player doubled as vocalist and the horn man switched easily from trumpet to clarinet and back again. They were playing "Blue Spanish Eyes." It was odd how many songs brought Ginny back to mind—perhaps because before Ginny he had never been aware of music, had never bothered to differentiate one song from another.

Ginny. Her face flashed in his mind again and disappeared as he stared hard at the dance floor. The women on the floor were all aglitter with costume jewelry, their hair bouffant, their bodies girdled. Even the younger women were brittle at the edges, their brows penciled, their eyes as bright as their fingernails. The men ranged in age from the early thirties to late middle age; they were dusted and pomaded, redolent with after-shave, many of them fashionably bearded and sideburned, their hair air brushed or false, their dark and maroon blazers freshly cleaned, their slacks newly pressed or forever creased, their shoes gleaming like small darting mirrors on the dance floor. "Blue Spanish Eyes." The trumpeter had a solo and the bodies on the floor wormed against one another—cigar-tinged breath wafting against gold earrings, bright-tipped fingers playing just above the collars of paisley shirts.

Threading through the dancers, Chapin Hope reached the bar as the song ended and the combo moved immediately into "Yesterday." Ginny once told him that "Yesterday" was a Beatles song and he had been surprised; it was too nice a song for him to associate it with a group so raucous, so corrupted. The senator suddenly felt naked, felt that everyone at the bar knew he was Harry. How many did know? How much would it cost? And what could he do about it?

"What'll it be, doll?"

A tall, blonde barmaid was looking at him attentively. He returned the look. Late thirties or early forties, he thought. Old enough for the face to have acquired a little character.

"Scotch on the rocks," he said.

At least he didn't have to fool with the Seagram's anymore—that had been Harry's drink and he wanted nothing more than for Harry to stay dead. He would have specified Chivas but the newspapers had mentioned the Chivas in Ginny's apartment. He didn't want to make any mistakes, not tonight. The drink came close to being a double.

"I like the way you pour," Hope said.

"I only do that for my handsome customers," the blonde said, smiling. The smile erased the age lines below her eyes. It was a stunning smile. A lovely smile. It reminded him fleetingly of another smile. Christ, he'd have to stay out of these places.

Chapin Hope swallowed and looked around. Most of the tables were filled and he had been lucky to snare a seat at the bar. The stools on either side of him were occupied. To his right a small, bald man who looked like Edward G. Robinson was asking the barmaid for a Canadian Club and soda. On the other side a bulky woman was tapping a cigarette. There was a sudden yelp and Chapin realized that the brown object in front of the woman was a Chihuahua and that she had just burned the animal with a falling ash. "God damn you, Pepe, you little fag," the woman snapped, and she dipped a cocktail napkin into what looked like a scotch sour and rubbed the animal's leg with it.

"Can I help?" Chapin said.

"Why don't you go fuck a duck?"

The woman was staring at him with the unblinking bleariness common to drunks. Chapin looked away and tried for an attitude of studied unawareness during the subsequent silence. Then the barmaid's voice filled the lull.

"Anybody here named Harry? There's a call for someone named Harry who's supposed to be at the bar."

"I'll take it," Chapin said.

114

"You're Harry?"

"No." He was careful. "But this is somebody's idea of a joke."

The phone was at the end of the bar. Chapin tried to keep his own voice low and pressed the receiver against his ear to make sure no one heard the voice on the other end. It was the same street-wise voice he had heard earlier in the day.

"How you doing, Harry?"

"My name's not Harry."

"Yeah, and that's why you came all the way down from Albany to answer a phone call for Harry."

"Let's just say you, uh, aroused my curiosity."

"We can say anything you want, Harry, as long as we talk about Virginia Hanson. Or were you one of the ones who called her Ginny?"

"Who?"

"C'mon, Harry, let's get with it. You know her name. Hey, you're the guy who was screwing her."

"This has gone far enough, mister." Chapin's voice rose. "There are laws against this kind of thing."

"Laws? Hey, Harry, what about the laws against what you did to Ginny?"

"What!"

"You know, the laws against chopping up your girlfriend with an ax."

Chapin slammed the receiver and stood there, staring at the phone, shuddering. The barmaid came over to him and seemed to be talking with genuine concern.

"Are you okay, hon?"

"I'll be okay," he said. "Just give me a minute."

"I don't mean to butt in, but you look a little rocky."

"No problem," he said. "No problem. Sometimes practical jokes go too far."

She reached over and patted his hand. "I know what you mean."

Chapin could feel himself quieting down but then the bar phone lit up and the blonde picked it up again.

"Wait a minute." She turned to Chapin. "It's for Harry again."

"The same guy?"

The barmaid held her hand over the receiver and nodded. Chapin Hope chewed his lower lip and tried to force a calmness. Self-control was as important as expediency to a politician and over the years Chapin Hope had learned to smile when he wanted to shout, to be cordial to people he despised, to hold back every normal reaction until he was sure it was also the politic one. Even during these past few weeks he had considered himself imperturbable. Now, however, it took enormous effort to put the panic aside.

"Tell him Harry doesn't want to talk to him," he told the barmaid. "Tell him to try Tom and Dick."

Teddi Bennett repeated the message into the phone. She waited for a second and then hung up. The pause was to allow Robert J. O'Malley time for an answer.

"That son of a bitch," he said; "is a lot tougher than I figured."

Teddi frowned as she put down the phone. Then she looked compassionately at Hope.

"C'mon," she said, "the next one's on the house."

The second scotch was, as the barmaid had promised, on the house, and Chapin bought the third. With each sip he could feel himself steadying down. He knew that this was the proper time to go home—there would be no further conversation with the anonymous telephone voice. But there was no way to erase that voice and what it had said. Someone knew. Maybe not everything, maybe it was just a clever guess, but someone knew enough to cause a great deal of trouble.

Chapin Hope looked again at the door, the way out. He felt that the moment he walked out that door he would step onto a roller coaster and hurtle forward, dipping and plunging and spiraling without the slightest control over velocity or direction. Here at the Blue Barn he felt at least temporarily safe. He was on an island removed from time and space and he liked the whiskey they served on this island, and the music, and the inane chatter, and the people dancing, and he especially liked the blonde barmaid whose name was Teddi.

"That's with an *i*," she said.

"Not like the bear then?"

"No," she said. "Do I look that cuddly?"

"I'm no expert," he said. "You could fool me."

"You know my name," Teddi said. "That puts you one up on me."

"It's Chapin," he said. "Chape."

"No last name?"

"Not yet," he said. "Not for the moment, if that's okay."

"That's okay with me," Teddi said. "I know too many names already."

"If it's ever important to know," he said, "just ask."

"I'll just call you handsome then," she said.

As he finished his third drink, Chapin found himself looking at her more closely. Probably in her mid-thirties. Sensual, but not overtly so—she didn't have to work at it. She was like Ginny that way. And other ways. They shared a quality. You could tell that

116

Teddi cared, that she was a . . . good person, an understanding person. She didn't belong in a place like this any more than Ginny had. There was a cliché that described her, someone found in a tawdry environment. A diamond in the rough. That was it. Both Teddi and Ginny were diamonds in the rough.

Teddi was returning the attention, sometimes allowing a regular customer's glass to go dry as she tended to Chapin Hope's needs. She wondered whether she was being to obvious, too coquettish. If so, Chapin Hope did not seem to notice. Maybe part of the reason was that it was not wholly an act; she could feel herself responding to some quality in him. As for what O'Malley suspected—that was hard to believe. After bringing Hope a new drink, Teddi excused herself and made her way to the pay phone in the outer corridor.

"I don't know what to tell you," she said to O'Malley. "For a minute there after he talked to you he was really shaken up, you know, angry but nervous too. Still, I don't think he's your man."

"Why?"

"It's just a feeling."

"That's a big help," O'Malley said. "Listen, I'm half tempted to come over there and try a less subtle approach."

"That could be cruel," Teddi said. "Look, maybe I could find out something for you. He seems to be going for me."

"Terrific," O'Malley said. "The last broad he went for in a big way was Virginia Hanson."

"Bob, I *can* find out for you. . . ."

"I don't even want to ask you what you've got in mind."

"Never mind that," Teddi said. "All I can tell you is that he's looking at me like they just invented girls. But I really don't think he's your man."

"He's our man. If he wasn't Harry, he wouldn't have taken that drive from Albany."

"I still don't think he did it," Teddi said. "Bob, I'll call you back in an hour."

Hope was still standing there beside the bar and Teddi threw him a small kiss. He waved his glass in return. Something about the senator's grin had been bothering her. When he smiled, Chapin Hope reminded Teddi Bennett of her second husband, an X-ray equipment salesman whose charm had never been more manifest than when he tried to persuade her to turn a trick for his bookmaker in payment of a gambling debt. When charm failed, he wept with fear and she had given in. The bookie had been a pig and she had locked herself in her bedroom for the next two days. There were more tears from her husband and finally he agreed to join Gamblers Anonymous. When she discovered that he used the meeting nights

117

to sneak off to a poker game, she went directly to Mexico for the divorce.

Chapin Hope's smile put Teddi on guard. The smile was pure con, a little boy's don't-be-angry-with-me smile. But nobody was perfect. And there was nothing in his attitude to generate fear. Chapin Hope, looking at the tall blonde on the other side of the bar, saw a way of salvaging something from the worst day of his life. No, one of the two worst days of his life. Chapin could feel the whiskey taking hold of him but he didn't care.

"That's the secret," he told Teddi. "Secret of success."

"What's that, hon?"

"Control. Never lose control."

He emphasized the pronouncement by flinging out his hand and accidentally knocking over his sixth drink. Teddi, again acting on behalf of the house, immediately produced a refill.

"That's very generous of you."

"We try to please."

"Sweetheart, you couldn't miss. I mean that in all . . . all sincerity." It was becoming hard to pronounce the words correctly but Chapin turned to the bar at large. "Friends, I want to make an announcement. I want to say for the record that Teddi here is the finest—one of the two finest—persons I have ever met."

A freckled man with red hair and dark glasses raised his glass. "I'll drink to that," he said. The three other men still sitting at the bar joined in and Teddi curtsied.

The Blue Barn was emptying rapidly and a chumminess born of loneliness and encouraged by liquor was enveloping the survivors. Most of those who had gone left in pairs. The bulky woman had gone with the Chihuahua, and Edward G. Robinson had disappeared with a woman in her late forties whose dark makeup and jet-black hair had given her the appearance of an Indian. Edward G. had won her heart with the disclosure that he was able to pay one of his ex-wives $450 a week alimony.

"I had a catered divorce," the woman had told him. "Hors d'oeuvres, drinks, cold cuts, turkey, evan a Viennese coffee hour, the whole bit. Listen, it was almost as good as our wedding, except that it was in a hall. I been to bar mitzvahs that weren't as nice."

As the two of them left the bar, Chapin felt an urge to wish them all well.

"You have my blessings," he said. Then he leaned over to Teddi to explain. "Everybody needs somebody."

"I think they make a beautiful couple," Teddi said.

Chapin felt he might have come up with a profound and original thought: *Everybody needs somebody*. He needed somebody. Not

Thalia. And not Greg or Norris or anyone else. He needed somebody who could make him forget the tiny dark stain on the trousers he had wadded up in the bottom of his golf bag, somebody who could erase the memory of the phone calls.

He needed Ginny. Ginny would have been at home here in the Blue Barn. She would have loved the dialogue between Edward G. Robinson and the Indian. She would have liked Teddi. She would have even enjoyed the woman with the Chihuahua. Ginny understood people. That had been another wonderful thing about her; when he was with Ginny, Chapin had liked people he would never have looked at before.

And the music. Ginny would have liked the music. He turned to the dance floor. Only four couples were left and the band was playing its final number, "Good Night, Sweetheart." The guitar player was crooning the lyrics and two or three patrons were singing along.

Chapin leaned forward, waving his glass to the rhythm, and then suddenly, inexplicably, he knew he was going to cry. Ginny, he thought. The name cut his soul. Ginny. Teddi Bennett saw Chapin Hope's face as it crumbled and she came quickly around the bar and led him by the hand into the vestibule. Somewhere she found a tissue and started mopping the tears from his cheeks.

"I'm sorry," Chapin said, his voice slurring the words. "Something . . . I don't know . . . it. . . ."

"You were thinking about someone, weren't you?"

Chapin nodded.

"You're a nice man," Teddi said, and she leaned forward and kissed him on the cheek. The kiss was as spontaneous as his tears had been; she couldn't help but feel sorry for him. Chapin reached out for her and buried his face in her neck and now she could feel the sobbing.

"I need you," he said. "Oh, God, how I need you."

"It'll be all right," she said. "I'll get off soon and it'll be all right."

Gently she pried him loose. Then she led him back to the bar and poured him a nightcap. He took it down dangerously fast and she excused herself for her final telephone call to O'Malley.

"I was about to call you," the reporter said.

"Why?"

"He's still there, isn't he?"

"He's here."

"Let him go."

"He's not the one, Bob."

"I think he is."

"No. He's not that kind of person."

"For Chrissakes, Teddi, this isn't the movies."

"Bob, I just don't think he did it," she said. "Maybe I can prove it. Anyway, he couldn't hurt a fly. Not tonight."

"Teddi, I'm coming right over there. Be there. I'm on my way."

He was talking into a dead telephone. Teddi had hung up, had gone back and asked a waitress to cover for her until closing. She took Chapin Hope's hand in her own and he squeezed hard.

"You're so beautiful," he said.

Teddi smiled her most dazzling smile and returned the pressure.

"Weren't you going to take me somewhere?" she asked.

15

The phone went dead as O'Malley was still shouting Teddi's name into it. He banged the receiver down and reached for the bottle and a coffee cup. He could understand his own concern over Teddi—what he couldn't understand was the intensity of that concern.

How long had it been since he felt intensely about anyone, about anything? He had no recollection of ever having been in love. His ex-wife had replaced him with a plumber she met at a Parents Without Partners meeting—a steady type whom O'Malley fervently wished she would marry, enabling him to escape the alimony hook. That had never been love. He had even lost all empathy with his children, a son and daughter he supported but rarely saw. O'Malley had worked hard at walling himself off from people and it was something of a shock to realize his failure; he cared very much about Teddi Bennett.

"Shit!"

O'Malley took a long swallow of bourbon and called back the Blue Barn.

"Oh, it's Mr. O'Malley." The waitress had answered the phone. "Teddi just left a minute ago."

"Was she with a guy?"

"Oh, hey, listen, I don't know if I should say anything."

"God damn it. . . ."

"Well, I'm sure it was okay," the waitress said. "He was a very nice-looking fellow. . . ."

It was O'Malley's turn to hang up. There was no time now to consider possible consequences and O'Malley dialed another, an unlisted number drawn from the file cabinet of his memory.

"Hello, Brownie," he said. "Bob O'Malley. I hope I didn't wake you."

"You didn't."

Brownstein wondered what O'Malley would think if he knew that the head of the Homicide Division was up late with a plate of stoned-wheat crackers and Boursin cheese, watching *Destry Rides Again* on the *Late Show*. Fortunately the call had come during a commercial break. Marlene Dietrich had just done "See What the Boys in the Back Room Will Have" and Brownstein had been humming the tune when he picked up the phone.

"What's up, Bob?"

O'Malley told him. He did it without preamble and without elaboration, straight, the way he might sum up a story for the desk. He spoke rapidly but he left nothing out. O'Malley began with the receipt of the photograph of Chapin Hope, concluded with the fact that Teddi Bennett had just gone off into the night with a potential killer. Along the way he touched on the conflict-of-interest material and the apparent links between the senator and the mob. Brownstein's near hum had died in his throat after O'Malley's first sentence. He listened to the reporter without interruption but a few times he shuddered with anger. When O'Malley finished, there was a pause.

"Bob," he said, "I think you better get right over here."

It was Robert J. O'Malley's first visit to Detective Lieutenant Charles Brownstein's home, a medium-sized ranch in what over the years had become an upper-middle-class development. Lived-in but expensive French Provincial furniture, framed prints of Manet landscapes and Degas ballet dancers, library shelves filled with books, a baby grand with a Beethoven sonata resting on the music holder. Brownstein seemed anxious to explain some of this away—he said that Manet had always been his wife's favorite, that the only one to play the piano was his daughter. Violet Brownstein, a slim and gracious woman with prematurely gray hair, clear brown eyes, and a cultured voice, placed a fresh pot of coffee on the table and excused herself shortly after O'Malley's arrival. Brownstein was in a crisp fury and wasted no more time with small talk.

"I thought we could trust each other."

"C'mon, Brownie, do I know everything you're doing?"

"There's a difference. And the difference is that I'm a police officer. What in the world makes you people think you have the right to play detective?"

"Take it easy, Brownie."

"I mean it. For instance, don't you think I know you've been hitting the bars asking about Charlotte? I didn't say anything because I figured you couldn't do much harm there, and you'd let me know if you found out anything. But this. My God, Bob, don't you realize you may have jeopardized an entire investigation?"

"Hell, Brownie, as it is, I'm telling you all this without my editor's permission."

"Yes, well, I should have a few things to say to him at some later date."

"Look, it's like you say, you're a police officer and that means there are some things I can do that you can't do. . . ."

"What? Lie? Bribe? What else? You've already admitted threatening a man with blackmail. You've withheld evidence that should have been turned over to the police. Bob, do yourself a favor—don't try to explain things, don't make it any worse on yourself."

"Hey, Brownie. . . ."

"I'm serious, Bob. You people don't know a damn thing about police methods. As far as I'm concerned, so far you've accomplished only one thing—you've alerted a murder suspect. I let it go when I discovered you were showing Hope's photo around. But there's no way I can countenance this latest escapade."

O'Malley spilled some of the coffee he was pouring. He leaned over the coffee table and blotted up the small puddle with the bottom of his jacket.

"You mean, you knew about him?"

"Just let's say we've been trying to connect him with Virginia Hanson."

"Have you?"

"Yes and no," the chief said. "We've uncovered some . . . tenuous linkups. For one thing, we've shown the photo to the same people you have. For another—and this is *not* for publication —Virginia Hanson had the habit of saving newspaper stories about the senator. If there's a more solid hookup than that, we'll find it. But obviously our investigation has to be discreet."

"Yeah, well, mine doesn't—and that's the point I'm trying to make."

"You've certainly made that point to the senator but what else have you really got so far? A man's not-unnatural reaction to a blackmail call."

"If he wasn't the one, he wouldn't have been so upset. Hell, he'd never have shown at the Blue Barn."

"That's debatable. In any case, it's not the kind of evidence we're looking for."

"Well, what about the conflict-of-interest stuff? The banks? The land deals?"

"What that all means to me is that we're investigating a politician. I don't think there's a one of them could stand up to a complete tax audit. It may make what you people call good copy, Bob, but it's got nothing to do with the ax murder of a cocktail waitress."

"Maybe so, maybe no—at least it tells you what kind of prick Hope is."

"I don't want to hear any more of that, Bob!" The coffeepot

123

jumped as Brownstein's hand came down on the table. "Nothing more. As far as I'm concerned, what you've done is reprehensible. If Hope isn't involved in this, you're guilty of harassment at the very least. If he is involved, you've done him the considerable favor of letting him know he's under investigation. And now you've even gotten an innocent friend involved. This Teddi Bennett, are you sure she's with Hope?"

"Positive."

"And I suppose you realize that you've put her life in jeopardy? If anything happens to her—anything—you're responsible."

"God damn it to hell, Brownstein, don't you think I know that? Why the hell else do you think I called you?"

Brownstein caught an unfamiliar note in O'Malley's voice. He looked closely at the reporter and saw something close to anguish on that broad face. His own voice softened.

"I'll get some men on it," he said. "We'll find her."

"I hope so."

"And who knows, maybe she can help us," Brownstein said. "Maybe this whole escapade will work out for us."

"Thanks for that, Brownie."

"One thing though, Bob, no more holding out."

"Okay. But that should work both ways."

For a moment Detective Lieutenant Brownstein felt like throwing his coffee cup at the reporter. But he grinned.

"You know what, Bob?"

"What?"

"You're worse than most cops."

16

When Teddi led Chapin Hope to her car, he offered no protest. He knew better than to try to get behind the wheel, and he couldn't remember the blonde having anything to drink. Her features, caught in the spaced illuminations of upcoming headlights, seemed set, resolute, sober. Chapin dozed off—whether it was for a minute or an hour he had no idea—but when he awoke, the car was parked in front of a Howard Johnson's Motel.

"Well," Teddi was saying, "do you want me to register?"

"No," he said. "Just give me a minute."

Walking unsteadily to the motel office, Chapin felt an acute sense of dislocation. What town was this? There was a Howard Johnson's in Westbury, another in Huntington, still another one in Brentwood —Jesus, they were all over the Island.

As he pushed open the door, Chapin felt a sense of his own relative innocence—or was he just being pompous? The point was that the simple act of walking into a motel office to register under an assumed name was not easy for him. And that had nothing to do with the drinks or the hour.

It didn't help that the clerk was a woman, a young woman scarcely out of her teens. But, of course, this was Howard Johnson's—he would have been able to tell by the orange roof if he hadn't seen the sign. This was a testimonial to wholesomeness, the kind of motel people *slept* in. He wondered briefly why the blonde had chosen the place; she was surely no innocent.

"Do you have a room for tonight?"

"Single or double?" she asked.

"Double."

"All we have left," the girl said, "is one where the television set isn't working."

"We'll just have to make do without television," Chapin said.

"Will that be for one night?"

"One night."

The girl slid the registration card toward him. Chapin hesitated for an instant. "Harry," he wrote, and then, without a second thought, "Hope." There was a space for an address, and he invented a number and street in Poughkeepsie. The next space asked for automobile identification and this necessitated a trip to the car. " 'Scuse me," he told the clerk.

The blonde leaned out the window as he approached, "All set?" she asked.

"Uh, not quite. I have to know what kind of car this is."

"A Dodge Dart," she said. "Nineteen sixty-nine."

He stared at the license plate, three digits and three letters, for an inordinately long time before successfully committing them to memory. Back in the office, he finished filling out the registration and started to search for his American Express card; suddenly he realized the name was not entirely right.

"I guess I'll pay cash," he said.

"That's twenty-six fifty," she said with a glance that was infuriatingly knowing. Chapin found three ten-dollar bills in his wallet. A close call. The girl counted out the change and smiled sweetly.

"Gee," she said, "I always thought there was an *h* in Pough-keepsie."

"Oh, yeah," Chapin said. "I always forget that *h*."

"I can imagine," the young woman said. Her smile took on a new degree of condescension, and Chapin reacted.

"As a matter of fact," he said, "if you want to know the truth, I started to write down Schenectady, but I didn't know how to spell that one either."

"What's the matter with Albany?" she said. "A lot of people use Albany."

"Fine," he said. "Next time I'll make it Albany."

Albany? Could she know anything? In his entire public life Chapin Hope had never been recognized by a stranger. The choice of Albany had to be a coincidence. Chapin smiled, and the smile became a laugh by the time he got back to the car.

"What's so funny?" Teddi said.

"My dumbness," he said. "I'm so damn dumb I don't even know how to register at a motel."

"That doesn't bother me a bit," Teddi said. "I think it's kind of nice."

"The room is down there at the end," he said.

As Teddi slowly drove her car the length of the parking lot, Chapin found himself studying license plates. Many were out of state, evidence that the motel was no oasis for local swingers. Why had she picked this one? Then, before Teddi had driven the final hundred yards to the last remaining vacant parking slot, Chapin was asleep again, his head resting uneasily against the car's side window.

"Are you all right, hon?"

"Huh?"

"Listen, hon, are you going to be all right?"

The blonde was shaking him. What was wrong with him anyway? Chapin struggled with the car door, made it to his feet, and then the blonde led him by the hand toward the room.

"I'm going to need the key, hon," she said.

"No key," he told her. "They didn't give me a key."

"They had to," she said. She reached into his jacket pocket and came up with the key. Chapin wondered why he hadn't remembered it and felt thankful that he wasn't going to have to fit the key into the lock.

Initially the spaciousness of the room surprised him—and then he remembered that this was not a room designed to encapsulate a pair of lovers; it was the large family size, a room large enough to contain the hopes and aspirations of road-show, middle-class America. He walked past the dressing room leading to the bathroom and found himself confronting two double beds.

"Which one is mine?"

Chapin was asleep before he heard an answer—face down on the nearest bed, spread-eagled, his suit jacket still tight around his shoulders. Later he stirred to the sound of a distant shower but the fact had trouble penetrating his consciousness. Eventually it struck him that the blonde was in there showering, getting herself ready for him.

Dizzy and weary, he somehow got to his feet and somehow got his jacket off and somehow wrestled free of shirt and trousers and T-shirt and shorts. He left the clothes on the carpet where they fell. A shower—he needed a shower. He opened the bathroom door and walked in and Teddi gave out a small scream.

"Hey, it's just me," he said. "What'samatter?"

"You surprised me," she said, stepping out of the shower and wrapping a towel around herself. "I thought you were out for the night."

"Not me," he said. "Hey, you don't have to leave. We could take a little shower together."

"I'm all done," she said, "but that's an interesting idea."

"Yeah, it is, isn't it?" he said. "And I'll tell you something that you probably won't believe—I've never done anything like it."

"I do believe you," she said. "And you know something? I especially like you when you tell the truth. The only thing you haven't told me is your name, your whole name. Here you are

127

asking me to take a shower with you and I don't even know your last name.''

"You're right," he said, "absolutely right. Just gimme a minute."

He stood then under the stream of water and allowed it to come down full force on his face. Then he turned the water up as hot as he could stand it and he thought of Thalia; Thalia would kill him if she could see him now. Well, what difference had that ever made? What the hell difference did anything make?

"It's Chapin *Hope*," he said.

"Chapin Hope?"

"Chape Hope to you," he said.

"That's nice," she said.

"Wait," he said. "Lemme give you the full particulars, the whole story. I'm also a politician, a state senator, in fact, and I'm married and I have two sons and I'm taking a hell of a chance telling you anything."

"No, you're not . . . Chape."

Chapin knew better than that, but he didn't care. The water seemed to be washing away some of the alcohol, and he took a closer look at the woman who was waiting for him. She was ripe, but it was not the ripeness of youth—a ripeness that included an occasional sag and wrinkle, breasts that, though medium sized, seemed somewhat pendulous. Her legs were the best feature; they would have looked fine on a woman half her age. What was it—forty, forty-five? The age didn't bother him but why should it? They were both the same age. That realization surprised Chapin. It had been many years since a woman his own age had interested him sexually; this Teddi was a good-luck piece (he smiled at the double meaning), who had transformed this worst of days into something that could be survived. If only he wasn't so damned drunk. The water was helping—but not that much.

"Are you about through?" Teddi said.

"Just about."

"I'll be in the room."

"Don't start without me."

It was a cheap remark and he was immediately sorry he had said it. Thank God she didn't respond in kind. It had been such a long time. Months. Ginny had been the last. He didn't count Thalia. Their infrequent couplings generated about as much excitement as a sneeze.

Teddi had chosen the bed beside the windows, the one he hadn't used. The only light in the room came from behind Chapin; it was a beam of light showing through the partially open bathroom door.

128

Chapin had some difficulty negotiating the distance to the bed.

"Chape . . ." Teddi said.

"I'm here."

"I know," she said. "Oh, you don't have anything on."

"Neither do you."

"Well, we're even." She didn't move as he put his arm around her. "Please don't think I'm a busybody," she said, "but I'd like to know some more about you."

"I'd like to know something too."

"Like?"

"Like why are you here?"

"You're stealing my questions."

"What do you mean?"

"Oh, I don't know. You, well, you don't look like the kind of man who'd pick up a barmaid. Let me ask you something—have you ever done anything like this before?"

"You'd be surprised. . . ." He stopped short.

"Tell me, I'd like to know."

"Maybe later. What about you—have you done this kind of thing before?"

"Probably less times than you're thinking," she said. "But I'm not exactly a virgin."

"Good."

"That's what I say."

"Mmmm."

"That's right, relax. Just close your eyes and relax. It's nice to talk this way."

Chapin closed his eyes. He was intensely aware of the woman beside him, of the fact that she was naked, of the slight pressure from her left breast as she leaned toward him. He was slightly surprised at his reaction, however. The thought of making love was in no way displeasing but he was not aroused.

Guilt? If so, it certainly wasn't prompted by any thought of cheating on Thalia. Not her. If there was guilt, it was prompted by someone else, by Ginny. She was there in his mind; he couldn't erase her. There were all those things he had wanted to do with her, all the fantasies that had never been realized. Their sexual unions now seemed incomplete; by the time Ginny had allowed him to come to her, by the time she was ready to admit him, they were both at an explosive stage and the actual contact, the touching, never lasted for more than a minute or two. Chapin had never known anything like their couplings, but it had been all explosive and now it was over.

The simple act of thinking about Ginny aroused Chapin. He

129

couldn't bring her face into clear focus, but he remembered the outlines of her body with exactitude and that body was in front of him now, young and intact and unblemished, and he recalled then the blue dressing gown.

This time it would last; this time he would make it last. He would do all those things there had never been time to do and in the dimness of this unknown room it no longer mattered that the woman beside him was a stranger. She was a woman and she was there, and his eyes opened as he touched her.

"Why don't we talk a little more?" Teddi was saying. "Why—"

"No talk," he said. "Not now."

Chapin could feel the woman tense as he reached for her, but he ignored the reaction. He lowered his head to her left breast and kissed her there. She remained tense as his mouth made love to one breast and then the other and then the space between. He held the breasts in his hands, kissing them desperately, doing finally all the things he had longed to do with Ginny, and he felt the woman end her resistance and relax, placing her head back on the pillow and breathing responses to his every movement.

He didn't rush anything. He licked her breasts and her shoulders and her ribs, waiting for her to offer a hint of encouragement or discouragement, but she didn't move. Slowly, Chapin cautioned himself, go slowly. He spent long moments moving toward her abdomen, nuzzling her gently one moment and licking her frantically the next. He had never done this with Ginny and he wondered if she would have remained as motionless as this woman. As he moved his position again, he could feel the woman holding her breath—actually holding her breath—but there was no stopping him now; he could not have stopped himself at this point.

Once Chapin did pull away from her for a brief moment, and he heard her breath come out in a gasp. He lowered himself then to the foot of the bed and, with his knees resting on the carpet, started slowly to work his way up. He kissed her instep, her ankles, the hollows of her knees. He marveled again at the length of her legs, and then he was at her thighs. He delayed and stalled, made every movement last; he didn't want it to end, not this time.

Chapin rested his head on the bed beside her. She was lying on her back and his face was parallel to her hips. He continued to nuzzle her as she turned suddenly toward him and reached out her hands to the back of his head and drew him into her and held him there. Chapin felt every shift and then it was rough and dry to his tongue, then silky wet, and then he was tasting her, loving her in a way he had never been able to love Ginny. He felt her start to

130

tremble and he felt her back arch and then her hands on the back of his head pressing him hard into her, and she was shuddering and her hands were steel bands on the back of his head and he was no longer the aggressor; the act had taken on its own life and it was in control of both of them.

Oblivion. Chapin Hope was so intent on what he was doing that he was hardly aware of the cries that came from above him from some great distance.

Then the woman was still, and he enjoyed even that, the pause. With Ginny it had been so quick, so violent; once he had gotten inside of her there had been only that urgency, that need to complete, but now he took his time and lived out the fantasy.

Chapin raised himself up above the woman, and he entered her and started the final act of love. Ginny, he thought, and then he corrected himself. This isn't Ginny, he told himself; this is some stranger, some pickup, some blonde he had met in a bar.

"Oh, God," he said. "Oh, God."

Chapin was fighting the act, fighting the idea of exploding inside her. He became soft, became hard, became soft, became hard again and even as the act finally started, even as he felt the warmth closing in around him, he thought of all the reasons why he must not love her, must not love anyone.

The current became stronger and it swept him along like a twig. Ginny, he thought, Ginny, and then the river became a waterfall and there was no time for thoughts.

Screams. The screams were his own and he could not stop them. At the very end the screams became sobs, great shuddering swallows of pain, and he did not understand them, would never understand them, did not even know for sure whether the pain had won out over the joy.

"Oh, Ginny!" he screamed. "Oh, God, Ginny. . . ."

As he said the name, he came back to a sense of what was happening, and he knew it was wrong, dreadfully wrong, that at the end he had been making love to a dead woman. Not to the borrowed blonde next to him.

"I'm sorry," he said. "I'm terribly sorry."

"Never mind," she said.

"But I am," he said. "I'm really sorry."

"Just give me a minute to freshen up," she said, "and I'll be all right."

Her voice was clipped. There was no trace of the torrent that had swept them both along. Nor was there any trace of forgiveness. There was something else.

In less than a minute he got a clue to what it was. The bathroom

131

door was flung open and he had just a fleeting glimpse of the blonde as she opened the door to the hallway and literally ran from the room. The expression on her face was one of pure fear.

It was past four o'clock when Teddi finally reached the apartment in Hempstead. She stopped the elevator at the second floor, saw the light beneath O'Malley's door, and stepped off there. She tested the door and it opened. O'Malley was seated at the card table and there was a half-filled glass in front of him.

"Hey, are you all right?"

"I'm all right."

"What happened?"

"Nothing happened," she said. "I told you there was nothing to worry about."

"Sure," O'Malley said, "that's why you look like there was a ghost in the elevator."

"You've got some imagination," she said.

"I've got to call Brownie," he said, picking up the phone. "He's got his bloodhounds out looking for you." And then in a half shout, "God damn it, Teddi, where the hell were you?"

"It doesn't matter," she said, looking away.

"Damn it, I told you not to take any chances."

"I'm here, ain't I?"

Brownstein picked up the phone on the first ring. "She just came home," O'Malley said. "And she's okay."

"Good," Brownstein said. "What happened?"

O'Malley looked at Teddi. "What happened?"

"He's your man," she said.

17

Sunlight pierced the room. Chapin raised his head and the room tilted. He stared with only partial comprehension at the disarranged bed across the room, at the clothes strewn on the floor. His clothes? He never did that, never was that sloppy. But they were his, all right. What the hell was going on?

He forced himself to a sitting position on the edge of the bed, held his head in his hands, tried to piece together his memories of the night. Later, after he went into the bathroom and stepped under a cold shower, the fragments began to come together. Not all of them, but enough—the night was a jigsaw puzzle with entire sections missing. The phone call to the Albany office, the other calls in the bar—what was the name of that bar? The Shed? Something like that. The Shack? No, that wasn't it. It would come later if he didn't strain for it. There had been too many drinks, a lot of scotch. A barmaid, a blonde—Teddi, that was it, Teddi. Yes. Registering at a motel, something about Poughkeepsie, something about her car. *His* car was still back at the bar, sitting there in broad daylight with the velvet cover on the license-plate shield. What *was* the name of that bar?

There was one peculiarly sharp memory and that was of the sex. He had never known a feeling like that, never realized that pain could be an additive to joy. Ginny was long dead and he had screamed out her name. At that thought, at the memory of the blonde running from the room, Chapin's headache turned into a steel ball banging against the sides of his skull.

Where was he? A Howard Johnson's, but where? The room was warm but Chapin started to shiver. He checked his wallet, found three dollar bills, and then called room service to order coffee. He had intended to ask room service where he was, but a woman's voice answered and Chapin suddenly couldn't find the right words. Postcards, there had to be postcards. In a bureau drawer, beside a Gideon Bible, there was a small stack of postcards picturing the famous orange roof on the front and an address on the back. In this manner did Chapin Hope finally learn that he was a guest at Howard

Johnson's Motor Lodge in Westbury on scenic Long Island. Okay, that was a start.

Now, the name of the bar. The Castle? No. He looked at his watch—nine thirty-five—and picked up the phone to call his law office. He was lucky; Greg was not going to court. At first, as the story unfolded, Greg laughed. He seemed especially delighted to hear that Chapin had woken up without knowing where he was.

"I've never gotten *that* drunk," he said. Nor did he seem particularly upset to hear that Chapin couldn't remember where he'd left the car. "There are a few of those make-out bars around there. How does the Hidden Cove grab you?"

"Nothing."

"The Bushes? The Stargazer?"

"No," Chapin said. "It's like a building. You know, it's named after a building, like a house or a cabin."

"The Barn," Greg said. "The Blue Barn."

"That's it, the Blue Barn. Hey, that's terrific."

"Elementary, my dear Watson," Greg said. "Just one of my many areas of expertise. But, for future reference, you would have been much better off at the Stargazer. Much younger stuff there. How come the Barn?"

When Chapin told him about the phone calls, Greg stopped laughing. When Chapin started to tell him about the blonde, Greg cut off the phone call and said he was on his way.

The coffee helped. Chapin had ordered a pot and he drank the first two cups black. As he added milk to the third cup, the impact of the phone calls finally hit him again. Somebody knew about him and Ginny. Somebody knew he was Harry. Somebody knew that State Senator Chapin Hope was the face on the police sketch. The thought that a stranger knew all this added a stab of fear to the headache.

"You look like hell," Greg Hammer said when he arrived. "First thing, tell me again about those phone calls. Somebody's on to you, but I don't think it's the cops or our investigator would have heard something. He's got a pipe into the department."

"Maybe somebody was making a good guess," Chapin said. "Maybe he was just trying to blackmail me."

"He may have been guessing," Greg said, "but I think we've got to assume otherwise. He had something to go on."

"That damn police sketch in the paper."

"It was more than that," Greg said. "You didn't admit to anything on the phone, did you?"

"Nothing."

"But you showed up at the bar. That was a mistake. But, of

134

course, that wasn't your big mistake. You know what your big mistake was, don't you? No? Well, your big mistake was not calling me right away.''

"I realize that now.''

"I hope so, Chape, I sincerely hope so.''

"I won't do it again.''

"That's right. From now on, you don't wipe your behind without telling me—not when it comes to this case.''

"I wasn't aware that this had become a case.''

"Well, let's call it a situation, not a case, if that makes you feel any better. The point is this: The next time anyone starts talking to you about Virginia Hanson, you call me. I'm your attorney and you're my client.''

"Okay. Okay. You're the attorney.''

As he said it, Chapin saw the smile of satisfaction on Greg's face. Why that smile? Why was it so important for Greg to establish a pecking order? Once again Chapin was impressed by how little close friends really know about each other. Greg was helping himself to what was left in the coffeepot.

"Now that that's settled,'' he said, "tell me about the blonde.''

"I knew you'd get to that sooner or later,'' Chapin said.

"That's not what I'm talking about,'' Greg said. "All I want to know is where she fits into all this.''

Chapin felt a small pang of disappointment. He was curious about whether Greg had ever gone through an experience remotely like this one. But it would be better not to ask; Chapin didn't know the proper words to ask the question. They had never discussed sex in terms of emotion or feeling. The locker-room conversations had always centered on technique, novelty, and eccentricity, never on anything quite so nebulous as passion.

"She doesn't fit,'' he said. "She was just someone I met.''

"Yeah. This gorgeous blonde saw you, mild-mannered Chapin Hope, sitting at a bar, bombed out of your skull, and she suddenly decided that you were irresistible.''

"I'm telling you, Greg, she felt it as much as I did.''

"So she was a good piece of ass,'' Greg said. "Although I wonder whether you were sober enough to know the difference, Chape. But let's keep the fuck stories for another time. I'm more interested in what she said, how she acted.''

"Why?''

"You should be able to figure that one out on your own.''

"You're thinking she had something to do with those phone calls?''

"You can bet your Senate seat I do. Get with it, Chape. If she was some cunt you picked up at the bar, maybe I'd consider the possibility of coincidence. Just maybe. But the *barmaid?* Not on your life. The barmaid at the place where you were told to go. Think about it for a minute, Chape. Who picked up whom?''

"I don't remember."

"How come *her* car?" Greg asked. "How come you picked this place?''

"She picked it," Chapin said. "Look, I was drunk. She was doing the driving.''

"That's what I mean," Greg said. "Okay, now let's take it from where you registered.''

As his partner talked, more fragments came back to Chapin. Greg kept pushing him to remember—what had he said and what had she said, what had he done and what had she done?

"Oh, no!" Chape said.

"What?"

"My name—I told her my name."

"She knew your name long before you ever got there. If she asked, she was just making sure. What else?''

Chapin told what he remembered and finished by describing the way Teddi had fled the room.

"What do you mean, *ran* from the room?"

"Just that," Chapin said. "She ran like she was scared out of her wits.''

"You didn't do anything to her you haven't told me about? You didn't hit her?''

"My God, no. I told you. It was great."

"Chape, did I ever tell you about the time my secretary went to Honolulu on her honeymoon, she sent me a telegram asking for an extra week off. The cable said, 'It's great here.' I sent her back a cable and it said, 'Come home at once; it's great everywhere.' ''

"You don't understand," Chapin said. "You really don't understand this time.''

"We'll see who understands," Greg said. "I'm just trying to figure why she ran from the room. You must have—''

"No, nothing."

"You didn't even say anything to upset her?"

"Well, there was one thing."

"You going to tell me about it?"

"You're going to think I'm crazy," Chapin said. "What happened was that I called her by the wrong name. I called her Ginny by mistake.''

"What?"

"Ginny. I yelled her name by mistake."

136

"When did you do that?"

"What difference does that make?"

"*When?*"

"At the worst possible time," Chapin said. "When I came. God damn it, when I came." Greg just shook his head. "I got confused for a minute there. I told you I was drunk. I was having this thing, this experience, you wouldn't understand, and I got mixed up. I thought I was with Ginny."

"Chape." Greg Hammer's voice was almost theatrically somber. "I hope Virginia Hanson was worth it."

"What do you mean by that?"

"I mean that you're still hung up on a dead woman and that fact has absolutely stripped you of reason."

"I was smashed," Chapin said. "I made a mistake. Listen, I feel lousy about it. I can understand why it might have upset her. But not frighten her. Hell, Greg, she ran out of this place like Jack the Ripper was after her."

"He was," Greg said. "Don't you understand? As far as she's concerned, you are Jack the Ripper."

"What are—"

"She knew Virginia Hanson. She knew whose name you were yelling. She knew whom you meant. What do you want me to do, draw a picture? She figured you did it. C'mon, put your coat on and let's get the hell out of here."

In daylight the Blue Barn stirred no memories for Chapin. It was one of those places that require darkness and neon to lift it from anonymity. But he had only to look at the parking lot to know he'd been there. The Blue Barn didn't open until lunchtime, and the lot was deserted except for a few cars that probably belonged to employees and a Mercedes with a velvet pouch over an official emblem.

"You okay?" Greg said.

"Just hung over. And worried."

"You should be."

"What I wonder is, who's after me?"

"We'll find that out pretty soon."

"Yeah." Chapin's sigh was a near moan.

"Drive carefully," Greg said. "We don't need any more problems."

"I'll second that."

"There's just one other thing," Greg said.

"What's that?"

"Take that silly thing off your license plate, will you?"

Chapin made good time getting home. He listened to a soft-music station during the ride and tried to avoid the questions attacking him; but that was like holding back the Miami Dolphins' defensive line. Who had called him? What did he know? What was he looking for? Was Greg right about Teddi? How could she believe him capable of doing a thing like that? The logical answers frightened him and he realized he would have to get rid of the bloodstained trousers at once. He hadn't told Greg about the pants, and he never would. The new lawyer-client relationship was humiliating enough without Chapin having to own up to another embarrassment.

The boys would be in school by the time he got home and Chapin was hoping that Thalia would be out shopping. Of course, he could tell her that he had come home early for the weekend and had left right after a breakfast meeting. Not that she would say anything; still, it would be better if he could change his clothes and shave before she saw him. The mirror in the motel room had shown him a Chapin Hope he barely recognized—a rumpled suit, a wrinkled tie, a stain on the shirt collar, a small difficulty in keeping his hands from trembling.

Driving through Stony Harbor, Chapin felt a little better. This was his village. Then he turned into his driveway and saw the station wagon. Thalia was in the living room, still talking to Lupe, who took one look at Chapin and dragged her vacuum cleaner from the room.

"*Chapin!*"

"In person," he said.

"What happened?" She was staring at him.

"Nothing," he said. "I decided to come home early."

"Bullshit!"

It was Chapin's turn to stare. The word was so out of character that it cracked across the room at him like a pistol shot, striking him in the temple, directly in the headache. What had gotten into her?

"Hey," he said. "There was a breakfast meeting. I decided—what the hell?—I could get an early start on the weekend."

"You went to a meeting looking like that?" she said. "Sure you did. Chape, you wouldn't rake the yard looking like that."

"There was no time to shave," he said. "Some thanks I get. I thought you'd be happy to see me. It seems to me a wife should—"

"Oh, please, spare me the bromides," Thalia said.

"Bromides?"

"You should know what they are, Chape. They're rapidly becoming your stock in trade."

She was smiling and Chapin suddenly filled in one of the missing pieces from the previous night. The "Poughkeepsie" exchange

138

with the desk clerk at the motel. It was the smile. Thalia's smile had that same infuriatingly superior quality that the desk clerk's smile had. Chapin could think of no response.

"I've got some errands to do," Thalia said. "If you need anything, ask Lupe."

A minute later she was at the hall closet getting her coat. And then he heard a car drive off. It sounded like the Mercedes.

18

After he put down the phone, O'Malley had just one question for Teddi.

"How do you know?"

"I know."

"How?"

"He yelled out her name."

O'Malley found himself thinking suddenly—inexplicably—of Isaac Alexander Grossheim, the shipping baron who founded the *Islander* and sold it to the Chicago corporation shortly before his death. Near the end of his life Grossheim's senility had interfered with the operation of the paper. Every ten days or so the crazy old man ran an editorial calling out for the castration of all morals offenders. Maybe, thought O'Malley, the old bastard hadn't been so crazy after all.

Teddi had been watching his face.

"I'm a big girl, Bob," she said. "I know what I'm doing."

There were a great many things O'Malley wanted to say, but he didn't say any of them.

"Brownie's going to want to talk with you," he said.

"Okay, but I don't want any publicity."

"There won't be any."

A white lie. O'Malley knew that he couldn't guarantee a thing. Teddi leaned over and kissed his cheek.

"You need a shave."

"Get the hell out of here."

As soon as the door closed, O'Malley settled into his oversized bed. When he didn't fall asleep immediately, he poured himself another drink. And another. And at 9:30 A.M., when Brownstein was pushing against his doorbell, O'Malley still hadn't been to sleep. The detective had just come down from Teddi's apartment.

"She's okay," he told O'Malley. "She'll testify if she has to. Otherwise I'll keep her name out of it. Bob, I appreciate the lead and I still expect to see you at my office at eleven. I've already notified your immediate superior and he'll be there."

"Yale?"

"Yes."

"Custer Yale is many things," O'Malley said. "But one thing he is not is my superior."

"Eleven o'clock this morning, Bob."

And at that hour Brownstein looked across the surface of an uncluttered desk at a bleary-eyed reporter and a remarkably modish editor. The detective began by saying that his office had been making a discreet investigation into Senator Chapin Hope's possible involvement in the Hanson case and that O'Malley had been getting in the way. Remembering that Yale was the one who had wanted to put pressure on him at the outset of the investigation, Brownstein didn't bother to attempt cordiality.

"I've told Mr. O'Malley and I'm telling you, Mr. Yale, I don't want you newspaper people playing detective. I don't want your newspaper jeopardizing an important investigation."

"I hope you're not trying to push the *Islander* around, Chief," Yale said.

"If you like, I can get the district attorney down here now," Brownstein said. "Or I can call in the rest of the media and describe to them precisely the manner in which the *Islander* is trying to obstruct justice."

O'Malley remained silent but he was impressed by Brownstein's bluff. He knew that the Homicide chief would not call Nassau County's glory-seeking district attorney, Norman Galton, into the case until he had to. He was equally certain that Brownstein wouldn't alert anyone else to the Hope lead. Yale, clearly not recognizing the bluff, switched to an executive-to-executive tone.

"Well, Bob may have gone a little too far," he said.

"As I said, I've told Bob and now I'm telling you—"

"Well, I think the *Islander* can promise you full cooperation," the managing editor said, offering his hand in surrender. "Bob, I'll want to talk to you about this back at the office."

Back at the office, however, the tone of voice changed once again. He sounded less like a frightened rabbit. What he sounded like, to O'Malley, was a courageous rabbit.

"Don't let that prick cop scare you off," he said. "Keep digging. This is our story and we're not sharing it with anybody. I don't mind telling you, Bob, this is one story that's got the brass in Chicago very excited."

"You know, Custer, for a minute there you had me going."

"What do you mean?"

"Well, up until that Chicago shit, you almost sounded like a newspaperman."

"Yeah, well. . . . ." Yale looked down at his desk and started to thumb through a stack of press releases. "Don't forget to call in."

O'Malley checked his mail and spent a few minutes at his desk before going to lunch at the bowling alley near the *Islander* office. He was joined by two younger colleagues, recent arrivals who dressed like twin bank clerks. Both of them ordered the diet-chop—ground round and cottage cheese—then watched enviously as O'Malley enjoyed the ham special, which came with gravy, mashed potatoes, and sauerkraut. O'Malley had two bottles of beer with the meal and then ordered coffee and a piece of coconut-custard pie for dessert. The two younger reporters discussed the usual topics—salary inequities, editors' failings, office politics, office sex.

"Fucking editors," O'Malley said, almost by rote, "they're always screwing somebody."

His luncheon companions chortled at that. A few weeks before they might not have joined him for lunch. But now that he had been detached from the police beat to concentrate on the Hanson case, Robert J. O'Malley rated a measure of respect. He had become a character instead of a lush. Some of his co-workers even remembered that he had won a Pulitzer Prize. As his two colleagues watched in awe, he topped off the lunch with a Benedictine and brandy, then reached for the check.

"I'll put it on the expense account," he said. Actually that was not the case, O'Malley was notorious for the size of his expense vouchers but no one ever questioned their honesty. His two fellow workers were mesmerized; under the provisions of the latest memo, they couldn't take the President of the United States to lunch without first receiving permission in triplicate.

Minutes after arriving home, O'Malley felt sleep catching up with him. He stripped down to his underwear and tumbled into the unmade bed. He would have slept through the night if the phone hadn't rung shortly after nine that night.

"Yeah?"

"Hello." It was a woman's voice. "Is this Robert O'Malley, the reporter for the *Islander*?"

"Yeah."

"The one who's been writing about the Virginia Hanson murder?"

"That's right." He had been half asleep when he picked up the receiver; now he was fully awake. "Who am—"

"I hear you've been looking for me. I've been out of town."

"Who is this?"

"I'm a friend—I *was* a friend—of Virginia Hanson's. My name is Charlotte."

142

"Oh, yeah, the famous Charlotte. I have been trying to reach you. Where are you?"

"Right now?"

"Yeah, right now. . . ." The woman seemed to be giggling.

"This is no joke."

"I know that," she said. "That's why I'm calling. I'd like to help."

"Have you spoken to the police? They're looking for you, too. They're looking like hell."

"That's a problem," she said. "I know there are detectives asking about me. It's a little complicated but I don't want to talk to them unless I absolutely have to. That's why I decided to call you. I'll talk to you but you've got to promise not to bring anyone else along."

"That's no problem."

"And no tape recorders. Nothing like that."

"That's only in the movies," O'Malley said. "Listen, I won't even take notes."

"Okay, where do you suggest we meet?"

"Someplace where we can have a drink," he said.

"An excellent suggestion."

"I guess we can eliminate the Pumpkin," he said.

"I should hope so."

They went through four or five clubs, including the Blue Barn, but Charlotte vetoed all of them.

"I'd rather not go anywhere there's a chance I'll know someone," she said. "I'll tell you what—Renée's, over in Great Neck. I've only been there once or twice and it's Friday; it'll be so jammed, no one will notice us. I'll meet you in the foyer. I'll be the brunette in the white blouse."

"I'll be the fat guy."

O'Malley had never been to Renée's before but he knew what it was. He had heard it called "the meat rack" by those who went to such places. When he arrived, there was a tall, handsome brunette in a white blouse and black skirt waiting in the foyer. She was the only woman in the place who didn't look frantic. As he walked into the bar with her, O'Malley felt momentarily self-conscious at the thought of his own rumpled appearance. But it passed.

The sound from the bar carried into the foyer. Friday was obviously Renée's night. At least three layers of people circled the long bar. They were jammed together, rush-hour passengers on a motionless but noisy subway car to nowhere. There seemed to be no one under the age of thirty in the room. The women were heavily jeweled and looked as though they were all overprivileged refugees

143

from the Miracle Mile in Manhasset. A sizable percentage of the men had midwinter tans acquired during a long weekend in Florida or a junket to Las Vegas. A few men had the unmistakable aroma of the mob.

Charlotte found a place to stand against the wall and O'Malley pushed his way up to the bar. While he was reaching for his change, a heavy blonde pressed against him and said, "When did you get your divorce? I got mine in September."

O'Malley took one look at the woman's desperate eyes and could think of nothing to say. He fought his way back to Charlotte, who was being besieged by a sixtyish dandy with long white sideburns and what O'Malley was sure was a silver wig. The man was wearing a print shirt open at the collar, beads, a yellow knit blazer, razor-creased maroon slacks, a sapphire pinky ring. He was in the process of inviting Charlotte home to try out his swimming pool.

"I got a dome over it, doll, and it's heated," he said. "Don't worry about a swimming suit, we don't believe in 'em."

"I'm sorry." Charlotte showed just the faintest trace of a smile. "I wouldn't want to take the chance of anything happening to you."

"To me?"

"Like a heart attack," she said.

"Don't worry about me, doll . . . I'm a tiger."

O'Malley allowed his hand to fall on the man's shoulder and then he spun him around.

"Hey, buddy," he said. "Get your hands off Officer Jones before I pull you in on a morals rap."

"Take it easy, Sergeant." Charlotte didn't miss a beat. "We're just supposed to be sizing this place up."

The old man looked at them in bewilderment.

"Well, you know how I feel about perverts," O'Malley said. "They oughta be in jail."

"Oh, I really don't think this one is physically able to do any harm," Charlotte said.

O'Malley released the man's shoulder.

"Okay," he said. "Get lost before I change my mind. And for Chrissakes, get a haircut, will ya?"

The man accepted the invitation and vanished.

"I like you, O'Malley," Charlotte said.

"Yeah, I'm known for my charm."

O'Malley's charm, thin at any time, was being stretched taut. The place was a madhouse. Every time he raised his glass toward his mouth someone gave him a shove. The noise was incredible. He could see Charlotte moving her lips but he couldn't hear a word she said. The only way to be heard above the Latin music was to shout and even that didn't always work.

"This is impossible," O'Malley said.

"What?"

"Let's get the hell out of here."

"WHAT?"

"Come with me."

He took her hand and led her toward the door. Directly across the street there was a diner, one of those all-glitter diners where the women wear expensive slack outfits and the men are in tailored sheepherder's coats and suede jackets. O'Malley and Charlotte found a booth in the rear. They both ordered coffee and O'Malley ordered chili and a baconburger.

"Go ahead," Charlotte told him. "I'll enjoy watching."

Before the food came, he took a good look at her. She knew what he was doing, sizing her up, and the process didn't faze her. She was a tall, not-quite-statuesque woman. Strong features, large brown eyes, full lips, and dark brown hair. She was wearing a good deal of makeup but it had been carefully applied. Everything about her, it seemed to O'Malley, was carefully put together; he could not tell for sure whether she was wearing a fall. Except for the sensuality, she reminded O'Malley of an executive secretary. The sensuality was almost opulent.

"I dropped by the Pumpkin the other night," she was saying, "and Baldy told me about you and the police. I was lucky that none of them were around. Actually, I've been in Europe for the last month with a friend. Before that I used to stop at the Pumpkin once or twice a week. That's how I met Ginny—Virginia Hanson. To tell you the truth, Bob, I've always liked the Pumpkin. Once you're accepted there, it's like a club."

"C'mon."

"No, really. There's a sort of warmth. Even the waitresses . . . the bartender, Bobby Kelly, the piano player, the singing, all that."

"Yeah, even Baldy, he's a sweetheart."

"Well, you can't have everything," Charlotte said. "But I mean it, I like the Pumpkin. I'm a people watcher and you meet some very interesting types there. One night I had a great conversation with an engineer from Grumman who helped build the LEM, you know, the vehicle they used on the moon. And even Bobby Kelly. Did you know that his real name is Stan Goldstone and he started out studying to be a what-do-you-call-it, not a rabbi, a cantor. And then he decided to be an entertainer instead."

"That's a hell of a name change."

"That's the best part. He was starting out and he got a chance to play a resort in the Catskills. An *Irish* resort. In the *Catskills*. Can you imagine? Anyway, the owner liked his style but said he would have to use an Irish name. So he came up with Bobby Kelly. I understand that you've had an interesting background yourself. Didn't you once win the Pulitzer Prize?"

"What? Have you been doing research on me?"

"No. I've got a good memory. I've always read the *Islander* and I know your by-line."

O'Malley felt that the only person who ever noticed a reporter's by-line was another reporter. Or an immediate relative. If Charlotte was out to butter him up, she was going about it the right way. But he didn't want her to think she was succeeding.

"That's very flattering," he said. "Why don't you begin by telling me anything you know about Harry."

"I can tell you a lot about Harry," she said. "But I ought to start by saying I don't think he's capable of something like this. I hate to be the one who involves him if he's innocent."

"He's already involved," O'Malley said. "Let me give you his initials: C.H."

"You're right," she said. "Chapin Hope. Well, you really don't need me then. . . ."

"More than you might think." Pay dirt. O'Malley wiped his mouth with a napkin. "How can you be sure that Harry is in fact Chapin Hope?"

"Ginny told me." Charlotte hesitated. "Look, I had no idea you were this close to him. You don't really need me. The one thing I want to avoid is going to the police, any kind of notoriety at all. I'm sure you're aware of the fact that I haven't given you my last name."

"I did notice that."

"I think I can talk to you off the record."

"Off the record," he agreed—a promise O'Malley gave more often than he kept. He knew that whenever someone said it was "off the record," they were getting down to the facts.

"The thing is, I have this friend. The one I was in Europe with. He's a very prominent man, you'd know his name right away. You'd also know that he happens to be married, very married. That's neither here nor there, but I don't want to do anything that would hurt him. If it got out about us, it would be very bad for him. If my name came out as some kind of witness in a murder case, or if my picture was in the papers, it could backfire on him."

"What is he, some kind of politician?"

"You might say that."

"Well, there's no reason for him to ever come into this, but I'm not about to argue with you."

146

"Good." Charlotte reached out and, for the briefest of moments, allowed her hand to rest on O'Malley's wrist. "He doesn't realize I even knew Ginny Hanson or that I make the bar scene as often as I do. There's a lot he doesn't know about me and there's no need for him to find out."

O'Malley understood. She didn't want to mess up the trips to Europe and whatever else the payoff was. What the hell. At least she was honest about it.

"That's fair," he said. "I just want the story. If I have to write anything at all, I'll just call you an informed source."

"Informed source—I kind of like that."

"One thing I don't figure," he said. "What made Virginia Hanson tell you about Hope?"

"She had to tell somebody, she was just bursting with it, with who he was. When I told her who my fellow is, she knew she could trust me. We were, so to speak, in the same boat."

"You were close then?"

"We were friends. But neither one of us is—was—the kind of person who let another woman get too close. I'm what you might call a man's woman, if you know what I mean, and Ginny was the same way. But we'd talk there at the Pumpkin and we even got together for lunch a couple of times. . . ."

"Did you ever meet Hope?"

"Just that night. I was there when he came in a little before eight and she introduced us. He's quite a nice-looking man, you know, and he was very pleasant. You could see that he was hung up on Ginny; you know, the way he watched her. I can't see him hurting her."

"Did you see him again that night?"

"No, but I came back later on, and then Ginny showed up just before closing. She told us—Baldy was there—that 'Harry' had just left her off and that something hilarious had happened. Baldy took a little walk and she told me they had been smoking pot and she'd give me all the details some other time. She just stayed a little while and she left."

"What was so funny?"

"It probably had something to do with the grass. I mean, I just start to think of Chapin Hope smoking pot and I get the giggles. Ginny told me that he was one of those behind the new narcotics law."

"Did she ever talk about Hope as a lover? You know what I mean, whether there was anything funny there."

"Nothing weirdo, if that's what you're getting at. She once told me that Hope was a very uptight guy, very repressed. She wondered whether she should bother shacking up with him or not. But Ginny really cared about him. She said he was a very unhappy man, and that worried her. He wasn't getting much satisfaction out of his family and she was afraid that he was using her for some kind of release. She said he was too intense."

"Too intense—those very words?"

"I think so. Who knows anymore?"

"Did he ever hurt her?"

"Not that I knew. I mean you never know what goes on in another person's bedroom, do you? Once I remember Ginny came to work with a bruise on her forehead but she said it was nothing, that she had hit her head on a kitchen cabinet. I wondered about that."

"That night she was killed, did she say anything about seeing Hope later on?"

"No. All she said was that she sure hoped he kept his sense of humor."

"What do you think? Do you think he paid her another visit that night?"

"How would I know something like that?"

"You're not talking to the cops," he said. "All I want is an educated guess."

"I just don't know."

"You think he was angry with her?"

"Well, she was laughing. And she did say that about hoping he kept his sense of humor. But to do what happened to Ginny. I don't know. He'd have to be crazy."

"Yeah, crazy. You had to be there."

"If it is Hope, I sure hope they get him."

"They will," O'Malley said.

He ordered blueberry cheesecake for dessert.

Charlotte had refused to give O'Malley a phone number where she could be reached but she promised to stay in touch. O'Malley's instinct was to believe her. The proper thing, the correct thing, was to tell Brownstein about the interview—but that could wait. Why get Brownstein angry again? The following Monday he did visit Brownstein, but only to tell the Homicide chief that he was going to interview Chapin Hope.

"I want to get him on tape," O'Malley said.

"I don't think so. . . ."

"Listen, Brownie, I won't even talk about Virginia Hanson. Not a word. I've got to get some reaction to that other stuff we've got on him, the conflict-of-interest stuff."

"I don't see how I can object to that. . . ."

148

"I've already set it up," O'Malley said. "I just wanted to clear it with you first."

"Incidently, I'd be interested in your impressions of him, Bob. His state of mind, that sort of thing."

"You going to put me on the payroll?"

"Who knows? After all, you've been handling this case like a rookie cop so far." He got up and filled a cup with boiling water from a coffeepot. "Ready for a cup of tea, Bob?"

"You go ahead," O'Malley said. "It's too early in the day for me."

19

Robert J. O'Malley was not a man given to nostalgia; yet when he came back to Stony Harbor and saw the village's main street, he felt a trace of . . . something. Old men holding fishing poles were standing guard over the town dock, and everywhere O'Malley could see the ties to the water and the ties to the past. He hated those modern, climate-controlled shopping centers with ties only to the almighty dollars.

The appointment with Chapin Hope was for four o'clock. O'Malley drove past Bobo's, went the length of Main Street, took a couple of lefts, and found himself on Pinnacle Drive. He drove slowly by the mailbox with the name Morgenthau, smiled briefly at the memory of his trip to the village clerk's office, and continued his drive about a hundred yards until he came to the unmarked mailbox at the foot of Chapin Hope's driveway.

At the end of the long winding driveway, two cars, a station wagon and a Mercedes. O'Malley parked his Pontiac on the opposite side of the driveway, beneath the basketball backboard. Before leaving the car and going up to the house, he reached into his glove compartment for a quick bracer.

The doorbell was answered by a woman with the pleasant, noncommittal face of a model in a Saks ad. O'Malley was impressed by her wholly unruffled façade—he figured she must have spent half the day working on her hair to get it looking that way.

"You're Mr. O'Malley," she said. "I'm Senator Hope's wife. Just a minute; I'll get him."

"Thank you."

O'Malley stood in the entranceway, filling it with his bulk, noticing that everything within eyesight—the tables, the chairs, even the woman—was supported by limbs that seemed just a trifle too slender. In her greeting, Thalia Hope had managed to offend O'Malley three ways. In the first place, she had not found it necessary to give her own name, implying that she had no desire to know the reporter on a personal level. Second, she had not invited him into the living room but had left him standing in the hallway like

150

a delivery boy. And, finally, she had not quite managed to conceal the repugnance in her eyes, the witheringly judgmental glance that thin people enjoy giving to people of O'Malley's girth.

When Chapin Hope walked into the room, O'Malley felt as if he were looking into a fun-house mirror and seeing his perfect opposite. The taut slimness of the man, the tidiness, the unwrinkled quality that seemed to pass from his starched shirt to his starched face. O'Malley realized that the contrast was not escaping Hope; the senator was studying the reporter with the same undisguised curiosity.

"I'm glad you had the time to see me," O'Malley began. "I'm sure there are a lot of other things you'd rather be doing."

"Not at all," Chapin said. "I'm just a little surprised is all. I can't remember an *Islander* reporter ever wanting to interview me in depth before. I'm actually flattered."

As the senator spoke, O'Malley took a miniature Sony cassette recorder from his pocket and put it on the end table beside Hope. "I hope you don't mind if I turn this on. . . ."

"Where's the microphone?"

"No microphone," O'Malley said. "This doesn't use one. I'll tell you, Senator, this is about the best piece of equipment they make and I can get it to work only about fifty percent of the time. Actually, I hate mechanical things. Here, let me test it."

O'Malley hit one button and a second, and then a third and both men heard the machine repeat, "Actually, I hate mechanical things. . . ."

O'Malley grinned. "Hey, what do you know?" he said.

"I don't think the recorder's a good idea," Chapin said. "It makes everything too official. I thought we were going to have a relaxed interview."

"I'm with you, Senator," O'Malley said. "I wouldn't use the damn thing except my boss says I have to. This way I can't possibly misquote you. And the thing is, we may get into some touchy areas."

"Oh?" Hope glanced over at Thalia and then back at the machine. "That sounds ominous. Look, Bob—it's all right if I call you Bob?—look, I'm not all that used to this sort of thing. If the questions get too sticky, although I can't imagine why they would, but if they do, I might want to call in my partner, Greg Hammer. Thalia, didn't you have something . . . ?"

"Oh, that's right."

Although the cue was a familiar one to Thalia, she was sorry to hear it this time. There had been an expression of something close to fear in Chapin's eyes, and she was amused at the contrast between

151

the two men. She couldn't help but think of a bear and a humming-bird—she knew Chapin would not be pleased to be thought of as a hummingbird. For a minute she thought about changing her mind and staying, but then she shrugged her shoulders. It wasn't worth the fuss. She excused herself and walked up the stairs to the master bedroom, closing the door loudly behind her.

"Okay, Bob, what's on your mind?"

"I hardly know where to begin," the reporter said.

"Well, I can't help you there."

O'Malley concentrated on looking earnest. "It's just that there seems to be more than one angle here," O'Malley said. "As you probably know, I've been looking into your background these past few weeks."

"No. I didn't know."

"I'm surprised," O'Malley said. "I figured one of your friends would tell you. Hell, almost everyone I talked to said he was your best friend. The fact is, I never knew a man who had so many best friends."

"That's a snow job," Chapin said. "Off the record, there's only one reason a politician has so many friends, and that's because he's in a position to do favors. Legitimate things, but favors. And let me tell you something—if I do a man a favor, he's grateful, all right, but he's also resentful. I've done men favors where they resented the hell out of it. I'll tell you how you can find out who your best friend is: Lose an election. The one who calls you two weeks later, that's the one you want to hang onto."

"Except you've never lost any elections," O'Malley said.

"I hope you're not holding that against me," Chapin said. "I know I'm considered a little too conservative by your paper's standards. Perhaps I should ask just what kind of profile you're doing on me."

"It'll be an in-depth piece," O'Malley said, and then he told an outright lie. "Actually, we may wind up with a series of in-depth pieces on several of the Island's most important legislators."

"I see," Hope said.

"The first thing," O'Malley said, "we've been doing a little checking, and we find that a great deal of your money, your campaign support, has come from the United Dairymen. At the same time, you've been voting at each session to raise the price of milk."

The expression of relief that had appeared at the mention of a series of articles remained on Hope's face. O'Malley figured that political corruption was the least of the senator's worries.

152

"Well, Bob, all I can ask you to do is watch for the kind of support they give me next time out. Between the two of us, my information is that I've been cut off their list."

"How'd that happen?"

"It's really quite simple," Chapin said. "I'm sure you know that special-interest groups are constantly trying to exert pressure on legislators. Let's just say that as a result of this kind of pressure, I learned recently that the dairy industry is going to try for another price hike this session. I also learned that these fellows are anticipating the day when they can charge a dollar a quart for milk. More than anticipating, actually; their timetable calls for this to happen within the next five years. As it happens, Bob, I found this outrageous—my feeling is that you've got to draw the line somewhere. And if it costs me a campaign contribution, so what? No one's ever going to be able to say that Chapin Hope took milk from the mouths of infants. It may be true that babies can't vote, but some things are more important than votes."

"Yeah," O'Malley said, "and of course mothers can vote."

"Well, you can look at it any way you like," Hope said. "My own feeling is that you could do a lot of good by simply warning your readers about the effort to raise milk prices. You could perform a public service."

"Senator, you've been explaining politics to me. Let me tell you something about newspapers. Newspapers are not in business to perform public services. They're—"

"It's never too late to start," Chapin said.

O'Malley admired the quickness of the riposte. "Touché," he said.

"I hope this isn't a contest," Chapin said. "Let me tell you, Bob, this milk experience has been something of an awakening for me. It's bad enough what the oil companies have been doing to us. And all those other shortages—can we assume that they're just natural occurrences? Or is everybody trying to get into the act?"

"Well, Senator, I think my editors are more interested in the donations the dairymen have been making to your campaigns."

"I can understand that, Bob. And you can tell your editors that Chapin Hope votes his conscience. Why, if those farmers thought for a minute that they were buying me with their lousy thousand-dollar donations, well. . . ."

"Five thousand dollars," O'Malley said. "At least that's what they reported."

"Was it? That shows how much it matters to me, I don't even know the amount. Look, Bob, I can assure you that there has never
153

been any connection between those contributions and my vote. My reason for voting for price boosts was simple—I was trying to help the little man, in this case the dairy farmer. I don't know if you realize what the average dairy farmer makes in New York today. . . ."

"Senator—"

"Damn little," Hope pressed on. "And my feeling is that in a business that basic, a man should be able to make a fair day's wage for a fair day's work. And that is the only reason I ever voted for a price increase for the milk industry."

It was a hell of a performance, O'Malley thought. Hope was probably dynamite in debate.

"Senator, excuse me, would you let me check this machine again? I don't want to miss this."

The reporter hit the buttons in sequence, heard the voice saying, ". . . fair day's wage for a . . ." and reset the machine. Now to step up the pace. "I suppose," O'Malley said, "you can explain your ties with Sonny Castor."

"I don't believe I've heard that name."

"James Castorina?"

"Jimmy? He's been a friend for years. But I've never heard of the other—"

"Same guy, Senator. Ask the DA's office about him. And I suppose you can explain how come your law firm does so much business with banks?"

O'Malley could see Hope stiffen. "There's nothing illegal about that," the senator said. "A law firm, even a law firm where a state senator is a partner, can do business with whomever—"

"And I suppose you could explain how come you bought seven acres off Main Street and, just a few weeks later, managed to get it downzoned. . . ."

"I must say, Mr. O'Malley, you've been doing some homework. But what is this? It doesn't sound like any kind of profile to me, it sounds like a witch-hunt."

From the start, O'Malley had known that he would do what he was about to do. He had known that the minute he promised Brownstein that he wouldn't do it. Although as far as that went, he felt the detective chief half wanted him to do it.

"You can still call me Bob," he said. "But there's just one other thing. I suppose you can explain what you were doing with Virginia Hanson the night she was murdered."

Chapin Hope crumbled. It was as if a room had been plunged into darkness by the sudden flick of a light switch. The light simply winked out of his eyes, the animation shorted from his face. Even

O'Malley was surprised by both the suddenness and the completeness of his victory.

"Mr. O'Malley," Hope said finally, "you might as well turn off that machine. I'm not saying another word to you."

As O'Malley reached for the recorder, Chapin Hope walked into the hall and looked up at the still-closed bedroom door. This gave O'Malley an opportunity to reverse the spools of tape. He put the machine out of sight by his feet and once again set it into operation. Hope was gone for another minute and then came back into the room, walking like a man suffering from physical exhaustion.

"I've called my law partner," he said. "I'm not going to say another word without an attorney."

"That's your privilege," O'Malley said, "but it's certainly not going to help you."

There was no answer, and O'Malley went on in hopes of trying to draw a response. "We've known for a month," he said. "That picture in the paper, that must have driven you right up the wall. And if you're thinking that's all there is, forget it. Virginia Hanson told people about you, Senator, she told people who you were."

Hope shuddered but said nothing, and O'Malley stopped talking. The two men sat there silently, eyes not meeting, as the room turned gray. The first sound was the opening of the upstairs bedroom door. Thalia came into the living room, touched the wall switch, flooding the room with light.

"Oh," she said, "I didn't know anyone was still here. I didn't hear a sound."

"We've got some more business," Chapin said. "We're just waiting for Greg."

"Well, I've got to go shopping anyway," Thalia said.

O'Malley watched Thalia leave the room. He could tell people who had money by the way they walked; there was a certain assurance to their carriage. O'Malley wondered whether Thalia Hope's walk would change when she found out about her husband. The reporter had no pity for Hope, but he could feel something for the man's family. Not enough to make him let up on the story, but something.

The silence continued. Hope seemed small, lost in the oversized chair while O'Malley overflowed the smaller chair and kept shifting his weight from one position to another. Even then Hope seemed wrinkle-free and dapper. O'Malley was rumpled and fidgety. He knew without looking that there was at least one food stain on his tie and he would have traded his soul for a drink.

Greg Hammer came into the house without knocking. He walked directly over to O'Malley and stuck out his hand; only then did the reporter realize that Hope had not shaken hands. Hammer's handshake was professionally firm, and his exuberance seemed exaggerated. O'Malley found it somewhat incongruous that the lawyer had bothered to shave before coming over but there was no missing the razor redness to his cheeks and the rich aroma of after-shave lotion.

Hammer took O'Malley by the elbow and guided him to the far side of the room away from Hope. There was something about that elbow grip that annoyed the reporter; it was the kind of grip a man used on caddies and porters. As Hammer started to talk, O'Malley remembered the tape recorder and moved back toward the chair.

"I'm just in the way here," Hope announced, standing up to leave. "I've got nothing else to say."

Greg Hammer waved his partner-client back to the easy chair. "Well?" he said.

"Well?" O'Malley said.

"Well," the lawyer said, "Chapin tells me you've been doing some tough reporting."

"That's what they pay me for."

"Well, I'd like to level with you, Bob. I can call you Bob?"

"Join the club."

"Fine. I really do want to level with you."

"A lot of people tell me that, counselor, but they usually mean just the opposite. It's like they always say 'truthfully' just before they tell a lie."

"I don't think there's any reason to make this any more difficult than it already is," Hammer said. "Truthfully, Bob—no, strike that. Damn it, I *am* going to level with you. The senator and I expected someone to come up with the sort of information you seem to have. I'm not going to tell you how wrong it is, but let me assure you of one thing: Chapin Hope is not guilty of any crime. If he ever touched Virginia Hanson, and I'm not saying he did, it was in love, not in anger. . . ."

"That's a nice line, counselor. You ought to save it for the jury."

"I'll make believe I didn't hear that. Look, O'Malley, I'm trying to help you. I'm trying to keep you from making a terrible mistake. To tell you the truth, I'm glad you're the one who's come up with this . . . theory, and not the cops."

"How do you know the cops haven't come up with it?"

"If they have, they've had the good sense to keep it to themselves. I'd expect you to do the same."

One of O'Malley's ambitions was that someday he would be able to rush into the news room and yell, "Stop the presses!" Now it was with a certain satisfaction that he unleashed another cliché. "In this

156

business, Mr. Hammer," he said, "you go with what you've got."

"Well, then, what you've got—and what the *Islander* has got—is a lawsuit that will put both of you where you belong, out of business."

"Can I quote you on that?" O'Malley said.

Hammer turned off his anger. "Look, Bob," he said, "let's try to talk sense to each other. You seem like a reasonable man to me. All I'm asking you to do is listen to reason."

O'Malley felt the tape recorder against his foot. "I'm known for my reasonableness."

"Okay. Chapin couldn't talk to you this way. Maybe I can begin by observing that a man like yourself, a reporter with your reputation, should be driving around in something a little more impressive than that beat-up Pontiac I saw out in the driveway. I'll tell you, Bob, I can't help seeing you behind the wheel of a new car, something more—"

"What the hell are you trying to say, counselor?"

"I'm just making a simple observation."

"That's not the impression I get," O'Malley said. "I get the impression that you might be offering me a new car if I do a favor for you."

"A favor?" Hammer said. "What kind of favor?"

"I hate to be crude, counselor, but I think you'll give me a new car if I kill this story."

"That sounds like bribery," Hammer said. "I'm not sure I understand exactly what you're talking about."

"Oh, you understand, Mr. Hammer. You hit it right on the head. Bribery's the exact word I had in mind. I think you were offering me a bribe not to write the story I'm going to write tonight—the one linking your Boy Scout partner with a murder victim."

"Okay, O'Malley, let me caution you—"

"I thought you were going to call me Bob."

"O'Malley, let me tell you something, and you get it straight. What you're about to do is attempt to ruin the career of an innocent man. *An innocent man*. Understand that, understand it good. You get one fact wrong, one little fact, and we're gonna sue your ass off."

"I think your ass is in more trouble than mine, counselor," O'Malley said as he reached down and picked up the tape recorder. "I think anyone who listens to this tape is going to think you tried to bribe me."

O'Malley stopped the car at the end of the driveway and opened the machine. He wanted to hear the exact words, and he depressed the button that rewound the tape. He pushed the Listen button; but what he heard were not the self-confident tones of Long Island's leading criminal attorney. What he heard was a shrill, piercing whine, the kind of whine you get when you have somehow managed to insert the cartridge incorrectly.

20

Even the cellar was immaculate in the Hope home. The walls whitewashed, the floor tiled, and the long room divided into sections. There was a workbench area complete with power tools that Chapin rarely operated but that the boys were beginning to use. There was a storage area lined with bins and shelves. Elsewhere there was a big floor-to-ceiling closet. The oil tank and burner were against the far wall. The golf bag was where Chapin had left it, wedged out of sight behind the oil tank.

Chapin, who had waited for Thalia to go to sleep before going down to the basement, turned over the bag, allowing the clubs to clatter out onto the asphalt-covered concrete, and there, at the bottom of the bag, wadded up into a musty ball, were the blood-stained trousers. How could they build a house this expensive without a fireplace? He took the trousers up into the kitchen, put them into a paper bag, put the bag at the bottom of the kitchen garbage container. Later he dumped this, along with the lamb-chop bones and orange peels and other refuse, into a larger garbage can that was wheeled down the long driveway to the curb.

Thalia had fallen asleep with the reading light still on beside her. The book left open in her lap was *Little Women*, by Louisa May Alcott. Thalia returned to her childhood favorite periodically, whenever she needed to be reminded of a world where women were charming and men were chivalrous, a world of needlework and balls and blossoming romance.

Chapin removed the book from her lap and put it beside the clock-radio. Before turning off the lamp, he paused and studied his wife's face. He was astonished to discover that she, too, was growing older. He reached out and held her shoulder.

"Honey, wake up," he said. "Wake up, Thal."

"Huh . . . Chape? What time—"

"It's only eleven fifteen," he said. "Wake up, Thal."

"What?"

"Please, Thal, I've got to tell you something."

"Oh . . . Chape . . . I'm sleeping."

"Thalia, it's important."

"Can't it keep until tomorrow?"

"No. It can't keep at all. Please, I've got to talk to you tonight. Here, I've made you a cup of coffee."

"It'll wake me up."

"That's the idea."

Thalia accepted the cup and without opening her eyes took a sip, then another. Her eyes fluttered open tentatively. Chapin was fully dressed, and she wondered what was wrong. As she came fully awake, he reached out and turned off the reading light.

"I thought you wanted me to wake up," she said.

"I don't want you to look at me," he said. "I don't want you to see my face."

The truth was that he did not want to see her face. Not when she heard what he had to tell her. In his mind as he turned off the light, he was still poking about for a way to start. Where does a man begin when he is about to be honest with his wife for the first time in fourteen years? Chapin thought for a few more seconds and found a place.

"Thalia, do you remember when we went to the library last spring and we heard that lecture, that professor from Hofstra, what was his name?"

"Chapin, if you woke me out of a sound sleep to help you remember the name of some professor, I—"

"Wait a minute, Thal. I don't really care about his name. It was what he said. Remember, he was talking about open marriage; he said that if both partners were unfaithful, it would be okay—that if a person was honest about infidelity, then it wasn't the same as cheating."

"I remember how angry you got," Thalia said. "I remember how you jumped up and started yelling about the kind of people they let teach our children nowadays—"

"Forget that," Chapin said. "I've been thinking about what he said."

Thalia snapped the reading light back on. "What are you getting at?" she said.

Chapin's mouth went dry, and he turned his head from the light. Then he plunged. "I've got to tell you something," he said. "Thal, I've been unfaithful."

The light went off and he heard her head hit the pillow. House noises filled the silence. "Thal," he said, "are you listening?"

"I'm listening."

"I've been unfaithful for the last fourteen years. With different women."

160

More silence. "I never thought I'd have to tell you," he said, "but I have no choice. Believe me."

There was still no answer. "Are you still listening?" he said.

"I'm still listening."

"The longest affair lasted four years."

"Four years." Her voice was flat.

"Not four solid years," he said. "On and off."

"How nice."

What the hell was the matter with her? he thought. Why wasn't she screaming?

"The woman was Margaret—Jack Dunbar's legislative assistant."

"The one you said was in love with Jack?"

"She was—she used to tell me that. But apparently he didn't feel the same way. And she said that anyway, she'd never sleep with her boss."

"But it was all right to sleep with someone else's boss?"

Even the sarcasm was a relief. "I don't blame you for being bitter," he said.

"What was it like, Chape?"

"What?"

"Oh, come now, Chape, you're not going to leave out the good parts. What did she do that I wouldn't do?"

"She wasn't as bright as you, Thal, and probably not as attractive. She was thirty-five, she was a divorcée. And I was alone in Albany a lot. You never spent much time there."

"You never asked me to, but there's no sense going into that. So those were the legislative meetings you phoned me about."

"A lot of times there really were meetings," he said.

"Of course there were," she said. "But I'm still waiting for the juicy details. I'm sure you want to tell me."

"If you must know," he said, cutting Thalia off, "I went to her apartment. She'd make a steak and I'd bring wine. We'd eat by candlelight, and she'd have the stereo on. She was very prim in the office, but in the apartment she was different. She'd wear a low-cut gown or a see-through blouse, and—"

"That's enough, Chape. I get the idea."

It was going all wrong.

"I'm sorry," he said. "I don't want to make this any worse than it is. Look, I'm trying to be as honest as I can."

"I can see that," she said.

"There've been others," Chapin went on. "Nothing serious. You know, someone you'd meet at an office party, and there'd be a lot of drinking, and afterward you'd wind up in the wrong apart-

161

ment. Then a day later you wouldn't even look at each other."

"How about prostitutes? Hookers, isn't that the word?"

"Once I went to a massage parlor," Chapin said. "It was after a campaign-committee meeting in the city. The parlor was on Eighth Avenue, and you went into a reception room and you could pick somebody out."

"I hope you made a good choice."

"She was a girl, a teenager. She was black."

"What did *she* do?"

What the hell was the matter with him? He wanted to tell her. "She took me into a cubicle and she rubbed me until I got an erection. Then she put a rubber on me and she started committing fellatio. . . ."

"You can be more explicit than that, Chape."

"She started blowing me. How's that? But I told her that wouldn't work—with the rubber on—and she said the taste made her sick and she wouldn't take off the rubber unless I gave her another ten. So I did, and she took off the rubber and later she got sick."

"Tell me, Chape, did you ever do it with anyone we know? Anyone I know?"

"Just one. What's-her-name, uh, Milgram."

"Edie Milgram? You're making that up."

"I wish I were."

"What would Edie Milgram want with you?"

"You remember the peace vigils in 1968. Well, she was assigned to my office. One morning it was snowing and she was outside reading her Bible, and I asked her to come in. And it happened. Right there in the office."

"On the couch?"

"No, on the rug."

"Edie Milgram on the rug?"

"It was terrible," Chapin said. "She started to cry about halfway through and she never stopped."

Thalia finally broke the silence that followed. "You bastard," she said, "you lousy bastard."

At last, he thought. "I'm sorry," he said. "I'm truly sorry, Thal."

"You don't understand," she said. "I'm not talking about the infidelity," she said. "I knew all about that."

"You what?"

"Oh, not the names," she said. "Not the details. I probably could have found them out if I wanted to, but to tell you the truth they didn't interest me. But I knew all the same. For one thing, you were always extra solicitous when you had something going on. For another, every time you make love, your cheeks get mottled. They stay mottled for hours. I bet you didn't know that, did you? Well, there were all those nights you came home with mottled cheeks. You really should check that out with a doctor, Chape. And all those nights you said it was one thirty and it was really four thirty—did you really think you were fooling me?"

"Thal, I—"

"And you think Priscilla doesn't talk to me? You think she doesn't know about Greg? We both know the kind of men we married."

"You never said anything."

"What should I have said? There was nothing to say. And what I resent now isn't the infidelity. What I resent is your dragging me into the mess you've made of your life. Let me tell you something, Chape. Your little affairs haven't bothered me all these years because they were just that, *your* little affairs. Oh, I guess there was an ego thing at first, but you'd be surprised how quickly that went away. They were your affairs, your sleaziness. But now, for what reason I still don't know, you're making them part of my life. You're forcing me to confront something I haven't wanted to confront. And I resent that very much."

"I told you," he said, "I had no choice. I had to tell you."

"Yes," she said, "let's get to that. Why? Why after all these years have you seen fit to burden me with your . . . filth? Has somebody else found you out? Has . . . wait a minute, that fat newspaperman who was here today, does it have something to do with him?"

Chapin nodded. "Yeah. You see, there's one more affair I haven't told you about yet. The woman's name was Virginia Hanson."

There was no reaction. Nothing. Obviously Thalia hadn't followed the story. It had never occurred to Chapin that there were people who weren't interested in the Virginia Hanson story.

"Am I supposed to know Miss Hanson?" Thalia was saying. "Or is it Mrs. Hanson?"

There was no way to sugar-coat it. "She was the one who was killed by an ax murderer," Chapin said. "The cocktail waitress."

"No. . . ."

"Yes. Ginny Hanson. The cocktail waitress. The one we talked about at the dinner party. The one someone did those terrible things to."

"My God, Chapin. . . ."

"I knew her for only eight months." Chapin was talking rapidly

163

now, almost as though he had memorized the script. "It was the first time in my life I was emotionally involved. I . . . I never met anyone like her before."

"A cocktail waitress?"

"She wasn't like that," Chapin said. "Not like you think. She was very bright. She. . . . Look, that's not important. The thing is, I was with her the night she was killed."

"I don't believe this. I simply don't believe it."

"The whole world's going to know tomorrow so you might as well believe it tonight. That O'Malley, that reporter, somehow stumbled across the fact that I was seeing her. He knows the whole thing, he knows I was with her that night, and Greg tells me he won't listen to reason. He's going to print it, he's going to print the story in tomorrow's paper."

"It's going to be in the *Islander*?"

"Unless I miss my guess, it's going to be all over the *Islander*. And that's not the worst. Greg is pretty sure I'm going to be a suspect, maybe even *the* suspect. The police are going to think I killed her."

"No!"

"Christ knows what it's going to do to us, to my career . . . everything."

"Did you?"

"Did I what?"

"Did you kill her?"

Everybody's favorite question, he thought. "My God, Thal, don't you know me at all?"

"How can you ask me that tonight?" she said. "Chapin, we've never even tried to know each other."

He didn't answer her. "I think it'd be a good idea for you and the boys to go to your mother's place until all this blows over," he said. "I can guarantee that when tomorrow's paper comes out, all hell's going to break loose around here. I want you to know, Thal, I won't blame you for anything you decide to do—not anything."

"You probably believe that," Thalia said. "I'll let the boys visit my parents but I want you to talk this over with them first."

"You're not going to make me do that, are you, Thal? Couldn't you . . . tell them?"

"They're your *sons*, Chapin, it's got to come from you."

"But how do you tell your sons something like that?"

"You haven't had much trouble telling your wife."

"Christ, Thal, they're just kids."

"There's one thing you could tell them."

"What?"

x

164

"You could tell them the truth."

"Couldn't I just tell them that Ginny was a mutual friend of ours? Maybe you could—"

"They'll read differently in the newspaper, Chapin. My God, it'll probably even be on television. No—no subterfuges this time, Senator. No press releases. Not even a 'no comment.' Not with your own sons."

"I can't," he said.

"The truth," she said. "You'll have to tell them the truth."

Chapin Hope looked at his wife's dimly visible profile in the darkness of their bedroom. "Thal," he said, "I don't know how to tell the truth."

It was a final admission. He got undressed then and climbed into bed beside Thalia. He knew there would be no sleep. The truth?

"Chapin," Thalia said. "I want you to understand why I'm going to stay. One reason is the boys. I don't think we should wreck their lives at this point any more than we have to. Another is that you've supported me and my children all these years. My staying will probably be helpful to you, and I owe you that much."

"Thal—"

"No, don't touch me, Chapin," she said. "Don't do that. Not now. I couldn't—I don't want you to touch me."

"I just want to tell you what it means to me."

"Don't tell me anything," she said. "You've told me enough. Neither of us has had much practice with honesty when it comes to each other, and it's going to take some getting used to. And don't misunderstand me. I've never resented you more. And right now I want very much to get even with you. Not because you've been unfaithful but because you've dragged me into all this."

21

When Frank Cappobianco's promotion to detective came through, he was assigned to Homicide. A friend at headquarters told Cappobianco that Brownstein had asked for him. And his first day on the new assignment he was called into the Homicide chief's office.

"I hope," Brownstein said, "you don't have any illusions about this being glamorous."

"No, Lieutenant, I don't think so."

"Well, just in case you have," Brownstein said, "and to disabuse you of any such illusions, I think we'll let you start out on the Hanson case. You were in the apartment that night and I'm sure you recall the situation."

"Yes, I do."

The new detective would recall that night the rest of his life. During his first weeks, as he followed down a succession of fruitless leads, the stomach-turning specifics would come back constantly. One day, as Brownstein was showing him the photo of Chapin Hope, Cappobianco thought of another head, a head that had been left in a bathroom sink. It was difficult for him to connect the two, the face of the state senator and the head of the cocktail waitress, but he had been on the force long enough to know that anything was possible. He had arrested a father who beat a year-old infant with a belt; he had seen two drunks attempting sexual congress on the front lawn of a church; he had administered first aid to an engineering executive who tried to drown himself in a toilet bowl. He had never seen anything to equal the butchery in Virginia Hanson's apartment that night—but why shouldn't a state senator be responsible?

Now, riding on the back of a garbage truck, Cappobianco couldn't help but remember Brownstein's comment about glamour. Cappobianco and a second Homicide detective had been on the truck for a week, picking up much of the garbage in Stony Harbor and carefully analyzing the garbage from the Chapin Hope residence.

"Routine," Brownstein had told him. "It's one of those things, you never know what you'll find." Brownstein had made the arrangements with the private garbage collector who served Stony Harbor, a man who had no objections: "Considering it's free labor, I won't even ask why." The only protest had come from the village police chief, who seemed to resent Brownstein's appearance in his community.

"I don't like the idea of people poking around in our residents' garbage," he had told Brownstein.

"We're not people. We're police."

"It's still an invasion of privacy," the chief said.

"And what in hell are you?" Brownstein said. "A police officer or a private guard?"

"Well, you haven't even told me what the case is," the police chief said. "I'd like to know if any of our residents are involved in criminal activities. Why don't you just tell me what's going on?"

"Take my word for it, Chief, you're better off if you don't know. And don't worry, if anything comes of this, we'll credit you with giving our department your full cooperation."

The chief had agreed but that first day on the truck Cappobianco noticed an unmarked car tagging along behind them. He recognized the driver as a young guy he had seen at the village hall the day they had talked to the chief, a local cop named Walsh. Cappobianco stopped at the first pay phone and called Brownstein; within ten minutes a police car pulled up beside Walsh's car and that was the last they saw of him.

Even the garbage was different in Stony Harbor. Tab cans and biscuit tins and copies of the *National Review*. Empty food containers bearing the Gristede's and S. S. Pierce labels. The whiskey bottles were all the good stuff—Johnnie Walker and Beefeater and Jack Daniel's. Cappobianco's practical streak rebelled at the sight of discarded clothes that could still be mended and worn, toys and appliances thrown out prematurely. Even the food leavings—partially spoiled fruit, vegetable leftovers, pieces of untouched roast beef and ham—reflected the superabundance of the community, the American dream come true.

It was hardly surprising the people in surrounding communities found uses for Stony Harbor's refuse. The truck's regular route ended at the town dump, where burnable garbage was put on the incinerator conveyer belt and the rest of the trash was pushed into piles and later bulldozed into the earth. The piles of refuse scattered across the sandy dips and plains of the dump attracted humans as well as ants. As he watched people poking through the trash, Cappobianco envisioned archaeologists of the future attempting to re-create twentieth-century suburbia through its artifacts. What would they make of the toaster casings, the play-gym chains, the

Tinkertoy remnants of broken barbecue grills, the rusting hulks that once were mowers, lawn sweepers, and motorized edgers? What of the broken Barbie dolls, the bed springs, the television cabinets?

Cappobianco watched the people ferreting among the mounds and he wondered whether anything would be left for the archaeologists. Some were professional scavengers who came with their own pickup trucks. A man wearing a beard and denim outfit was a local sculptor who worked in junk. But most of the people searching through the piles were hunting for their own creature comforts. That first day, as Cappobianco was studying the movements of a Puerto Rican family through the midden, the father suddenly came across a pair of battered work shoes and he held them up in triumph.

The truck driver had been told that his two new assistants were police officers; the other thing he had been told was not to ask any questions. The two detectives worked the back of the truck, heaving the garbage from the curbside cans onto the truck floor, where it was compacted by hydraulic rams. Four different times along the route they asked the driver to stop the machinery and pull over to the side of the road, allowing them to scan the refuse before it was compacted. Three of the stops were camouflage; the only one that mattered was the one that followed the Hope pickup.

During the first week there had been nothing solid. The sole item worth noting had been an empty Chivas Regal bottle. And on this day, as they tossed Hope's garbage into the truck, Cappobianco spotted a second empty Chivas bottle. The fact that Chivas seemed to be Hope's brand and also the brand favored by the Hanson killer may not have been evidence but it was the sort of small detail that helped fill in background spaces.

Then Cappobianco noticed a paper bag lying beside a black-currant-jelly jar and he grabbed it up. The minute he looked inside the bag, he sensed that he had something. It was not the first item of clothing found in Hope's garbage—there had been a torn pair of boy's Levi's and a Shetland sweater frayed at elbows and cuffs. But neither of these had been stuffed into a bag and both had been put out on trash days, not on days given over to the collection of noninflammable garbage. Cappobianco held the trousers by the waist and allowed them to unroll. They were men's trousers and they were in perfect condition. Almost perfect condition. There was a small stain, just a smudge, really a small dark spot of irregular contours that may or may not have been blood.

"I guess we've got something to show the lieutenant," Cappobianco said.

22

O'Malley was typing as he always did, on the attack, his short stubby fingers punishing the typewriter. The sidebars were in the bank and there was just the main story to complete. It would be typed one more time, no more, and then it would be done. As he sat there, hitting at the machine, a deskman who had been getting the story one take at a time counted out the major headline (SUFFOLK POLITICO DATED AX VICTIM) and a news editor was adding the "bug" reserved for potentially prizewinning stories ("Copyright, the *Daily Islander*").

State Sen. Chapin Kirk Hope of Stony Harbor, one of Long Island's most respected legislators and a quiet power in the Republican hierarchy, was revealed yesterday to be a suspect in the ax murder of red-haired cocktail waitress Virginia Hanson.

The forty-year-old lawmaker, married and the father of two children, had been seeing the attractive twenty-five-year-old divorcée for several months prior to the killing and was with her only hours before she was hacked to death in her Mineola apartment.

The senator's involvement in the case—described by authorities as one of the most brutal murders in Long Island's history—was uncovered by the *Daily Islander* in the course of an investigation into Hope's political activities and associations. (See story on page 3.)

Meanwhile, it was learned, police have also been looking into the six-term legislator's connection with the slain woman. Det. Lt. Charles Brownstein, head of Nassau's Homicide division, concedes that such an investigation is being made but refuses to elaborate.

During an interview at his Stony Harbor home yesterday Hope refused to discuss the Hanson case with a *Daily Islander* reporter. When asked about his involvement with the cocktail waitress, Hope phoned his law partner, noted defense attorney

Gregory Hammer, who hurried to the Hope house. Obviously upset by the *Daily Islander's* inquiry, Hammer said Hope was innocent of any crime but did not deny the senator's involvement with Miss Hanson.

"If he ever touched Virginia Hanson, and I'm not saying he did," said Hammer, a longtime friend of the senator and the best man at Hope's wedding, "it was in love, not in anger."

The relationship between Suffolk Republicanism's Mr. Clean and the red-haired waitress was confirmed by several sources. Habitués of the Pumpkin, a so-called cheaters' bar where Miss Hanson was employed, identified a photograph of Hope as being "Harry"—a self-professed insurance salesman who had been coming to the bar "every week or so" for about eight months prior to the murder. They said that it was obvious "Harry" and Miss Hanson were seeing each other and that the couple left the Pumpkin together the night of the slaying. Miss Hanson returned alone several hours later as the bar was closing. She said she had just left "Harry" and that "something funny" had happened while they were together. It was shortly before 3 A.M. when Miss Hanson said good night. At 5:30 A.M. police found her chopped to death less than a mile away in her blood-drenched apartment.

In the wake of the murder, police circulated a computer-aided sketch of "Harry," who was described as a suspect. Except for a few minor details, the sketch looks like a drawing of Hope, chairman of the Senate Appropriations Committee and a conservative Republican with sufficient moderate support to have been mentioned as a possible candidate for Congress or statewide office.

Last night Lt. Brownstein refused to divulge the nature of the investigation aimed at Hope, nor would he characterize the senator's role in the case. One of the first questions police are expected to put to Hope is why he failed to come forward after the slaying—especially in light of the widely circulated "Harry" sketch.

The disclosure that "Harry" was actually a high-ranking state senator came as a surprise to friends of Miss Hanson, but not as a shock. This was especially true among regulars at the Pumpkin, where, as one patron explained, "Lots of people ain't what they seem."

People who had met "Harry" at the cheaters' bar described him as a pleasant, quietly sociable man who found it difficult to take his eyes off Virginia Hanson. They said that the miniskirted waitress repaid the attention.

"Ginny had a thing for him," said Stanley Davits, manager of the Pumpkin. Although there were no reports of the couple quarreling, their relationship bore hints of tension. Miss Hanson had told close friends that "Harry" was married, and she was known as having "a history of picking losers when it came to men." According to one informed source, "Harry" may have been another loser. "She really cared for him," said the source, "but she thought he was too intense. . . ."

O'Malley finished typing the main story, carried the last page to the copydesk, then went back to his own desk and opened the drawer and reached for the bottle. At midnight, when it was too late for the *Times* and the *News* to get the story, too late for *Newsday* and the *Press* to do a quick rewrite, he put in a call to Brownstein.

"Brownie, I hope I didn't wake you," he said. "But I thought you ought to know—we're going with the story tomorrow."

"We're not ready to move yet," the homicide chief said. "It's too soon. Why don't you hold off the story until—"

"If it was up to me, I would," O'Malley said. "But there's no way to hold it back now. This has become Custer's special project and he says we're going with it, no matter what. I just thought you might want me to read it over the phone. . . ."

"Bob, do me this favor, bring it over here. I want to see what you've got."

Barely a half hour later Brownstein was sitting back thumbing through the carbons of a half-dozen stories. There was an interview with an aunt, Brigid Grady, and the neighbor, Roland Feebe. There was the main news story, an article that would begin on page one, jump to page three, jump back to both pages of a double truck, where it would be featured along with side-by-side photos of the original police sketch and the senator. There was a second major story headlined, HOPE'S RECORD: POLITICS FOR PROFIT, and this was preceded by an editor's note describing it as the first part of a four-part series. The initial article explored "Sen. Hope's remarkably profitable two-way relationship with the banks." Further articles, it was promised, would "deal with the senator's performance of favors for the dairymen's lobby, his involvement in land deals, his association with mob figures."

"Well," Brownstein said, "this makes pretty good reading."

"I wonder what that means," O'Malley said.

"I'm not going to con you, Bob—we've known each other too long for that, for politeness. You've got some fascinating stuff on Hope there. All that you don't happen to have is a case that will

171

stand up in court. Neither do we. We're coming pretty close to it, but when this comes out in print tomorrow, we may never get Hope.''

As Brownstein went back to the stories one last time, O'Malley picked up his freshly poured cup of tea, took a sip, made a face, put it down on the coffee table. Brownstein thought once again that O'Malley would have made a good cop. Not that he would admit this to the reporter, but the Homicide chief was impressed by the amount of digging that went into the story chronicling the senator's financial wheelings. The murder story was the flashier of the two, the story that would get all the attention, but it was the other story that was the most impressive. Secretly Brownstein wondered how anyone could get the facts—the dollars and cents—without having a badge to flash.

There was something else that impressed Brownstein: how much easier it was for a reporter to reach his goal than it was for a cop to do the same. All the information that made such spicy reading would make inadequate evidence. It was the great difference between journalism and justice; it was easier to bring implications into print than into court, easier to convict a man with words than with evidence.

"This is pretty strong stuff," Brownstein said.

"Well, you've been fair with us," O'Malley said. "I just wanted you to know ahead of time that they decided to run with it; I figured you might want to be ready when Galton jumps all over you tomorrow."

"I appreciate that—and I'm impressed by your grasp of our district attorney's character."

"He's an asshole."

"Now, now, Bob, you're talking about our chief law-enforcement officer." In spite of himself, Brownstein laughed. "But I must confess, you writers do have a way with words. Still, there is a point or two I might quibble with in your story, if you're interested."

"Go ahead."

"Well, right in the beginning here, where you say the senator was revealed as a 'suspect.' You don't say who revealed him or even who it is that considers him to be a suspect. It seems to me you may be opening yourself up for something. . . ."

"Yeah, Custer checked that out with the libel guy and he said it would be okay, that a person can be a suspect without being arraigned."

"Something bothers me here toward the end of the story. You have an 'informed source' telling you what Miss Hanson was thinking, that whole business about Harry being a loser. Who was she?"

"Who said it was a she?"

"I'm assuming that much from the language," Brownstein said. "It's not the kind of observation that most men would make. Unless, of course, it was Feebe. . . ."

"Brownie, I'll level with you. It was just some broad at the Pumpkin."

"Bob, you're still holding back on me."

"Scout's honor."

"I find the thought that you may have been a Boy Scout vaguely terrifying," Brownstein said. "Who was she?"

"Okay," O'Malley said, "but do me a favor and try to hold down the righteous wrath. It was Charlotte. Look, Brownie, she called me and we set up a meeting. I had to agree not to bring anyone along."

"Righteous wrath is an understatement," Brownstein said after letting out a long breath. "I should be furious. I've had men looking all over the place for her. What else did she have to say?"

"Not much," O'Malley said. "And I still don't even have a last name."

"The reason I'm not chewing you out, Bob, is that I appreciate your coming here tonight. But we've got to cooperate. If she calls you again, we've got to know. Is that understood?"

"Understood."

"Fine. Now let's get back to your story. There's another point. Back here, here you have me being strangely uncooperative: 'Last night Lt. Brownstein refused to divulge the nature of the investigation aimed at Hope, nor would he characterize the senator's role in the case.' It seems to me that you're taking liberties without even asking me about it."

It was O'Malley's turn to smile.

"Let me ask you," he said, "and this is for the record, Brownie—what kind of investigation have you been running and how would you characterize the senator's role in the case?"

"Now, Bob," he said, "you know I can't comment on something like that."

The truth was that Brownstein was not particularly upset by the story's appearance. He knew it was coming. Even when he had cautioned O'Malley not to mention the Hanson case in his interview with Hope, he suspected that the warning would be useless. By the time he was ready to join his wife in bed Brownstein was feeling that the story might even be useful. It was time—past time—to call Hope in for direct questioning, but he had lacked enough evidence

173

to make an arrest; now the story would provide him with an excuse for speaking with the senator.

The following morning Brownstein learned he would need no excuse to contact the senator. Soon after he arrived at his desk, he received a phone call from L. Gregory Hammer. Hammer explained that he was calling as Chapin Hope's attorney.

"I guess," Brownstein said, "that we both read the same story."

"What story?"

"In the *Islander*."

"I haven't seen the paper today," Hammer said. "It doesn't get out here until noon or so—but we suspected they would run something. Senator Hope just wanted to let you know that he was available to clear up any misunderstandings."

"Tell him we're glad you called," Brownstein said. "In light of the story, it would seem to make sense for us to get together."

"I'm sure you realize that the story is pure character assassination. It's an obvious smear—but I'm sure that kind of yellow journalism outrages you as much as it does me."

"I thought you hadn't seen it. . . ."

"We haven't," Hammer said. "But we spoke to that fellow O'Malley yesterday and we both have a pretty good idea what we're up against."

"That's not my province, counselor," Brownstein answered. "I'm simply conducting a murder investigation."

"Of course. Of course. The senator realizes that, Chief, and he wants to cooperate in any way he can."

"Let's say between one thirty and two o'clock."

"Fine," Hammer said. "Uh, just so we understand each other, I hope you're not taking any of the insinuations in that scandal sheet seriously."

"I hope this won't sound too pompous, counselor, but we don't deal in insinuations over here. We still deal in facts. One fact we're pretty well sure of is that the senator was involved with the murder victim. Maybe he'll have some information that will help lead us to the murderer."

"My client will of course cooperate fully," the lawyer said. "Of course he's innocent. We know you want to solve this case and we'll try to give you whatever information we can. There's a killer loose, a madman apparently, and if we can help bring him to justice, so much the better. You'll see, Chief, that we have nothing to hide, absolutely nothing."

174

"One thirty, then?"

"That sounds fine," Hammer said. "I take it Norm will be there?"

"The district attorney's office will be notified."

As soon as Brownstein put the phone down, it rang again. Cappobianco was on the line. They had found something, a pair of trousers with a stain that could be blood, and they thought they should take them right to the lab. Brownstein said he was thinking right and after putting the phone back, he looked toward the ceiling. He was reminded of a rabbinical student he had known in the Army; they had been playing poker together on a troop train and the rabbi-to-be had just filled an inside straight. "Jesus Christ," he had shouted, "there *is* a God!" If the stain was blood, the victim's blood, it would restore Brownstein's faith as well—you keep peeling and chipping and sooner or later something shows through.

His mood was shattered by a third call, this one from District Attorney Norman Galton's assistant, Chuck Ferris.

"Damn it, Brownstein," he began, "I've been trying to reach you all morning."

"I tried to call Norman earlier," Brownstein said, "but there was no one in his office. I thought that the district attorney would want to know that Chapin Hope is coming in for questioning today—he's a suspect in the Hanson case."

"What's going on here, Brownstein?" Ferris was yelling into the phone. "What the hell are you trying to pull?"

"I'm not following all this, Chuck."

"Don't try to bull me," Ferris said. "Don't you think we read the papers? Why haven't you notified the district attorney before? Or didn't you think he'd be interested in the fact that you've got a state senator tied in to an ax murder?"

"I'm sure he'd have been *interested*, Chuck, but I don't know that any other purpose would be served. There was no reason for me to contact your office until we had a definite suspect and the possibility of an arrest. I'm sure you're aware that with any other suspect we would have conducted a preliminary interrogation before asking you people to sit in. In this case, I was calling you so that an assistant district attorney can be here from the start."

Ferris forced his voice back to normal.

"Well, let's try to cooperate on this from now on."

"That's fine with us," Brownstein said. "I've asked Hope's attorney, Gregory Hammer, to have him here between one thirty and two."

"I wish you would let us know before you set up anything else.

175

The district attorney is very busy with his welfare-cheat investigation, but I'm sure that he'll want to be there in person. He'll also want to go over the case with you beforehand.''

"Fine. If he doesn't have any lunch appointments, tell him to come by around twelve thirty. We can order sandwiches.''

23

Nassau County District Attorney Norman Galton stopped to admire his reflection in the well-waxed limousine that the county provided for his official use. The car had begun life as just another black Cadillac, but at Galton's instructions it had been ennobled with twin golden seals of office, a two-way police radio, a telephone, a portable bar, a siren, blinking red lights, and four American flags—two mounted on the front and two mounted aft.

Trailed as always by Chuck Ferris, Galton slid into the backseat of the limousine. The moment the door was closed, the car began to move from its reserved parking place and the four small flags stirred with the motion.

"Do you want the flasher?" the driver said.

"No, I'm just going home, Al," Galton said. "You can take it easy."

Before keeping his appointment with Brownstein, District Attorney Galton had to do something very important. He had to go home and change clothes. As he left the car to go into his house, he turned to Ferris.

"The new suit?"

"Why not?" his assistant said. "The TV people are sure to be around."

Galton enjoyed the preparation. He showered and shaved for the second time that morning. His black hair was brushed flat with twin military brushes until not a single hair was out of line. Galton knew that his slicked-down, parted-in-the-middle hair would never be considered stylish. The year before, he had let his hair grow longer and had it styled. Chuck Ferris had taken one look and laughed his dry laugh and that had been Norman Galton's last flirtation with modishness. As always, Ferris had been right. This way he looked harder, tougher, more the old-line prosecutor—a man more interested in substance than appearance. Which was ironic because Galton knew that substance was minor, that nothing was more important than appearance. The whole concern with hair was proof—he was creating the *appearance* of a man unconcerned with appearance.

His costume was chosen with equal attention to detail. When he had been looking at suits a week earlier, Galton had tried on several of the new Italian styles with pinched waists and flared lapels, but had finally selected a black, pin-striped suit with slightly squared shoulders. The shirt was pale blue, a color that photographed well on television. His one concession to his own inner taste was the tie, a red-and-blue foulard from Bloomingdale's men's department. He put on his horn-rimmed glasses and returned downstairs to the car.

"That's a hell of a tie," Ferris said.

"Don't tell me there's something wrong with this tie?"

"It's very impressive," Ferris said.

"It cost fifteen dollars," Galton said, "it should be impressive."

"It's very pretty," said Ferris, whose own sartorial style could be described as Rotary conservative.

"By that you mean it's too pretty?"

"Now that you mention it," Ferris said, "it just might be."

"Well, I like it," Galton said. Then he changed the subject. "Chapin Hope! I still don't believe it. I guarantee you one thing, we're going to straighten out Brownstein. Why in the hell didn't he bring us into this right away?"

"Who knows?" Ferris said. "Maybe he things you're too political."

"That no-politics stuff is crap. That kind of thinking means just one thing to me; it means Brownstein will never be district attorney of Nassau County. This really galls me. That snotty son of a bitch—who does he think he is?"

The drive back to the county center was accomplished in silence, a silence that did not indicate any lack of harmony between the two men. Quite the opposite. This was a partnership of some duration and, as in any good match, words had become less than essential. Galton and Ferris used words simply to underscore the obvious. What ensured the success of the relationship was their shared assumption that one day, with everything breaking right, Norman Galton would be elected governor of New York State. Or United States Senator. Or even—why not?—President of the United States.

Brownstein had waited fifteen minutes and then had eaten a sandwich at his desk. When Galton and Ferris showed up at the squad room a half hour late, the Homicide chief offered to send out for something.

"Nothing for me," said Ferris, a lean man who was one of the stars of the annual prosecutors-defense lawyers softball game. "I'm staying in shape for squash."

"Nor for me," the district attorney said. "I'm trying to drop a few pounds. I'll tell you, Brownie, I saw myself on television the other night and I didn't recognize myself. Half the trouble is that I'm always photographed standing next to Chuck here and the contrast is too much. If he doesn't start to fatten himself up, I'm going to have to hire a new assistant—a flabby one."

Ferris smiled with his lips, but Brownstein did not even reward Galton's efforts with the trace of a grin. The Homicide chief knew he had just been subjected to one of the basic opening gambits in a politician's repertoire—the old self-deprecation *shtick*. He was expected to play along, to deny Galton's plumpness, to laugh along with the overbearing jackass. Or to make a remark about himself that would be denied in turn. Brownstein said nothing.

"Well, then," Galton said. "What Chuck and I would like to know, basically, is just what the fuck has been going on around here?"

"If you've seen the *Islander*, you know almost as much as I do," Brownstein said.

"Oh?" Galton said. "Well, then I didn't read the paper closely enough. I didn't see anything explaining why the chief of Nassau County's Homicide Division failed to notify the district attorney that he suspected a state senator of chopping up a cocktail waitress. Was that in there somewhere and I just missed it? For Christ's sake, Brownie, it seems to me that at some point someone somewhere should have asked themselves, 'Why don't we let the district attorney know about this?' "

Ferris' smile pleased Galton. He could always tell when he had done something properly by the way Ferris reacted.

"I think, Norman, the answer to your question should be clear. We didn't have enough—"

"Brownie, I don't want to hear your answer. I know you're a good cop, and I know you're going to have a good excuse. But that's all it'll be—an excuse. The truth is that the minute you heard the name Chapin Hope—and I don't care whether it was in connection with butchering a broad or shoplifting at Macy's—the minute his name came up, you should have gotten hold of me. You didn't do that, and there's no excuse. So don't try to give me any."

Brownstein looked over at Ferris, who was staring at a Wyeth print on the far wall as though the conversation was of no particular interest to him. The only indication that he had heard a word was that tight smile of his. Here we go again, Brownstein thought, and he tried to keep his voice even as he answered. "Look, Norman, I've already pointed out to Chuck that there was no procedural reason for me to notify you. If you'd like me to repeat the lecture, I'm more than willing."

"Take it easy, Brownie. I just think you should have told me. I mean, Chapin Hope! Do you know how long I've known Chapin? I can't count the number of political affairs we've been to together. Frankly I can't even picture him screwing a cocktail waitress."

"We share your difficulty," Brownstein said. "It's not easy to connect a man like Hope with a crime of such violence. But that very fact is one reason to suspect Hope."

"I'm not sure I follow you."

"Well, exactly what type of person does one see chopping up a good-looking young woman? It's not a common killing, and my guess is that we won't find a common killer."

"So what *do* you think—do *you* think it was Hope?"

"At this point I would have to say yes. It's a qualified yes, but he is our only suspect. Let's say I think it *could* be Hope, but I'm not sure. The fact of the matter is that he was indeed carrying on with the murdered woman. He was carrying on an affair with her for several months; he was using an alias and living a double life and probably doing many other things that no one in this room would have felt him capable of. And all this financial wheeling and dealing that's coming out now. . . ."

"But what've we got on him?"

The *we* made Brownstein smile. He knew what he had, and he knew what Galton had. What he had was evidence that might be described as flimsy—incriminating, perhaps, but flimsy. What Galton had was an insatiable appetite for higher office and headlines.

"Our evidence is slim, Norman."

"Add it up for me."

"I'm waiting for a lab report right now that may alter the situation," Brownstein said. "What we can talk about now may sound better here than it would sound in a courtroom. One, we know he'd been seeing Virginia Hanson for quite a while. Two, Virginia Hanson led an active sex life and was probably once a prostitute. Three, we're certain he was with her until nearly three o'clock the night of the murder, and we have a witness who will place him inside her apartment that night. Four, there's the fact of his never coming forward to identify himself—not even after his sketch appeared in the paper."

"It sounds sexy, Brownie," Galton said. "But what we need is some hard evidence, something a prosecutor can wave in front of a jury. How about the weapon, the ax?"

"Nothing yet," Brownstein said. "Moreover, we're just assuming it's an ax. According to the coroner, it could also have been a butcher's cleaver or something similar. So far, no weapon. Of course, we haven't searched Hope's house yet either."

"You said something about a lab report."

"We're waiting on one right now," Brownstein said. "We've got a pair of the senator's trousers with a possible bloodstain on them. We know that Miss Hanson and Hope have different types of blood—if it's Miss Hanson's type, then we're in business."

"How did you come up with—"

"We've been going through his garbage for the past week. He was throwing the trousers away."

"Garbage?" the district attorney said. "You've been going through a man's garbage?"

When Chapin Hope and Gregory Hammer arrived at the squad room, Norman Galton greeted each of them with his two-handed handshake. Chapin was starting to feel the lack of sleep, a burning sensation behind the eyes, but his mind was never more alert. The austerity of the squad room—drab aqua walls, plain wooden chairs, scarred table and desks—depressed him, emphasizing, as it did, that he was very much the outsider here. His eyes moved from Brownstein to Ferris to Galton and stopped there. Galton put his hand on Chapin's shoulder and guided him over to the corner of the room.

"This is a hell of a mess, Norm," Chapin said. "A hell of a mess."

"I couldn't be sorrier," Galton said. "I hate to put anyone through this. And a friend—I'll promise you this, Chape, my office will give you every consideration."

"I know you will, Norm, and I won't forget it."

Almost reluctantly the two men walked back toward Brownstein and their roles in the drama that followed. It was a strange drama in that the two principal figures, Galton and Hope, remained silent while the secondary players exchanged the lines. The final figure, Ferris, crew-cut and brown-suited, remained a prop. Brownstein was in his usual working clothes—white shirt, dark tie, trousers, and shoes. Set against him, Hammer seemed to be garbed in neon; he, like Galton, had dressed for the cameras—blue-striped, French-cuffed shirt, bright blue tie, and maroon blazer.

As he sat down, Chapin thought that as far as his career and marriage were concerned, there was nothing Galton could do to help. The damage had been done. All that remained to be determined was the extent of the damage. As he listened to Greg and the detective—the Homicide chief, Brownstein, he had read about in the papers—Chapin realized that the damage might be extensive indeed.

"I want you to know that we're here to cooperate," Hammer was saying. "My client is absolutely innocent, and we're here to help you do justice. We have nothing to hide."

"I appreciate that, counselor," Brownstein said. "I couldn't ask for more." He turned to Hope. "Senator, I'd like to begin by asking you how long you knew the late Miss Hanson—"

"Excuse me just a moment, Lieutenant," Hammer said. "I've advised my client not to make any direct statements at this time. However, I believe this in no way negates what I just said. I want to assure you of our fullest cooperation and I believe that I can address myself to these matters on the senator's behalf."

"Perhaps, counselor, you had better redefine what you mean by fullest cooperation."

"My client is innocent of any crime," Hammer said, "and, of course, must take certain precautions to protect his reputation. It's that simple. But let me address myself to the question of the late Miss Hanson. Senator Hope *did* know the late Miss Hanson. The senator knows many people from all walks of life. As a politician he's in the business of knowing people. His friendship with Miss Hanson might best be described as a very casual relationship. There was nothing wrong with it at all."

"I think that'll be all," Brownstein said. "I think you two can go now."

"Just a minute, Brownie," Galton interrupted. "I'm sure the senator would like to cooperate—maybe if we got into another area—"

"I'm not especially interested in talking to Mr. Hammer," the Homicide chief said. "If the senator wants to talk to us, that's something else."

"That would have to be against my advice," Hammer said. "My client has not been indicted for any crime. In fact, you haven't told us whether or not you consider him a suspect in this case."

"Maybe I can clarify that," Brownstein said. "Right now Senator Hope is *the* suspect in this case."

"Well, then," Hammer said, "I can only conclude that you don't have a shred of real evidence or you would have indicted him. If you want to try the case in the press, that's your business. But I think it's highly likely that my client is wasting his valuable time here. Senator, our business with these gentlemen is at an end."

Chapin was not at all sure that he followed Greg's strategy; he saw no reason to anger men who held such power over him. And he was numbed by what Brownstein had said about him being *the* suspect. Despite everything that had happened, Chapin still found it difficult to accept the idea of anyone really believing him capable of . . . of slaughter. Chapin flashed Galton an apologetic look and followed Greg out the door.

"Keep cool, Chape," his partner said. "When we leave the building, we're going to walk into reporters, and I want you to look as innocent as you know how. And let me do the talking."

To Chapin Hope the media was like an army. Greg beamed as though they were being greeted by long-lost friends. He gave the television people time to set up their equipment, and then he spoke without having to pause for any reason other than effect.

"Unfortunately Senator Hope can have no comment at this time," the lawyer said. "He would like nothing better than to tell you the full story right now and set the record straight. I promise you he'll do that as soon as possible. He simply came here today to offer help to the authorities. A psychopathic killer is at large in our community, and like all law-abiding citizens, Senator Hope fervently wants him apprehended."

Greg paused and went on. "I might emphasize that Senator Hope came here voluntarily at his own insistence. He has not been indicted for anything, he has not even been accused of anything—except by your less responsible colleagues in the press, who, incidentally, may find themselves answering to the libel laws. I'm sure you have a lot of questions, but if you'll just hold them until we can deal with them, gentlemen and lady, we'll bid you good day."

Chapin tried a smile then and hoped that it would photograph better than it felt. What Greg had said about his wanting the killer apprehended was true, although his motivation went far beyond that of an ordinary law-abiding citizen. There was a homicidal monster loose, a butcher who had killed the one person in the world who was closest to him and who might be a threat to other human beings he cared about. To say that Chapin fervently wanted the murderer caught was no exaggeration, but he wondered if the "gentlemen and lady" would believe that. It was like Greg to be precise—and Chapin turned to look at the only female reporter on hand, a youthful blonde in a red coat, a familiar figure from the Channel 5 evening news. She had always seemed fresh and innocent to Hope and, as he was seeing her for the first time, she met his eyes and called out her question.

"Senator, were you sleeping with Virginia Hanson?"

"See you, fellows," Hammer said.

In the squad room Norman Galton was losing his temper for the second time in an hour.

"I have to hand it to you, Chief," he said, "you certainly handled that beautifully. You certainly got a lot of information out of him."

"What should I have done?" Brownstein said. "Look, Norman, I don't try to tell you people what to do inside a courtroom and I'd appreciate the same courtesy—"

"If I may interrupt here." It was the first time during the meeting that Ferris was more than an echo. "Lieutenant Brownstein established one thing for us. We found out what we wanted to about Hope. He did know Virginia Hanson; there's no doubt he was the 'Harry' in the case. No jury in the world is going to think. . . ."

The rest of the sentence was lost in the ring of the desk phone. It was the police laboratory reporting that the stain on the trousers was, indeed, human blood, type O. Virginia Hanson's type.

"Well, it looks like you'll have something to wave in front of a jury," Brownstein said. "The blood on the trousers matches Miss Hanson's, not Hope's."

"Great," Galton said.

"The courtroom won't be big enough to handle the reporters," Ferris said.

"I still don't know if we have enough to make an arrest," Galton said.

"You could let a grand jury do it for you," Ferris said.

"Why don't you let me set up a walk-through? We could bring in an indictment the day after tomorrow."

"I wish there was more evidence," Brownstein said.

"I thought you liked the trousers," Ferris said.

"I do, except apparently there's just the one small stain, not what you would expect if you had seen the apartment that night. Of course, he could have committed the murder itself while they were both naked and then gotten dressed—which could explain why the pants weren't splattered with blood. One thing I will do is get somebody out there with a search warrant as soon as possible to go through the house."

"Don't worry about evidence," Galton said. "Have you ever seen a grand jury in operation? They don't need evidence. They're going to love this one, they're going to eat this one up. Chuck, put in a call to the chief of the Indictment Bureau and tell him we want to walk this thing through tomorrow. Then get me Hammer and I'll tell him to bring in Hope tomorrow."

"What makes you think he'll testify?" Brownstein asked.

"I'm betting that Hope will figure he can't afford not to," Galton
184

said. "And we'll get the indictment either way. Look, Brownie, what were you telling me before? Weren't you saying something about you doing your job and me doing mine?"

By the time Galton was on the phone with Hammer the district attorney had softened his voice.

"Yeah, Greg, that's right, we all know Brownie can get a little uptight"—the district attorney winked broadly in the direction of the Homicide chief—"yeah, it's the Irish in him. Listen, Greg, something has turned up. The chief has come up with something new, and I think we've got a case against the senator. In any event, we're going to send it to the grand jury. No, I can't tell you what it is. No. Sorry. Brownie doesn't want me to say. We're giving it to the grand jury tomorrow. Right. Have Senator Hope here at one o'clock."

As Galton put down the telephone, he couldn't hold back the smile. Beautiful. He could almost taste the case, a case that would be reported everywhere—not just in the *Islander* but in the New York *Times*, not just on Channel 67 but maybe even on the networks. And waiting for him now, waiting just outside was a crowd of reporters. Before going out, Galton turned to his assistant one last time.

"Chuck," he said, "if you don't mind, why don't we trade ties? This one seems just a trifle . . . splashy."

24

Greg Hammer and Chapin Hope had been allowed to use a private elevator in case any members of the press were around the building. Then they spent five minutes in a futile search for comfort on a wooden bench just outside the grand jury chamber.

"What in the hell are they waiting for?" Chapin asked.

Before Greg could answer, the door beside the bench opened and a man wearing a dark business suit appeared.

"Mr. Hope, the grand jury would like to see you now."

As he got up, Chapin glanced at Greg, who shrugged in mock resignation. He had advised Chapin not to testify. "There's no point to it," Greg had said. "It's six of one, a half dozen of the other that you'll get indicted whether you testify or not."

"At least they'll hear the truth," Chapin said. "I didn't kill Ginny, and I'll tell them so. Maybe then the cops'll wake up and start looking for the real killer."

"That's wonderful, that's really going to impress them. Chrissakes, Chape, how many times do I have to tell you that truth doesn't mean a damn thing? Besides, you should know enough about the law to know that a grand jury is a prosecutor's forum. Hell, I'm not even allowed to go in there with you. This is the DA's game—he's playing in his ballpark, and it's even his ball. Chape, he can have you indicted by tomorrow if he wants to. He can move that quickly."

"But if I don't testify, it looks bad."

"Bullshit. You were *invited* to testify, not ordered. You don't have to show."

"So then he'd subpoena me."

"Never. It gets technical, but the fact is that grand juries rarely subpoena defendants. In New York if a grand jury subpoenas the target of an investigation, he can't be prosecuted. Not unless he signs a waiver of immunity."

"Okay," Chapin said, "look at it the other way. What harm can I do by going in?"

186

"Not much, except that they can use your testimony against you at a trial."

"I still want to do it."

"You still don't realize that I'm the lawyer, do you, Chape? Maybe you *should* testify. Maybe that'll be the lesson you need."

"Maybe you're the one who needs the lesson, Greg. Maybe I'll be able to show you that people still do listen to people."

"I only wish I could go in there with you," Greg said. "I only wish I could be there when you convince them of your innocence. I'm sure it's going to be a stirring moment and I hate to miss it."

As he walked into the grand jury room, Chapin began to sense what his partner had been talking about. The very architecture of the room emphasized who was in control. It was the kind of room that might be used for staging cockfights.

The room had been constructed vertically instead of horizontally. The witness sat at the base of the room beside the court reporter, and rising directly in front of him were the benches holding the twenty-three members of the grand jury. And up at the very top of the room—Hope had to tilt his head back to see him—was a young man he didn't recognize, an assistant district attorney with a sharpness to his features, Kip Farnsworth. Galton had surrounded himself with lean and angular young men, almost all of whom were Republicans. Normally that fact might have comforted Chapin, but there was nothing in Farnsworth's face that he could identify with—the young man looked about as compassionate as a knife edge.

"I'll be with you in a minute, Mr. Hope." The microphone in front of the assistant district attorney amplified his words into small explosions. "Just another moment or two and we'll be with you."

Hope turned to the court reporter at the desk beside his. "Christ," he whispered, "they really stick pins into you around here."

The man's eyes registered shock and as Chapin heard the rumble of laughter from above, he realized that the microphone in front of him had been left on and had magnified his whisper into every corner of the room. He was thankful that Greg wasn't there to enjoy his embarrassment.

Why should he be so nervous? These were his people. The grand jury was just as Greg had predicted it would be. Not a single black, not a single sweater, not a single beard, only an occasional sideburn. The grand jurors were white, elderly, most of them well into their retirement. They were conservative in appearance, but they had all dressed for the occasion. Several of the women wore hats and the men all wore neckties. It had to be an event. A grand jury could function with just thirteen members present, and attend-

187

ance varied from day to day. But everyone had shown up for Chapin Hope—for the chance to see a state senator who might have murdered his girlfriend. And as he examined them, Chapin realized that they were looking at him that way. They were looking at him as if he were Jack the Ripper.

"Mr. Hope, if we may proceed now." Farnsworth's voice was resonant and sure of itself. "If the foreman will swear in the witness."

The first steps were dry and mechanical, devoid of surprise. The giving of the oath. The taking of name, address, occupation. Chapin looked up at the grand jury steadily; perhaps a steady gaze would be seen as a sign of innocence.

"Mr. Hope," the assistant district attorney began, "did you kill Virginia Hanson with an ax or a similar instrument on or about November eleventh of last year?"

"No, I didn't," Hope said. "I could never have—"

"A yes or no will suffice," said his interrogator. "Now, you understand that you are not required to testify here, that you have voluntarily agreed to appear."

"Yes."

"And I'm assuming that you also understand that we may get into areas here that we would not explore in a courtroom."

"I've been so instructed."

"I think it only fair to tell you that it is not our business here to determine your innocence or your guilt. Our sole business here is to determine whether there should be a trial or not. Whatever is said here is said in complete confidence. Our purpose here is to arrive at the truth, and we can best do that if we have your complete cooperation."

"I'm happy to have the chance to set the record straight."

"Fine. Now, let's start at the beginning." The resonance in the young man's voice was really quite remarkable. "Did you know the late Virginia Hanson?"

"Yes, I did."

"Was she, in point of fact, your mistress?"

"Pardon me?"

"Perhaps I'm not speaking clearly. Let me repeat the question. Was the late Virginia Hanson your mistress?"

"No, she wasn't."

"No?" Farnsworth said. "Mr. Hope, I feel I must remind you that you've just sworn an oath to tell the truth in this chamber and that oath is just as binding here as it would be in a courtroom. You can be held for perjury here just as—"

"I think I know what a mistress is and she was not my mistress.

188

A mistress is someone . . . uh, someone whose bills you pay, someone you keep."

"We appreciate the lesson in semantics, Mr. Hope." The young man's voice was well suited for sarcasm. "We may save a lot of time here if you just describe your relationship with the late Miss Hanson as completely as you know how."

Chapin Hope took a deep breath and looked at the faces skewering him from above. There was a peculiar intensity to the silence in the room. There was no throat clearing, no rustling of paper. There was just dead silence. "We're waiting for your answer, Mr. Hope."

"This isn't easy," Chapin said. "I'm going to have to ask the people in this room to forget their preconceptions and prejudices and—"

"Please address yourself to the question, Mr. Hope. Would you just describe your relationship with Miss Hanson in any terms you like?"

"Yes, of course," he said. "I . . . we . . . were lovers."

"You were lovers," the young man said, "but she was not your mistress?"

"The word 'mistress' is all wrong," Chapin said. "It's connotations are wrong. Miss Hanson and I . . . well, we loved each other." As he said it, he knew he sounded fatuous. And he wished he had said it to Ginny.

"I see," Farnsworth said. "That's very poetic. Tell me, Mr. Hope, you are married, am I right?"

"Yes."

"You were and are living with your wife?"

"Yes."

"I mean, you're not separated or considering a separation?"

"No."

"And you have two children?"

"Yes."

"And yet you were meeting with Miss Hanson in a clandestine manner."

"It wasn't clandestine," Chapin said. "I met her at her place of business and we'd talk."

"Oh, yes, her place of business. Is that the Pumpkin?"

"Yes."

"What sort of a place would you say that is?"

"It's a cocktail lounge."

"I suppose you could call it a bar?"

"I suppose so."

"As a matter of fact, Mr. Hope, isn't it known as a so-called cheaters' bar? A place where men and women pick each other up? A place where married people, especially men, cheat on their spouses?''

"I really wouldn't know about that."

"But you did meet Miss Hanson there?"

"Yes."

"Now, maybe you can tell us what the name 'Harry' means to you?"

"That was a joke between Ginny, between Miss Hanson and myself. She called me Harry and I called her Gertrude."

"And that was a joke?"

"That's exactly what it was."

"Are you telling us that you didn't use the name Harry as an alias? You didn't introduce yourself around that bar, the Pumpkin, as an insurance man named Harry?"

"Yes, but it was partly a joke."

"Partly?"

"Well, uh, I am a state senator."

"Yes, you are, aren't you, Mr. Hope. Now, let's move on to another area. Perhaps you could tell us how often you were seeing Miss Hanson."

"When I was on the Island, once a week, even twice. Less often other times."

"And on those occasions were you intimate?"

Words, Chapin thought. He and Ginny could be intimate when they were standing on opposite sides of a room. "Intimate?"

"I'll be more specific," Farnsworth said. "Did you have sexual relations?"

"Yes. Uh, maybe not every time, but usually."

"And did Miss Hanson ever attempt to blackmail you?"

"Blackmail me?"

"Did Miss Hanson ever attempt to blackmail you on the basis of your having repeated sexual relations with her?"

"Of course not. She wasn't that kind of person."

"Oh? Do you know what kind of person she was? Are you familiar with her background?"

"I knew all I had to know. I knew she was a fine person."

"I'm sure she was. But did you know that you were one in a long string of married men? Did you know that Virginia Hanson was once a prostitute?"

"That's a lie!"

"I think we can show otherwise, Mr. Hope," the young man said. "But at any rate, you insist that Virginia Hanson never tried to blackmail you in any way. Did you ever give her large sums of

190

money for any reason whatsoever?''

"No, I did not. She would never take a penny from me."

"Well, perhaps we're quibbling over words again. Are you telling us that you never arranged for Virginia Hanson to receive a sizable loan from Federated Security? That you never cosigned that loan? That you didn't recently pay off that loan, a loan for four thousand dollars?"

"Miss Hanson was dead when I paid off the loan," Chapin said. "I had cosigned and I had to pay it off. But if she'd lived, she would have paid it herself."

"But she never tried to blackmail you?"

"Look, I tried to give her money a number of times and she wouldn't take it. She didn't even ask me to arrange the loan; I knew she needed the money, and I set it up without her even knowing I was involved. It was just a favor."

Even to Chapin the words sounded hollow. Greg was right. Tell his story? He hadn't been able to *tell* anything.

"Okay," the assistant district attorney continued, "you were with Miss Hanson one or two times a week, and you were usually intimate with her on these occasions. Tell me, did you ever have a lovers' quarrel? An argument?"

"No. We never had a hard word."

"I see. Were you with her the night she was killed?"

"Yes."

"But you were not with her when she was killed."

"No, I certainly was not."

"At what time did you leave her?"

"Late," Chapin said. "It was after two o'clock."

"That night, that last night in her life, were you intimate with her? Did you have sex?"

"No, I didn't. I did not."

"Oh? Why was that? Why precisely were you *not* intimate with her? Had you perhaps been having a fight that night?"

"No, that wasn't it."

"Well, an earlier witness had recalled Virginia Hanson saying that something 'funny' had happened between the two of you that night. Perhaps you can tell us what that something 'funny' was?"

"I have no idea. I was not intimate with Miss Hanson that night."

"Are you aware then that she had sexual relations with someone else that night? I'm sure you read in the newspapers that there was seminal fluid found in her body that night."

Chapin felt slightly nauseous. "I read it," he said.

"And you are telling us that this seminal fluid was not yours?"

"It was not mine."

191

"Well, do you think perhaps Miss Hanson was seeing one of her other married lovers that night?"

"There were no other married lovers."

"Well, then, are we to assume that the seminal fluid just appeared out of nowhere?"

"Whoever murdered her must also have raped her," Chapin said.

"We may not be in disagreement on that," Kip Farnsworth said. "Let me ask you something else, Mr. Hope. You said that you read about the seminal fluid in the paper. Since you were reading the papers, you must have seen the police sketch of the man known as Harry. Is that a fact?"

"Yes."

"And did you recognize it as a sketch of you?"

"Yes."

"Good. Since you knew the police were looking for you, why didn't you come forward? Why didn't you just come forward and offer your help?"

There was no answer.

"We're waiting for your answer, Mr. Hope."

"I was afraid," Chapin said finally. "I was afraid of what people would think."

"I think we can understand that," Farnsworth said. "Let me go back to another area. Earlier that same evening, the night of November eleventh, something kept you from being intimate with Miss Hanson, from having sex. What was that?"

"I fell," Chapin said. "I stumbled on her living-room carpet and hit my head on a table. I was out cold for—"

"Were you drunk?"

"No, I wasn't drunk. I didn't have that much to drink."

"But you stumbled on a rug and hit your head on a table. And you weren't drunk?"

"No."

"Well, then could it have been all that pot you were smoking? Was it that?"

Chapin felt as if he had been punched in the thorax. How did they know that? God, had they found marijuana butts in the apartment?

"That's a question, Mr. Hope. Maybe you don't understand the word 'pot.' Maybe you call it grass. Or perhaps you stick to the more formal term, marijuana. Isn't it a fact that you were smoking marijuana that night? Isn't it a fact that a New York State senator was indulging himself that night in an orgy of booze and pot and sex and violence?"

"No!"

192

"No? No to what, Mr. Hope? No to the booze? You've already said you were drinking. No to the pot? You were on marijuana that night, Senator. You know it and we know it. No to the violence? No to the sex?"

The jurors' faces were studies in rapacity. If it was this bad here, what would it be like in a courtroom? Chapin wanted to run.

"Never mind," Farnsworth was saying. "We'll confine ourselves to the marijuana. We can all understand your reluctance to respond, Senator. We know you're a member of the Senate Subcommittee on Narcotics Control. We know that you supported the state's antidrug legislation."

"I know what you're thinking," Chapin said. "I know what you're all thinking. Yes, I did smoke marijuana that night but it was the first time in my life, the very first time."

"It must have had a powerful effect on you. There were a lot of firsts that night, weren't there? Your first joint of marijuana. Perhaps the first night you were with Miss Hanson without being intimate with her. Were there any other firsts that night? Were there any other firsts you'd care to tell us about?"

"Nothing else happened," Chapin said. "Nothing else happened to me that you don't already know about."

"Tell me, Mr. Hope, do you recall what you were wearing the night of the murder?"

Where was the young man going now? "A suit," Chapin said.

"Do you remember what color it was?"

"As I recall, it was gray. Yes, gray."

"Oh, the same gray suit you have on now?"

"No, it was another one. Gray flannel."

"Would you mind telling us where that gray flannel suit is right now?"

Some of the jurors were actually leaning forward. What the hell was going on? Was it possible the assistant district attorney knew something about the trousers? But how could he? They were gone. If anything was left of them now, it would be ashes. "I have no idea where it is now," he said, picking his words carefully. "It seems likely that it would be home with my other suits."

"You're sure of that?"

"Well, I'm not sure, but as I said, it seems likely."

As he answered, Chapin looked at one of the jurors, a gray-haired woman who had been making notes on a pad. She was smirking.

"Well, I think that'll be all, Mr. Hope. I think you've helped us as much as you're going to."

"But—"

"You're excused, Mr. Hope."

As he got to his feet, Chapin felt moisture running from his hair down into his collar. It was as cold as ice. Up above him the faces of his twenty-three judges were solemn, faintly triumphant. They all seemed so confident, so sure of themselves, so certain of their ability to determine what was truth and what was justice.

Outside, Greg took one look at his partner's face. "I told you," he said.

Chapin sighed. "I should have listened," he said. "God, how I should have listened."

"Well, look at it this way, you got a lesson in the system."

"What system?" Chapin asked.

"The one politicians and lawyers are always talking about," Greg said. "Justice."

Chapin made the call to Nassau Republican Chairman Rocco Porcina a few hours later from his home. Justice had turned out to be farcical; he'd try the system he knew best. Politics. He'd gone out of his way for the Nassau organization any number of times; Porcina owed him. That was still the system; there was no new politics. I help you. You help me. And in this case Porcina was the only one who could help him. Nassau was Rocco Porcina's protectorate; even the State House couldn't cut it there. And certainly no one from Suffolk could.

Not that anyone in his county or up in Albany seemed ready to stick his neck out for him. One of the things that had surprised him in the wake of the *Islander* stories was the absence of calls from colleagues. He hadn't expected a deluge, but there had been nothing at all. No commiseration, no sympathy, not even anyone asking him to say it wasn't so.

"Hello, Rocco?"

"That's me."

"This is Chapin Hope."

"Who?"

"Christ, I said, this is Chapin Hope. Listen, Rocco, I thought you could do me a favor. A big one."

There was silence at the other end, and Chapin continued. "Your man Galton is trying to indict me for . . . for murder . . . in the Hanson case. The, uh, cocktail waitress. I know Norman's hungry, I can appreciate his being motivated by the newspaper stories. But I'll tell you straight out, Rocco, I had nothing to do with it. Nothing. Now, I hate to put it this way, Rocco, but I've done things for you people in Nassau and I think I deserve better than to be charged with a crime I didn't commit. If there was an iota of guilt, that would be different. But there isn't—I'm absolutely innocent."

He paused but there was no response; what the hell was the matter with Porcina? "Quit the games, Rocco," Chapin said, and he could hear himself shouting. "If Galton goes ahead with this, he's not only going to make a fool of himself but he's going to hurt the party."

"Who'd you say this was?"

"Damn it, Rocco, cut it out. This is Chapin. Chapin Hope."

"Okay, Hope, now you listen if I've got to spell it out for you. What you're involved with is no ordinary problem. A goddamn murder charge *and* a newspaper series on a whole network of conflict-of-interest accusations. You've been around long enough to know you can't expect anyone to advertise their association with you after the kind of mess you've let go public. Make it all go away, Senator. Make it never have happened. Then give us a call. Until then, Senator, you're the goddamn invisible man."

Chapin stared dully at the dead phone.

25

People of the State of New York v. *Chapin Hope.*
Indictment number 450019.
The Grand Jury of the County of Nassau in the State of New York accuses the defendant, Chapin Hope, of murder under 125.25 of the penal law. On or about November 11th, the defendant did, with the intent to kill, with a sharp-edged instrument kill Virginia Hanson in Mineola, New York. . . .

Jerome Hill
Foreman, Grand Jury

Norman Galton read the indictment a second time, then allowed the single piece of paper to flutter down onto his glass-topped desk. Before placing the phone call that had to be placed, he cleared his throat and composed his thoughts.

"Greg, I won't beat around the bush," the district attorney said. "I'm afraid I've got some bad news for your client. They indicted him."

"What?"

"I just got the paper. The grand jury indicted the senator for murder."

"Well, it doesn't come as that much of a surprise. Grand juries being what they are."

"Personally, I couldn't be sorrier, Greg. I'll have to ask you to bring him in tomorrow. We'll get him arraigned then. Around ten."

"I appreciate the courtesy, Norm. What're you going to do about bail?"

"We don't want to go hard on the senator. Do you think he could make fifty thousand?"

"Isn't that a little steep, Norm?"

"What can I tell you, Greg? It's murder. If we ask for less than fifty, someone's sure to say we're doing favors."

"Well, thanks for warning me."

Galton's next call had been suggested by Chuck Ferris, although the district attorney would have made it sooner or later on his own.

This was to Rocco Porcina. As the party's county chairman Porcina had earned a national reputation by having elevated the dispensation of patronage to an art form. "Clear it with Rocco" was more than a slogan; it was an unwritten law. If a lifeguard was being hired or a county commission chairman was being named, Porcina approved before the appointment was rubber-stamped by a county executive who concentrated his attention in a continuing struggle against international communism. The net result to Porcina was power. So many people owed Porcina and his machine favors, if not livelihoods, that even in the midst of a Watergate or a depression he could be expected to deliver a Republican majority on short notice. Although Rocco Porcina had become virtually inaccessible to the press, he could be seen and reached by anyone else at all. Rocco felt close to the little people, the ones who came and asked for jobs for their children, but he had no great affection for the politicians, the officeholders. They were no more than Lionel trains on his hobby table; if one went bad and malfunctioned, he was simply replaced by a newer model.

"I thought I better let you know," Galton was saying. "They've indicted Chapin Hope on that murder case."

"Did he do it?"

"We've got a case."

"That's not what I asked."

"I'd have to say it looks like he did it."

"What does your Homicide chief think?"

"He thinks Hope did it."

"That fellow is one snotty son of a bitch but he's usually right."

"I just thought you'd want to know, Rocco."

"I'm glad you called, Norm. By the way, who's going to handle the trial?"

"We're still discussing that. I was thinking it might be the right time to get back in front of a—"

"It's none of my business, of course, Norm, but I'd hate to see you take a chance personally. It might be a good idea to let one of your bright young men take care of the trial itself while you run the investigation. Your man Farnsworth looks like a comer, Norm."

"To tell you the truth, Rocco, I've been thinking along those very lines."

"I knew I could count on your natural instincts. And, Norm?"

"Yes?"

"Let me tell you what I am thinking about Chapin Hope. We've all gotten along with Chapin in the past. He's done us favors, we've done him favors. Chapin has always paid his dues. But he has just become too expensive for us. The *Islander* has got him with his

197

hand stuck in the cookie jar, you know, up to the elbow on that bank stuff and with those land deals. He's a sinking ship, Norm, and he can't take us anywhere but down."

"I see what you mean, Rocco."

"What I'm saying is that no one owes him a goddamn thing, Norm, nothing."

"Right."

"What I'm saying, Norm, is the quicker this whole thing is over, the better it is for the rest of us."

The rest of the calls that morning were made by Chuck Ferris. They were made to the news directors of six television stations, to two news magazines, to a half-dozen newspapers. Each call transmitted the same information. It might be a sound idea to have top people at the district attorney's office the next morning at a quarter of ten. It might be a good idea to have cameramen as well. Ferris said that he would be only too happy to outline the story over the phone but, of course, that was against the law. Did it have to do with a certain state senator? he was asked. He couldn't say anything that specific, but he knew they would be interested.

It was the tail end of the morning rush hour. Greg was driving and Chapin was sitting beside him, looking out at other cars, other people. What would they think if they looked back and recognized the face they had seen in the papers the night before? What would their reaction be? Surprise? Distaste? Curiosity? Pleasure? Probably some mix of emotions, the same division of feelings one might experience when seeing a drowning victim on the beach. Compassion or sympathy? Not likely. Not for someone accused of chopping a woman apart with an ax.

The trauma of the grand jury room was still with Chapin Hope. So was the recent indignity of having police finecomb his house in what was obviously a search for the murder weapon. It did not soothe his feelings that they came up empty-handed; the search was too humiliating. They even went through the boys' rooms. Whoever it was who said that self-pity was a luxury didn't know what he was talking about. Self-pity was a necessity. At the moment, Chapin seemed to be the only one feeling sorry for himself.

Greg was still angry because he had gone into the grand jury room at all. Thalia had been treating him the way she might treat a stranger. The boys, before being shipped to the in-laws upstate, had been unforgiving and Chape Jr. had asked him, "How could you do that to my mother?" It seemed as though even Daisy, the family's poodle, had become chillier. And now he was worrying, among other things, about his family's safety—worrying that they might be threatened by a maniac, a nightmarish figure at large with an ax.

Chapin turned from the traffic and studied his law partner. Greg's red tie gleamed above the rich brown leather of his overcoat and above the blue, pin-striped vest. It was a big day for Hammer and he was exuding a heavy aura of self-confidence as he spurred the Buick along the parkway. He realized Chapin was looking at him.

"Don't worry," he said, "it won't take long."

"Yeah," Chapin said.

"And please remember, this time let me do all the talking."

"You won't hear a word from me."

From the moment of arrival Greg was like a fighter striding through the crowd toward the ring—waving, smiling, radiating confidence. The newspaper and television reporters were everywhere outside the building and all over the lobby in front of the district attorney's office. Chapin recalled some of the same faces from the day before. The blonde, now wearing a fur-trimmed green coat, was on hand. And today there were many new additions. One of the cameras bore the open-eye symbol of CBS-TV—what in the hell would Walter Cronkite have to say about Chapin Hope?

Galton and Ferris were waiting in the district attorney's office with several aides. This time there were no handshakes, no cordial asides, no expressions of sympathy. Today it was "Senator Hope," not "Chape." Today he was taken at once to a second room, where he was to be booked. He stood, shifting his weight from one foot to the other, while a uniformed policeman typed out his "pedigree." His name and date of birth. His height and weight. The color of his eyes and hair. His occupation. ("State senator," he said, and the man typed in the words without so much as an upward glance.) His parents' names. (Thank God the old man was not alive to see this.) And finally, did he have any prior criminal record? ("No, no prior criminal record.")

Then it was time for the fingerprinting. His fingers went numb in the hands of the technician. Hammer and Galton stood aside, making small talk, and two men, plainclothes officers apparently assigned to guard him, were watching with openly bored expressions. Didn't anyone realize what was going on? Chapin wished the numbness in his fingers would spread, would blot out the moments that were crowding him. Each step in the arraignment process was predictable enough; Chapin could have anticipated them without difficulty. What he couldn't have anticipated was his own reaction. Never had he felt more alone, more vulnerable, more at the mercy of strangers.

But they were all caught up in the process now and there seemed no way to step out of it. The process didn't care that Chapin Hope was a state senator, a respected member of the community, a family man. That he had loved Ginny Hanson—that Ginny had been viciously murdered by some insane person who was still at large. The process cared about nothing and no one.

But the process was all part of justice, all part of the great American traditions. And since he had killed no one, since he had done nothing really wrong, why, then, at one point in the process he would be set free. If not this day, the next one. If not then, another time. To believe anything else would be to join in the cynicism of the times, in the skepticism of those who once ripped up draft cards and burned flags.

"What're you thinking about?" Greg said.

"You really want to know?" the senator said. "I'll tell you. For the first time in my life I was thinking it was a good thing that I never quite managed to get the death penalty restored."

"It's not that bad."

"Not yet."

Then the senator was seated on a tall stool in front of a white backdrop and, in the glare of floodlights, was photographed in profile and full face. The "mug shots." Surely this would be the final indignity. No, not quite. He saw the flash of the handcuffs in one of the officer's hands and he couldn't remain silent.

"No!" he said, but it was too late; his hands were locked together in front of him.

"Come on, Norman," Greg was asking. "Is this really necessary?"

"I'm sorry," Galton said. "I really am. But it is a murder case. These things are called for in a murder case and the law makes no exceptions. And there's a lot of press out there today. I'm sure you understand, Greg. You, too, Senator."

"Yeah, I was going to ask you about the press," Greg said. "You must've been on the phone all morning."

"I didn't call one of them," Norman Galton said.

Chapin didn't say a word. He thought of the number of times that he and Norman Galton had shared a dais and of the nice things they had said about each other. The cuffs were heavy on his wrists.

"Try not to let them bother you," Galton said. "It's just for a few moments."

"Just long enough," Greg said, "so that every photographer out there will get a picture of them."

"They come off the very minute we get into the courtroom," the district attorney said. "The very minute."

"Beautiful," Chapin said.

200

"This'll be the hard part," Greg warned as they left the room. "They're a pack of wolves."

Cameras. Lights. And he was the action. The most rapacious reporter was the young woman he had seen the night before. As they walked through the crowd, Chapin could distinguish her voice. "How does it feel?" she wanted to know. "How does it feel to be indicted for murder?" He lowered his head deeper into his black cashmere overcoat. Why weren't they moving faster? Then he realized that everyone else in the group was enjoying it, actually enjoying the thought of getting his picture taken.

Greg hadn't been entirely accurate. The reporters didn't bring to mind a pack of wolves; they more resembled a gaggle of geese—honking, pecking, trying to nibble him to death with the most inane questions he had ever heard. The photographers were the worst of them all. "Over here, Senator," and "This way, Senator," and "Let's have a big smile, Senator." Any minute now he expected one of them to ask him to sit on a railing and cross his legs.

Finally they escaped into a car and moments later they were at the county courts building. The photographers had to remain outside but the reporters tagged right along and one of the officers had to shove them forcibly from the elevator car.

"The arraignment's a snap," Greg was saying. "I've got the bail bondsman all set. You should be home for lunch. Galton will ask for fifty thousand, which wouldn't cause any problems, but we'll probably get him down to twenty-five."

As promised, the cuffs were removed from the senator's wrists once he was standing in front of the judge. Galton was nowhere to be seen and the same assistant district attorney who had conducted the grand jury session was representing "the people." A blue-uniformed court officer called the case. "Chapin K. Hope," he said, "charged with 125.25 and 130.65 of the penal law." As Chapin remembered the state's penal law, the 125 series related to murder. The other number probably referred to sexual abuse. Everything by the numbers.

Like churches, courtrooms are dedicated to litany and ritual. Chapin joined Greg and the assistant district attorney inside a railing and faced up at the judge, a black-robed man who seemed vaguely familiar. Had they, too, shared a dais? The desk area in front of the judge was lit by a tensor light and a silver water pitcher sat nearby. An American flag was off to the side.

"The defendant waives the reading of the indictment," Greg was saying, "and pleads not guilty to the charges, Your Honor."

The judge adjusted his glasses and glanced at the papers in front of him.

"Does the district attorney have a recommendation as to the dispensation of bail?"

"Notwithstanding the fact that there is no prior record," the young man said, "this is a most serious crime, Your Honor. The people ask bail of a hundred thousand dollars."

Galton's first shaft. Hammer almost smiled when he heard the figure; he never underestimated the opposition and he took this as a warning.

"The defense feels that twenty-five thousand would be more than equitable, Your Honor," he said. "As the district attorney has pointed out, my client does not have a prior record. He has roots in the community and holds high public office and, in fact, has a long and proud record for public service. Nor is he a wealthy man, Your Honor. My client is presumed innocent. He wants to be free to fight this charge and clear his reputation."

The judge was staring down at Chapin. Was that a look of recognition or one of distaste? Chapin couldn't be sure. Then he turned back to the assistant district attorney.

"What about the nature of the people's case?" he asked. "Would the district attorney care to comment about that?"

"No, no, Your Honor, we don't want to comment." The voice lost some of its resonance. "Uh, we would simply point out that the grand jury has seen fit to indict the defendant."

The judge looked at Greg.

"Counsel, do you have anything else to say on the subject of bail?"

"The district attorney's reluctance to comment only demonstrates the thinness of his case, Your Honor, if indeed it can be called a case at all. I repeat that my client is not a wealthy man and that if he remains in custody, his ability to prepare his defense will be severely impaired."

The judge shuffled the papers in front of him. He took off his glasses, wiped them with a tissue, and put them back on.

"All right," he said, "after listening to counsel for both sides, the court will put bail at fifty thousand dollars."

After that it was a matter of following a familiar script. Greg said that the bond would be posted. He asked for twenty days in which to file motions. The judge asked if there were any objections and the assistant district attorney said no. The judge set a hearing date two months in the future. Greg nodded to a small ferretlike man standing nearby and Chapin realized he was the bondsman. They joined a court clerk in another room; the $50,000 bond cost the senator

$1,500 in cash; he turned over the deed to his house as collateral.

"Just one more thing now," Greg was saying.

"What now?"

"The press one more time," he said. "This time it's our show. They've got all those pictures of you with the cuffs on. A couple of pictures without them won't hurt. But for Christ's sake, stop looking so guilty. Try to remember that you weren't the one who killed the broad."

"*I* know that," Chapin said. "It's the rest of you I'm worrying about."

"That's better," Greg said. "Much better."

"Give him a chance, fellows," Greg said. "Give the senator a chance."

"How about a statement, counselor?"

For a few minutes they stood side by side on the top steps as the cameras clicked and buzzed. Then the microphones were at their faces. Greg did the talking.

"I'd like to answer all your questions," he said, "but as most of you know by now, I make it a practice not to argue my cases in the press. As I said in court just a few minutes ago, the district attorney's refusal to comment on the nature of his case shows that Mr. Galton has, at best, a very thin case. If indeed he has any case at all. The mere existence of this case represents the commission of a great wrong against an outstanding public servant. One fact stands out above all others. That is simply that Chapin Hope is innocent of any wrong-doing. And it is also important that a horrifying murder has been committed, and nothing is being done to catch the real killer."

"Maybe you can tell us then"—Greg Hammer turned to face the shrill voice of the young newswoman and this time he was ready for her—"is it true that Senator Hope was sleeping—"

"*Bullshit!*" The attorney spat out the word he knew would prevent that question from being heard on television that evening. "That kind of sophomoric question doesn't deserve the dignity of a response. Maybe you'd like to tell us if it's true whether you've been sleeping with your executive producer?"

Hammer had no idea how accurate the guess had been until he saw the young woman's cameraman double over in laughter.

"Don't feel bad, honey," he said. "Everyone's got to sleep somewhere."

"The hammer strikes again!" a male reporter from a rival network called out.

Then they hurried down the steps, carrying the newspeople along with them. On the sidewalk Chapin almost bumped into a familiar figure. Robert J. O'Malley had been watching the spectacle from a distance. For a moment the two men stared at each other. Hope opened his mouth to speak, then closed it and pushed past.

After the departure of Gregory Hammer and Chapin Hope the press drifted back to the district attorney's office, where Norman Galton was readying his statement. The district attorney was splendid in gray herringbone, blue shirt, and blue-and-gray-striped tie. It was difficult to tell whether his glasses or his teeth shone the most.

"As you know," he said, facing the cameras with his jaw thrust forward, "it is not the practice of this office to argue cases in the press. And I'm certainly not going to break that precedent. Our interest is in justice, not publicity. Because of the unusual nature of this case, however, and the prominence of the defendant, it's vital that I make one thing emphatically clear. I want the people of the county to know that there will be no special privileges shown to anyone. I promise the people of this county that the district attorney's office will give this prosecution its fullest attention."

Galton walked from the cluster of microphones out to the waiting limousine. As the car moved from the curb, its siren growled a low warning to the newsmen clustered ahead. Galton rolled down his window and smiled toward the last television camera. O'Malley took one look at the car's flags fluttering in the breeze and he drew himself up and saluted.

"*Four* fucking flags," one reporter said.

"Thank God it's one of ours," O'Malley said wryly.

26

The pressure was getting to Norris Whitlaw. His name was appearing with some regularity in the *Islander* stories. The name could be found deep in the stories, on the jump pages, in the long lists of friends and associates, in the corporate structures. Norris Whitlaw was there as a lesser character, a functionary, an attendant lord—but he was always there, always trapped in the amber of journalese. If Norris Whitlaw ever had doubts, he could now be sure that he was "a prominent mid-Island construction executive" and a "builder with strong ties to the Republican Party."

It was ironic that this should happen to him when things were working out for him so well on another level. Eighteen-year-old Donna Martinelli had finally succumbed to his charms and granted her boss what he thought of as her virtue. It had been a fine moment, the best thing ever to occur on the deep-pile aqua carpeting of Norris Whitlaw's office. The girl had not cried, had not carried on, had not shown a trace of resentment, had in fact been very good about the whole thing.

But always, as if to mar what otherwise would have been an idyllic existence, there was the newspaper. Not just his name, but Rhoda's. Land purchased by the Rhoda Corporation; loans floated by the Rhoda Group; mortgages held by Rhoda Whitlaw. And now there was a series of telephone calls from the reporter O'Malley. After each call Norris would call Greg for advice.

"Say nothing to no one," the lawyer said one day. "I don't care if that fat bastard finds you in bed with Chapin, I want you to deny everything."

"What if he gets to Rhoda?" Norris said. "She's getting very upset by all this. She keeps asking me why her name has to be in the papers."

"What can I tell you, Norris? You should have married a starlet."

"Yeah, but the thing is, I didn't."

"Are you trying to tell me that you can't control your own wife?"

"I'm not trying to tell you anything," the builder said. "No one's trying to tell you anything at all. It's just that Rhoda is back sucking the bottle worse than ever. Rhoda's just not right, you know?''

"Maybe if you'd come home some nights, she'd get right. Norris, maybe you better start spending some time with your wife.''

"Yeah, well, what'll I tell this O'Malley?''

"You tell him just one thing. I mean this, Norris. You tell him that your attorney is L. Gregory Hammer and that if he has any questions at all, he should come to me, that I will be doing all the talking for you.''

"He left a message today. He wants to know about the proposed high-rise apartment. What do I tell him about the high-rise?''

"Exactly nothing, Norris. Look, if he asks you whether there is a God in heaven, you tell him he'll have to check that out with me.''

"You know, Greg, I never felt good about that high-rise.''

"Never felt good?'' Hammer gripped the phone tighter. "Norris, no one ever felt good about that high-rise. That's the trouble with putting an apartment house in the middle of a historic community like Stony Harbor. No one anywhere feels good about it. But what we feel good about is the money we're going to make.''

"Well, I just went along on that because Chape said it would be a good thing. I didn't know there was going to be any publicity.''

"For Christ's sake, Norris, wipe your nose and grow up! We've had a pretty good ride so far. We hit a little rough weather and you start looking for a life preserver.''

"Not me, Greg. My God, the three of us have been best friends since we were kids.''

"That's right, Norris. If it wasn't for Chapin—if it wasn't for your old buddy Chape—you would still be laying bricks, not receptionists. You might even be swimming in an unheated pool.''

"I'm not going to do anything.''

"That's my advice, Norris. Just remember this—if it's Chapin's ass, it's your ass, too. There is no way they are going to send Chapin off to jail for conflict of interest without them hanging us at the same time.''

"Even if we said we didn't know what we were doing?''

"We don't say anything. When O'Malley calls you, you're not in. If he finds you, you can say that it is a terrible shame that anyone could accuse Chapin Hope of anything because he happens to be the finest man you have ever known. And so far as anything else goes—*anything* else—you would like to be of help to him but he has to speak to your attorney.''

"Okay,'' Norris said.

It all made sense. But, then, it had all made sense from the

206

beginning. It had been one sensible step after another and somehow it had led to the edge of a cliff. And behind him, coming up strong, was a fat reporter named O'Malley. He hit the intercom.

"Donna? Could you stay late tonight?"

"Tonight?" the girl's voice came from the box.

"Yeah, tonight," he said. "There's something you could do for me."

"It's the wrong time of month," she said.

"Oh, I'd forgotten," he said. "Okay. Thanks anyway."

Robert J. O'Malley was, in fact, coming closer and closer to an inevitable confrontation with Norris Whitlaw. For two weeks he had been knocking on doors in Stony Harbor. Never had he seen so many doors opened by black women wearing white starched uniforms. When he finally spoke to the senator's neighbors, he got what he knew he would get, little more. The Hopes were active in civic affairs; they kept a nice home; they always seemed happily married; they gave to every charity drive. It was difficult to connect a man like Senator Hope to such a terrible crime.

O'Malley could have written the story in his sleep. The basic neighborhood-reaction-to-scandal story. Complete with recommended quotes. "They've always been good neighbors," O'Malley was told. "I just can't believe he would do anything like they say in the newspaper," O'Malley was told. "They've always been a quiet couple," O'Malley was told. One of the reporter's minor fantasies was that one day he'd run into a neighbor who would give him a quote along these lines: "If there's a dollar involved, that son of a bitch would stick his grandmother in the oil burner." But no, the story was as standard as the once-a-year hurricane sidebar, the two-days-without-electricity story, or the tearjerker about the small child facing a delicate heart operation, what O'Malley called the "hole-in-the-heart story."

The only one willing to depart from the script at all was the senator's next-door neighbor, Norman Morgenthau. The president of his own mini-computer company and one of Stony Harbor's few Jews, Morgenthau was something of an outsider himself.

"I've lived here five years," he told the reporter, "and I've never seen the inside of his house." He also told O'Malley that the Hope boys had been taken out of the school. "My kids tell me they were taking a lot of flak." He had always been impressed by Thalia: "She's got class." And now he was impressed by the extent of the senator's financial manipulations: "I don't know if he killed the girl—it's hard to imagine anyone doing a thing like that—but he sure turned out to be a *gonif*, didn't he?"

From Morgenthau's house O'Malley worked his way down toward Main Street and finally to Bobo's, where he was warmly welcomed by the cop who had once made the mistake of stopping the senator for speeding.

"Hey," Walsh said, introducing the reporter to the other regulars, "here's the guy who finally put the boots to Senator Hopeless."

The afternoon crowd at Bobo's grunted approval. As far as O'Malley could see, they were the same faces he had seen during his visits some months earlier. One of the regulars—he was the elderly outpatient from a nearby veterans' hospital—beckoned to O'Malley with drunken confidentiality.

"I can tell you why he did it," he said.

"What?"

"I know why the senator killed that cocktail waitress."

"Oh?"

"Because she wouldn't blow him."

This time O'Malley turned around to study his informant. The old man nearly knocked him off his stool with his breath.

"How do you know that?"

"All them politicians want are blow jobs," the patient said. "You know what an Albany sixty-eight is, don't you?"

"I don't think I know what that is."

"That's what those politicians up there do with their friends. They say, 'Listen, I don't have time for a sixty-nine. I just got time for a sixty-eight. That's where you blow me and I owe you one.' "

Despite the fascinating nature of the old man's pronouncement, O'Malley did not see it as an investigatory lead. The young cop, Walsh, was talking at him from the other side.

"I don't know about Hope," Walsh said, "but I keep hearing about one of his buddies and he's some kind of disaster."

"Who's that?" O'Malley asked.

"His buddy, Norris Whitlaw. The construction guy."

"Yeah, I've been trying to reach him."

"Well, when you reach him, you're gonna reach a big nothing," Walsh said. "A friend of mine, he's got this garage in Patchogue, never mind his name. He knows Whitlaw's receptionist, this Donna, and according to her, Whitlaw has been sniffing after her since the day she shows up for work. This Donna, the way I hear it, has done it with everything including fire hydrants. But Whitlaw is a fucking weirdo; he figures she never did it before, so he's been doing everything to her *except* screw her. Like he even takes her out to dates at the pizza place there in Patchogue."

"Norris Whitlaw?"

` "Yeah, my friend there says you gotta see it to believe it. This Whitlaw is some dude. And he sits there in his fancy clothes playing the jukebox and getting pizza all over himself."

"And your friend knows all this for sure?"

"He ought to," Walsh said. "He's been boffing that Donna for the past three years, since she was fifteen."

"Yeah, well, excuse me, buddy, I think I'll make a phone call."

O'Malley eased himself from the stool and went to the booth at the back of the bar. Rather than go through the ordeal of trying to squeeze himself into a container designed for humans of more modest girth, he reached into the booth and dialed the number of Whitlaw's construction firm. This time he didn't mention that he was Robert O'Malley; this time he was calling "from the district attorney's office."

"Hello," Norris Whitlaw was saying. "Can I be of any help to you?"

"Yeah," O'Malley said. "You can stop being nervous. This is O'Malley from the *Islander*. I have a few questions for you."

"I'd like to help you, Mr. O'Malley," he said. "But I don't really see how I can. Actually, I'm in the middle of a conference right now—why don't you call me in—"

"Yeah, I guess you are pretty busy," the reporter cut him off. "I guess you're pretty busy thinking about building that high-rise apartment in Stony Harbor."

"What high-rise apartment?"

"That one that you and Hope and Hammer are going to build right there—"

"I really don't know what you're talking about, Mr. O'Malley. If you have any questions about any matter at all, I would ask you to refer them to my attorney, L. Gregory Hammer."

"Well, do you think he's going to be able to tell me about that pizza place in Patchogue?"

"What?"

"Well, I wanted to ask you to recommend one of your favorite pizza places in Patchogue, somewhere we might sit down and talk and play the jukebox and you know. . . ."

"I'm very busy," Norris said. "I'm too busy for this."

As he put down the telephone, he knocked over a cup of coffee. The possibility of being involved in a land scandal was bad enough —but how could O'Malley know anything about Donna? Damn Chapin anyway! What had he gotten them into? He reached for the button on his desk and in a few seconds Donna Martinelli was at the door.

"Yes, Mr. Whitlaw?"

209

"Donna, I seem to have spilled some coffee," he said. "Would you mind terribly?"

"Oh, on *our* rug!" she said. "I'll get it."

After mopping up the dark puddle with paper towels, Donna brought in the half-dozen letters she had typed that afternoon. She had spelled it "sincerly" on every letter. She had made it "you're" instead of "your." She had punctuated each letter with erasure smudges.

"Great," Norris said. "Just terrific."

"Thank you, Mr. Whitlaw."

She was leaning over him then and he realized she was wearing the perfume he had gotten for her two days earlier.

"By the way, Donna, do you think it would be all right to stay a little late this evening?"

"Today I'm all right," she said.

"Fine," he said, "I've got a little something that needs doing."

Shortly after five o'clock that evening O'Malley parked his car across the street from the business offices of Norris Whitlaw & Associates, Heavy Construction. The firm's nerve center was housed in a new brick-and-glass building on Route 110 in one of the business-industrial parks that had become the hubs of commerce and manufacture on Long Island. The parks were the business equivalents of housing developments—sudden communities of similar buildings that replaced farms and fields and brush. They represented a nationwide move of industry from cities to suburbs and they symbolized the growing independence of Long Islanders, especially those who no longer had to commute to the city for their livelihoods. They were male enclaves dominated by men who attended breakfast meetings of the Long Island Association and who lunched in overpriced diners and topless bars. These intersuburban commuters drove their own cars to work, coached Little League baseball teams, bowled in company leagues, and belonged to boating groups, church groups, school committees, and civic associations. Some of them worked out in gyms once a week. Others got together periodically in motel cocktail lounges, where they either talked shop or sought out extramarital liaisons or did both simultaneously. Few, if any—other than Norris Whitlaw—took teenagers to pizza parlors.

O'Malley shook his head at the thought. He had seen Norris Whitlaw once and he had some trouble making the connections. That had been at a breakfast meeting of the Long Island Association—a super-Rotary whose membership embraced both

Nassau and Suffolk Counties—at which Whitlaw had introduced the main speaker. The speaker was a Long Island Railroad flak who made the usual speech about how the line intended to improve its services.

Norris Whitlaw stood out in O'Malley's memory as he had stood out at that breakfast meeting. Resplendent in a Cardin blazer, a mod haircut, an ascot—he had actually been wearing an ascot—Whitlaw had been the embodiment of the word "fop." He looked like a high-priced gigolo, the sort who would appeal to a bejeweled and aging widow hungering for a dance partner at a resort hotel. How, O'Malley wondered, did Whitlaw come off in the eyes of a Patchogue teenager?

Cute, in point of fact. At the very moment O'Malley was parking outside the office building, Donna Martinelli was thinking that Mr. Whitlaw was cute. Something seemed to be bothering him but whatever it was, it did not interfere with his intrinsic cuteness.

She knew it was silly to keep thinking of him—and, for that matter, addressing him—as Mr. Whitlaw, but she couldn't help it. She just couldn't bring herself to call him Norris. In the first place, that didn't even sound like a real name and, anyway, he was older than her father. Still and all, he was cute. And he was the first man she had ever had sex with who smelled good.

And the way he dressed was out of sight. And he gave her real tough presents—expensive perfume and dresses and even jewelry and lingerie. She had a whole schoolbag filled with things she had to hide from her mother. He was even cute when he made love. The only trouble was that he got so excited—she had never seen anything like it and when he started yelping like a dog, she worried about him.

Donna was thinking all this as she sat in her employer's private office watching him make the drinks. He had just complimented her again on the letters she had typed that afternoon. She had gotten them all exactly as he had dictated them. Donna wished her high school steno teacher could have heard that; she never would have believed it. She wondered what her steno teacher would say if she could see Donna at that moment—sitting on an orange leather couch while her boss mixed drinks.

"I'm making the usual," Norris said.

"Oh, *good!*"

"It's a reward for those letters," he said.

The usual was a whiskey sour with two cherries. Everything needed for the drink was stored in the concealed bar—a bottle of Seagram's, ready mix that frothed when stirred, grenadine, orange slices, and, of course, maraschino cherries. As he whipped up the

211

concoction, Donna walked over to the office door and pressed the little button that set the lock and then she came over to her employer and kissed his ear.

"Mr. Whitlaw, you really are cute."

"Let's relax with our drinks first," he said.

Donna pouted—mock exaggeration—and she took her foaming drink back to the couch. Norris turned to reach for the Johnnie Walker Black and when he looked back, she was sucking on an orange. Norris looked away, tried to think of something that would permit his erection to die down a little, but could think of nothing but Donna sucking that damn orange slice. Donna went over to the stereo and fiddled with the dial on the FM band and Norris casually walked over to the door and depressed the button that he was certain would lock it. And then he thought of Robert J. O'Malley and his erection vanished.

The reporter was sitting in the parking lot, inflicting steady damage on the flask from his glove compartment. He watched as the last group of workers came out of the building, found their parked cars, and drove off into the darkness. In the slots reserved for the Norris Whitlaw & Associates executives there was a maroon Cadillac and a few spaces away there was a yellow Gremlin.

By five thirty O'Malley concluded that something was detaining Norris Whitlaw. He lumbered across the street and pushed his way through the plate-glass doors into the building. The lobby directory listed Norris Whitlaw on the second floor. The unmanned elevator deposited him in front of an empty reception desk and the carpeting muted his footsteps as he walked down the corridor. The entire second floor was unlit except for a narrow white streak of light coming from beneath the door at the end of the hall. He stopped in front of the door and read the lettering: NORRIS WHITLAW— PRESIDENT. Bingo! From within the office the reporter could hear the sound of music, or what passed for music among the younger generation.

O'Malley opened the door quietly and allowed it to swing slowly in. There was a long polished walnut desk and behind it a swivel chair upholstered in orange leather. The chair had been turned around and O'Malley was looking at the back of Norris Whitlaw's head and bare neck.

Facing the reporter and sitting astride Whitlaw's lap was a lithe and quite naked young woman with long brown hair that curled softly onto slim shoulders. The young woman was going up and down in an unmistakable rhythm that never faltered as her dark eyes widened and she uttered two words to her employer.

"Who's he?"

The chair swiveled around sharply and Norris Whitlaw stared at the fat man standing in the open doorway. The girl was still rising and falling in Whitlaw's lap and the executive's face was a curious mixture of horror and delight as he stared at the man who could only be Robert J. O'Malley.

"I locked the door," he said.

"*I* locked the door," Donna said.

"Oh," Norris said.

"I can see you're busy," O'Malley said. "I'll wait outside."

Ten minutes passed before Norris Whitlaw walked into the reception area, where Robert J. O'Malley was waiting, his feet propped up on the desk, reading a copy of *Time* magazine. The construction-company president was fully dressed and looked as though he had just stepped from the window of an exclusive men's store. There was only that slight nervous tic beneath his right eye to indicate his recent ordeal.

"Hi, there," the reporter said. "I'm O'Malley."

"Your arrival was, to say the least, inopportune," Whitlaw said. "But, uh, I'm sure you're a man of the world and you realize how these things happen."

"Not often enough, if you ask me," O'Malley said. "Hey, that's some kid you've got there."

"Yes, in fact she still is a kid. An incident like this could be terribly upsetting. I've told her to stay there in the office. I think inside she's scared silly. . . ."

"She didn't look scared."

"At any rate, I trust this incident will be forgotten."

"Yeah, I'm sure it will be," O'Malley said.

"Let me be precise," Whitlaw said. "I trust that you won't find occasion to use something like this in that . . . newspaper of yours."

"You must be kidding," O'Malley said. "Do you think I could write up something like that in the kind of story I write? Mr. Whitlaw, I don't write about people's personal lives. I particularly don't like to write about a middle-aged man carrying on with a girl young enough to be his daughter. The very thought offends me."

"I'm happy to hear it."

"Yeah, I don't write that kind of smut," the reporter went on. "But, as luck would have it, one of my best friends is Allison Newmark—you know, she writes 'Allison's Alley'—and she just loves to write that kind of smut."

"Mr. O'Malley, you have no scruples."

"Sometimes I worry about that," the reporter said. "I worry about my not having any scruples when I meet someone like you,

213

someone who has so many of those scruples. Whitlaw, I thought maybe you and I would talk about Senator Hope.''

"I can't talk to you about him," he said. "If you want to ask me any questions, you'll have to call my attorney, Mr. Hammer.''

"The thing about Allison, if she decided to write about you humping that little girl in your swivel chair, she wouldn't embarrass you by using your name. She'd probably just use your initials. What's Donna's last name anyway?''

"O'Malley, do you think I would compromise that—''

"Look, never mind her last name. Just give me the initial.''

Norris Whitlaw thought back over his long friendship with Chapin Hope. He recalled the phone conversation with Greg Hammer. He thought about his business, his home, his position. He thought about the high cost of divorce, the risk of putting so much property in a wife's name. He thought of the girl behind the closed door at the end of the corridor.

"Tell me, Mr. O'Malley," he said, "just what was it you wanted to know?''

27

Damned if it didn't smell like spring. As he walked from his car to the front door of the Hope home, Greg Hammer inhaled deeply. The morning air was a tonic. Almost golf weather. On Greg's scale of one to ten the day was starting out as nine and rising.

"Greg, you should have called." Thalia was still wearing a housecoat. "Chape is up at my mother's with the boys for a few days."

"Yeah, I spoke to Chape yesterday," Greg said. "You're the one I wanted to talk to now."

"Come on in and I'll plug in the coffee." Thalia opened the door. "But don't you dare tell Priscilla what the house looks like. I gave Lupe a few days off, and I'm not lifting a finger." She stopped for a moment and touched her hair. "I really didn't expect anyone," she said, "that's why I look this way."

"You look fine," he said. And the funny thing was, she did. She looked good enough so that Priss would have killed him if she could have read his mind at the moment. This was the first time he had ever seen Thalia like this, her hair down, nonautomated, and there was something about her that had escaped his notice in the past.

"Black?" Thalia was saying as she came back with two cups of coffee.

"How did you know?"

"I just guessed," she said. "I always think of you as a black-coffee type."

"Well, I like it with cream and sugar," he said.

"You *do* surprise me," she said.

"It just goes to show." Greg felt as comfortable as he did when making a point to a jury. "You should never take someone for granted. But we all do, you see. We take people and put them in little boxes, and we don't really know a thing about them. All these years you've had me in a little black-coffee box."

"I know what you mean," she said. "Look how long I've lived with Chape—I thought I knew everything about him."

"The coffee's good, Thal."

It was the first time that he had ever called her that, Chapin's pet nickname, and the fact was not lost on either of them. It led to a moment of silent consideration.

"Tell me something, Greg," she said then. "I haven't really had a chance to speak to you about this whole thing. What's going to happen?"

"You mean, will Chapin get off?"

"That mostly."

"I think so," he said. "As nearly as we can tell—unless Galton has some surprises up his sleeve—they have a weak case. However, as far as politics is concerned, I think Chapin ought to start considering another line of work. Actually, I think the public is capable of forgiving a man for screwing a cocktail waitress . . . sorry about that, Thal."

"That's all right," she said. "It's a fact . . . I've gotten used to by this time."

"Okay, when it comes to that, the public is willing to look the other way and maybe even sympathize with him for getting caught. There but for the grace of . . . you know. But murder is something else. And unless the real killer turns up, a lot of people are always going to be sure Chapin did it—it won't matter if he's acquitted; the damage was done the minute he was indicted. On top of that, what's sure to finish him in politics is all this other stuff, the land dealings, the bank business. It doesn't matter that people figure that most politicians are crooks. What they can't forgive is a politician getting caught at it. That's wiping the constituents' faces in the mud because they're the ones who voted for him. And it's also a demonstration of something else they can't stand—dumbness."

"I wondered how this would affect you and Norris," she said. "I keep seeing your names coming into it. You know, it's a funny thing, I've read every word of those land stories and I still don't understand how some of those deals worked."

"I'll tell you something," the lawyer said. "There are some things that I don't understand. I'm on the boards of some corporations that I barely knew existed. I knew what was going on generally—don't get me wrong—but I never stopped to add it all up."

"Then you can guess how surprised I am," Thalia said. "I had no idea that so much was in my name."

"I guess it didn't seem important enough to tell you," he said. "The interesting thing is that very little of it is unusual. Not just the land deals, but the bank stuff, the milk-lobby contributions, the whole *schmear*. It's all pretty well standardized—hell, they could print a manual if they wanted to. I don't think there's a solid

216

indictment in all of those stories; there aren't laws to cover most of that stuff. There are dozens of politicians the papers could write similar stories about. The only reason they went after Chapin is that his name came up in a murder case."

"But can anything happen to you?"

"I don't see how. Most of my colleagues—especially the ones in civil practice—are doing things a lot worse. I'll tell you, other than Chape, the only one really sweating this is Norris. Everytime his name gets into the papers he calls and asks me what we should do."

"But what about your *reputation?*"

"Thal," he said, "all those stories mean to me is that I'll get my name in the papers a few more times than I counted on this year. Maybe you didn't know it, but criminal lawyers are like actors—the public doesn't care what you do on your own time."

"It's incredible, when you think what one unfortunate set of circumstances can lead to. . . ."

"It all depends on how it ends. It's like a fairy tale—the ending is everything. There's no way that Chapin can come out of this smelling like a rose. But I don't think he's going to have to spend a single night in prison. Actually, that's what I want to talk to you about."

"There's something I can do?"

"I think there is. First, though, I'd like you to tell me something honestly."

"I'll try."

"How do you feel inside about this whole thing? Specifically, how do you feel about Chape?"

"I guess I'm still sorting that out."

"Let me put it this way. Are things very bad between you?"

"They're not very good. Look, Greg, why don't you just tell me what you want?"

"I'm thinking of introducing you to the press," he said. "They've been asking, especially the television people. I was thinking of letting them come over here this afternoon. But it all depends on how you feel about Chape. If you're still mad at him, well, then you're probably not going to do him a hell of a lot of good."

"Mad?" she said. "This goes a lot deeper than that, Greg. It goes so deep that every time I start to think about it I put it out of my mind. I'm waiting until I feel ready to think about it. But I have myself and the boys to think about, too. I told Chape I'd keep up appearances. If you really think I can help with the press, okay."

"Well, the very fact that you're still with him indicates that you

217

don't think he's an ax murderer. I think if you could tell the press that you think Chape is innocent, that would probably be enough. . . ."

"Chape's the one who makes the speeches," Thalia said. "I've watched those reporters on television; they seem so crude."

"The reason they seem crude is that they *are* crude," Greg said. "They have no time for subtleties, they give their viewers what they want—they assume guilt, not innocence. They can be crude as hell with someone like Chape, but you're different. You're not an accused ax murderer. You're the Innocent Victim. The Wronged Woman. With you they have to go gently."

Thalia looked at him. "I'll bet you *are* a hell of a defense lawyer," she said.

"You better believe it," Greg said. "Anyway, you'll be all right. Now that that's settled, could I bother you for another cup of coffee?"

"Of course. What was that, one sugar or two?"

"Oh, I'll take it black."

"What?"

"I always take it black," Greg said. "Before—that was just to tell you that I don't like being put in a box."

As he was talking, Greg Hammer reached out to Thalia and allowed his hand to rest on her wrist. Lightly. She made no move to pull away and, in fact, seemed not to notice his hand. He kept talking.

"I could get them here this afternoon. Not in the house but out on the lawn. You could stand at the front door and just chat with them. You know, we could keep it all very relaxed. Homey."

"What would I say to them?"

"Oh, that your husband made a mistake, but he's not the first man to make a mistake. That sort of thing."

"Why do we have to do it today?"

"I found out from somebody they called that the *Islander* is going with a blockbuster corruption story tomorrow. It's got to have come from Norris. It's got the names of every bank that ever did business with our firm. Every one, every transaction, every fee. We need something to offset it."

"Does Chapin know . . . ?"

"He knows about the bank story, but he doesn't know a thing about this. To tell the truth, I'm not sure he'd go for it. Chapin still doesn't quite understand that I know best."

Thalia gently slid her arm away from Greg's hand.

"I'll do it," she said. "But to be honest, I don't think I'll like it."

218

"That's settled, then," he said. "I'll tell them three o'clock."

Thalia got up. "Gregory," she said, "if I'm going to be greeting the press this afternoon, I'd better start doing something about the way I look."

"You look fine."

"My hair is a wreck."

"I like it that way," he said. "I've never seen it that way before."

"Gregory, there is no end to your surprises this morning."

"All I'm saying is that it'd be a mistake to get yourself all dolled up. Don't go to the beauty parlor or anything. Don't wear a suit. The more casual, the better. Maybe just a sweater and some slacks and your hair down. . . ."

"Mr. Hammer, how *do* you know about these things? How do you know what I should be wearing?"

"A defense lawyer has to be an expert on everything. Do you think I'd let a client go on the stand without telling him what to wear? Believe me, Thal, this isn't the first time I've told someone not to look too glamorous."

"Too glamorous?" She laughed. "I'd love to have that problem."

"Let me tell you something," he said. "You're looking pretty damn glamorous to me this morning."

"Oh, Greg, I really have to get going now," she said, allowing mock impatience to cover genuine concern. "I really have to get ready."

"I'll be here about two," Greg said. "We'll have time to run through some questions and answers."

"No," Thalia said. "I know this is going to sound strange, Greg, but as long as I've got to speak to the press, I'd like to do it on my own. I never was much good at remembering lines."

He stared at her face, thinking again that there was something there he'd never noticed before. "All right," he said. "Damned if I don't think you can do it. But look, Thal, I know you'll be alone here for a few days. From time to time I may just pop in and see how you're doing."

"You really don't have to," she said. "I think it's time I learned to do things for myself."

"Okay, but if you need anything at all. . . ."

"I'm not going to need anything."

"I mean *anything*," he said.

Thalia had trouble concealing her smile until Gregory Hammer turned and walked toward the door. Subtlety had never been his strong point. It was all so incongruous. At this level, at this station,

219

after all these years, it was simply incongruous. Not only that, but it was bad form.

What would have happened, she wondered, if she had returned Greg's look, if she had said yes? What would Greg have done? What would it have meant to him? And never mind Chapin or Priscilla, forget the balance of their lives. Just think about her and Greg. Thalia conjured up a mental image of the two of them together, and the whole idea was sufficiently ludicrous to prompt laughter.

She had to get a move on. Thalia studied herself in the mirror and in a strange way she could understand what Greg had been reacting to. A person cannot pass through a holocaust without being marked. Thalia saw something different in her face. Not strength—not that, not yet. Character, perhaps, a trace of character. What if suffering led to beauty? If it did, by the time this whole thing was over she might be able to run for Miss America.

At three o'clock Thalia Hope opened the front door of her home, and the sight flashed her back to another time, to her wedding reception, which was held outdoors. But she took a closer look and the memory dissolved as quickly as it had come.

The people waiting outside the Hope house were carrying notebooks and tape recorders and clipboards; they were standing beside a battery of television cameras, all aimed at the front door like cannons. Some of the neighbors, attracted by the unfamiliar sounds of a crowd, were grouped together on the outskirts of the reporters. Thalia recognized a woman from the next road, a woman who hadn't exchanged a word with her for years, and there was no mistaking the smugness that enveloped her features. The microphones had all been taped to a single tripod and it stood off to the side of the door, a forsythia of cable and chrome. There was among the reporters a man of immense girth and she nodded to him, a nod that came as no small surprise to Robert J. O'Malley.

"Mrs. Hope, Mrs. Hope?" The first question was coming from a television reporter who had always reminded her of a bit player in gangster movies. "Mrs. Hope, I think we're all interested in how you're taking this experience personally."

"Well enough," she said. "At least, I think I'm taking it well enough. Of course, I know that my husband is innocent of this terrible crime and we're confident that the rest of the world will also discover that fact."

"How can you be so sure?" The question was asked by a blonde woman in a vivid red coat. "How can you be so sure that your husband didn't kill Virginia Hanson?"

"I know my husband." She was afraid that sounded less than

220

convincing, and she decided to amplify it. "At least, I know him well enough to know that he is incapable of such an act, that he is not a violent man, that he never even raises his voice in anger."

"How did you react"—the blonde wouldn't let up—"when you discovered that your husband was involved with another woman?"

"I suppose I reacted the way anyone else would," Thalia said. "I was hurt. More than that. I was shattered. But I really don't want to go into all that."

"Have you gotten over it?" The blonde's voice was syrupy with sympathy. "Do you find that—"

"Young lady, I knew my husband was having an affair with Miss Hanson because he told me about it some time ago. But it seems to me that that's not what's important here. The important thing is whether he committed this horrible crime, and I know he didn't. My husband is being pilloried for infidelity and because of his station in life. Maybe all of you should ask yourselves whether having an affair is that much of a crime. For all I know, the only difference between my husband and some of you is a question of luck."

"Are you saying—"

"I've said all I really want to say." There were a few more questions along the same lines, and then it was over. "Thank you all for coming," Thalia said. As she turned from the microphones, she heard the cameras switch off, one by one, then she turned to the fat reporter. "Mr. O'Malley, if I might see you for a moment?"

O'Malley followed her into the house, to a dining alcove in the kitchen. She sat down on a stool and the reporter took a stool on the opposite side of the counter. After several moments she looked up and seemed surprised to find him sitting there, waiting. Then her face softened.

"Why?" she asked.

"Don't ask me, Mrs. Hope," O'Malley said. "Television reporters are trained to ask those questions. They take shallowness tests before they're hired."

"I wasn't asking about them," she said. "They asked the same questions my friends would ask if they had the nerve. I'm assuming that's why all reporters get paid. For having the nerve to ask questions that no polite person would ask. I don't blame them in the least. It's you I'm curious about. Why did you go ahead with the original story?"

"Mrs. Hope, that's my job," he said. "That's what I do."

"It's funny," she said, "but I'm not angry at you. What you're seeing is simple curiosity. Chape told me that they offered a bribe but that you didn't go for it. Why?"

"Who knows?" he said. "It wasn't the first time. Sometimes I

221

kick myself all over the lot."

"I don't believe that at all," she said. "But I'm curious as to why. I'm sure Chape and Greg could have scraped up a great deal of money."

"Maybe they should've been clearer," O'Malley said. "I didn't hear anyone say anything about money. I thought Hammer was talking about a car. I've already got a car."

"Mr. O'Malley, I wish you could give me a serious answer."

"I know," he said, and he would hate to admit to himself that he was struck by her sincerity, "it's almost too serious. Maybe what it comes down to is that everyone should have something in his life that's not for sale."

"I guess I knew it would be something like that," she said. "In a way, it's almost reassuring. Despite the pain you've caused in this house—and you have caused pain, Mr. O'Malley—despite that, it's nice to know that somebody still has a commitment to something."

"Yeah," he said. "Mrs. Hope, I've got to call the paper and tell them what went on out there today. Do you mind if I use your phone?"

The desk put him on to rewrite and O'Malley talked out the facts from the scribbles on some folded-up copy paper. The bulk of the story consisted of the quotes from Thalia. He gave a brief description of the setting and tried to characterize Thalia.

"She's an attractive suburban matron," he said.

"Oh," Thalia interrupted, "is the 'matron' part absolutely necessary?"

"Just a minute," O'Malley said into the mouthpiece. "Do me a favor and change that to 'strikingly attractive woman.' " Then he hung up. "That better?"

"Much better," she said.

Dusk had arrived and the kitchen was dark. Thalia, however, made no move to get up and turn on the lights.

"I understand you have another story tomorrow," she said.

"That's right."

"How much longer will it go on?"

"Not too much longer. It shouldn't matter anymore. This stuff, no one can understand it anyway."

"Do you want to know something, Mr. O'Malley? Most of those things you've been writing about—I don't understand them either. Sometimes I wonder whether Chapin even understands them."

It was a good quote. O'Malley repeated it to himself silently until he had it down, then filed it away for later reference. It would make a strong top on the story he had just dictated.

"I'll tell you," he said, trying to keep his tone casual, unofficial, "I'm doing one story that I'm having trouble adding up. This one involved your husband as an intermediary. This is also about Rocco Porcina, you know, the Nassau Republican leader. Last year around this time Rocco transferred eight million dollars in party funds to Federated Security and put it in a noninterest-bearing account. Chapin represented the bank on the deal. Do you remember him saying anything about that?"

"I'm sure you realize that I wouldn't say anything if I did," she said, "but as a matter of fact, I don't. Anyway, that doesn't seem illegal. Is this another of Norris' stories? It seems to me that Mr. Porcina should be able to put the money in whatever bank he chooses. What difference could it possibly make to anyone?"

"I can answer that," O'Malley said. "About three-quarters of a million dollars a year."

"But there's nothing illegal—"

"Maybe not," he said, "but not everything that's wrong is illegal."

Something in O'Malley's manner suddenly alerted her. "Are you interviewing me, Mr. O'Malley?" she said.

"What do you mean?" he said.

"I was assuming that this wasn't an interview," she said. "I'd hate to read about this in the paper tomorrow. You could make me look like a perfect fool."

"I won't go with it, then," he said, and to his own surprise, he realized that he was telling the truth.

"It's hard for some people to know where their job ends and their life begins," Thalia said. "You may not believe it, Mr. O'Malley, but my husband is like that, and I suspect you are, too. In your case there must be times when it gets very difficult. These stories you're writing. Don't you ever worry about the possibility that you're ruining people's lives?"

"I'm not going to ruin any lives that aren't already ruined," he said.

"That's a very cruel thing to say."

"But it's true," he said.

"It's still cruel."

O'Malley stood up to go. "Let me tell you what I think," he said. "I've got the feeling that you weren't involved in any of this, that your name was used without your knowledge. If you want to tell your story, I'll make sure it's told right."

"Thanks, but no thanks," Thalia said, reaching for a wall switch and dousing the kitchen with fluorescent light. "If any more damage is doing to be done, it'll have to be done without my help."

28

Greg Hammer was a thoroughly organized man, a shortest-distance-between-two-points man, a two-birds-with-one-stone man. When Thalia Hope appeared on the television screen that night, he was watching while loping easily along the conveyor belt of his new electric Jog-a-Matic machine. Without breaking stride, he reached out in front of him and switched off the power. Priscilla, hearing Thalia's voice, came in from the kitchen.

"She looks great," Priscilla said. "You know, I never thought of Thalia as particularly attractive before."

Greg said nothing. By this time he knew enough never to comment on another woman's good looks. He listened closely as Thalia's televised image spoke.

"The important thing is whether he committed this horrible crime, and I know he didn't. . . . Maybe all of you should ask yourselves whether having an affair is that much of a crime."

Greg smiled. Thalia was saying the words just right. More to the point, they were just the right words. Sooner or later people were going to have to start feeling sorry for Chapin Hope. Even Greg found himself feeling sorry for his client and partner. Chapin was bright enough, plenty smart enough, but all the smarts in the world don't help when luck runs out. What had he done that was so wrong anyway? Put his thing where it didn't belong. Big deal. If that was a crime, they'd have to give Greg Hammer the chair. He smiled a second time.

"I can't get over the way she looks," Priscilla said. "Maybe I should go on a diet."

"And lose that figure?" Greg's right hand brushed casually over his wife's breasts but his eyes never left the television set. "Not on your life. You're fine just the way you are."

"Good," she said, "because I have some plans for you this evening."

"Oh-oh."

"What's that mean?"

"I thought I told you," he said. "I've got a client's meeting after

224

dinner. There's no telling when I'll get back.''

"You don't want me to wait up for you?''

"There's nothing I'd like better," he said. "Believe me, Priss. But I'm afraid it'll be for nothing. Let's hold it for the morning. It'll be a nice way to wake up.''

"Mmmm.''

As Thalia vanished from the television screen, replaced by a team of miniature horses being chased across a kitchen floor by a dog, he turned on the jogging machine again, and this time he moved the belt speed up to its maximum setting. His thoughts kept time with his pace. Who knows? Maybe it wouldn't. Be a late night. Maybe he was. Misjudging Thalia. Maybe not. Only one way. To find out.

The sweat poured from his body in small rivers and when he could stand it no more, when he thought his lungs would explode through his chest, Greg Hammer reached out and turned off the machine. Priscilla came in then carrying his martini on ice cubes and he took the drink into the sauna with him. The worst that could happen was that Thalia would say no.

Greg drove the length of Main Street and stopped at the Sunoco station to make the call. It was a well-lit phone booth and he felt vulnerable. Whenever he saw one of his neighbors making a call from a public booth, he automatically assumed that someone was trying to get laid. Otherwise why not make the call from home? The phone bleeped a busy signal at him and he hung up quickly. He drove on to the Shell station, tried again, got another busy signal. To hell with it; he'd appear unannounced.

Driving up the long winding driveway, Greg switched off his headlights. That was one of his usual precautions. Although what difference would it make in this case? What if he were seen? There was no reason on earth why Chapin Hope's lawyer and partner shouldn't be visiting his home at night. Greg parked the car beneath the backboard and walked up the unlit path toward the front door.

As he was walking past the living-room windows, Greg suddenly stopped and froze. The living room was dark but a lamp had been left burning in the den and he could see Thalia there beside the lamp, talking into a telephone nestled against her neck.

She was no more than thirty feet from him and separated only by thermopane windows. He stood motionless, studying her, feeling very much like a Peeping Tom even though Thalia was fully clothed, still wearing the slacks and sweater that he had recommended. It was, he realized, the first time he had ever really seen her, the first time he had been able to see her when she wasn't wearing any of her masks—her official hostess mask, her upper-

225

class exurbanite mask, her senator's wife mask. There was an animation to her face that he had never seen before. Was she talking to Chape? Could Chape provoke that kind of unshielded gaiety? Greg doubted it. He wondered whether Chape had ever seen her this way. Fully dressed but naked. Damn it, she *was* attractive!

The doorbell set off distant chimes. There was a brief delay and then the light above Greg's head went on, as did the lights bordering the path and the driveway. The face peering out at Greg registered clear relief on recognizing him, but by the time the door was unbolted and opened there was the beginning of a frown.

"I was just talking to Priss . . ." Thalia said.

"I thought maybe it was Chape," he said. "I've been trying to reach you."

"Oh? Priss said you had to go out on business."

"Yeah," he said. "I have a late appointment. But I thought I'd check in with you first. Did you see yourself on television?"

"I took one look," she said. "And then I closed my eyes. My hair—are you sure I should have worn it like that? Anyway, I *heard* myself on television."

They were standing in the hallway. She made no move to invite him in and he made no move to step in. She seemed to be waiting for him to come to the point. Did she have any idea what was going on in his mind?

"Was there something specific, Gregory?"

"Yes, Thal, as a matter of fact, there is."

"Well, come in and sit down," she said. "I'm expecting a call from Chape. Maybe you'll want to say something to him."

"Yeah, let me think about it," he said. "You know, Thalia, nothing helps my thought processes as much as a glass of something."

"Oh, excuse my manners," she said. "You know where Chape keeps it. Help yourself."

Greg knew where Chape kept everything. He had been in the Hope house often enough so that he could have found his way around in the dark. But this time it was different, it *felt* different. His own expectation, probably; Thalia still hadn't rolled out the welcome mat. Not yet. Of course, some women never got around to unrolling mats. Some women had to be persuaded and some women had to be directed and occasionally, once in a rare while, there would be a woman who took the initiative herself. Which would Thalia be? Before all this had come to a head, she would have had to have been directed. But now? He couldn't tell.

Without asking, Greg poured two identical drinks. Chivas over ice cubes and a splash of club soda. This time Greg ignored the easy chair and sat down on the sofa beside Thalia. Surprise was still in her eyes as he handed her the drink.

"Not for me," she said. "I never drink after dinner. You know me, Greg, one drink and I forget who I am."

"Would that be so terrible?" he said. "Besides, you have to join me in a toast. A toast to Thalia Hope."

"Me?"

"To one of the best performances I've ever seen on television," he said. "They should give you an Emmy."

"I can see it now," she said, taking a drink. "Best performance by a suburban housewife whose husband has been charged with murdering—"

"Thal, you were just great. And you didn't need my advice at all. You said all the right things and you looked . . . perfect."

"Whatever I am today," she said, "I owe to my costume designer."

"Splendid," Greg said. "Then let's drink to him."

Thalia took a second long swallow and felt the effect immediately. It always seemed to hit hardest when she was tired— and she couldn't remember being more tired. She had earned this drink. As she went for the third swallow, she knew she wasn't going to need the Valium, not tonight.

"Let me get another," Greg said.

"Oh, I really shouldn't," she said.

"Yes, you should," he said, getting up. "Admit it, you're feeling better already."

Greg did not seem to hear her protests. He drained his glass, then carried both over to the bar for refills. Thalia accepted the drink, took an automatic sip, then put it down on the coffee table. The first drink had made her dizzy. The second would knock her out. There was something about the way Greg was looking at her.

"I am tired," she said, feeling her eyes closing.

"Does this feel better?"

His right hand was at the nape of her neck, gently massaging the soreness away. The hand was both gentle and strong and, like Greg, it was sure of itself.

"That does feel better," she admitted.

"It's my specialty." He reached over and put his own glass on the coffee table. "One of my specialties."

Now Greg was using both hands, working his way from her neck to the base of her spine. She had never felt such strength before. The weariness was being rubbed away and Thalia felt her body relax.

"Lie down," he said. Later, in trying to reconstruct the evening, she realized that she should have drawn the line there, should never have allowed Greg a moment of dominance. She lay face down and his hands continued their methodical stroking. The first indication that something was wrong was a harsh quality to his breathing.

"How does that feel?" he said.

"That was fine," she said. "That felt just fine. Thanks."

It was as if by putting the words into the past tense, she could bring the act to an end. But he went on.

"Yeah, it feels good." There was a thickness to his voice. "Now relax, Thal. Allow your whole body to go limp. That's right. That's fine."

Thalia desperately wanted to say something, something cool and impersonal and matter-of-fact, but she could think of nothing. The last thing in the world she wanted was limpness and yet her body seemed to soften under his hands.

Greg Hammer's hands had lost none of their purposefulness. They were, in fact, moving more slowly now. He didn't want to rush things. His hands moved from her shoulder blades to her sides. Then they went to her legs, massaging each leg from ankle to thigh. Thalia wanted to say something to stop him but the words stuck in her throat.

Besides, Greg seemed to be observing all the proprieties, going just so far and no further. He had done nothing truly out of line. Possibly he wouldn't. In point of fact, Thalia was mildly curious about the mechanics involved in taking that next step. What on earth would he say as he tried to insinuate his hand beneath the back of her sweater, how would he explain it as he allowed his hand to go from her leg to her inner thigh?

But perhaps the entire scenario existed only in her mind. Maybe Greg was just being his usual self. After all, he couldn't buy a magazine at the stationery store without being flirtatious—a glance from Greg Hammer was the equivalent of a direct proposition from most other men.

"Thank you, Greg," she said finally. "That felt just fine."

He didn't respond; nor did he stop. His hands kept up their relentless stroking and his breathing had not lost its peculiarly labored quality.

"Greg," she said, "that's enough now."

"Is it? Enough for who?"

"Enough for me."

Again he seemed unwilling to hear her. Thalia briefly debated whether she should try to pull away but decided against any sudden movements, any challenges. Right now it was cat and mouse and she didn't have to be told who was the mouse—or the danger involved in angering the cat.

"Oh, Greg." She tried to make it sound casual, an afterthought, but it was an effort to regain some control. "My neck is killing me—would you mind doing my neck?"

Without hesitation Greg moved his hands up to the back of her neck and as he did so, Thalia shifted her weight and returned herself to a sitting position. Greg's hands tightened on her neck.

"Good old Thal," he said, "always thinking. I'll bet you were always the smartest kid in the class, weren't you?"

"One of us better be smart." For the first time Thalia allowed her voice to reflect the coolness she was feeling. "Greg, you can let go now."

"That's right," he said. "I could let go now. Then again, I could decide not to let go now."

"I think what you need—what we both need now—is a drink. Maybe that's what we both need. . . ."

"Do you really want me to stop?"

Christ, he *meant* it. There was a genuine questioning quality to his voice, a tone of authentic surprise. For a minute he seemed very much the little boy and it was Thalia's first indication that she might be winning the battle.

The irony of the moment was inescapable. If it had been anyone else except her husband's partner, if Priscilla were not her best friend, if it had been a male approaching her with sweet reason instead of brute force, if . . . if . . . if— there were so many ifs, so many reasons she might have accepted a lover. Lord knows she wasn't fighting for Chapin's honor; infidelity was no longer an issue. But there she was, defending her virtue like some . . . nun. Perhaps it was because the honor she was defending had nothing whatever to do with Chapin; it was her own.

"Yes, Greg, I really want you to stop. And now."

That quickly it ended. As he withdrew his hands from her, Thalia turned to look at him. She scarcely recognized him. Never before had she seen Greg Hammer in a moment of uncertainty, less than sure of himself. That very morning, all that byplay with the coffee, that was the Greg Hammer she had always known.

"Would you like that drink now?" she said.

"Yeah, I could use one." His breathing was back to normal. "A double."

"Gregory, I think we both better forget what just happened. It never happened. Nothing happened."

"That's the truth. Nothing happened."

Thalia heard the bitterness in his voice and noticed the dots of color as they popped out in his cheeks. Until then she hadn't realized just how angry he was.

"I don't know why you had to make such a big deal of it," he said. "All I was going to do was fuck you."

Thalia had always hated that word. And when she heard it used then, used in its literal sense, she knew why. It was a word filled with ice. What had been happening had nothing to do with romance or even seduction. Greg Hammer had not the slightest desire to make love. He was intent on just one thing, fucking her.

Thalia leaped to pick up the ringing telephone.

"Hello," the voice on the other end said, "I'm calling for Park Vale Estates, the new year-round vacation center in the Poconos."

"Hello, Chape," she said. "No, not at all. I'm glad you were able to call. No, you picked a fine time."

She looked over to Greg and he was holding a finger up to his lips, shaking his head.

"Excuse me," the voice on the phone was saying. "Can you hear me clearly? We'd like to invite you and your husband to spend a free weekend as our guests at Park Vale House. We'd like to show you our choice homesites. And all you have to do is—"

"Oh, I miss them, too," she said. "When will you all be coming home?"

"This must be a bad connection," the voice was saying. "I'm calling for Park Vale Estates in the Poconos. Hello. . . ."

"Oh, absolutely," she said. "Greg has been keeping in touch. Oh, yes, as a matter of fact, I *do* know where he happens to be tonight. . . ."

Thalia turned to look at Greg but she was looking at an empty chair. A second later she heard the front door slam.

"This is Park Vale Estates," the voice was trying again. "In the Poconos."

"I'm sorry," Thalia said. "We're not interested. But I appreciate your calling."

As she hung up, Thalia heard the sound of Greg's motor racing, an angry sound in the nighttime stillness of Stony Harbor, and then there was a squeal of tires and he was gone.

29

Chapin Hope couldn't wait for his visit with his two sons to come to an end. Lord knows, he did his best. He spent the better part of a week exercising his genius for building bridges and reconciling differences. He explained the ways of the world to his sons, told them of the weaknesses that human flesh was heir to, was at times painfully honest with them. At the end of that time—after six days of ducking his mother-in-law and crawling before his sons—he got the verdict from Chapin Jr.

"You know what you're doing?" the boy said. "You're just trying to rationalize away what you did."

Rationalize? Where in the hell did a fourteen-year-old boy get that kind of nonsense? Rationalize! He was simply explaining the way things were, simply articulating reality. That's what Chapin was thinking. What he said was something else.

"Perhaps you're right, son," he said. "But there's another possibility. Maybe, when you're a little older, you won't be quite so hard on your old man as you are now."

Driving away from the boys, Chapin felt only one strong emotion: relief. There was nothing more depressing than waging an extended war without prospect of victory. Of course, he was doing nothing more than racing from one battlefield to the next. Oh, there was one difference—two nights earlier he had seen Thalia on television and for the first time he felt there might be some hope of salvaging something.

It was not just what she said, that business about anyone being capable of infidelity. It was more the way she said it. She seemed more philosophical somehow, more tolerant. What he saw on the television screen was at least the possibility of another chance. But what he found waiting for him at home was a woman who sidestepped his attempted embrace.

"I saw you on television," he said to her, "and I want to thank you for the things you—"

"By this time you should know better than to believe everything you see on television."

231

"You were very convincing," he said.

"To everyone except myself, then. Chape, you may as well know it—I haven't changed my thinking. I've spent a lot of time considering the life we've led and one thing I do know—I'm not at all interested in turning the clock back."

"I'm not asking for that. Maybe if we could just start over again, if we could at least love each other a little."

"That would solve nothing. That would just confuse the issue. One thing I don't want is to have the issue any more confused than it is now."

"Thal, I want you. When I saw you on television, I couldn't wait to get here. I know we could—"

"I suppose your other women friends don't want to have anything to do with you anymore. Well, you really can't blame them."

"Thal, it's you I need."

"Oh, I don't know," she said. "I'm sure you could get your pal Greg to fix you up with one of his."

"What's that supposed to mean?"

"Whatever you want it to mean. Greg left a message for you this morning; you're supposed to come down to the office as soon as you get home."

"Thal, I really do need you."

"Not yet, Chape," she said. "You go along down to the office. Look, don't expect too much from me. Not now."

A month earlier Chapin Hope might have ignored the meter in front of his office; now he was careful to insert the nickel. In the old days he couldn't have stepped out of the car without hearing a chorus of hellos; Stony Harbor had been Chapin Hope's preserve the way Sherwood Forest belonged to Robin Hood. On Saturdays Chapin had delighted in walking the length of Main Street with Chape Jr. and Tommy, had felt a sense of squireship as he exchanged greetings with the storekeepers. The voices then had been eager, fawning, admiring. At the soda parlor the proprietor would give the boys free chunks of broken chocolate and sometimes they would stop at the hobby shop for the latest car models or at the stationery store for the current *Mad* magazine. In summer they brought their poles down to the dock, where they fished for snappers—baby bluefish that Chapin would later roll in flour and fry in oil.

This time there were no greetings as he hurried past the Village Hall to his office. His junior partner, Jack Battalini, was leaving the building as Chapin entered; there was a brief nod from the younger man, a cursory "Chapin." In the days that Chapin thought of as

BI—Before Indictment—Jack would have stopped, no matter how pressing his engagement, and would have paid court. Christ, thought Chapin, the ethnics were all ganging up on him. He was up against a veritable United Nations force. O'Malley, Brownstein, Battalini, and even that bastard Galton, who was half Jewish although he attended the Episcopal Church. And the latest word was that the trial was being assigned to Frank Barrows, the show nigger on the Nassau bench.

It would be easy to become paranoid. Chapin could sense that everyone—even his secretary—treated him in a different way. It would be different if he were the killer, but he wasn't, damn it, he wasn't. Grace, who worked part time for him, mumbled something about no messages and made believe she had some pressing business at the file cabinet. Greg's secretary looked at him as if he were carrying leprosy symptoms: "Mr. Hammer's been *waiting* for you."

He pushed open the door to his partner's office.

"You son of a bitch!" Greg Hammer slammed his fist down on his desk. "You stupid son of a bitch!"

It took a moment. Chapin stood there, his hand still on the doorknob, trying to grasp the fact that his partner was being serious.

"Easy," he said. "Take it easy, Greg."

"Chapin, you are such a fucking idiot."

"Hold it right there. I don't have to take this from anyone. The last I hear, we were partners around here—so stop treating me like one of your flunkies."

"Bullshit!" The veins at Greg's temple were purpling. "After the stunt you pulled, buddy, you take whatever you get. You and that pain-in-the-ass wife of yours, too. Take it or get yourself another lawyer."

Greg got to his feet then and at that moment Chapin wondered whether he was going to throw a punch.

"What are you talking about?" Chapin said. "What the hell are you talking about?"

"You don't know? You have no idea?"

"What's this game, twenty questions?"

"Suppose I tell you that the judge ruled on our motions and that one of the things he granted was our demand to see the physical evidence. I suppose that doesn't give you any ideas?"

"What ideas?"

"Let me give you a hint, Chape. A key word. Something you find around the house. Trousers. How's that? Trousers."

Chapin sat down. He had known all along. He had known ever since the grand jury appearance when the assistant district attorney

233

asked him about the suit. He had known it but he had not wanted to believe it.

"How?"

"They were going through your garbage."

"What? They what?"

"They went for the long shot and they hit the daily double. They found the pair of gray flannel trousers that you put in your garbage. But I'm sure you can explain it. I'm sure you can explain right now why you put a perfectly good pair of gray trousers in the garbage."

"Jesus!"

"And I'm sure you can explain what the spot on it is, the spot on the left pant leg."

"I'd hate to have to explain any of it."

"That's unfortunate, Chapin. That's truly unfortunate."

"Greg, this is all a surprise to me."

"Well, it's as much a surprise to me, even more. And it isn't the kind of surprise a lawyer likes to get. The worst thing a client can do is hold out on his attorney. I thought you might understand that. You *do* have a law degree? Well, to spare me any future surprise, maybe you'd like to take this opportunity to tell me where you put the ax."

"Let up, Greg."

"No, you grade-A-fucking moron, I don't think I will let up. I don't think I'll let up one goddamn bit. You just sit there and listen. First, we got the notice on the motion. The ruling. It said that the only thing we couldn't see was the list of prosecution witnesses. That won't bother me unless there is someone you have neglected to mention, maybe someone who sold you an ax the day before the murder. . . ."

"Christ, Greg, that's an awful thing to say."

"Not at all. Not considering what you pulled. Anyway, we were home free on the autopsy report, which is wonderful reading and tells about everything from the jism that was left in your lady-friend's vagina to the condition of her head. Here, let me give you an idea." Greg picked up a xeroxed sheet and started reading: " 'Specimens taken: Brain and stomach contents for toxicology; clothes and hair to Meadow Glen laboratory.' But that's not the good part. Here's something that might interest you. A little diagram."

This sheet of paper carried line drawings of various parts of the body.

"My God!"

"Don't turn away. Take a good look. It's about time you understood what this case was all about. Maybe if you understand that, you won't pull any more of this kind of shit. You know, of course, there's a new nickname for you going around town. Maybe you've heard it. Hopeless. Senator Hopeless. At first I thought it was unfair but now it's beginning to make a certain amount of sense. It has a kind of ring to it.''

Had they ever been friends?

"Get it over with, Greg.''

"I told you. Don't *you* ever tell *me* what to do. Not if you want me to save your ass. Chapin, allow me to let you in on something. Yesterday afternoon I was on the phone with Lenny Wexler. I hate to think of Lenny Wexler getting all the headlines that are going to go to the guy who defends you. I hate to think of Lenny Wexler getting any more fame but you want to know something? He couldn't find the time to handle your case. It's possible that he is that busy but I'm wondering if he didn't know who he'd be dealing with. Chape, it looks like I'm stuck with you. But you start doing what I tell you to do, or I'm going to drop you like a hot potato.''

Chapin was tempted. He was tempted to tell Greg Hammer to go fuck himself. He was tempted to say the words in a tone of quiet contempt and then walk out of the office.

"Okay," he said.

"That's better," Greg said. "Let me go back. We had no trouble on the autopsy request; we were also given permission to examine the physical evidence and the prosecution's lab reports. The first thing I noticed was what isn't on the evidence list—they don't have anything resembling a murder weapon there. Unless, of course, you sliced her up with marijuana butts. They're also on the evidence list. Obviously they were found in the apartment. But we can handle that. You're not on trial for smoking pot, you're on trial for murder. There're also newspaper clippings that the cops found in your girlfriend's place—did you know she was keeping a little memory box on you? Sweet. Very touching. But that's not going to be a problem either. We'll concede that she knew you and that you were banging her. Except, of course, we'll call it love. Maybe the jury will look at it as the last fling of a forty-year-old man searching for his youth. I was just beginning to wonder if they had anything worthwhile at all when I noticed the last item—a pair of men's gray flannel trousers. Whose? Obviously they'd have to be yours to make any sense as evidence. Only, why hadn't you told me about the missing pants? That, old buddy, is when I began to get the first glimmerings of your capacity for shitheadedness. When I checked the lab reports and saw that there was one on the trousers, I got an even better idea of the sheer scope of that capacity. Because it said that the pants contained a bloodstain and that the blood was type O, which does not happen to be your type but does happen to be Virginia Hanson's.''

"I should've told you."

"Anyway, so we're allowed to see the evidence, even conduct our own tests on it. I decided not to wait until you got back. I wouldn't have taken you along in any case. Yesterday I picked up my lab man and drove into Mineola. Galton sent Ferris over to the evidence vault to help us—actually, I think they were looking for some kind of reaction. Ferris seemed to take a certain pleasure in telling me how they came up with the trousers. When the guard came out with the trousers, no one had to tell me that they belonged to you. I could practically see you in them. Forgive me, Chape, but you've never been much of a dresser. My technician made the same tests the cops had and got the same results. Suddenly it looks like they've got a case against you. Not the strongest case in the world—because if you were the killer, you'd expect the pants to be covered with blood—but not the weakest either. Of course, I haven't heard your explanation yet. Since we all know that you didn't do it, I'm sure you have a marvelous explanation. I'm sure you can tell me how the broad's blood got on your pants."

"She cut her finger on a soda can."

"Come again."

"A flip-top can. She cut her finger on it. I helped her patch it up. That's how the blood got on my pants."

"A flip-top soda can?"

"That's what I said."

"Yeah, but I didn't quiet believe it." Greg laughed and shook his head. "Actually, it's not so bad. It's so fucking stupid we may even get away with it. A flip-top soda can—I think that'll play."

"Is that about it?"

"Pretty much. I hope you've got things straight now. Just try to keep in mind that you're facing a murder charge. The minimum sentence for murder in our great state is fifteen to twenty-five and the max is life. If you don't want that to happen, don't pull any more shit. What we're going to do now is go over the whole thing again from start to finish. From the moment you walked into that god-damn bar and your lady love introduced you to that broad no one's been able to find, that Charlotte, to the moment she dropped you back at your car and you saw her through the window when you drove out of the parking lot. We're going to make sure there isn't anything else you neglected to tell me. Or that you haven't pulled any other idiocies. Not telling me about the trousers was dumb but putting them in the garbage, that's simply incredible. I almost hate to ask you, but what'd you do with the jacket?"

"It's still in my closet."

"Jeezus!"

"I know all this seems a little stupid, Greg, but let me ask you, what would you have done with the pants?"

"Are you kidding me? Those pants are evidence. I'd have taken the whole fucking suit, put it in the fireplace, and had a wienie roast."

"Okay," Chapin said, "that's something I've got to live with. One thing bothers me. It seems to me like they're the ones who are making all the moves—now's the time we ought to be doing something."

"We are doing something."

"Like what?"

"One thing, I'm trying to do Brownstein's job for him and solve the fucking case. We've got investigators breaking their backs trying to find out who else was cozy with your little girlfriend. You'll see how much we're doing when the bills start to come in."

"How about the trial itself? Shouldn't we be rounding up our own witnesses?"

"*Our* witnesses?"

"You know, character witnesses. . . ."

"Character witnesses, hey, that's a terrific idea." There was no mistaking the sarcasm in Greg Hammer's voice. "Okay, I've got a pencil. Fire away."

"What're you talking about?"

"All those character witnesses," he said. "I'm ready to start listing them. Who should we start with?"?

"I don't need this, Greg. You know them as well as I do. We could start with some of the senators—Jack Dunbar, the others—and maybe we could scare up a judge or two. . . ."

"Chapin, are you still smoking pot? What had happened to your—okay, I spoke to Jack. Also to Clark. Also to Roger. Also to any other members of the club who would still return my call. Some of them would go so far as to wish you good luck. But not one of them is willing to come into the courtroom and—"

"Well, of course, I can see where a politician would have to keep hands off, but surely we can get—"

"Chapin, let me level with you here. I've spoken to a dozen people—no, more—people who've known you most of your life and not one—no one—will willingly go into court and speak on your behalf. Some of them we can lean on and make them, by God, appear but there are so few it might be worse to have them there. That fucking O'Malley has not exactly been helping our cause. I'll tell you true, if your sainted mother read O'Malley's stories, she'd

237

think twice about coming forward.''

''Jesus, Greg, I had no idea.''

''You may as well know what we're up against,'' the lawyer said. ''In fact, I asked everyone I thought might be remotely possible. We've spoken to dozens of people. Nothing. In fact, through it all, there was only one person who volunteered to say something about you. Funny thing was that he came to me. I didn't even have to call him. He came here and asked if he could be a character witness for you.''

''Who was that?''

''Leroy Wilkins.''

''Leroy Wilkins. Hell, I don't even know a Leroy Wilkins.''

''No?'' Greg said. ''Think about it. *Leroy. Lee*-roy. The spade who brings the drinks to the locker room at the club.''

30

The selection of a jury in the Chapin Hope murder trial was accomplished in less than a week. Defense counsel Hammer's primary question to prospective jurors was whether they would allow evidence of marital infidelity to prejudice them against the defendant. He also made sure that they accepted the theory of reasonable doubt. "Even if you think it probable that a defendant is guilty," he explained, "you would have to vote for acquittal if there were the slightest reason for doubt." District Attorney Galton's questions were aimed at determining if the prospective jurors would be able to convict someone on the basis of circumstantial evidence. He also asked whether they felt that a man of Chapin Hope's political prominence was immune to criminal acts. The answer was invariably "no."

The day the first witnesses were to begin testifying, Norman Galton stayed under the sunlamp an extra five minutes. He was going to need all the color he could muster up. It was not just that he would be facing the cameras; on this particular day he would also have to face up to Chuck Ferris and Rocco Porcina.

Norman Galton had come to an independent political decision. For the first time in his career he was turning his back on instructions from above and advice from below. Here he was, involved in the kind of case that most prosecutors only dream of, and he had been lingering in the background like some teenage wallflower. Norman Galton didn't know what you call someone who avoids available spotlight but the one thing you never called him was "Governor."

"You're what?" Ferris said.

"I'm handling the case myself."

"It's a mistake, Norman, a bad mistake."

"Damn it, Chuck, how long have I been here?" Galton asked. "Right here in this job? Nine years. Building a reputation and waiting for a break. Something that would generate the next move up—the big move."

"I understand your thinking," Ferris said. "But this isn't the case. There are too many risks."

239

Galton was adamant: "This damn case is in the papers every day. Whoever prosecutes Hope is going to cash in. If it's some new guy—say I give it to Farnsworth—you know what that'd mean. That'd mean that every other morning I'd open the paper and see Farnsworth's picture. And one day it wouldn't just be the picture of my most promising assistant, it'd be the picture of the next Congressman. Or the next Senator. Or governor."

"What about Rocco?" Ferris said. "Or do you think he was just kidding? I thought he told you plain and simple that he didn't want you involved in this case."

"Rocco isn't God."

"The point is, Norman, Rocco *is* God, at least in this county, and you know it. The last politician around here to come out against Rocco was the famous Arthur J. Stainbeck."

"Who?"

"My point exactly."

"I get the point, Chuck, but I've thought a lot about this. We simply can't let the Hope case slip by; we may never get another chance like it. In any event, I'm going to do it. Look, I've drawn up a statement for the press and what it needs is that old Ferris touch."

"What it really needs is a match. The fact is that unless you win this case, it can destroy you. And to win it, you're going to have to do a top-notch job in court and you haven't been there for a while. There can't be any mistakes."

"But I *have* been there, Chuck, and you shouldn't overlook that point."

Indeed, he had been there. There had been a time when Norman Galton had been the fourth-ranking editor of the *Harvard Law Review*; the way one became the fourth-ranking editor of the *Harvard Law Review* was by being the fourth-ranking student in the class. The career that followed Harvard was at least marked by flashes of brilliance. Others had gone to work for Supreme Court judges and for large corporations but Norman Galton had chosen to slug it out in the slums of the legal profession, in the criminal courts, representing anyone who would have him. Then he discovered politics. No one ever confused him with Clarence Darrow but Galton could not look at his brightest young assistant, Kip Farnsworth, without thinking of himself at an earlier time. Where had it gone?

"There's one more thing," Ferris way saying. "While you've been junketing around the country these past eight years speaking at law-and-order banquets, L. Gregory Hammer has been trying cases—and winning them. You go in there against him and he just might cut you up bad."

"Are you finished, Chuck? Are you quite finished?"

"Yes."

"Good. Then will you take a look at this statement? I think it needs something a little lively near the end."

Rocco Porcina was letting his four-year-old grandson sip from his glass of Tab when Norman Galton appeared on the screen, his tan showing up nicely on Rocco's twenty-seven-inch Zenith. The district attorney was reading from a piece of paper.

"Because of the importance of this case," he said, "and because of its political overtones, I have decided personally to prosecute the case against Chapin Hope. This is the first trial I have prosecuted in several years and the only reason I would undertake this arduous task now is to ensure absolute fairness, to make sure that justice is served in Nassau County."

Rocco Porcina's already-narrow eyes narrowed further. He reached for the remote-control gun, aimed it deliberately at the television set, and slowly squeezed his district attorney into oblivion.

"Carmela!" he called into the kitchen.

"Yes, dear."

"Do me a little something tomorrow," he said. "Pick me out a nice get-well-soon card, something very nice with flowers, and send it to Norman Galton. Put my name on it. Just 'Rocco'—and he'll know who it is."

"Is Norman sick?"

"It looks that way," he said. "Very sick. It looks like maybe he's not going to make it."

The statue that Norman Galton walked past on his way into the Nassau County Courthouse was of Christopher Columbus, a man whose connection to law and order escaped the district attorney. But then there was little about the building's exterior to indicate its purpose. From the outside the courthouse might have been taken as a school or an office building. Or even a jail.

When he got inside, Galton was not particularly surprised by the number of people crowding into the courthouse's central corridor. It had even been that way during the jury selection. It was a hot-ticket trial and the buffs had come early—women carrying satchels large enough to hold their lunches and their knitting, women trading in their soap operas for a dose of reality. Some of those competing for the 150 available seats recognized Galton and the district attorney smiled as he heard his name whispered by strangers.

Damn that Ferris. Galton missed Ferris. His assistant had asked to be excused from courtroom duties and Galton had agreed reluctantly. He made sure Ferris had a seat in the spectator section, however. At Ferris' suggestion, he had assigned Kip Farnsworth and another of his bright young men to help him with the trial, and they were already seated at the prosecution table when he arrived. He was not entirely pleased with them. It seemed to Galton that they eyed him in much the way a pair of lean barracuda might watch the death throes of an aging whale.

Nor would matters improve when the judge arrived. The plaque on his desk said, COURTROOM OF HONORABLE FRANK H. BARROWS. Barrows had emerged from a welfare family in Harlem, had been discovered there by Princeton University's inner-city recruiter, had been educated at Princeton on full scholarship, had won a second grant to Yale Law School. Galton felt that all this largesse should have instilled a sense of gratitude in Barrows' soul. But that was not the case. At forty-four Frank Barrows was a belligerent, whip-thin black who ran his courtroom like Genghis Khan.

Sitting beside his two assistants, Galton glanced over toward the jury. Fourteen strangers—twelve jurors and two alternates—all seemingly middle-aged; the men wearing neckties, the women in pearls and beads. Two blacks, one woman who might or might not be black. Six of the fourteen were wearing eyeglasses.

Turning toward the table directly behind him, Galton could see Chapin Hope and Greg Hammer. As he glanced at them, Hammer took a pencil from behind his ear and filled in a space in the morning *Times* crossword puzzle. There were three sharp raps, as of a nightstick hitting a wooden bench, and Hammer folded up the newspaper to rise with the rest of the court.

Judge Frank Barrows' no-nonsense style was immediately apparent. Ignoring everyone else, he turned to the jury and began his instructions—outlining legal procedures familiar to anyone who ever owned a television set.

"There may be a particular difficulty about a piece of evidence," the judge was saying. "Say, the admissibility of a certain piece of evidence. In that case I may excuse you. As you know, the jury is not involved in determining questions of law. You determine the facts and I'll determine the law. You do your job and I'll do mine."

Galton noticed that Hammer had again taken his pencil to fill in other spaces in the crossword puzzle.

"There may be a situation that will arise," Barrows went on, "when the answer is given to a question and one or another of the attorneys will object. If that objection is sustained—if I grant that—I will say, 'The jury will disregard that last answer.' Now, I know we are all human beings, that we can't completely forget something we have already heard. Okay, don't strike it from your mind—but do strike it from your consideration."

It had been a long time. Galton had forgotten so much of it. The words the judge was saying. The kind of hum—expectancy—that fills a courtroom during a big trial. Even the courtroom itself; the slender twenty-foot frosted windows on one side of the room, the six overhead chandeliers, the large American flag decorating the wall behind the judge. Had the flag always been that wrinkled?

He was snapped back by Hammer's voice.

"I have a motion," the defense attorney was saying, "that all witnesses be excluded from these proceedings."

"Well?" The judge seemed to be looking at Galton.

"Your Honor?" Galton said.

"Do you have any objection, Mr. Galton?"

"No, no objection."

"Very well, so ruled."

And so the process began. Galton walked to the lectern directly in front of the jury box. The reading light was off but he didn't want to begin by fumbling around for a light switch. Instead he strained to read his notes in dimness.

"After several days of jury selection," Galton began, "we are now at that stage of trial where we are about to begin considering the evidence. Now, as the judge has told you, I am required by law to make an opening statement to you. My opening statement has two aims. I want to read you the indictment. And then I intend to tell you in rough terms how we are going to prove that indictment."

Galton paused. The reason he stopped was that from the corner of his eye he could see Hammer blocking an enormous yawn. Frowning, the district attorney picked up his copy of the indictment and held it up so that he could read it from the light of the chandeliers.

" 'The County Court of Nassau County. The People of the State of New York against Chapin Hope. The Grand Jury of the County of Nassau in the State of New York accuses the defendant, Chapin Hope, of murder. . . . On or about November 11th, the defendant did, with the intent to kill, with a sharp-edged instrument kill Virginia Hanson in Mineola, New York. The Grand Jury of Nassau County by this indictment further accuses the defendant, Chapin Hope, of the crime of sexual assault on the victim, Virginia Hanson, in Mineola, New York, on the same date."

Galton folded the indictment and slipped it into his jacket pocket, then turned so that, at the proper moment, he might point his hand toward the defendant.

"The indictment is an accusatory document," he said. "It points the finger of accusation at State Senator Chapin Kirk Hope. And now it is up to us, as prosecutors, to explain the reason for this indictment, this accusation. How do we propose to do that?''

He was sure Hammer would have used a different approach, something a little less pedestrian. Well, Norman Galton could do that, too, could go beyond the Dick-and-Jane approach, but unless juries had changed radically in the past nine years it would not be worth the effort. Juries were still not selected on the basis of wit or intelligence. What you had to do was draw a picture for them.

"Now, one way we will do this is by calling witnesses. Some of these witnesses will be policemen and some of them will be police experts. We will call the county coroner—the medical examiner—who will describe the manner in which Virginia Hanson was abused and murdered. This will not be pleasant for any of us and I will apologize in advance to the ladies of the jury because this is not a pretty crime.

"We will call a bartender who will tell us that the defendant was intimate with the late Virginia Hanson for months before the murder. We will call other witnesses who will testify to their relationship. We will call a bank executive who will tell us how the senator arranged a sizable loan for the victim—and then paid it off himself. We will have a fingerprint expert place the senator in the dead woman's apartment. We will have a neighbor of the victim tell us the senator was in Miss Hanson's apartment the night she was murdered. And we will have a close business associate of the senator tell us that the senator knew he was wanted for questioning weeks before his arrest and yet he refused to come forward.

"Another way we will explain this indictment, this accusation, is through the presentation of evidence. We will offer evidence taken from the dead woman's apartment, and I will again apologize in advance for upsetting those of a squeamish nature. And we will produce a pair of trousers worn by the defendant on the night of the murder. Trousers stained by blood—the same blood as that of the victim, the late Virginia Hanson.

"We will in effect reconstruct the last night in Virginia Hanson's life—a night of drugs, liquor, sex, and slaughter. And in doing that, ladies and gentlemen of the jury, we will demonstrate beyond all reasonable doubt that the murderer of the late Virginia Hanson was her married lover, State Senator Chapin Kirk Hope.''

Leaving the lectern, Galton congratulated himself. Oh, it was not the kind of thing you heard on television, not the kind of presentation that emits sparks, but appealing to a jury was like appealing to a voter. The important thing was to be serious and somber, even at the risk of seeming a little dull. And that wouldn't hurt—juries tended to trust the lawyers that seemed incapable of outwitting them. Galton could anticipate the reactions, could guess how they would respond to the "drugs, liquor, sex, and slaughter." That had been Ferris' phrase, one of his very few contributions. The district attorney had been especially pleased by the way he had curled his lips around the phrase "married lover." He made the mistake then of looking over toward Greg Hammer and he felt his confidence evaporate.

Hammer was smiling broadly and pouring himself a glass of ice water. Judge Frank Barrows was busying himself with paperwork, and if he had reacted at all to Galton's opening statement, he was not indicating the nature of his reaction. Nor did Galton's two young assistants offer any sign of approval. Almost in desperation then, Galton singled out Chuck Ferris in the spectator section; it seemed to him that Ferris was frowning.

Then it was Hammer's turn. He walked up to the same lectern, seemed to notice that the lamp was off, and reached over to switch it on. He did this even though he was not reading from notes.

"Chapin Hope killed no one and is guilty of no crime," the lawyer said. "That will be proved shortly."

And then he sat down. The courtroom buzzed and Galton wondered why. It was too underplayed, too simple. Norman Galton, for one, was not impressed. His feeling that Hammer was overrated grew stronger as the first few prosecution witnesses testified. The defense lawyer seemed under no compulsion to shine. He allowed witnesses to come to the stand without suffering an intensive cross-examination; his infrequent questions seemed designed simply to clarify points that had been previously made.

From time to time Galton himself tried for a moment of drama—by asking a question that was not in his script. The fingerprint technician had described the volume of prints taken from the dead woman's apartment when Galton enjoyed what seemed to him to be a flash of real inspiration.

"Tell me," he said, "did you happen to find any of Chapin Hope's fingerprints on the remains of the marijuana cigarettes?"

"Objection," Hammer said. "The defense is perfectly willing to concede that Senator Hope had been a visitor to the dead woman's apartment. What the senator may have smoked during those visits is immaterial."

"Sustained," the judge said.

"Well, then, let me reword the question," Galton said. "Did you happen to take anyone's *fingerprints* from the marijuana cigarettes?"

245

"No way," the technician said. "How could anyone take a print from something like that?"

There was something about the man's incredulity that caused a low rumble of laughter to fill the courtroom. Why not? If it had been another attorney, Galton would have participated in the merriment. Now he could feel the flush creep up his cheeks, threatening to ignite his ears. He had forgotten so much of it; what he had forgotten most of all was the necessity for restraint.

"No further questions," he said.

Hammer got to his feet and spoke from the table.

"Tell me," he said, "all those fingerprints you took from Virginia Hanson's apartment. How many different people did they come from?"

"A dozen or so," the technician said.

"And I assume that you've checked out the identities of the other visitors to Miss Hanson's apartment."

"We've been able to link the prints with three or four known visitors."

"Now, correct me if I'm wrong," Hammer said, "but that means that there's another half dozen or more prints that you've been unable to identify."

"That's correct."

"No more questions."

Immediately following the lunch recess, Leonard McCoy went to the stand. The timing left something to be desired. More than one juror felt a certain queasiness as the county medical examiner began a long, detailed description of the condition of the body on his arrival. He mentioned such items as "the abdominal cavity" and "exposed frontal bones" and "exposed gullet, with windpipe missing" and "blood running from all orifices" and "solid food particles remaining in stomach" and "right lobe of liver severely shredded" and, finally, "decapitated head with both eyes missing — orbits appearing normal." Although he stuck with technical terms, the doctor seemed to linger just a trifle lovingly over some of the details.

"Thank you, Doctor, that seemed a complete report," Galton said. "Your witness."

"Tell me, Doctor," Hammer said, coming forward, "you mentioned the presence of spermatozoa in the corpse. But I don't see any mention of the test in which spermatozoa are compared to the defendant's blood type."

McCoy was nettled. "That test isn't done in Nassau County," he said.

"Really?" Hammer said. "That's standard police procedure

246

now in much of the country—a test that enables authorities to determine a donor's blood type by examination of spermatozoa.''

"I've heard of it," said the coroner.

"But you don't perform it?"

"That is correct."

"Then your report is not quite as complete as we might have wished, is it?"

"Objection," Galton said.

"Sustained."

"No further questions."

At the prosecution table Farnsworth whispered to Galton. "Get him on redirect. McCoy obviously doesn't think it's a definitive test."

"Forget it," Galton said. Who wanted to hear about spermatozoa? Although you never knew what the press would pick up. But he had a much better idea than keeping the medical examiner on the stand. What he needed now was a little . . . blockbuster. Yes, that was it. He turned back to Farnsworth.

"Let's call Cappobianco next," he said.

"That's not the game plan," Farnsworth said. "We haven't laid out the rest of the physical evidence."

"We need something *now*," Galton said. "I don't want everyone going to bed tonight thinking we've got no case. Call Cappobianco."

Frank Cappobianco took the stand as the light on the other side of the long frosted windows was dimming. Slowly Galton led him down the trail to the bloodstained trousers. He wanted maximum effect. Finally, as his witness was talking, Galton walked over to the evidence display and picked up the pair of trousers; he wished that somehow the bloodstain was larger, that it was more than a smudge, that it was the kind of thing that would turn a couple of stomachs.

"Do you recognize these?" he said to Cappobianco.

"Yes, sir."

God damn it, didn't Cappobianco understand what he was there for? Galton almost had to take him by the hand and he wasn't entirely successful in keeping the sarcasm out of his voice.

"Would you care to tell us about that, Officer?"

"I was working the garbage detail—"

"Excuse me, Detective Cappobianco," Galton said, "but it might be helpful if you would tell us what the garbage detail is and what its assignment was."

"We were assigned to accompany the garbage truck in Stony Harbor. It was our job to examine the suspect's garbage."

"By 'suspect,' you mean the defendant, Chapin Hope."

"Yes, sir."

Damn it, the man was as bad as Brownstein. "So you went through Chapin Hope's garbage every day. . . ."

"Objection," Hammer said. "Leading the witness."

"Sustained."

"Well, Officer Cappobianco, why don't you tell us more precisely what this assignment entailed?"

"We went through Senator Hope's garbage every day."

Was the bastard being sarcastic? "And. . . ."

"And?"

"Let's take the morning of February sixth. Do you think you could tell us what happened on the morning of February sixth?"

"On the morning of Tuesday, February sixth, we noticed a brown paper bag in Senator Hope's garbage. This bag was rolled up tight and—"

"Objection!" L. Gregory Hammer was on his feet. "We must object to the prosecution's attempt to introduce improper evidence. The court has not yet been informed as to whether Detective Cappobianco had a search warrant."

"A search warrant?" Galton yelled. "What's the matter with you, Hammer! What kind of cockamamy—"

Barrows' voice cut Galton into silence. "Will counsel please approach the bench?" the judge said.

Hammer and Galton took separate paths to the desk. They were joined by the court reporter, who placed his machine between the two of them and started recording the conversation. The voices of the three men were no more than a low rumble to the rest of the courtroom.

"Mr. Galton," the judge began, "I never want to see a display like that again. I should think you would know better. This is a courtroom, not a saloon. It is not a forum for shouting matches. I hope I make myself clear."

"I'm sorry, Your Honor, it's just—"

"Now, Mr. Hammer, why don't you tell me what this is all about? I'm sure you realize that this is the wrong time to object to evidence; the proper time would have been before the courtroom proceedings had actually commenced."

"I would have introduced my objection earlier, Your Honor," Hammer said, "but I had no way of knowing how this so-called evidence was discovered. I had no idea that the police were searching the senator's garbage without a search warrant. There's a precedent here, Your Honor, a case in California recently in which—"

"As a matter of fact," Judge Barrows said, "I'm aware of that case and it did involve a similar search. The determining factor was, as I recall it now, whether the garbage can was covered or uncovered. Mr. Galton, what was the exact condition of the garbage can?"

Norman Galton may have appeared confused at that moment but his mind was finally functioning with a sharpness he barely remembered. He did not want to rush this moment, particularly when he glanced over at his adversary; one could not help but be impressed by the breadth of L. Gregory Hammer's grin. The district attorney took a deep breath and Hammer made his first real mistake of the day.

"Your Honor," he said, "since it's now apparent that the state's entire case depends on a single piece of fraudulently acquired evidence, I'm going to move that all charges against my client be dropped immediately."

"Perhaps, Mr. Galton," the judge said, "I should recess the trial and give you an opportunity to marshal all the necessary facts before I comment on Mr. Hammer's motion."

Galton couldn't decide which of the judge's two attitudes impressed him the least—his anger or his condescension.

"Oh, I shouldn't think there'd be any need for that," Galton said. "As a matter of fact, the evidence was acquired *after* the garbage cans had been emptied onto the truck. At this point, of course, the contents of the containers would have to be considered municipal property and there was clearly no need for a search warrant."

Galton turned to Hammer and treated him to his most sincere expression and Hammer was, for the moment, speechless. It was by no means the first time he had lost a courtroom skirmish and now he knew something; he would not again be careless with Norman Galton.

"Detective Cappobianco," Barrows said, addressing the witness directly while motioning both Greg and Norman to remain before the bench, "would you kindly describe the exact circumstances of your discovering the trousers?"

"They were in the senator's garbage," the detective said.

"We already know they were in the senator's garbage." The judge sighed. "What we want to know now is precisely—and I will stress *precisely*—how they came into your possession."

"Well, the garbage was dumped out onto the loading chute and then I sliced open the plastic bags and—"

"That's enough," Barrows said. "I guess, Mr. Hammer, I won't have to wait before acting on your motion. The court sees no reason to disallow the evidence or to drop charges against your client. Your motion is dismissed. And, considering the lateness of the hour, I think this might be an opportune moment to recess for the day.''

Norman Galton glanced at his two young assistants and he could see that Farnsworth was impressed. ''Not bad, Chief, not bad at all,'' the young man said. And then the district attorney saw something he hadn't seen in many days, something he had sorely missed. Chuck Ferris, still seated in the spectator section, was giving his boss his official smile of approval.

31

The press was at them the minute they got out of the car. Reporters followed them to the court building and a television camera crew had set up its equipment at the base of the statue of Columbus. Greg waved.

"The *Niña*, the *Pinta*, and *Channel Two*," he said.

Chapin and Thalia worked at their smiles but Greg's came without effort. He traded jokes with the reporters, played up to the cameras, and winked at the blonde from Channel 5. He only wished that Norman Galton could be there catching his act. Yesterday had been Norman's day but today Greg had a little surprise for him. It would be a gamble, but a good one. That is, of course, if Chapin was finally telling him the truth. Chape had reaffirmed the story and Greg tended to believe him this time.

This second day they were a half hour early but the bustle in the courthouse lobby reminded Greg of Madison Square Garden prior to a Knick game. Even the ebb and flow around the glassed-in relief map of Long Island was similar to the movement around the glassed-in floor plan of the Garden. Trials drew the kooks from their cubbyholes. Greg laughed out loud as Chapin brushed away an elderly woman who pulled a pad and pen out of her satchel and thrust it at him.

"At least she didn't give you an ax to sign," he said in a low voice.

The courtroom was jammed again. Galton and his assistants were already at the prosecution table. Galton was turning around, obviously counting the house. Transparent *schmuck!* The combination of Galton's sunlamp tan and Mr. Square haircut was too much. He was probably trying for the straight-shooter, crime-buster look but he came off like some refugee from a barbershop-quartet contest.

Uh-oh, Galton caught his eye and waved. Greg nodded brusquely. He hoped that none of the jurors had caught the exchange. Laymen didn't go for the professionals-together horseshit; they did not like the idea of prosecution and defense cozying up to each other.

The judge entered and Greg nudged Chapin to rise.

"His Honor, the nigger," Greg whispered.

The room was still as Galton finished with Cappobianco, taking him through the discovery of the trousers, the spotting of the stain, and the immediate delivery of the pants to the police laboratory. As Greg stood up to cross-examine, there was a buzz—an almost electric response—from the spectators. It was at moments such as this, only at moments such as this, that attorney L. Gregory Hammer felt one with the world. This was what he did better than anyone he knew.

He started easily, almost gently, reviewing Cappobianco's discovery of the trousers, asking once again the exact circumstances, following the trousers to the lab.

"Tell me, Detective Cappobianco," he asked then, "is this a routine procedure with you?"

"I'm not sure what you're getting at."

"Excuse me, Detective Cappobianco. I'll be more specific. Peeping into people's garbage. Do you do a lot of that?"

Galton was up.

"Objection."

"Counsel might have phrased the question a little less editorially," Barrows said, "but the objection is overruled."

Greg nodded at the judge.

"Let me rephrase that. Are garbage searches a routine practice for you, Detective Cappobianco?"

"For me personally or in the division?"

Greg assumed an expression of weary tolerance.

"For you personally."

"No."

"In fact, have you ever conducted such a search before?"

"No, sir. But I've only been in the—"

"Just respond to the question. Prior to going through Senator Hope's garbage, had you ever been assigned to such a detail? Yes or no."

"No."

Greg glanced over at Galton. The district attorney was now more red than brown. Somehow Greg was making the police department look like the KGB. Some of the jurors were undoubtedly thinking about cops going through *their* garbage.

"Now, about that stain you saw on the trousers. Would you say it was large or small?"

"I didn't measure it."

"I realize that, Detective Cappobianco, and I'm sure we'll get the dimensions when we hear testimony on the laboratory report.

252

But I'd like to know the way it appeared to you. Would you say it was large or small?''

"It was large enough to notice."

There was a ripple of laughter, and Greg joined it.

"Very good, Officer. Very good indeed. Let me put it another way. Was this stain on the trousers you pulled out of a private citizen's garbage the size of a half-dollar? Or was it even smaller than that? The size of a quarter, perhaps?''

"It wasn't round, it was irregularly shaped."

"I know that. But, even so, was it more like a half-dollar or a quarter?''

"A quarter, I guess."

Greg paused for a moment and then continued.

"About the size of a quarter." He reached into the pocket that contained the quarter he'd put there earlier in the day. "About this big?''

"Objection," Galton said. "The defense counsel is putting on a show.''

"I think you've made your point, Mr. Hammer," the judge said. "Objection sustained."

Greg put the coin back in his pocket. Galton had been right to object, but he had only heightened the effect. Another pause.

"And this stain the size of a quarter was the only trace of blood on the trousers?''

"Yes."

"Don't you find that curious?"

"Pardon?"

"As a detective, doesn't it bother you that there is just a single, small spot of blood on a pair of trousers supposedly worn during the commission of an ax murder? Wouldn't you expect a great deal of blood to be on such trousers? Wouldn't you expect them to be literally drenched with blood?''

Galton started to object but held back as Cappobianco answered. "Not necessarily. He might not have been wearing the trousers when he actually committed the murder. He could have been nude.''

"Or he could not have been," Greg said, frowning. "Okay, who told you to take the trousers to the laboratory, or was that something you did automatically?''

"Lieutenant Brownstein directed me."

"Lieutenant Brownstein is your superior, the head of Nassau's Homicide Division?''

"That's right."

"You've been under his command for how long?"

"Six months."

"And what division were you in before that?"

"I was a uniformed officer in the Second Precinct, sir."

Greg had deliberately chosen the roundabout route to his destination. Now he closed in.

"Yes, I'd almost forgotten that. Weren't you one of the officers who was called to Virginia Hanson's apartment the night of the murder? One of the patrolmen who was dispatched to the scene after a neighbor called headquarters?"

"That is correct."

"It must have been a terrible scene. Would you say it had an emotional effect on you?"

Galton was up again.

"Objection. I fail to see what my esteemed opponent intends to accomplish through this line of questioning."

"Sustained."

"I was simply trying to establish the possibility that Detective Cappobianco has an emotional attitude about the case, that he might—"

"The court is aware of your motive, Mr. Hammer," Barrows snapped. "Objection sustained. The jury will disregard counsel's last remarks."

Greg held up his hands in surrender.

"Sorry, Your Honor." He was almost on target. "Now we have already had testimony on the crime scene, Detective Cappobianco, and I won't ask you to go over that same ground. What does interest me, however, is whether you have anything to add to the description already offered."

"I'm not sure I understand your question."

Greg looked toward the windows and then turned back to the witness.

"Do you recall finding anything at the scene in the way of physical evidence that has not yet been mentioned?"

"Not to the best of my knowledge."

"Objection!" Galton called out. "Mr. Hammer is clearly off on some kind of fishing expedition."

"Your objection is not without merit," Barrows said. "Do you have something specific in mind, Mr. Hammer?"

"Detective Cappobianco has given direct testimony on the finding of what the prosecution claims is physical evidence, Your Honor. My line of questioning is germane to that finding."

"I don't see how," Galton said.

254

Greg raised his eyebrows.

"All the district attorney has to do is listen, Your Honor, and I'm confident that even he will understand."

Barrows' gavel silenced the laughter as it was forming.

"If opposing counsel are trying to work up a vaudeville act," he said, "they will have to find a forum other than my courtroom. Is that understood?"

"Yes, Your Honor," said Galton, thinking that it probably looked good for the party to have a black on the bench but that Barrows was too high a price to pay for that kind of public relations.

"Yes, Your Honor," said Hammer, thinking that the black bastard knew how to run a court.

"Splendid," Barrows said. "Objection overruled for the time being, but the court expects the point of your questioning to become apparent, and very soon, Mr. Hammer."

"It will, Your Honor. Now, Officer, let's get back to Virginia Hanson's apartment the night you discovered her murder. Was there any other physical evidence you remember?"

"Not that I'm aware of."

"Let me see if I can't help you out, then. Do you remember finding an empty soda can?"

"A soda can?"

"Yes, an empty can. To be precise, an empty Fresca can."

Cappobianco closed his eyes for a moment.

"Yes," he said finally. "Yes, there was a can. Fresca; maybe two or three of them. One was on a table in the living room."

Bang! He had counted on Cappobianco's alertness and he had been right.

"Very good, Officer. Let's just concentrate on the single can whose position you recall so precisely. What kind of can was it?"

"Just like you said, Fresca."

"No, no. How did it open?"

"Oh, yeah, it was a flip-top can."

"You're sure of that?"

"Yes, sir. I definitely remember that it was a flip-top can. I remember putting it down at the log book in headquarters."

"You're positive, then? It was a flip-top, an empty flip-top?"

"Yes, sir."

"Do you happen to know where that can is now, Officer? Or was it thrown out?"

"No, sir, it wasn't. It was turned over to the police property clerk's office with the other stuff."

"Objection!" Norman Galton would tolerate no more. "I'm

255

sorry, Your Honor, I've been listening to Mr. Hammer's questions very closely and I can't see what some soda can has to do with physical evidence linking the defendant to the murder of Virginia Hanson.''

"It has everything to do with it," Greg said. Cappobianco's last statement had been part of the gamble. Greg had been willing to bet that the can would be in the property clerk's office. Brownstein ran a thorough division. He had, however, missed one thing in not having the can analyzed at the lab. And Greg was sure it hadn't been analyzed. Because if Chape was telling the truth—and he goddamned well better be telling the truth this time—there had to be some trace of blood on that can. Virginia Hanson's blood.

Barrows beckoned to them.

"Would counsel please approach the bench?"

As he and Galton walked up to the bench, Greg looked at the flag above the judge; someone really should take that flag down and iron it. As the stenographer again placed his machine between the two lawyers, Barrows looked to Hammer. "All right, counselor," he said. "It's time for you to tell me precisely where you are taking us."

"The soda can is vital, Your Honor. We concede that the trousers found in Senator Hope's garbage were his and that the bloodstain on them was Miss Hanson's type. In fact, we'll go further and admit that the blood came from Miss Hanson. However, I'm positive that the can will demonstrate that the blood did not get onto the trousers through any act of violence. The fact is that Miss Hanson cut her finger on the can when she and Senator Hope were together earlier in the evening, and he attended to the cut. That's when a drop of blood fell onto his trousers."

"Tell me, Mr. Hammer," the judge said, "do you know if the can has been tested for blood?"

"That's my next question to Cappobianco," Greg said. "I don't know whether he'll have that information—he wasn't a detective at the time of the murder. And I might add, the can wasn't listed on the prosecution's evidence sheet."

"Do *you* know, Mr. Galton?" the judge asked.

"Well, I must admit that this whole development is new to me, Your Honor."

"According to the testimony of your witness," the judge said, "the can does exist."

"I know, but, uh. . . ."

"It was mentioned in his report, he says."

"Yes, Your Honor, I just don't know about it."

"Mr. Galton, far be it from me to tell you how to run your office, but I think this is something you might find out for us."

"Just a minute, Your Honor, and I'll check with Chief Brownstein."

Greg watched Barrows carefully. If anything, the judge's expression became more austere. It was obvious that Galton was attempting to pass the buck. The district attorney beckoned to Brownstein and the two men had a whispered conversation at the police benches. Watching them, Greg was struck by the contrast—Brownstein's calm and Galton's consternation. He looked for Ferris in the spectator's section and spotted the aide leaning forward with a frown on his face. Galton walked back to the bench slowly.

"We do have the can, Your Honor," he said. "But it was never sent to the lab."

"Mr. Galton, I am going to call another recess and I suggest that you obtain the can and send it to the police laboratory immediately."

"Of course, you realize, Your Honor, this may have no bearing on the evidence. Even if her blood type is on the can, that doesn't prove anything."

"You're trying my patience, Mr. Galton."

The district attorney wouldn't let up.

"I don't see why we have to recess. This is a smoke screen by the defense, Your Honor, a red herring. Mr. Hammer is famous for—"

"Not another word, Mr. Galton." Frank Barrows looked at the district attorney of Nassau County as though he were about to spank him. "I'm calling a recess. I want that can tested. And I want the lab report and the technician who makes the test in court first thing on Monday morning. Do I make myself clear?"

"We'll get right on it, Your Honor."

Barrows announced the recess, giving the "examination of new evidence" as his reason. There was a buzz of annoyance from the spectators, who reacted like fans watching a ball game called because of a drizzle. As the courtroom emptied, Galton and Brownstein huddled at the prosecution table. Greg couldn't hear the words but there was no mistaking the ferocity in the district attorney's face. Then he spotted Chuck Ferris hurrying up from the spectator section and as he went by, Greg grabbed his arm.

"Hey, Chuck, what's the hurry?"

Ferris shook him off with the muscular quickness of a good halfback. "Get your hand off me, Hammer."

Greg was surprised by the force in Ferris' voice.

257

"Sorry, Chuck," he said. "I just wanted to ask you how you let Norman get into this."

Greg wasn't sure that he caught Ferris' answer. The district attorney's hatchet man had a reputation as being highly self-controlled. Still, the last word he said was "you" and the first sounded very much like "fuck."

32

Although there was a full weekend to analyze the can, Galton drove to police headquarters with flags flying and sirens screaming. Brownstein sat up front, embarrassed merely by being part of the sideshow, but even more embarrassed by the circumstances that caused him to be there. A detail had been neglected. He knew better and his men knew better. A few minutes later, when he finally saw the can, when he noticed the tiny dark smudge on one side of the opening, his embarrassment grew. And so did the shard of doubt about Hope's guilt that had been scratching at his mind over the recent weeks as the trial grew closer.

The three of them—Brownstein, Galton, and Ferris—waited in the anteroom while the technician took the can into the laboratory with him.

"God damn it, Brownie," Galton snarled, "you better get back to that birdcage you call a Homicide Division and shake some people up."

"I told you before, Norman, I'm responsible for my division. I'm the one to blame. If you want someone shaken up, you go to the commissioner and tell him to shake me up. But you be damn sure you know what you're talking about."

Galton threw up his hands and looked to Ferris for approval.

"Let's not worry about whose fault it is," his aide said. "The important thing is to see whether it *is* blood, whether it's her type. If so, it certainly knocks a hole in the case. Look, Norman, are you sure you want to go on handling this trial? You could turn it over to Farnsworth—you could say that another investigation has come up or that the overall operation of the office is suffering with you devoting all your time to the Hope prosecution."

"God damn it, Chuck, get off that. Get fucking off it. What do you want me to do, destroy myself politically?"

"If that hasn't already been accomplished, it never will be."

Brownstein was not the only person in the room astounded by Ferris' temerity. Norman Galton stopped pacing and stared at Ferris as if his assistant had just hit him. When he finally spoke, his voice

259

was as cold as the April wind whipping the street outside.

"I'll tell you something, Chuck. I'm beginning to think that when this is all over, you and I are going to sit down and re-evaluate our relationship."

"What bothers me," Brownstein broke in, "is what it means if her blood type is on the can."

"It means we take a screwing with the jury," Galton said. "It means that jury may not buy our best piece of evidence. Christ, Brownie, you never came up with the murder weapon, you can't even find that friend of Virginia Hanson's, that Charlotte, and that leaves us with the pants as the strongest thing we've got. Hammer may just luck out yet."

"I'm thinking about Hope," the Homicide chief said. "About just what did happen that night. If her blood type is on the can, he just may be telling the truth about the pants. I still think they could have been nude, but I'm not sure. Maybe we should reassess the whole case."

"So why don't you go over and work for Hammer?" Ferris snapped.

"Yeah," Galton said. "Damn it, Brownie, sometimes I—"

Brownstein had risen as the door opened and the lab man came out holding the can. All three men looked at him.

"Well?" Brownstein said.

"It's blood, all right."

"What type?"

"The victim's type, type O."

"Shit!" Norman Galton's voice was accompanied by the sound of his right fist smacking into his left palm.

"If you insist on staying with this thing, Norman," Ferris said, "we're going to have to come up with something else. You're right about the jury's reaction. We've got to have something to counter this with."

"Well, let's get something!" Galton said. "You got me into this, Brownstein, now you figure a way to get me the hell out."

For the first time in the case the Homicide chief felt defenseless against Norman Galton. There was no way he should have missed the flip-top can.

"I'm afraid our case is pretty much laid out," he said. "We're still trying—for instance, we haven't given up on locating the woman who was with Virginia Hanson at the Pumpkin prior to the murder—but I seriously doubt that any new evidence is going to turn up."

"Yeah," Galton said. "Including the weapon."

"We've been all over Hope's house and office and the Nassau

Overlook apartments," Brownstein said. "Perhaps you'd like us to dredge Long Island Sound."

"Let's not panic," Ferris said. "It's not going to do any good to start looking for scapegoats. What do we have, the one big thing we *do* have, is the murderer. This little flip-top stunt doesn't have to convince the jury that Chapin Hope didn't do it. We have a lot going against him."

"And there's still stuff that we haven't gotten into," Galton said. "We haven't even mentioned any of that financial stuff that the *Islander* has—"

"No way," Ferris said. "It's one thing to get Rocco mad but if you start in with that stuff, you couldn't run for councilman. You'd be opening a Pandora's box."

Brownstein grimaced in distaste. "That stuff doesn't relate to the murder," he said.

"Well, the goddamned jury is going to need some . . . distraction," Galton said. "I want something to take their minds off the flip-top can and I'm going to need it on Monday. I'm going to call Teddi Bennett."

"I don't think so," Brownstein said.

"Brownie, do me a favor," Galton said. "Don't think. Period. We made a deal at the start of this and I'm going to remind you of it now. You do your job and I'll do mine."

"I gave my word," Brownstein said. "I told Miss Bennett she wouldn't be called except in an emergency."

"If this isn't an emergency, what is?" Galton said.

"Bringing her in isn't going to prove anything. The only thing she can demonstrate is that Chapin Hope confused her with a woman named Ginny. It doesn't seem to me that the defense is making any effort to deny Hope's involvement with Virginia Hanson."

"The chief seems to be missing the point," Ferris said, speaking past Brownstein to Galton.

"Seems to be," the district attorney said. "Chief, the point isn't just that Chapin Hope was sleeping with Virginia Hanson. The point is that Mr. Respectable also slept with someone named Teddi—and that's another reason for bringing her to the stand."

"That's not a crime."

"No crime at all," Galton said. "From what I hear about Teddi Bennett, no crime at all—but a mistake. We can show just what kind of an immoral bastard he is."

"I'm not following this," Brownstein said.

"C'mon, Brownie, don't get cute with me."

"Let's say I'd rather not follow it," Brownstein said.

261

"Let me spell it out. Hammer is going to say that Virginia Hanson was the great love of Hope's life, that this was no ordinary fling. We'll show that this true love isn't even cold in the ground when he has another broad lined up. Broad number one is killed and our senator can't wait to climb on broad number two—"

"That stinks," Brownstein said. "That really stinks. I have an alternate suggestion. I repeat that maybe it's time we sat down and reviewed the case. It wasn't the strongest case to begin with, almost entirely circumstantial, and now the defense is going to destroy the credibility of our strongest piece of evidence. Maybe what we should do is give some thought to dropping this mess before it gets worse."

"Absolutely not," Ferris said. "The district attorney's office is not about to quit now. What the hell would that look like?"

"Absolutely right," Galton said. "Brownie, there's nothing unethical here. We're simply showing the jury what kind of man Hope is."

"We could have Teddi Bennett in court on Monday," Ferris said.

"Chuck, take care of that."

"I'm dead set against this," Brownstein said. "I don't want anything to do with it."

"At least we all agree on that," Galton said. "Brownie, why don't you just relax for a while? No one's going to ask you to do anything from now on."

Further talk would be senseless. As he got up to leave the room, Brownstein felt drained. Back in his office, Detective Lieutenant Charles Brownstein finished one of the least pleasant days in his career by calling Robert J. O'Malley and telling him that Teddi Bennett was going to be called to testify about her night with a state senator.

The reporter put the phone down and stared at it. The thing to do now was pick it up and tell Teddi, but he knew he wouldn't do that, not over the phone. He hated telephones. Sometimes it seemed that he had to rely on them even more than typewriters for getting stories into print. Now he took his jacket from the back of the chair, threw it over his shoulders, and went out to the elevator.

He waited a moment before knocking on the door to Teddi Bennett's apartment.

"Who is it?"

"Bob."

"It's unlocked."

"Jesus, you live dangerously," O'Malley said, opening the door.

"Optimistically, you mean," she said from the bedroom.

The floor plan to Teddi's apartment was a replica of the reporter's. There all resemblance ended. For one thing, Teddi had gone to the trouble of putting in a sofa and chairs that matched. She had, in addition, turned the apartment into a kind of greenhouse; all available window space was filled by hanging baskets of greenery and there were ferns sprouting from bookcases and vines sending tendrils out along the ceiling. In one corner a tree was growing, a gray ornamental tree with outsized glossy leaves and a single horizontal branch that served as a clothesline for a pair of pale blue underpants and matching brassiere.

"This neighborhood," O'Malley said, "you really should lock the door."

"You know where the stuff is," Teddi called out. "Help yourself."

Teddi Bennett's entire liquor collection consisted of a single bottle of Jack Daniel's, a bottle reserved for the sole and exclusive use of her neighbor when he came up to visit her. O'Malley half filled a juice glass, then set himself down gingerly in the middle of the sofa.

As he was getting settled, Teddi came into the room. At least, it looked like her. What O'Malley saw was not much more than a blur, a dervish in a terry-cloth bathrobe and a white towel wrapped around her head. She raced into the room, scooped the undergarments from the branch of the tree, and disappeared back into the bedroom. The entire round trip, lasting no more than a few seconds, was accompanied by a shrill squeal.

"I was going to telephone you," he began, "but that seemed chicken."

"Uh-oh."

"Believe me, it's even worse than that."

"They've decided to call me to the trial?"

"Yep, that's what they've decided to do."

"Well, it's not all that much of a surprise," she said. "When you told me my name was going on the witness list, I figured I'd be called. I'll tell you, Bob, the only thing that surprises me nowadays is good news."

"Brownie apologized," the reporter said. "I was a little hard on him. But, what the hell, it's not his fault. It's that bastard Galton."

"Look, no one has to be upset over me."

"I am."

263

"Bob, it's not all that bad," she said. "Someday, you're going to have to stop worrying about me. I'm able to handle things myself. You told me not to go off with Hope—you warned me beforehand."

"I got you involved in the first place."

"No one gets me involved in anything except for myself. Bob, we never really talked about that night."

"You don't have to."

"I know that, but no one made me do what I did. I've done dumber things in my life. Not many, but some. And if I've learned anything, it's don't expect someone else to look out for you. I made a mistake, I clean up the mess."

"Yeah, but it's not really your mess," O'Malley said. "It's Galton's. He's desperate, he needs a score the worst way."

"What can I do for him? All I can tell them is what happened. I'll have to watch my language, that's all."

"I should never have called Brownstein."

"You know it's not his fault," she said. "What're you doing, Bob, fooling yourself? C'mon, I've got to get dressed. You were just looking out for me."

"I shouldn't have put you through any of this."

"You're not putting anyone through anything. I don't even feel bad about going to court. It'll give me a chance to wear my new blue dress. I mean, all it means to my bosses is that they'll have to handle a bunch of extra customers next week. Big deal. Anyway, if it helps put Hope behind bars, that's what it's all about, isn't it? That's the bottom line."

"I wonder."

"You *wonder?*"

"That business I told you about with the flip-top can," O'Malley said. "That surprises me. At first I figure Hammer is playing games with the jury but when they come up with her blood on that can. . . ."

"They did?"

"That's what Brownstein just told me," the reporter said. "I'll tell you the truth, I don't know what to think now."

"That night," Teddi said thoughtfully, "the night that I left with him, I was sure he couldn't kill anyone. I suppose just the fact that he called out her name—that doesn't *necessarily* mean he killed her. I'll tell you something, Bob, he really didn't strike me as someone who could hurt anyone. . . ."

"I hate to think of you up there."

"But what's the worst that can happen to me? They put me on the stand and I tell all and the people find out I'm not a virgin. But all

264

they really find out is that Chapin Hope had an affair with Ginny."

"That's the trouble," the reporter said. "They already know that Chapin Hope was making it with Ginny Hanson. So why belabor the point? Galton is after something else."

"Hey, Bob, you *are* worrying about me. Jesus! I'm forty-one years old and I no longer care what anyone else thinks about me. Present company excepted. My parents are dead and gone and all this would have done anyway is confirm their suspicions. There's only one person on earth I worry about, Bob, and you already know the whole story."

"Yeah. Well."

"Somehow it doesn't seem fair to blame Hope for what happened that night. I hardly ever meet a guy who doesn't try to do the same thing. I mean, let's face it, you don't exactly have to be Raquel Welch. There's another way of looking at it. Maybe all it tells about Chapin Hope is that he's a human being."

"The jury won't see it that way. That's the funny thing. Any guy on that jury would love a tumble, you know, but the minute they get on a jury they become official. Official Human Beings. And if someone does something they'd like to do, they figure he has to be some kind of creep."

Teddi came out of the bedroom wearing the dress provided by the Blue Barn's management. They were no more generous with the costume than they were with the salary check. O'Malley took in the legs.

"Sometimes I wonder," Teddi said.

"Yeah?"

"I wonder what you thought," she said. "Sometimes after work, I'm sitting here watching the late movie, and I wonder what you thought that night. When I came back and told you what happened."

"It happened," he said. "I forgot it soon enough."

"Yes, but at the time, what'd you think of it then? I worried about that later. If I thought it was going to bother you, I would never have done it."

"The only thing bothering me that night was the thought that some maniac was going to chop you up. Teddi, you and me, we don't have to impress each other anymore. We *like* each other."

"I just wondered what you thought. That time we made love— that was so long ago, it was like two different people—"

"We're friends. I'd rather be that." He stopped there, but she seemed to be waiting for him to go on. "I came to the conclusion a long time ago that I'm not much as a lover boy. My wife—hell, she wasn't much of a wife and not much of a woman either—but I

265

couldn't even hang onto her. I didn't want the same kind of thing with you. I didn't want to louse us up. I mean, if we were having to be good lovers, what chance would we have to be good friends?"

"I'm not complaining either," she said. "Bob, I wouldn't louse this up for anything. But I always wondered. You never seemed to mind if I had a guy or what I did."

"A woman like you, you should have a guy," O'Malley said. "And you never said anything about me, my life."

"I knew you had a visitor."

"Yeah. Well."

"I'll tell you something I wasn't going to tell you, Bob. At first it bothered me. It seemed so impersonal. You know, I used to see your visitor in the elevator sometimes. She was always staring at the floor, always chewing gum. Can I tell you something? I think I used to be jealous."

"Jealous of her? That was like getting your car serviced."

"I haven't seen her in a long time."

"Yeah, she gave up the business. Became an airline stewardess. I missed her for a while. But now, you know—nothing. I think I'm getting old."

"I know what you mean," Teddi said. "I never loved one of them. But a long time ago I figured things weren't going to work out like in the movies. I'll never be your basic Doris Day. Let me tell you, Bob, oh, God, I'm talking too much."

"It's okay."

"It's enough for me that there's someone who gives a rap for me, someone who cares that I make it from one screwed-up day to the next. Believe me, that's enough."

"What the hell," O'Malley said. "You're talking about me."

"Yeah," she said. "I've got to shove."

"I'll just finish my drink."

"Do me a favor," she said. "Leave the light on in the living room."

"Sure," he said. "Look, I'm sorry about the trial."

"Forget it," she said.

Robert J. O'Malley did not rush the drink. He sat there for a long time, resting his eyes against the walls of Teddi Bennett's apartment. Someday he'd have to get around to doing something about his apartment. Wallpaper was a nice idea. Someday. He didn't think, though, that he'd bother with a tree. The tree, stripped of its drying undergarments, seemed bare and lifeless, as dead as driftwood.

"Hello," the voice said, "is this Chapin Hope?"

"Speaking," he said.

"Chapin. . . . Chapin . . . I'm not even sure if you remember me. This is Teddi. Teddi Bennett. The barmaid at the Blue Barn."

"Yes?"

"We . . . oh, do you remember?"

"I remember very well," he said. "There may be some things about that night I'd like to forget. But I remember you."

"Look," she said, "I've got to see you."

"What happened that night, at the end, you have to understand, I was under a terrible strain. I was drunk . . . that wasn't me."

"You don't have to explain anything to me. I'm the one who should apologize to you. For calling you at home, for calling you this late. But I got off work early tonight—I just told them I wasn't feeling well. But I know that I have to see you. I have to talk to you."

"Why?"

"Because of what's going to happen. I feel just terrible about it. I have to testify at the trial, you know, for the prosecution. They want me to tell about what happened that night."

Chapin thought he had become immune to fear but it came back at that moment and sent a shock through him. More. There was still going to be more. If her testimony was allowed, it could kill him. And the newspapers! O'Malley would have another field day.

"Chapin?"

"I heard you," he said. "I guess I should have expected it from the beginning. I guess that s what that whole night was all about."

"No," she said. "There are some things about that night I'm ashamed of. You probably don't believe me, and I can't blame you, but I like you, Chape, and I really don't want to do you any more harm. This whole thing is not going to be very pleasant for me either."

"Why do you have to, then?"

"The district attorney has subpoenaed me, that Mr. Galton."

"What good would it do for us to get together?"

"Chapin, I like you and maybe I can tell you some things you don't know about that night. The least I can do is tell you what they expect me to say on the stand."

The first days of the trial had gone well, almost too well. Maybe his luck was still holding. Thalia would never know; she was out with Priscilla, taking in one of those new disaster movies. Chapin had stayed home because if there was one thing he didn't need in his life, it was another disaster. Chapin took down Teddi Bennett's address, agreed to meet her, and left a note for Thalia. She wouldn't understand but what difference did that make? Nothing was apt to make matters worse. On the outside, in public, Thal was more than ever the brave-wife-who-believed-in-her-husband-and-would-stick-by-him. On the inside, in private, she was more than ever a stranger.

Teddi Bennett. Should he believe her? Well, he knew one thing. There had been a genuine liking that night. To use one of Ginny's favorite expressions, they "made waves ." Christ, but it had been a long time since he had made waves with anyone. What would that be like, making love to that one again, to do it when he was cold sober?

No matter what, it made sense to go over there. She said for him to come by himself, but this time he would call Greg. Every time he had gone off on his own there had been trouble. A machine answered Greg's phone. Priscilla's recorded voice. The Hammers were out for the evening but if there was any message, the caller should wait for the tone. Chapin waited.

"Greg, this is Chape. This is a little weird, but it may be a break. I just got a call from Teddi Bennett—the barmaid at the Blue Barn, the one I met that night after I got threatening phone calls. Our friend Galton apparently has got his hooks into her; she says he's calling her as a witness right away. She wants me to come over to her apartment and she'll tell me about it. She says she wants to help me. I don't have time to go into detail, but I believe her. If you get home in time, here's her address. I'll be leaving in about five minutes. . . ."

He gave the street address of the Hempstead apartment building and hung up. He pulled on a sweater and grabbed his golf jacket. Before getting into the Mercedes, Chapin breathed in the spring night. It was pretty out; tree branches soft in the shadows and stars glinting like jewels in a velvet sky. He wished he could roll back time to other springs and that he and Thalia were going to the beach to watch the stars stretch across the sound. No, that wasn't what he wished at all. What he really wished was that it was last spring and he was going to see Virginia Hanson.

34

What surprised Thalia most was the absence of fear. Even as she drove toward the rendezvous, she felt calm, sure of herself, in control. Control was the key word. She was in complete control of her decision to be unfaithful to Chapin Hope.

It was, in fact, one of the most cold-blooded decisions she had ever made, a decision not made out of any sense of need, not to satisfy any emotional or physical requirement. Possibly that explained the absence of guilt. Guilt? Guilt toward Chapin? The thought made her laugh. If anything, she felt quite the opposite. In her entire lifetime, in forty years, most of them spent on Long Island's North Shore, Thalia had made love to only one man. Chapin Hope. Now, at least, a curiosity was about to be satisfied.

And, in a sense, she was doing this for Chapin. Although he might not see it that way. He might not see it as such a great favor. He might not understand that this was the last chance for their marriage.

The idea had occurred to her a few weeks earlier. Clearly there was no way that she and Chapin could get together on the same terms as before. By confessing to a string of adulterous relationships, he had upset a delicate and long-standing balance. And by doing what she was going to do, she might take one small step toward equalizing the situation. If she tore just one page from Chapin's book, maybe then she would be able to go back to him and try a new start, a new arrangement, a new balance.

Chapin had, of course, suspected she would do this. In fact, his one request had been that she not do it with one of his friends. That was an easy stipulation. She wouldn't let Greg Hammer near her again if he were magically transformed into Robert Redford. She had toyed with the idea of Norris Whitlaw—in point of fact, Norris could no longer be considered a friend—but he always gave Thalia the impression that he was about to burst into tears and that wouldn't do, that wouldn't do at all.

Thalia finally decided to leave the man to chance. The next man to demonstrate a male interest in her would be in for the surprise of his life. Oh, not if he were, say, a garage mechanic or a construction worker. But if he were someone more . . . suitable.

It happened this very day, Friday, in the courtroom—just when she had begun to wonder whether she would ever find an opportunity to test her plan. She was not about to make the first move. Despite the difference she had been feeling in herself lately, she still thought that her image was sometimes forbidding, that she was not at all the kind of woman who attracted male flirtations.

The man was sitting in the courtroom, just across the aisle from her. She felt his eyes on her and she turned to meet them. Initially, following the habit of years, she looked quickly away and returned her attention to the trial.

But a moment later she steeled herself and looked back. He was still staring directly at her and this time he was smiling—smiling in a manner that seemed more friendly than suggestive. Thalia allowed herself a brief smile in return but was unable to hold it for long. She returned to the trial.

Time and again Thalia was tempted to look back at the young man but after all those years of being cloistered, after a lifetime of doing what was expected, she didn't dare. Damn, damn, *damn!* Robert J. O'Malley had been right the first time; she was nothing more than a suburban matron.

Suburban matron, suburban matron—the thought stayed with her until the midday recess. Then she practically charged at the young man, allowed herself as much of a smile as possible, and said the least characteristic thing she had ever said in her life.

"Would you like to make love to me?"

"Pardon me?"

He seemed shocked and suddenly young. He pulled back as though stung by a bee. Something went on in his eyes, a kind of refocusing, and then he whispered back to her.

"I don't believe I heard you correctly."

"I just asked you if you would like to make love with me."

"Certainly," he said—all hesitation gone.

She still wasn't letting herself think. "Would tonight be all right with you?"

"That would be fine," he said. "Just fine."

He wrote down a few notes on a scrap of paper—"Hungry Bull Diner, just W of Smithtown, Jericho, 8 P.M."—and handed her the note.

"It was nice to meet you," he said, calmly turning his attention back to the trial.

Thalia took the opportunity to study him more closely. Young. At least ten years younger than she was. He was bearded but the beard

270

was neatly trimmed. He wore a three-piece tweed suit. All in all, he was not a bad choice.

Soon afterward the young man disappeared—leaving Thalia with a piece of paper in her purse and the wildest notion she had ever entertained.

Now, driving toward a man she didn't know, Thalia began to appreciate what Chapin had gone through all those years. Even constructing her little lie for the night—she said she had to get out and she was going to see the big new disaster movie, *Avalanche*—even that had hurt somehow. She was not accustomed to telling lies and the words sounded hollow even to her. All the lies that Chapin had been forced to tell, poor man. Or did he get used to it? Did deception ever become a habit?

Ten minutes later Thalia was parking the station wagon beside the Hungry Bull Diner just west of Smithtown on Jericho Turnpike. Inside, just a few customers—one a bearded man wearing a vested suit and stirring sugar into a cup of coffee. She took the stool beside him.

"You did come," he said. "I was going to give you five more minutes and then I was going to disappear into the night. I was almost sure it was a practical joke. Coffee?"

"No, thanks."

"My name is Dave," he said. "I—"

"Don't tell me," she said. "I don't want to know your name and I don't want you to know mine. In fact, I don't want to know anything about you except that you're here."

"Well, we're going to have to talk about something," he said. "Maybe you'd like to know what I do for a living."

"Only if you insist."

"I'm a lawyer."

"Oh, are you?"

"See, you do want to talk."

"If you find it necessary to talk, please go ahead. Just don't expect me to talk back."

"Too much," the stranger said. "Very attractive, very stylish, and a good listener to boot. As nearly as I can tell, there's only one flaw. You're married."

"How do you know that?"

"I'll tell you what gave me the first clue," he said. "The fact that you're wearing a big golden wedding band on your left hand. Hey, I thought we were going to talk about me. Let's not digress. Where was I? Oh, yes, I was just saying that I'm a lawyer—just a humble Legal Aid lawyer, nothing like the high-priced talent we were watching today."

271

"Legal Aid—that's for poor people, right?"

"A poor lawyer for poor people," he said. "No, I'm being too modest. That's always been a fault of mine, perhaps my only fault. Hey, did we come here to talk or make love?"

The directness of the question startled Thalia just as her directness must have startled him. The answer was slow in coming. God, it was hard enough propositioning a man once—why did she have to do it twice?

"We came here to make love," she said.

"Then I should have asked for a booth."

"Pardon me?"

"Well, surely it would seem a little brazen, making love right here at the counter. . . ."

Why had it taken her so long to realize he was joking? She started to laugh then and realized, at the same moment, that it would be all right. He paid for the coffee, leaving a dime tip, and Thalia wondered at that. Was it proper to leave a dime for anything these days? Maybe he was as poor as his clients.

Thalia followed him to his car and sat beside him until he came to a motel without a name—unless it was called the Vacancy Motel because those were the only two words appearing in neon. The young lawyer drove a Volkswagen with a dented fender; funny, young men can get by with old cars but old men seem to require new cars. Thalia found some comfort in the dented fender.

He did not drive to the motel office; he drove directly to the back and parked outside unit number 18.

Sudden misgivings. The room smelled bad, musty, as though the carpet was suffering a terminal case of mildew. A large bed, a large color television set, nothing else of note. What was she doing in this strange room with this strange young man? What would it really prove? That she was still capable of attracting a male? No, Greg Hammer proved that beyond all reasonable doubt. Surely it went beyond that. Maybe what she really wanted was a demonstration that this part of it wasn't all that important, that Chapin's infidelities were not symptomatic of something that went far deeper. But if this wasn't important, why was her stomach filled with sudden flutterings?

"I thought you were almost sure it was a practical joke," Thalia said. "You came here before and reserved the room. You must have been pretty sure that I'd show up."

"Let's say I hoped you'd show up," he said.

"You seem to know just how to do things like this."

"I'll tell you the truth," he said. "This kind of thing doesn't happen to me all that often."

"But I am trusting you to know what to do," she said.

"The only thing I forget is how to start. How do we do that again?"

"I was kind of hoping you'd know," she said.

"I *do* remember," he said. "The best way to start is to take our clothes off."

"Could we turn the lights off first?"

"Well, we could," he said. "But then we'd probably leave our clothes on the floor and they'd get all wrinkled. Would you mind if I undressed before we turn off the lights? Then we can turn the lights off while you undress."

"If you want."

Moving slowly, he took off his jacket and his vest and hung them up in a small alcove off the room. With no apparent modesty at all he then removed his trousers and put them on an adjacent hanger. It was a peculiarly masculine striptease done for Thalia's benefit, and she didn't bother averting her eyes. Shirt, tie, shorts, shoes, socks. He was naked but somehow he didn't seem naked; his beard joined with hair on his chest, back, and shoulders and seemed to extend over him like a shawl.

"You can turn the lights off now," he said.

In the darkness Thalia debated briefly about what should come off and what should stay on, then decided not to be coy. She took off everything and slid into the bed, bumping into the unknown naked male who was waiting for her. His voice came to her through the darkness.

"Why don't you tell me your name?"

"No," she said.

"But you're making this more difficult—I should be able to call you something."

"What do you usually call a woman when you're making love to her?"

"Usually? Usually I call her Jennifer."

"Fine. Call me Jennifer."

"But you don't feel like Jennifer."

His hand was on her now, on her breasts, tracing their outlines with feathery fingers. Who was Jennifer? Wife? Girlfriend? What did Jennifer feel like? Quite likely Jennifer was closer to his own age, probably firmer and younger and more appealing. Was she going to be a disappointment to him? "You feel so good," he said, as if sensing her concern. "I wonder if you taste as good."

His mouth was on her then, very carefully moving from one breast to the other. She thought briefly of her encounter with Greg Hammer, the contrast, and then she settled down and allowed the

273

warmth to cover her. It was so easy. Thalia relaxed then and let it all happen to her, let the young man's mouth go where it wanted, let his hands coax more warmth out of her.

"Touch me," he said.

"What?"

"You heard me," he said. "Just touch me."

"I—"

"Don't talk," he said. "Just do it."

Thalia reached over to him and even in the darkness she blushed. She did touch him—the young man seemed large to begin with and grew immediately larger in response to her touch. She could feel him throbbing.

"No, don't stop," he said. "Stay there. Take me in your mouth."

"Please," she said. "I don't do that. I just want you to make love to me. I've got to explain something. I haven't done this before, nothing like this, not ever before. I'm not doing this for pleasure."

"Oh?"

"If I told you the reason I'm here tonight, you wouldn't believe me."

"But you're not here for pleasure?"

"No."

"Well," he said, "I certainly wouldn't want to ruin your plans and I sure hope this doesn't give you too much pleasure."

He was moving his mouth down her body and Thalia decided to remain still and let him do whatever was necessary for him. He seemed to have all the time in the world. He was so slow, so gentle, and then suddenly he was aggressive, harsh, and his tongue was filling her up.

"Don't stop," she said. "Please don't stop."

He stopped. He got up then and reversed himself on the bed; now his face was near her knees and his beard was silken against her thighs.

"I really ought to apologize," he said. "I could tell I almost gave you some pleasure there. I'll be more careful in the future."

What future? What next? His beard was against her belly. The thought of the two of them there, of what they would look like to anyone else, embarrassed Thalia. Even in the unbroken darkness of the motel room she closed her eyes. And then he was into her again with his mouth and there was no way to escape him; she held him in her two hands and he started to move slowly against her. The man slowed his movements and Thalia felt herself falling, slipping—a lazy, slow-motion fall, a fall without hurt—and then she felt the shudders in her stomach and the trembling across every part of her

274

body. She felt free; the act itself cut away all the troubles of the past months, cut away all the burdens, and she felt afloat somehow, lighter than air. Not thinking then, only responding, she took the man in her mouth and felt him move against her. When he was ready, he pulled back and went on top of her and she didn't do anything after that but be there, be there for the thrusting that gathered strength and momentum; be there for the trembling; be there for the explosion, be there in the quiet after.

"Dave," she said. "David."

"I was trying so hard not to give you any pleasure," he said. "I'm sorry if I didn't succeed."

"You made me aware of something I didn't know," she said. "I had no idea."

"No idea?"

"No idea how much I needed that," Thalia said. "I needed to feel alive. I haven't felt alive for so long."

"I'm happy to have been of help," he said. "I have to admit it felt good to me, too."

"Are you married?"

"I thought you didn't want to talk."

"I want to listen."

"Yes, I'm married. I'm happily married."

"That's good," she said.

"I'm happily married and, believe it or not, the truth is that this is the first time I've ever . . . strayed. I guess I've been curious about it for a long time."

"May I ask you something else?" she said. "How come you're at the trial?"

"I told you I was a lawyer. I'm just there to see the pros work. That guy Hammer is too much. I swear, for someone like me, the kind of cases I get, it's like watching a television show. It looks like he's going to get that poor son of a bitch off."

"Do you think he's guilty?"

"Who can tell?" the young man said. "But that guy Galton, he hasn't proved a thing yet."

"I guess not."

"But the real surprise is you."

"Me?"

"Coming to me like that."

"You mean women don't proposition you all the time?"

"Would you believe you're the first one all week?"

"Would you like to make love one more time?" Thalia asked.

"I'm not sure," he said. "Do you think you can manage to get my interest up one more time?"

"Let me try."

Thalia was astounded at her own audacity. Feeling good, feeling free, feeling brazen, she bent over and calmly put her mouth on the stranger.

"I thought you told me you didn't do that."

"That's what I thought," she said.

She could feel him growing then and moving in her mouth and then he pulled away from her and turned her over onto her stomach. Thalia was surprised at how easy it all was for him, how ready she was for him to enter again, and how ready he was for her. One night, two times, and she was already learning to anticipate the young man's rhythm—it was direct and strong, almost to a fox-trot beat. Chapin had always been so indecisive, compromising even there, always stopping to ask was she ready, was she all right, was she coming? Well, this young man knew enough not to ask and when he was ready, so was she.

And then it was over and she asked him what time it was. He turned on the lamp and looked at his watch. Thalia made no move to cover herself, she just lay there and enjoyed being looked at.

"Almost midnight," he said.

"I guess the movie has let out by now."

"I suppose we both have to go," he said.

"I think I want to thank you," Thalia said.

"Why don't we just thank each other, then?"

"Thank you, Dave."

"Thank you, Mrs. Hope."

Thalia felt the bottom fall out of the night.

"You *know*," she said. "You knew all the time. I thought you said you didn't know what to call me."

"Well, that was the truth, strictly speaking, which is what we lawyers are famous for," he said. "I mean I'd have to be pretty stupid not to know who you were but I still don't know whether it's Thalia or Thalia, whether it rhymes with 'tail' or 'pal.' "

"I think you're being clever with me," she said. "Actually, it rhymes with 'fail.' "

"If I were a sensitive sort," the young man said, "which, believe it or not, I am, I might take that personally."

"Oh, you didn't fail," she said. "Anything but. The only thing that failed tonight was a theory, a little experiment."

35

T. Bennett, the name on the door said. The door was slightly ajar but Chapin pushed the buzzer anyway. Then he knocked. Finally he called in.

"Miss Bennett."

He tried again.

"Miss Bennett?"

No answer. Just the afterfall of his voice on the corridor of an old apartment house in Hempstead. A corridor that was suddenly lonely. And intensely quiet—as if someone had pushed a button marked Silence and turned up the volume.

Gingerly, Chapin pushed the door all the way open. He went in.

Two steps and he was at the edge of the tiny entrance foyer staring at the living-dining room. At first the scene didn't register. Then it registered but his mind refused to accept it. For a full second he stood there frozen like a moving figure suddenly arrested by a camera. Then time began again and he staggered forward.

His arm slammed against the nearest wall for support. He looked toward the source of his pain and saw a wide-eyed Keene painting of a little girl staring back at him. It wasn't right for a child to see what was in the room—an insane thought. It wasn't right for anybody. Chapin screwed his eyes closed and willed the thing in the room to go away. But when he opened them, it was still there.

The disarranged furniture, the toppled artificial tree, the overturned plants, even the blood that formed rivulets in the dirt from the knocked-over pots—he could grasp all of that. But he could not deal with the thing sitting in front of him in a ladder-back chair at a small dinette table. The nude mutilated body of a woman—mutilated in a manner that was almost inconceivable. The only way he could begin to come to grips with the mutilation was to express it out loud in the dead room.

"There's no head," he said to the silence. "There's no head."

Chapin closed his eyes again, and in the blue-blackness of his squeezed-together lids there was a head on the body. A head with orange-red hair and green eyes and the faint trace of freckles across the fine-formed nose. But no, that was wrong, that was Ginny's head, and it didn't match this body—the long-legged body he had known one alcohol-ridden night and never forgotten. Teddi Bennett's body.

He opened his eyes, took another step forward, and stopped again—trying desperately to keep his thoughts coherent. He looked slowly around the room, looking for something he did not want to see. It was nowhere in sight and he knew he would not look in any other room in the apartment for fear of finding it.

Especially not in the bathroom. In court the day before—only the day before?—he had hidden his revulsion but he had almost gotten sick when the medical examiner testified about what police found in the bathroom sink in Ginny's apartment. And this, was this the same thing, the same as Ginny? When had it happened? Had it happened right after the telephone call? Had someone been listening to her—hiding in her apartment or lurking by the door? Then doing that to her, doing it and knowing that Chapin Hope would find the body. Arranging . . . leaving her like that in the chair for him to see when he stepped through the foyer into the brightly lit living room. But why? Why would someone hate him that much?

Being there was the worst thing that could happen to him. Coming there was the craziest thing he had ever done in his life. They would think he had done it. They would be sure it was him. God! This time they'd be positive.

His instinct was to turn and run. His instinct was to run the hell out of there, to forget the elevator and find a stairway and race down it. To run screaming into the street. To run until he burst.

Chapin turned but he didn't run. He knew he had to hold onto himself. He had to hold himself together. At least partly. He knew there was something he had to do. The phone, that was it. There was a phone right in front of him. He had to use the phone. Greg. He had to call Greg.

What the hell was wrong with his fingers? He misdialed the call and caught himself before he completed it. That was the first time. The second time he got a voice telling him to please dial his call again. The third time he got it right. A ring and then Priscilla's voice. Thank God! He had always liked Priscilla's voice. She always sounded calm . . . controlled.

"This is Priscilla Hammer," she said, "Greg and I—"

"Hell, Priscilla," Chapin said. "Greg . . . I need Greg. I have to talk to him right away. . . . I'm here, right here, and she's dead. . . . God, I don't know what happened. . . . Teddi Bennett, she's dead. . . . I don't know, there's no head. . . . I don't. . . . I can't. . . . No head. . . . I. . . ."

As he stopped, Chapin realized that he was talking to a recording. The same one he had heard earlier in the evening when he called from the house. They were still out.

He put down the phone. He knew he was losing control. The police, he could—he should call the police and report the crime. But he knew he didn't dare. Not the way his head was. Not without Greg or somebody else there to help him. Because they'd never believe him—not the police. They already thought he killed Ginny. They'd never believe he walked in the door and saw the thing at the dinette. They'd question him and look for his fingerprints and . . . wait a minute, fingerprints. Did he touch anything?

The telephone. He touched the telephone. Chapin pulled his sweater over his hand and rubbed the telephone with it until he was sure he'd removed his fingerprints. Next the doorknob.

Then he gave up trying to hold himself together.

He ran.

36

How long had the phone been ringing? O'Malley was dreaming about a phone ringing, but now he was awake and the phone was still ringing. He reached over and stopped the noise.

"Bob, are you awake?"

"Brownie?"

"Yes, listen, Bob, I want you to wake up. You've got to wake all the way up and take in what I've got to say to you. I'm in the apartment building now."

"What apartment? What time is it?"

"Get awake, Bob. Get awake. It's two ten in the morning and I'm right here, in your apartment building. I'm upstairs in Teddi Bennett's apartment."

Brownstein's words came at O'Malley like random pieces of a jigsaw puzzle. Why did it take such an effort to put them together? O'Malley remembered coming down from Teddi's apartment and finishing the better half of a fifth. Teddi's apartment. What in the hell was Brownstein doing in Teddi's apartment?

"Brownie?"

"Yeah, Bob, now listen to me. Someone got to Teddi tonight. She's been killed."

"What?"

"Bob, I hate to tell you this. Believe me, I hate to be the one. But Teddi Bennett was killed in her apartment tonight. We found her when someone called the precinct to complain about noise in the place. It looks like the same kind of thing that—"

"I'm coming up, Brownie."

"No." The Homicide chief's voice was sharp. "No, Bob, don't do that. I don't want you up here."

"Give me a minute, Brownie," he said. "Give me a minute and I'll be up."

"No, Bob, I'll come downstairs as soon as we've done a few more things up here."

O'Malley put the phone back and turned on the light. Teddi dead? The clock said just a few minutes past two. The sleep was thick in his eyes and his throat felt rusty. Teddi dead? It was still too early for a hangover to set in. Teddi dead? What in the hell was that all about? *Teddi?* O'Malley got into his clothes, the same ones he had stepped out of two hours earlier, and stumbled toward the elevator. Teddi dead? Killed? He wanted to get up there and get this thing straightened out. He had just left Teddi—what was it?—a few hours ago.

A uniformed policeman was standing outside the door to Teddi's apartment. O'Malley fished around for his press pass but he had left his jacket downstairs.

"Tell Brownstein O'Malley's here," he said.

The policeman left him in the hall. *Teddi* dead? A second later Brownstein came out.

"Bob, I'm sorry."

"What's all this? What. . . ." O'Malley waved his hand aimlessly.

"Someone got to Teddi tonight," Brownstein said.

"What're you talking about? Let me go in there."

"No, Bob, don't go in there."

Brownstein had no right to keep him out. No one did. Not if Teddi was in some kind of trouble. O'Malley shoved past Brownstein and pushed open the door. He could feel someone trying to hold him but he wasn't going to be held. He saw blood on the wallpaper, a splattering of blood, and he closed his eyes but it was too-late. Brownstein had both hands on one of O'Malley's arms and the cop held the other and the two of them managed to tug him out into the hall but they could not hold up the 320 pounds of Robert J. O'Malley as he slid straight down to the floor. Brownstein thought at first that O'Malley was passing out, but it wasn't that. The fat man was sitting on the floor of the hallway and crying like a baby.

The reporter's eyes had been open for only a second or two but the scene was frozen there. A flashbulb going off. A detective opening a desk drawer. A cop on the telephone. The medical examiner inserting a shining, chrome-covered instrument into a portion of a woman's torso.

O'Malley couldn't stop the tears. They rolled unchecked from his eyes and down his cheeks and finally the others began to go about their business. Much of the police business was transacted over the phone in Teddi's apartment. A detective asking the Identification Division to rush over a full set of Chapin Hope's fingerprints. Brownstein calling Galton, telling him what had happened. And then it was the *Islander* calling for O'Malley, an editor asking him to give the facts to a rewrite man. For the first time in his life the reporter turned down an assignment. For the first time something loomed larger than the next day's newspaper.

"Get somebody else," O'Malley told the desk.

"C'mon, Bob, you're right there."

"Get somebody else," he said again, and he hung up.

"Bob, I know this is a hell of a time to bother you," Brownstein said, "but we've got to move fast. Just bear with me, and it won't take long. When was the last time you saw Miss Bennett?"

He was numb, but he was awake. "Tonight," he said. "I was with her until she left for work. She was running late and I locked up for her."

"That would be about seven, then," Brownstein said. O'Malley nodded, and the Homicide chief continued. "She showed up for work and then she got a call from someone—we don't know who—but she said she had to go home and she cut out early. Was she doing anything special tonight, seeing anyone special?"

"She was just going to work," O'Malley said. "That's all."

"Had she been having any trouble? Was she—was there anyone who didn't like her?"

"Are you kidding? Brownie, you met her—you had to like her." O'Malley stared at the chief as if looking for reinforcement. "She was—she was somebody, Brownie."

"I know that, Bob. She was a fine person. A very fine person."

"I don't know who could hurt her, Brownie, I don't know who could hurt Teddi."

"It's so much like the other one, Bob," Brownstein said. "It's hard to believe it wasn't the same person. But I want to see what the ME says."

The numbness was O'Malley's salvation. "Hope?" he said.

"I don't know," Brownstein said. "You've seen him in court; he's seemed very cool, very contained. I can't connect him with this."

"He was with Teddi only that one time," O'Malley said. "She told me the whole thing."

Suddenly Galton appeared, striding up the hallway from the elevator, his camel's-hair coat sailing behind him in the small breeze created by his own motion. Ignoring Brownstein and O'Malley, the district attorney opened the door and looked into the apartment. He backed slowly from the door and out into the hallway again.

"God damn it, this is terrible," he said. "This is just terrible."

"I've never seen anything—" Brownstein began.

"This could throw a fucking monkey wrench into our case," the district attorney said. "This'll be all over the papers, this'll be everywhere—how're we gonna keep this from the jury?"

Neither Brownstein nor O'Malley said a word. They stood

silently as Galton went on speculating about the impact of the slaying on his case. He was finally stopped by the arrival of the medical examiner.

"What'd you find, Doc?"

McCoy looked at his notes. "Female subject, late thirties or early forties, killed with an ax or a cleaver, although I'm inclined to believe, from the nature of the wounds, that it may have been a cleaver."

"Is it the same as the last time?" Brownstein asked.

"Yeah, what is it," Galton came in, "another Chapin Hope psycho special?"

The medical examiner looked beyond the district attorney and talked to the Homicide chief.

"It looks the same, Brownie, but there's a difference that might mean something."

"What?"

"Well, the victim was mistreated in approximately the same fashion with what may well be the same instrument but there's absolutely no indication of sexual abuse."

"She wasn't raped?" Galton seemed mildly disappointed.

This time McCoy addressed himself to the district attorney. "There was no evidence of sexual molestation," he said. "Absolutely none."

"That doesn't make sense," Brownstein said.

"Wait a minute," Galton said. "This time the bastard had a motive. He didn't want her to testify against him—he didn't want everyone on the jury to know—"

"There's no way he would know that you were going to call her on Monday," Brownstein said. "Bob, you didn't mention this to anyone at the paper?"

"No one."

"It just doesn't fit," Brownstein went on. "Say—just say—it *was* Chapin Hope. Say he *did* know. Say he *decided* to kill her. Then why did he find it necessary to kill her in a manner certain to cast suspicion on him?"

"Because he's a goddamn nut," Galton said.

"Hey," the medical examiner said, "we found something in her hand. She may have grabbed it from the killer. Here."

The cuff link that McCoy was holding out was distinctive, black coral forming a backdrop for a single white pearl.

"Attaboy, Doc," Brownstein said. "If Hope has a pair of those, people are sure to remember him wearing them."

O'Malley scrutinized the cuff link. "No good," he said. "I'm pretty sure those were Teddi's. I've seen them before."

"Damn it to hell," Galton said. "Are you positive?"

"I'm telling you, I remember seeing it before."

The fingerprint man interrupted them both. "Chapin Hope was here," he said. "We got one perfect thumbprint."

"Where'd you lift it?" Brownstein asked.

"Not where you'd expect," the technician said. "A picture glass—the plastic frame by the foyer. The picture of the bug-eyed kid."

"That wraps it," Galton said. "We know Hope was here. Beautiful."

"You found just the one print?" Brownstein asked.

"Don't start that shit, Brownie," Galton said. "How many does he have to find?"

"That may be enough to arrest him," Brownstein said. "But you and I both know it's no conviction."

"Someone was careful," the fingerprint man said. "The phone was wiped clean, so was the doorknob. We got another set from a drinking glass but they're not Hope's."

"They're probably mine," O'Malley said.

"You were here tonight?" the district attorney said. "Why was that, Mr. O'Malley? What business did you have here?"

The reporter took a long look at Galton.

"Galton, why don't you go fuck yourself?" he said finally.

"Leave him alone, Norman," Brownstein broke in. "They were friends."

"Well, this really confuses the issue," Galton said. "What in hell are we gonna do when we go back to the trial on Monday? What the hell do we do with Chapin Hope now? The one thing we can't do is arrest him. Not unless he makes a full confession. If the jury knows he's under arrest—or even under investigation—it prejudices the case and that fucking Hammer'll get a mistrial."

"The least we can do tonight is ask him some questions," Brownstein said. "And we can stake him out. We can put him under heavy surveillance."

"Jesus, the irony of the system really kills me," Galton said. "We've finally got him and we can't do a thing. The jury can't even hear about this. They're sequestered—but it'll be harder'n hell to keep this from them."

"There's one more thing," the medical examiner said. "There's evidence of someone else's skin under the fingernails of the victim's right hand—it's more than likely that she scratched her assailant before succumbing."

"Good work, Doc," Brownstein said. "I'm sure we can find out if Hope has scratch marks."

284

"Good," Galton said. "If Hammer gets lucky and gets his buddy off on the first murder, then we'll make this one go down. And I mean we'll make it go down. But now, whatever you say to the press, I don't want this case linked to Hope in any way."

"Who're you kidding?" O'Malley said. "Not linked to Hope in any way?"

"Why don't I refer all press to your office, Norman?" Brownstein said. "After all, you and Ferris have had so much experience in that area."

"Don't get smart, Brownie," Galton said. "Just keep Hope's name out of it. And as far as you're concerned, Mr. O'Malley, I don't want to read about any of what we've been saying in tomorrow's *Islander*. I'm assuming our conversation is privileged and off the record."

"I told you, Norman, lay off O'Malley," Brownstein said. "He's gone through enough tonight. Bob, why don't you go and hit the sack?"

"Yeah," the reporter said, "why don't I?"

What in the hell? As he stepped into the elevator, O'Malley could feel his eyes getting hot again. O'Malley couldn't remember the last time he had cried. As a kid he didn't even cry much.

The reporter turned the light on in his apartment and got the bottle of bourbon down. The glass had not been rinsed since the evening but O'Malley didn't bother rinsing the glass often—alcohol was a germ killer, wasn't it? He poured the glass full to the top. He felt alone then, truly alone. No one would be looking in on him now. He stared at the glass for a long moment, then decided Teddi deserved better than that. She would have a wake without booze—without booze but not without tears.

The reporter waited for the wave to pass and then he reached for the phone and dialed a number he had first memorized years earlier.

"This is O'Malley," he said. "Get me rewrite."

37

At first he seemed to be asleep. Chapin was sitting in his easy chair, hunched in the direction of an unlit television screen, motionless. The sole light in the room came from a corner lamp. As Thalia started to walk onto the stairway, she was stopped by Chapin's voice.

"Enjoy the movie?" he said.

"Very much," she said. "I really didn't expect a great deal, not with a title like that, but it turned out to be exciting. In a Hollywood sort of way. Anyway, I'm exhausted, I was just going to turn in."

"What was the movie about?"

Was he being polite or suspicious? Thalia couldn't decide.

"Oh, you know. Boy meets girl, boy loses girl, boy gets girl—all of it in between landslides."

"Sleep well."

There was something about the way Chapin said that, something in his tone of voice, that made it sound very much like farewell. Thalia stopped before leaving the room.

"Is something the matter?"

"I'll tell you about it tomorrow."

"Chape, aren't you about ready to go to sleep now?"

"You go ahead," he said. "I'll wait up."

Wait up for what? Perhaps the turmoil of the past months was finally catching up with Chapin. Not that Thalia cared. Not tonight.

Chapin knew what he was waiting up for. He was waiting up for them. He didn't know precisely who they would be; all he knew was that they would come and accuse him of murdering Teddi Bennett. They would come and tell him that this time there was no way out.

Every twenty minutes Chapin reached out for the phone, dialed the number, listened to the recording: "This is Priscilla Hammer. Greg and I are out for the evening. If you have a message, wait for the tone and we will return your call as soon as possible."

At two in the morning he stopped calling. He just sat there, waiting. What difference would it make now whether he reached Greg or not? What difference would anything make?

Until the last few weeks Chapin Hope had never been an intro-spective man but now there was no way to avoid introspection. He had always been interested in where he was going, not why he was taking the trip. It had especially been that way in politics, in which introspection is a liability. And it had been that way in business and it had been that way in marriage and it had been that way in life. He had gotten to all the right destinations, always right on schedule, and now he was nowhere.

From nowhere the next logical step was nothing. Why not? Why not suicide? Why not take the full bottle of Valium he had seen in the medicine cabinet—apparently Thalia no longer needed it—and simply tranquilize himself out of existence? What would be the loss?

It hardly seemed worth the effort but Chapin sat there and went over the balance sheet one last time. This time he was seeking the black ink, a single plus factor, a conceivable justification for con-tinuing his life.

Politics. His political career was over no matter what. But what kind of career had it been? The people who elected him voted for him because they knew he was one of them, because he shared their fears and their hungers. He was their discovery, perhaps even their creation. In a time that reveres statesmen the people will find a Thomas Jefferson but in a time that reveres money they will turn over the nearest rock and discover a Chapin Hope. He may not have represented all the people but he did represent his time and now even that hollow triumph was gone. Never again would he hold public office, never again would he find so much as a local committeeman eager to return his telephone call. Politics—add a big fat zero to the ledger.

Marriage. What marriage? Where had Thalia been that night? She said she was seeing a movie with Priscilla; but Priscilla's recorded voice was coming over the telephone every twenty minutes to call his wife a liar. Boy meets girl, boy gets girl—and why not? It was hard to believe of Thalia, but why not? Who could blame her? For most of their marriage he and Thalia had been strangers on the same train, two not entirely dissimilar people who exchanged occasional greetings and trafficked in small politenes-ses, and perhaps it was reasonable for her to consider stepping off the train before it reached its destination. The marriage? Another nothing for the ledger.

The family. It was no coincidence that the family was as rocky as the marriage. He had always tried to be a pal to the boys—a weekend, game-playing father—and now he was learning the dif-ference between palship and fatherhood. The difference was a matter of depth. If he had been a real father instead of a pal, there might be a reservoir of love to draw on now. But the two boys were X-ing him out of their lives. His family, zero.

Friends. At one time, back in high school, you could have drawn a straight line from the catcher to the pitcher to the center fielder, and that line would have intersected with Greg and Chapin and Norris. What had happened to them, to the straight line? Norris had taken the first opportunity to go over to the enemy. And perhaps Greg had always been a petty tyrant unable to see beyond the perimeters of his ambition. The rest of them—the glad handers, the favor seekers, the golf players—they had all scurried for cover at the first appearance of a storm cloud. Add nothing for friends.

What else? Who was there to even notice the disappearance of Chapin Hope? Chapin had always surrounded himself with things instead of people; things were safer but they didn't mourn you when you died. A home doesn't care who lives in it and a Mercedes doesn't care who drives it and a suit of clothes doesn't care who walks around in it. And, yes, by God, a coffin doesn't care who's laid out in it.

So why not suicide? Was he even too cowardly for that? Was he just flagellating himself for some perverse satisfaction? Was there anything preferable? The debate went on without resolution; it went on until it was interrupted by a knock on the door. Them. Chapin felt no surprise. He opened the door and outside, in the driveway, he could see the revolving beacons atop a police car and a black limousine, red lights bouncing off the trees. Standing at the door; Brownstein, Galton, three uniformed policemen.

"I expected you," Chapin said right away. "Would you mind turning off the beacons? I think we've already given the neighbors enough to talk about."

"Turn them off," Galton said to one of the policemen. "We have a search warrant, Senator. I want to inform you that—"

"You won't need the warrant," Hope said. "Although it'll be the same as last time, you won't find anything. Just let me do one thing—just let me go upstairs and warn my wife. I don't want her to wake up and find strange men wandering through the house."

When Hope returned downstairs by himself, the district attorney started right in on him.

"You *do* know why we're here?"

"I have an idea," Chapin said.

"Senator Hope," Brownstein said, "it's no time to play games. If you want to call Hammer and get him over here, please do it. But no more games. I'll tell you that you have the constitutional right to remain silent and that anything you say can be used against you—

but I think it might be wise just to tell us what happened tonight.''

"Fine," Hope said. "And why don't you lay it out, too? Why don't you say you're here because you think I killed Teddi Bennett?"

"So you do know about that," Galton said. "Now how about telling us how come you know the lady is dead?"

Chapin was so very tired of Norman Galton. "I'll be precise," he said. "I was in her apartment tonight and I saw her, or at least part of her."

"Perhaps, then, Senator, you'll tell us why you were in her apartment."

"I can explain it," Hope said. "But I don't know whether you'll believe a word. Not, to be frank about it, that I really give a damn what you believe, Norman. The truth is that Teddi Bennett phoned and told me she was going to have to testify against me on Monday and she felt bad about it. She said she wanted to help me so I went over there."

"You didn't call her?"

"Nope, she called me."

"The information we have," Brownstein said, "is that someone called Miss Bennett around ten at her job and she took off—"

"That's a little before she called me. I went to her apartment and I saw—well, I guess you've seen it, too. How'd you know I was there?"

"We've got your fingerprints," Galton said. "You weren't thorough enough, Senator, you only wiped them off the phone and the doorknob."

"I panicked," Chapin said. "I figured you'd try to put it on me."

"They were on a picture, Senator," Brownstein said. "On the glass."

"A picture? Oh, yes, when I came in and saw the body, I must have hit it. I was shaken, it was a kind of reflex action."

"Senator," Brownstein said, "would you mind taking off your shirt?"

"My *shirt?*"

"Please, Senator," Brownstein said. "We have reason to believe that Miss Bennett may have scratched her assailant."

Chapin obliged by first removing his shirt, then his trousers. There were no marks.

As Chapin was getting dressed, Brownstein suddenly glanced at the floor. "Oh, Senator," he said, "you must have dropped this."

The Homicide chief bent down to the rug and seemed to pick up a small object. It was a cuff link, black backdrop and a white pearl. Brownstein handed it to the senator.

"Nope, not mine," Hope said, passing it over to Galton. "It must be yours."

"Enough!" Galton said. "No more games. Hope, I don't mind telling you that I think you killed Teddi Bennett tonight. You say she called you. What did your wife say when you told her where you were going? Or has she gotten used to that sort of thing?"

"She was out."

"Where was Mrs. Hope?" Brownstein asked.

"She said she was going to the movies," Hope said. "Maybe you better ask her yourself."

Chapin thought he saw a flicker of pity in Brownstein's eyes. Pity, if that was all that was left to him, suicide might make a certain amount of sense.

"So," Galton was saying, "you have absolutely no corroboration that you got a call from Teddi Bennett. And, of course, no witnesses as to what happened later at Miss Bennett's apartment. And, naturally, you didn't bother to call the police."

"Senator," Brownstein said, "is there anyone who can corroborate your story?"

"Not exactly," Chapin said, "but I tried to tell someone. I kept calling Greg Hammer, but he was out all night. I told him what was—I told his answering machine what was going on."

"What's Hammer's number?" Brownstein asked.

Greg Hammer answered the phone on the second ring. He and Mrs. Hammer were asleep; they had gotten home an hour ago; they had not bothered to play back the messages on the answering machine; no, they wouldn't touch it until the police got there. Hammer had only one question: "Just give me a hint, Brownstein, what'd the poor schmuck do this time?"

Within ten minutes the three of them were at the Hammer house. Greg, awake but bleary, took them to the answering machine. As he was rewinding the spool, Brownstein showed him the cuff link.

"Do you recognize this?"

"Never saw it before in my life," Hammer said.

As the senator's voice came on, Brownstein took notes: "Greg, this is Chape. This is a little weird, but it may be a break. I just got a call from Teddi Bennett—the barmaid at the Blue Barn, the one I met that night after I got threatening phone calls. Our friend Galton apparently has got his hooks into her. . . ."

"Beautiful," Hammer said. "See, keed, that's what I tried to tell you. Always let your Uncle Greg know what's going on and you'll never get into trouble. The smartest thing you've done in months is pick up that telephone tonight. . . ."

"That crack about me having my hooks into her," Galton said, "what's that supposed to mean?"

"Just what the man said," Hammer snapped back. "Galton, you've got a lot of nerve. There's only one reason you were calling that poor broad to the stand and that was to try to scare up a headline or two. If anyone in this room should assume responsibility for what happened tonight, it's you."

"We'll just see about that," Galton said. "As far as I'm concerned, this tape doesn't prove a thing. It could be a fake. The only thing that's going to impress me is if that machine gives me a play-by-play of what happened when Hope got to the broad's apartment."

"Maybe it can," Hope said.

"What do you mean by that?"

"I made another call from the apartment," he said. "I was trying to get hold of Greg and ask him what to do."

"Do you remember what you said?" Brownstein asked.

"I don't remember anything," he said. "All I know is that I was on the phone."

There was another call first, someone asking Priscilla to be block captain for the cancer fund drive, and then Hope's voice came on again. There was no escaping the contrast between the two Chapin Hope recordings. The first call had been in the senator's normal measured tones; there was even a slight hint of optimism. The second voice was something out of a nightmare, more a collection of chokes than a collection of words: "Greg . . . I need Greg. I have to talk to him right away. . . . I'm here, right here, and she's dead. . . . I don't know, there's no head. . . . I don't. . . . I can't. . . . No head. . . . I. . . ."

No one spoke for a minute after that and Brownstein played the tape a second time.

"That doesn't prove anything," the district attorney decided. "It doesn't say whether Hope did it or not. That could have been someone who just finished killing the broad."

"Or it could have been someone who just stumbled across a mutilated corpse," Hammer said.

"Let's play it one more time," Brownstein said.

"You gentlemen can play it till it comes out your ears," Hammer said. "I've heard enough to know what I think happened. I'm going to bed. You can let yourselves out."

As the tape started to play a third time, Chapin Hope had to get up and leave the room. He walked into the kitchen and sat down and tried not to hear.

"It could have been faked," Galton said later. "He could have figured this would be a way to set up an alibi."

"If he had done that," Brownstein said, "he might have bothered to do just that, give himself an alibi. He might somewhere have mentioned that he found the body or that someone else had killed her. Besides, he sounded too real."

"What's the matter with you, Brownie?" Galton said. "Are you practicing to be a defense lawyer?"

"I don't think he did this one," Brownstein said. "And if he didn't do this one, we've got to wonder about the first one."

"It's a little late to start wondering," Galton said. "A little late for second-guessing."

"The time is more than right for a little healthy second-guessing," Brownstein said. "You don't have enough to make a charge stick."

"Just make sure he's kept under constant surveillance," Galton said. "If he kills another broad, think what that would look like."

"His house is already staked out," the Homicide chief said. "But that's not what worries me."

"I know I'm making a mistake asking," Galton said. "But just what is it that does worry you?"

"That if it wasn't Hope, there's somebody else at large who may kill another woman."

38

O'Malley slept through Saturday and that night he sat up staring at television movies he didn't even try to follow. Sunday the numbness started to wear off and it was replaced by a pain that made him long for the numbness. He knew he couldn't spend the day in the apartment. Not Sunday.

On past Sundays Teddi had been his alarm clock. She had made it a practice to show up around noon carrying the newspapers and a brunch of cream cheese, lox, and fresh bagels. On clear Sundays they might take a drive down Meadowbrook Parkway to Jones Beach, where they walked the boardwalk and watched the ocean break on the lonely sand. Sometimes Teddi left him standing at the simulated ship's rail that ran along the edge of the boardwalk while she wandered along the shore picking up shells and stones, just like some kind of kid.

On this Sunday when Violet Brownstein called to invite him to dinner, O'Malley didn't need any coaxing. It saved him from a slow trip through a bottle. It saved him from something even more idiotic, something like going down to Jones Beach one more time to throw stones at waves.

O'Malley sensed that the dinner served by Violet Brownstein was excellent but he was not able to taste a thing. Almost any other time, the reporter would have come up with a funny line about the ethnic diversity provided by the main course—a superlative lasagna. He also would have returned for seconds and thirds. This time he felt neither funny nor hungry—just grateful for the company. At the end of the dinner, as Violet was pouring the espresso, he tried to express his gratitude.

"Being here today," he said, "I. . . ."

"It's okay, Bob." She sensed his embarrassment. "It's good having you."

Then, with what O'Malley would always remember as infinite grace, she leaned over and kissed his cheek. The fat man knew that he was blinking away tears. Christ, what was happening to him? For a second no one said a word and then Detective Lieutenant Charles

Brownstein's voice erased the silence.

"Before I have to sue for divorce, Bob, finish your espresso and we'll take a ride down to the office. There's something I want you to listen to."

O'Malley looked up.

"The famous Jericho Turnpike prostitution tapes," Brownstein said.

The reporter started pulling himself together. He stood up and turned to Violet.

"I wish I had been hungrier," he said. "The lasagna was terrific."

Violet Brownstein's laughter bordered on song.

"Don't thank me," she said. "Charley made it."

"What're we looking for?" O'Malley asked. They were in Brownstein's office and the Homicide chief was putting a tape on the machine.

"I'm not sure, Bob," he said. "Anything relating to Virginia Hanson."

"You don't think Hope did it, do you?"

"He could have, Bob, but there's room for doubt. More and more room. I told Galton from the beginning we should hold off on the indictment. We didn't have enough evidence then. And now there's this soda-can thing—it sounds legitimate to me. As for the second"—the chief hesitated—"crime, well, he could very well be telling the truth. For one thing, we searched his house again and we didn't find anything resembling a weapon. For another thing, we put him through the mill and he came out looking pretty good. There were no scratch marks at all and I don't think he ever saw the cuff link before."

"I'm pretty sure that was Teddi's," O'Malley said. "But there's one thing he's lying about."

"What's that?"

"Teddi never called him. You could take bets on that."

"You're right, Bob, but that doesn't mean he's lying."

"You figure it for a setup?"

"Again there's room for doubt. He could be lying. Perhaps he did find out somehow about her testifying and he called her—remember, we know she got a call at work. But it's also possible that he was set up. The same person could have called Teddi, then gotten a woman to call Hope and pretend to be Teddi. Or perhaps he forced Teddi to make the call. Also there's the complaint call to the precinct about noise in Teddi's apartment. We talked to her neighbors, and nobody admits making the call. And the crime itself—

well, someone could have been trying to make it look like Hope."

"So after this, all this, you're back where you started."

"I don't know, Bob, all I know is that sometimes I envy people like Galton their single-mindedness."

"So let's hear the tapes."

The Jericho Turnpike tapes consisted of call girls talking to their Johns and their madam, either on the phone or in motel rooms. The women had included professionals, cocktail waitresses, secretaries, a few schoolteachers, and more than a few suburban housewives whose recruitment had evidently not been so difficult. One housewife was heard explaining her availability to the madam: "Oh, no, Fred never asks questions—I might have a few questions to ask him, too. I'll tell you, my real worry is that you'll slip up some night and fix me up with my husband."

Each of the tapes was introduced ("October fourth, 1965, Nassau Maples Motel, telephone conversation") by a voice that was familiar to both O'Malley and Brownstein.

"Can you imagine Chuck Ferris listening to this stuff?" O'Malley said.

"Galton probably didn't trust anyone else," the Homicide chief said.

The tapes were studded with erasures and deletions but what proved most surprising to O'Malley was the number of inclusions. He recognized voices belonging to a few local politicians, some show-business personalities, a police official, and even a newspaperman. This conversation focused on the writer's somewhat unorthodox sexual needs and O'Malley had some trouble linking that with the slightly solemn and pontifical young man who still wrote editorials for the *Islander*; well, this tape probably explained all those editorials through the years praising Norman Galton as a crime-busting district attorney.

Just once during the three hours they spent listening to the tapes did O'Malley and Brownstein play back a sequence. Before one of the erasures there was this two-word segment spoken by the madam: "Hello, Ginny." They played it several times, but there was no more to it, just "Hello, Ginny."

"Ginny Hanson?" O'Malley said.

"Maybe," Brownstein said. "But it's a common name. Ginny. Virginia."

"Yes, Santa Claus," O'Malley said, "there was a Virginia."

"Early in the case you told me about somebody up high keeping Virginia Hanson's name out of the scandal. What was your phrase? A favor for a favor? It could explain the erasure. What was your source on that?"

"Teddi," the reporter said. "She used to be friendly with Ginny Hanson. But all Ginny ever said to her was that he was some guy whose libido was off the wall."

"We'll have to look into that," Brownstein said.

The last tape they listened to consisted of a phone conversation between the madam and one of the moonlighting housewives. The housewife was explaining why she had to turn down a trick.

"I have to go to a PTA meeting," she said. "They're holding elections and I'm running for president."

The trial resumed on Monday and the bloodstained soda can dominated the day. Galton was unable to dampen the effect of the lab technician's testimony. There was no mention in the courtroom of Teddi Bennett's murder and ostensibly, at least, the jury was unaware of it. No matter what, O'Malley doubted that Hammer would angle for a mistrial—the defense attorney was looking too good. The only member of the defense team showing strain was Hope himself; the weekend had obviously taken a lot out of him. All the newspaper speculations couldn't have helped much. O'Malley wondered how the senator had reacted to one headline in particular: WHERE THERE'S DEATH THERE'S HOPE?—it was the kind of line that won the $25 monthly headline contest at the paper, also the kind of line capable of destroying a man.

During the noon recess O'Malley saw the woman from Channel 5 coming at him—"Hey, O'Malley, how well *did* you know her?"—and the reporter hurried into his car and escaped to a Burger King stand for a solitary lunch. The stories on Teddi's murder—all except the one O'Malley phoned in—had speculated heavily on the senator's possible involvement in the crime.

To questions comparing the two killings, Galton was delivering a curt "No comment." The phrase was hard for him to manage, however, and he announced that a press release was being prepared and would be released at the end of the court session that day. When O'Malley reached the district attorney's office, Ferris was penciling the reporters' names on the copies of the release.

"A little extra service for the press," he said.

"Terrific," O'Malley said. "Only you spelled my name wrong. There's an *e* before the *y*."

"Sorry about that."

O'Malley grunted and scanned the paragraph, which, despite a few rhetorical flourishes, said nothing more than the fact that a trial was in progress and the district attorney did not feel it proper to comment on any possible similarities to any other case then in progress except to say that all avenues of investigation were being explored.

"Beautiful," O'Malley said. "That certainly clears everything up."

The reporter took the mimeographed sheet back to his apartment and placed it beside the Olivetti on the kitchen table. He rubbed his hands together, adjusted the margins, delayed some more, and then realized there was something playing games in the back of his mind. Something was not meshing properly. Custer Yale called then with his standard question—"What are you writing about today, Bob?"—and received his standard answer—"Oh, about six hundred words"—and when O'Malley returned to the typewriter, there was still something preventing him from starting. This time he picked up the phone on the first ring.

"Hello," she said, "this is Charlotte."

"Where the hell have you—"

"Please don't do that," she said, "don't ask me where I've been. I've been following the trial and it doesn't look to me like our friend Hope is going to be convicted."

"They need you in court," O'Malley said.

"That's why I'm calling," she said. "I remembered something else that Ginny told me, something that might help."

"Why tell me? You should be talking to the DA."

"I'm telling you. My, uh, friend—I don't see any way I could go into a courtroom."

"You're going to have to."

"I'm afraid, Bob. The only reason I'm calling you is that I trust you. Listen, this second murder, the barmaid from the Blue Barn, do they think Hope did it?"

"They're not sure. Why?"

"He must have," she said. "At least that's my hunch."

"What about Virginia Hanson?"

"That's more than a hunch, Bob. What I want to tell you—it's about the murder weapon. They never found one, right?"

"Right."

"Well, the police must have searched Ginny's apartment, right?"

"With a fine comb."

"And they didn't find a meat cleaver with a wooden handle, the kind they use in butcher shops?"

"Nothing like that."

"Well, Ginny had one."

"How do you know?"

297

"I was at her place a few times and I saw it. I kidded her about it once—you know, at today's prices how could she afford a piece of meat big enough to use it on? The thing is, she got it from the chef at one of the places where she worked. The Grotto. The name was stamped right there on the handle."

"No," O'Malley said. "They never found anything like it."

"They searched Hope's house, didn't they?"

"Twice. And they've been all over Nassau Overlook."

"Well, it still might help if they knew about the cleaver."

"I'll tell them. But listen, I'd still like to talk to you. There are some other things. . . ."

There was a moment's hesitation. "I'd like to see you," Charlotte said.

"What about now?"

"As it turns out, I'm free," she said. "We can try Renée's again. It shouldn't be crowded tonight. Let's say in a half hour. But, Bob?"

"Yeah?"

"Just you. Promise you won't bring anyone."

"Cross my heart," O'Malley said.

The minute he put down the phone the reporter picked it up again and called Brownstein.

"I told her I'd be alone, Brownie," he said. "Give me about ten minutes before you come in."

39

O'Malley waited for the elevator. Even though he distrusted all machinery and even though he lived on the second floor and even though he was in a rush, the reporter didn't risk moving his girth from one floor to another on foot. It gave him a chance to consider Charlotte's call. She seemed as anxious to put Chapin Hope behind bars as all the forces of law and order combined.

She was some cookie, all right. How had she managed to stay out of sight all these months? It bordered on magic—at least until this evening it did. Maybe she'd be able to make some kind of deal with Galton, something that would keep her off the stand, but what the hell, that was her problem.

What could Charlotte have, anyway? O'Malley no longer believed that Hope was guilty of anything except every kind of political chicanery known to man. The hell with Hope, he wasn't important. What was important was finding out who killed Teddi. Undoubtedly the same person who killed the other one.

Well, he would have ten minutes alone with Charlotte and that would be time to pursue at least two lines of inquiry. First, the phone call—what did Charlotte really know about the murder weapon? Second, did Charlotte happen to know who it was who did the favor for Virginia Hanson, the official who erased her name from the Jericho Turnpike scandals?

As he stood there waiting for the elevator, O'Malley could feel a shadow stalking the back of his mind, a shadow looking for a shape. The elevator stopped and he stepped inside and then it happened. There was one other occupant, an elderly man wearing a black overcoat and carrying a large manila envelope. O'Malley glanced over at the man and there was a click, a connection. He looked at the manila envelope a second time and thought back to another one, the one that had brought him the picture of Chapin Hope in the first place, the one that set all the wheels in motion. The shadow began to take form.

"Jeezus!" the reporter said and the second man in the elevator looked the other way.

O'Malley considered calling Brownstein right then but there was no time. Besides, it was still conjecture and he wanted to let the idea roll around a little more. And there were still those other shadows playing around in his mind.

Perhaps talking to Charlotte would help. Did she really imagine he wouldn't tell the police about this meeting? Maybe she figured that he had been charmed out of his senses. Well, okay, they had hit it off—he remembered the way they had put on that old letch at Renée's that night.

O'Malley hit a button on the car radio and caught the end of the news. A flash from the White House, the new unemployment figures, violence in the Middle East, all that and a wine commercial, and then he was at Renée's.

It was clearly an off night. No combo and only a dozen customers scattered around the bar. Also, no sign of Charlotte. Only after the reporter was seated and sipping a drink did she suddenly materialize beside him; perhaps she had been waiting to see whether he was alone. Charlotte was wearing a long-sleeved white blouse and a solid red skirt and something new, a pair of round, oversized sunglasses.

"How nice to see you again, Mr. O'Malley," she said with mock formality.

"And you, miss—I don't believe you ever told me your last name."

Charlotte laughed.

"Nice try, Bob," she said, "but I think I'll just keep that a secret."

"Yeah, the mystery lady. What's with the shades?"

"Part of my disguise, of course."

How much of that was kidding? Maybe she really was afraid somebody would recognize her. But who? Charlotte asked for a ginger ale. There was a pot of cheddar on the bar and she spread some on a cracker and handed it to O'Malley.

"So let's talk," he said.

"Yes," she said. "Let's talk about how I can help you get Chapin Hope."

"I just write the facts, ma'am."

"Don't kid a kidder, Bob," she said. "You were the first one to blow the whistle on Hope."

"I wasn't blowing the whistle on anyone," he said. "It was a story and I wrote it."

"You're not that ingenuous, Bob."

"I'm not that devious, either."

"Touché."

O'Malley couldn't quite tell if she was flirting with him.

300

"Listen," he said. "That last night you saw Ginny Hanson at the Pumpkin, was there anything else, anything you forgot to tell me?"

"Not really," Charlotte said. "But what I told you on the phone about the cleaver—shouldn't that help?"

"Not unless they find it," he said. "Still, knowing what to look for might help."

"They've got to find it," she said. "They've got to find something. Chapin Hope's a killer, Bob."

"What's happened?" O'Malley said. "You weren't that sure the last time I saw you."

"Nothing's *happened*," she said. "I just *know* it. Hope killed Ginny, and he probably killed that other woman, too. He's a killer, a murderer. He can't get away with this. He *can't!* They've got to get him, Bob. They've got to convict him."

Charlotte was leaning forward and there was an intensity in her voice that O'Malley had not heard before. It was almost as if her voice was changing. Not knowing quite why he was doing it, O'Malley reached out and took off her dark glasses. Charlotte's eyes were bright with anger.

"I'm not kidding, Bob. They've got to get him and put him away."

Her hand was squeezing O'Malley's wrist now and he looked down. The white sleeve ended in a wide cuff held together with a big gleaming ruby-colored cuff link. He looked at the cuff link, stared at it, and with the suddenness of a lightning bolt, everything came together. Kaleidoscopic images became a picture. The envelope the man had carried in the elevator. The same kind of envelope as the one in which the photo of Chapin Hope had been sent to him a millennium ago, the one on which his name had been misspelled "O'Mally." The same misspelling as that penciled by Chuck Ferris on the press release. Ferris' voice on the Jericho Turnpike tapes—the tapes from which Virginia Hanson had been erased. Ferris was the man who kept Virginia Hanson's name clean in return for intimacies—sex acts that she wouldn't even tell Teddi about, a favor for a favor. Only no man answering Ferris' description had ever been linked to Virginia Hanson, had ever been seen with her. That had bothered O'Malley during the drive to Renée's—someone would have seen them together.

But now Charlotte. The voice, the expression—and then he had looked down at the cuffed wrist and he remembered. The cuff link in Teddi Bennett's hand, the one for which the police had never found a mate, the black coral framing a white pearl. O'Malley *had* seen it before. But not on Teddi; she had never owned that cuff link.

She had never owned anything like that. He hadn't seen it on Teddi but he had seen it on a woman. He had seen it the last time he was in Renée's. He had seen it on Charlotte. And he knew. At that moment he knew everything.

The sound started deep in Robert Joseph O'Malley's gut—it was a roar, a bellow, the war cry of a wounded lion. It transfixed the people in the room, pinned them to their seats with shock and fear. It held them immobile as the fat man in the rumpled suit reached out and yanked at the head of the tall brunette sitting opposite him, yanked at her head and came away with a marvelously fitted wig that he threw into the bar as he pulled his hand back, laying bare the crew cut that was hidden beneath it.

"You fat bastard, I'll get you!"

A new voice was coming from the red-skirted figure opposite O'Malley. It was a wild voice, wild with rage and hysteria, but it was obviously and irrefutably a man's voice. Then both of them were off their seats and the skirted figure was holding a cheese knife in its right hand and stabbing forward with it.

It was no contest. The knife blunted against the jacketed flesh of O'Malley's shoulder and then clattered to the floor as the fat man, still bellowing, slammed his assailant's arm aside with his left hand and smashed a hamlike right fist into the mascaraed face in front of him. The skirted figure crumpled against the bar and then O'Malley grabbed it by the throat with his left hand and smashed his right fist into the face one, two, three times, and then they were on the floor and O'Malley was banging the crew-cut head on the floor when somebody finally grabbed him and he could hear Brownstein's voice telling him to stop.

"It's enough, Bob," the voice said. "It's enough."

As they pulled him off, O'Malley's hand grabbed the white blouse and ripped it away, exposing the shaved, padded chest beneath it. On his back were visible scratch marks. The figure on the floor was half sobbing, half screaming. Its face was twisted by rage. Blood mixed with the makeup, turning the face into a nightmare.

Beneath the crew cut—with the falsh lashes gone and the makeup running—was the man who had killed both Virginia Hanson and Teddi Bennett. The features were unmistakably those of Chuck Ferris.

40

"What the hell is this?" Cappobianco said, holding up the contrivance he had just found in a bureau drawer in Chuck Ferris' bedroom.

Lloyd Oakland, MD, staff psychiatrist for the Nassau County Police Department, looked up from the tape recorder he was fiddling with and glanced in the detective's direction.

"Use your imagination, Frank," he said. "That's a penis suppressor."

Well, live and learn. Cappobianco was wondering whether a detective ever did manage to get off garbage details. Detective Lieutenant Charles Brownstein was wondering approximately the same thing; the Homicide chief shook his head as he riffled through a drawer filled with slips and panties, a silken trove of prints and pastels. Alongside in the double bureau was a drawer stuffed with padded bras.

"What surprises me about this business," Brownstein said to the fourth person in the room, "is that I can still get surprised."

"Yeah," said Robert J. O'Malley, "I'm still not sure I understand it all."

"I can explain a great deal of it for you," said Lloyd Oakland, "although I want to talk to Ferris in more detail. But first let me play some of these tapes I found in the hall closet. I've been listening to them in the living room and—well—just listen. Ferris put dates on them so I can play them chronologically. Here, I'll start with this one—it's about a year before Virginia Hanson met Chapin Hope."

Oakland slipped a cassette into the recorder, pushed a button, and then the calm, matter-of-fact voice of Chuck Ferris cut into the sudden silence:

"I bought a new dress today. It was on sale at Lord & Taylor's in Manhasset. Red with long tapered sleeves and an Empire waist and a narrow skirt. And the fabric is lovely; a soft polyester that feels wonderful on your body. I couldn't wait to get home and put it on in front of the mirror. Just looking at myself, I felt warm—I actually glowed. It was as good as sex, although I had that too before the day was over.

"At night I wore the dress to Ginny's new place, the Pumpkin. I must say, I was a hit. Four offers. After a while I had an urge to stand on the bar and strip—that's all I'd need. Anyway, Ginny loved the dress. She said the color was just right for me. At her place later she put on her blue dressing gown and we did it on the bed. She got on top and did all the work. While she was coming, she called me Charlotte. She obviously has no trouble thinking of herself as the man. When I think of the way I had to threaten her at the beginning! I wonder what it's like to have a sex drive as strong as hers."

The only sound in the room was that of Oakland stopping the tape and removing the cassette. "There's more along the same line," he said, "but I'll skip to the day after the Hanson murder. Let's see . . . yes, here it is."

Again the voice was Ferris' but this time it was more animated:

"I just read the story in the *Islander*—they must have gotten that fat drunk, O'Malley, out of some alley to write it. Now I have two secrets. I'm the only person in the world who knows that I killed Ginny, and I'm going to make sure it stays that way. If they blame anyone, they'll blame that bastard Hope. If they don't find him by themselves, I'll lead them to him. I hate him, I really hate him. He's the reason I had to kill her; he's the one who came between Ginny and me. He deserves whatever happens to him. Last night at the Pumpkin I met him for the first time. At least I met him for the first time when I was dressed as Charlotte; I've met him as Chuck a few times at political affairs. He had no idea, of course; they never have. As for that Harry business of his, that's too much. Every time he smiled, I felt like spitting in his face.

"He was an ass letting her give him marijuana. That's something I'd never do—just dressing up is enough of a high for me. Anyway, after she dropped him off and left the Pumpkin, I had another drink at the bar and then followed her to her apartment. I could tell she wasn't happy I had come and I was even more annoyed when she let me in and I saw the joint in her mouth. To be nasty, I told her it was the wrong kind of joint and she got angry; she hates that kind of talk. Then she told me we couldn't do anything, that she wouldn't cheat on Hope. She actually said that—she wouldn't *cheat* on him. For the first time, I hit her. I kept hitting her until she gave in. She said it was rape and I suppose she fought me most of the way, but I know I enjoyed myself. Afterward she was furious—she told me she'd never even let me in the apartment again. She said it was her turn to do some blackmailing, that she would tell Norman about me, as well as anyone else who would listen. I know Ginny—she wasn't kidding. She would have told everyone. She would have told Norman. She. . . ."

Ferris' voice trailed off, and then there was a click indicating that the tape had been stopped and restarted. The voice that came back on sent a chill through the men in the bedroom. It had Ferris' rhythms but it was different. It was a woman's voice, and O'Malley gave it a name.

"Charlotte!"

"I was getting a little upset," the woman's voice was saying, "so I just took off my shirt and trousers and changed into a dressing gown. And I put on some makeup; that always makes me feel better. Actually, I don't know why I got upset—making these tapes gives me satisfaction. They say confession's good for the soul but that's not it because you only confess sins and I haven't committed any. I've only done what I had to do and what gives me pleasure. Ginny would have told the whole world about me; I had no choice. I remembered the cleaver and I went into the kitchen and got it. Luckily I always wear gloves as Charlotte. She was in the living room, and I got her in the neck with the first blow. My intention was to make it look like a crime of passion, and then suddenly it was. The truth is, I couldn't stop chopping. The way it made me feel— well, it was even better than dressing up and having sex with Ginny. Putting the head in the sink was messy but I thought about the police finding it and I had to laugh. When I left, I took the cleaver with me. Nobody saw me come in and nobody saw me leave."

"Jeezus!" It was Cappobianco.

"I'll just play one more tape," said Dr. Oakland. "This is after the second killing."

Again the voice was Charlotte's. "I thought sending that picture to O'Malley, the one I got from Ginny's place the night I killed her, would be enough, but it wasn't. The jury's thinking acquittal. And if Hope gets off, Brownstein will keep digging and who knows what he'll find? What I had to do was obvious. I had to kill Teddi Bennett. And I'm not ashamed to admit I wanted to—I wanted that feeling again.

"If I say so myself, I set it up beautifully. I called Teddi as Charlotte and told her to meet me at her apartment—that I knew she was a friend of O'Malley's and I could tell her something about the Ginny Hanson murder. Then I called Hope. I told him I was Teddi and I set him up. I even called the police after the murder and complained about noise in Teddi's apartment. I had to kill her the same way as Ginny so they'd think it was Hope again. But the minute she let me in I knew I didn't need to have sex. I had the cleaver in my hand behind my back and it was almost alive. I couldn't wait to use it. She must have seen something in my face because she dodged the first blow; I think it glanced off her side.

305

She put up a fight and that only made it better. After I killed her, I took her clothes off and I propped her body up at a table. What a high! It was even better than with Ginny; I can't begin to describe it. Just thinking about it gets me excited. . . ."

"I guess that's enough," Oakland said, turning off the recorder.

"You okay, Bob?" Brownstein said, looking at O'Malley.

"I will be in a second," the reporter said. He closed his eyes and swallowed and then he let out a long sigh. "Okay," he said. He turned back to Brownstein. "Before the doc does any explaining, tell me something, Brownie. As I remember, you weren't all that surprised to find out it was Ferris. How come?"

"I'd found out about his relationship with Virginia Hanson," the detective said. "I was following up on the Jericho Turnpike thing, and I finally tracked down Bunny Silver, the madam. Honey Bunny, to use the nickname you people gave her. As it turns out, Bunny's changed her name and moved to Detroit. She's gone back to schoolteaching. Fifth grade. I got hold of her about ten minutes after you phoned to tell me you were meeting Charlotte. She said that Ferris was the one who kept Virginia Hanson out of the case. Virginia Hanson told Bunny pretty much the same thing she told Teddi—that Ferris was strange, but not much else. I planned to talk to Ferris after we made the pickup on Charlotte. But I certainly didn't expect anything like this."

Brownstein motioned around the room. His meaning was clear. The extent of the division in Chuck Ferris' life was reflected by the division in the apartment. One side of the bedroom closet was given over to a modest collection of men's clothing: functional suits and sports jackets and trousers. The other side was filled with skirts, dresses, gowns, sweaters, and blouses. The shoe tree beneath the men's clothing contained a pair of loafers, a pair of black dress shoes, a pair of tennis sneakers, and even a pair of cleated baseball shoes. The area beneath the skirts and dresses was jammed with a miniature women's shoe store; a polished, multicolored assortment of heels and flats, everything from pumps to evening slippers. A his-and-hers closet for one person.

It was obvious that Ferris spent much of his time in the bedroom. The color television set was beside the water bed and the night tables were piled high with dress and wig catalogues and copies of a magazine called *Transvestia*. One entire wall of the bedroom was paneled in mirrors, and the mirror over the dressing table was ringed by low-wattage light bulbs, a copy of a theatrical dressing-room mirror.

A table beneath that mirror held a dozen bottles of cologne and perfume—Arpège, Shalimar, Joy, others. The rest of the table top and the drawer beneath it were crowded with pots, bottles, vials, tubes, and cases of makeup—lipstick, pancake-makeup stick, mascara, eye shadow, eyeliner, cold cream. Makeup pencils, brushes, and daubers. A special receptacle on the table held a variety of false eyelashes in neatly arranged rows, and nearby on a wooden pedestal was a brunette wig—similar to the one O'Malley had ripped from Ferris' head only hours earlier.

There was all that, and yet on a small vanity in the bathroom there was a leather case containing a military brush-and-comb set, an injector razor, a hot-lather set, and a wax stick used for grooming crew cuts.

At times the division was so stark as to border on humor. Frilly curtains, French Provincial furniture, Impressionist prints, a new dress still wrapped in tissue paper and draped over a living-room chair. A few steps away copies of *Sports Illustrated* and *Esquire*. And in a hall closet a squash racket and a fielder's mitt.

There had been other, grimmer discoveries. The missing coral-and-pearl cuff link, photos of Charlotte arm in arm with Virginia Hanson, a note pad on which Ferris had jotted down Teddi Bennett's address and the cassettes on which Chuck-Charlotte had recorded the full details of a double life, including two murders. Now the men in the bedroom looked at Lloyd Oakland. The psychiatrist moved over to where Brownstein was standing and picked up a pair of sheer, blue, bikini-style panties from the bureau drawer. "Ferris was always wearing something like this," he said, "even when he was dressed as a man. Ferris is a transvestite, a person who obtains primary sexual satisfaction from cross-dressing, from masquerading as a member of the opposite sex. Unlike a transsexual—a physically normal male who believes he's a woman—Ferris doesn't think he's a woman, nor does he especially want to be a woman. He knows he's a man and, in a way, that's the whole point—his satisfaction comes from the fact that he's a man *passing* as a woman. He's more comfortable in female clothes and he usually assumes a role that fits the masquerade; he has another name and his personality changes. As Chuck, Ferris was colorless, if competent. As Charlotte, he was outgoing, even glamorous. A true transvestite like Ferris becomes letter-perfect at his impersonation. Not just his appearance but even his actions. He could fool almost anyone."

O'Malley started to say something but stopped. There was no interrupting Lloyd Oakland, who had become completely absorbed in his subject and was lecturing as if he were in a classroom.

"Now, you have to understand that Ferris is not homosexual, at least not overtly so. When he does have sex, it's heterosexual, although there may be homosexual fantasies—making believe that he's the woman, for instance, and that the woman is a man. Generally transvestites have low sex drives. This is because their basic satisfaction comes from the act of cross-dressing. Like many transvestites, Ferris was probably capable of consummating the sex act only when he was dressed as a woman. His sex drive was extremely weak until Virginia Hanson came along. He had a hold over her—he could force her to go along with his desires, to be a party to his masquerade. And then her own sexuality took over and she didn't require much coaxing. At least not until she met Chapin Hope. Before Hope the men in Virginia Hanson's life didn't inter- fere with her relationship with Ferris. But Hope was different. She found herself deeply committed to Hope, in love—if you prefer that term. And when she told Ferris that their affair would have to stop, he couldn't take it.

"And there was another element at work," the psychiatrist continued after a pause. "Ferris was not a rational transvestite. He was and is psychotic. I don't know the causes yet but the need to kill had probably been building in him for some time. And when he killed Virginia Hanson, when he literally chopped her up—the cleaver was obviously a penis symbol—he found a new high. An ultimate high, if you will. And once he experienced that high, there was no stopping him. He had to use the cleaver on another woman —that's the real reason for the second murder. Nor would he have stopped there. If he hadn't been caught, he would have done it again. He would have kept on doing it."

There was a long silence, and then Oakland shook his head as if to clear it. "Sorry," he said. "I got carried away."

"Just one thing, Doc," O'Malley said. "Why did he take a chance on meeting me again as Charlotte?"

"That's on the last tape," the psychiatrist said. "He made it just before he left to meet you. It was the kick he got out of fooling you. Incidentally, Brownie, about the cleaver—you should find it in the trunk compartment of Hope's station wagon. Ferris planted it there yesterday while the car was in the courthouse parking lot."

"I wonder what Galton thinks about all this," O'Malley said. "By the way, where is our esteemed DA?"

"Probably under sedation," Brownstein said. "He and Ferris had a reunion at the hospital. Galton came in, took one look at Ferris' panty hose, and tried to take up where you left off. He actually had to be physically restrained. He told Ferris that he was worse than a pervert; he was a traitor."

"What'd Ferris say?" O'Malley asked.

"At first, nothing. Then Galton screamed something about putting him away for life, and Ferris looked right at him and said, 'I wish I'd used that cleaver on you.' "

Cappobianco shuddered. "Two murders," the young detective said, "and he almost got away with them."

"Brownie would have gotten him," O'Malley said.

"That's academic, Bob," said Brownstein. "You did get him."

"When you pulled that wig off his head," said Dr. Oakland, "it must have turned him wild. That had to be the single most devastating moment of his life."

"Because we knew he was a murderer."

"No, there was a stronger reason. One that hit the very core of his being."

"What was that?" O'Malley asked.

The psychiatrist tapped the tape recorder.

"The masquerade was over."

41

The last day of Chapin Hope's trial was given over to formalities. The district attorney stood up to say that new evidence forced the people to request the dismissal of all charges against the defendant, Chapin Kirk Hope. The judge dismissed the jury, then left the courtroom with the same angry stride that had carried him into it each morning.

Chapin Hope sat at the defense table long after the judge had left the room. He could hear calls of congratulation but most of them were not directed at him; they were for his attorney, L. Gregory Hammer. Chapin sat there, still, as the courtroom emptied behind him, sat there and wondered what he might conceivably do with the rest of his life.

Norman Galton stood on the courthouse steps waiting for the television people to set up their equipment. The statement he planned to deliver didn't seem quite right, seemed leaden. It lacked that old Ferris touch. And as he started to deliver his statement, Norman Galton worried about the necktie he had chosen—was it too garish, too loud? Would it photograph as a blur?

"The people of this state," he said, "are in the debt of the Nassau County police force for its superb detection work, for leading us to the solution of this horrendous crime. My office will, of course, continue to prosecute the case with great vigor. I want to assure everyone listening that the suspect's former ties with this office will in no way influence our determination to bring this case to a just conclusion.

"I must, at this point, mention that Senator Hope has been put through a considerable ordeal. But I'm sure that he would wholeheartedly agree with me in saying that the American system has again proved to be a system in which justice and truth will out, no matter what the obstacle. We can, all of us, sleep easier tonight, secure in the knowledge that justice has been served in Nassau County."

Detective Lieutenant Charles Brownstein saw the gathering of reporters on the front steps of the courthouse and he ducked out the rear exit. By noon he was back at his desk, where a message was waiting for him. Rocco Porcina wanted him to call.

"Thanks for calling back, Chief," Porcina said. "I know it's been a big day for you—and I'm about to make it bigger."

"Is that right?"

"In two months and four days we're going to nominate a candidate for the office of district attorney. We are not going to nominate Norman Galton. If you tell me now that you want that job, I can tell you now that it's yours."

"Maybe the voters will want to have a say in that."

"Oh, they will." Rocco Porcina laughed. "The voters will have a say in it *after* we have a say in it. Brownie—they call you Brownie, right?—well, Brownie, I understand the system and you understand the law. Together we can do one hell of a job."

"I'm not so sure we can, Mr. Porcina."

"Well, be sure," the party leader said. "*Be* sure. Because I'm telling you. I know you're not especially wild about people like me. Okay, maybe I feel the same way about people like you. But that doesn't matter."

"No deal," Brownstein said.

"Deal? Who's talking about a deal? The only deal I know about is this: We support you and you win. That's all. That's not such a complicated deal, is it?"

"I've got to run," the Homicide chief said. "My wife's making a special lunch today."

"Well, you run," Rocco Porcina said. "You run right along because, believe me, Brownie, that's all the running you're gonna do this year."

Chapin Hope felt the emptiness of the courtroom around him. He stood up and turned to leave; then he saw there was one person left in the spectators' gallery.

"Maybe we should go out the back door," he said to Thalia. "Try to avoid some of the—"

"You go on," Thalia said.

"What do you mean?"

"Chape, I was going to write you a letter and try to explain. But that seemed too cowardly. The thing is, I'm leaving you."

"Now? That doesn't make much sense."

"I would have left before this," she said. "But that might have hurt your chances."

"Let's at least talk," Chapin said. "You know how sorry I am to have put you through these past few months. Why don't we get away, take a little—"

"Chape, I'm not sorry about what has happened to *me* these past few months, not in the least. They've been the most valuable months in my life—it's the previous twenty years that bother me. I'm not sure just what the future holds for me but I can tell you one thing it doesn't hold, and that's the past. Chape, we were living a make-believe marriage in a make-believe world. I don't know what I want to be, but one thing I don't want to be is a make-believe person."

"I need you," Chapin said.

"More than you know," Thalia said. "I'll tell you something, Chape. I feel sorry for you. Truly sorry. But I just can't take the chance and stay around. Our life together was a diminishing experience—we were becoming less and less. I was diminished almost out of existence. I think I better find out if there's any of me left."

"I'd try and make it up—"

"Go," she said. "Just go, Chape."

L. Gregory Hammer had replaced Norman Galton in front of the microphones. He was all smiles.

"I couldn't agree more with what the district attorney has just said," Hammer began. "What we have seen here is a superb example of the American system at work. Speaking on behalf of both my client and myself—Senator Hope is, at this moment, overcome with joy and wants only to be with his family—I want to say that we never had any serious doubts about the outcome of the case, about the eventual establishment of innocence."

Hammer stopped then and chatted easily with the reporters as the television crews began to pack their equipment. The crowd in front of the courthouse began to dissipate and finally there were only a few of them left. The young woman from Channel 5 was looking at him.

"Why don't we get together?" the lawyer said. "Do you feel like something to eat?"

"Why not?" she said.

"And then later we could go out and have lunch," he said, and the young woman laughed.

Robert J. O'Malley jotted down the last of his notes on a piece of copy paper and put it into his jacket pocket.

Despite the knowledge that Custer Yale was waiting for him, O'Malley felt at home as he walked into the *Islander* building. It *was* home, the only place on earth he belonged. He and the old dame who did the pet column and a former city editor who handled obits—they had been there almost since day one; they were as much a part of the place as the teletype machines.

Custer Yale—floppy bow tie and plaid slacks—would not fit into the *Islander* if he stayed there a hundred years. O'Malley could imagine him selling shoes or walking dogs; but whenever he saw him sitting in the managing editor's office, he looked like someone who was lost and waiting for help.

"That was a marvelous job, Bob," he was saying. "And it didn't pass unnoticed. In fact, I can tell you now that there's going to be a little something extra in your paycheck from now on."

O'Malley said nothing in response. He knew he was supposed to offer some form of thanks for the raise, but what the hell, they got their money's worth.

"And when you get back to your desk," Custer went on, "you may find another little surprise."

O'Malley got up and walked over to his desk. Surprise was hardly the word. At first glance it appeared to be a television screen and it stood on a pedestal where the old typewriter stand had been. At the base of the screen was a typewriter keyboard—only it had approximately twice the number of keys as a typewriter.

"Where's my typewriter?" O'Malley asked.

"Your typewriter is obsolete," Custer said. "Before the year is out, everyone in the place is going to have one of these. It's a new VDT machine, *Video Display Terminal*."

The initials sounded vaguely obscene to O'Malley, as though they might stand for a cross between a social disease and acute alcoholism.

"There're only three of them in the place so far," Yale was saying. "It takes only a day or two to get the hang of it—wait'll you try. All the machines will be tied into a single computer—I'm telling you, we won't even have copy paper any more."

"I've got a story to do," O'Malley said. "Where's my typewriter?"

Custer Yale seemed not to notice the reporter's resistance. He quickly explained the machine—pointing out keys that deleted words, substituted words, rearranged whole sections, and so forth. There was a button that automatically corrected spelling, buttons that changed wording the way a pencil did on paper, buttons that made editing easy. The computer thought of everything except when to send out for coffee.

"At the end of the story," the editor was saying. "You don't type out 'thirty' anymore. You just hit the letters ST for Store It. What

313

happens then is the computer simply stores the copy electronically until an editor wants to check it over.''

"What happens if I type out *SH*?"

"SH?"

"That's short for Shove It," O'Malley said. "Which is what the computer can do with this whole goddamn machine."

"I knew you'd fight it," the managing editor said. Yale sat down at the new machine and immediately demonstrated his virtuosity— he showed how the reporter could get a printout of the story by striking the PI button. And how the machine would correct the reporter's mistakes by flashing the Syntax Error or the Improper Command lights. And finally he showed him how the machine could play ticktacktoe and even draw cartoon figures on the electronic screen. Using a combination of keys, Yale was able, in less than a minute, to produce the image of a dancing bear.

"Dancing bears," O'Malley said. "Dancing fucking bears."